CHARLAINE HARRIS

Grave Sight

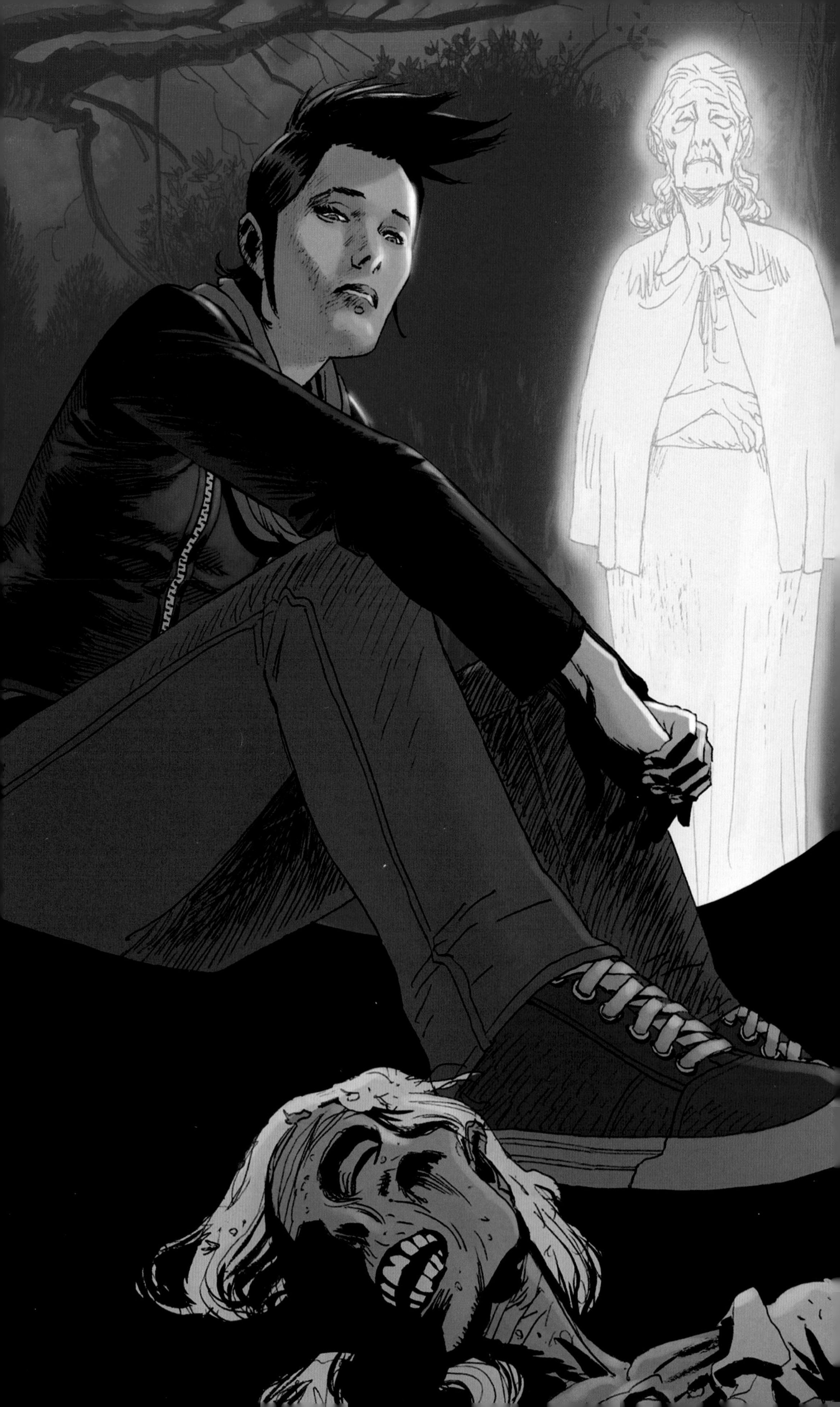

CHARLAINE HARRIS

Grave Sight

text adaptation by **WILLIAM HARMS**

art by **DENIS MEDRI**

colors by **PAOLO FRANCESCUTTO**
Gotem Studio

letters by **BILL TORTOLINI**

front jacket and title page art by **BENOIT SPRINGER**

issue covers by **BENOIT SPRINGER**
& DENIS MEDRI

collection design by **JASON ULLMEYER**

contributing editor **RICH YOUNG**

consultation **ERNST DABEL & LES DABEL**

special thanks to **JOSHUA BILMES**

THE BERKLEY PUBLISHING GROUP
Published by the Penguin Group
Penguin Group (USA) Inc.
375 Hudson Street, New York, New York 10014, USA
Penguin Group (Canada), 90 Eglinton Avenue East, Suite 700, Toronto, Ontario M4P 2Y3, Canada (a division of Pearson Penguin Canada Inc.) • Penguin Books Ltd., 80 Strand, London WC2R 0RL, England • Penguin Ireland, 25 St. Stephen's Green, Dublin 2, Ireland (a division of Penguin Books Ltd.) • Penguin Group (Australia), 707 Collins Street, Melbourne, Victoria 3008, Australia (a division of Pearson Australia Group Pty. Ltd.) • Penguin Books India Pvt. Ltd., 11 Community Centre, Panchsheel Park, New Delhi—110 017, India • Penguin Group (NZ), 67 Apollo Drive, Rosedale, Auckland 0632, New Zealand (a division of Pearson New Zealand Ltd.) • Penguin Books, Rosebank Office Park, 181 Jan Smuts Avenue, Parktown North 2193, South Africa • Penguin China, B7 Jaiming Center, 27 East Third Ring Road North, Chaoyang District, Beijing 100020, China

Penguin Books Ltd., Registered Offices: 80 Strand, London WC2R 0RL, England

GRAVE SIGHT

Published by arrangement with Dynamite Entertainment

Contains materials originally published in *Charlaine Harris' Grave Sight* Books 1–3.
Based on *Grave Sight* by Charlaine Harris copyright © 2005 by Charlaine Harris Schulz.

First edition: January 2013

InkLit hardcover ISBN: 978-0-425-25564-3

PRINTED IN THE UNITED STATES OF AMERICA

10 9 8 7 6 5 4 3 2 1

CHAPTER ONE

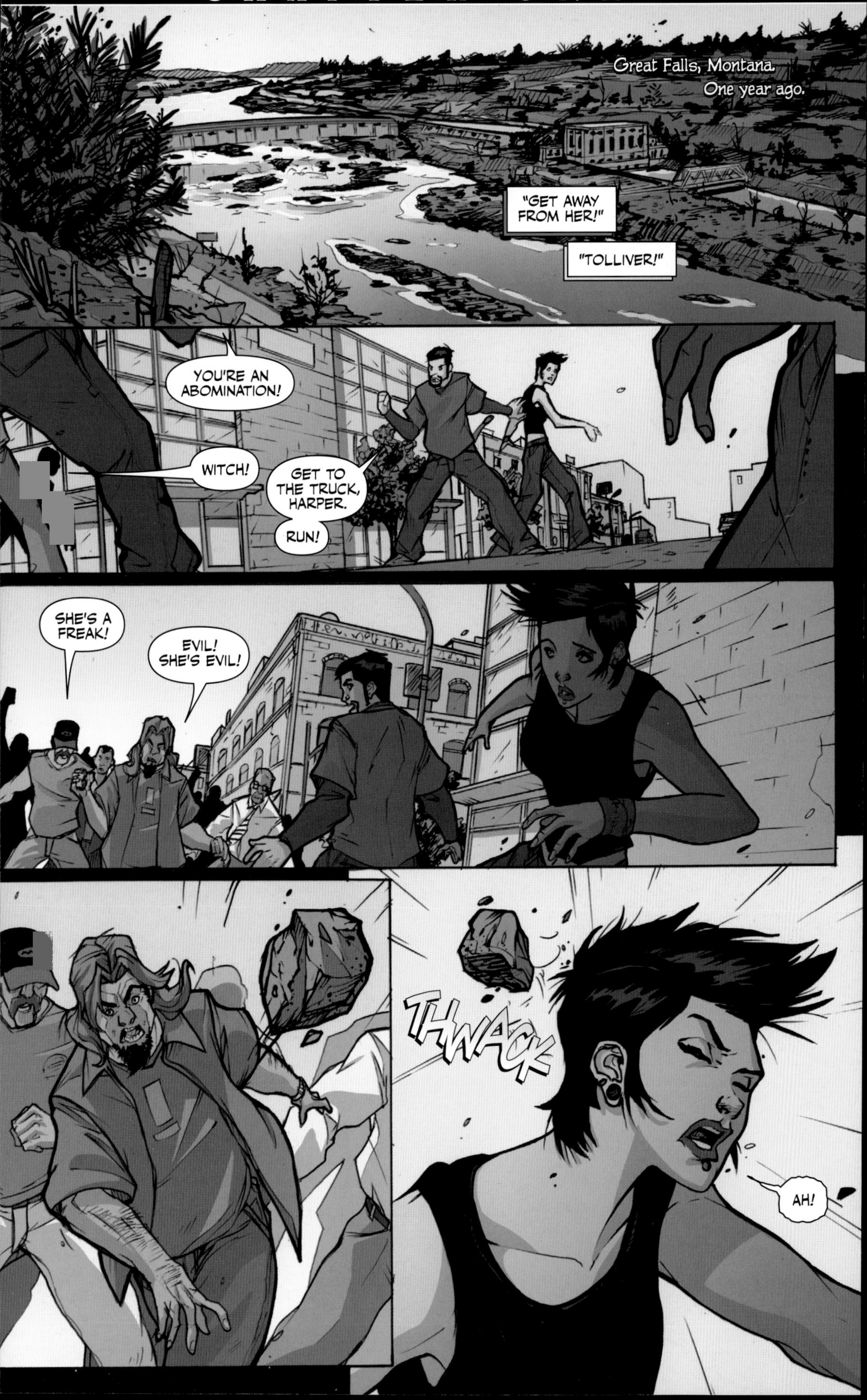
Great Falls, Montana.
One year ago.
"GET AWAY FROM HER!"
"TOLLIVER!"
YOU'RE AN ABOMINATION!
WITCH!
GET TO THE TRUCK, HARPER.
RUN!
SHE'S A FREAK!
EVIL! SHE'S EVIL!
THWACK
AH!

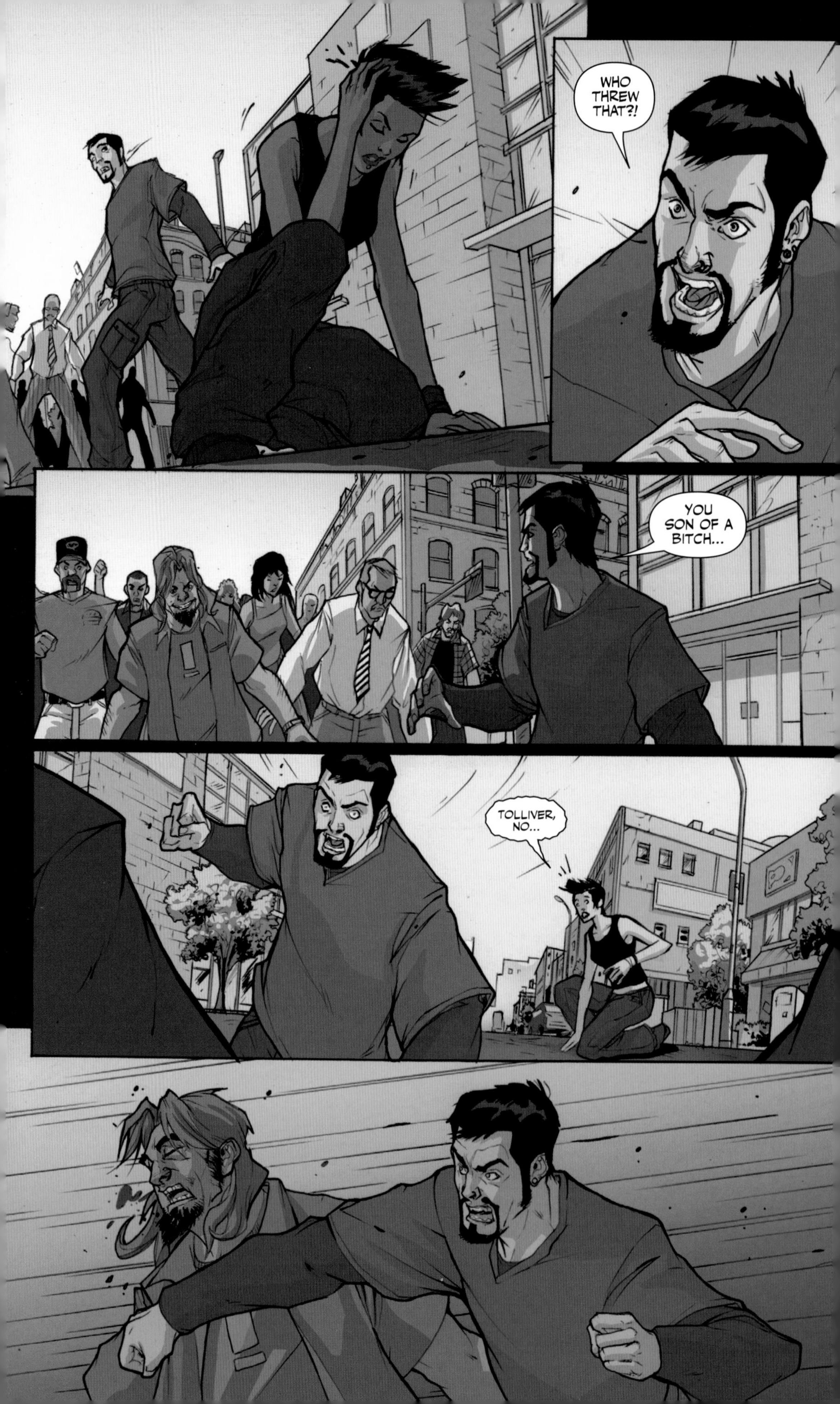
WHO THREW THAT?!
YOU SON OF A BITCH...
TOLLIVER, NO...

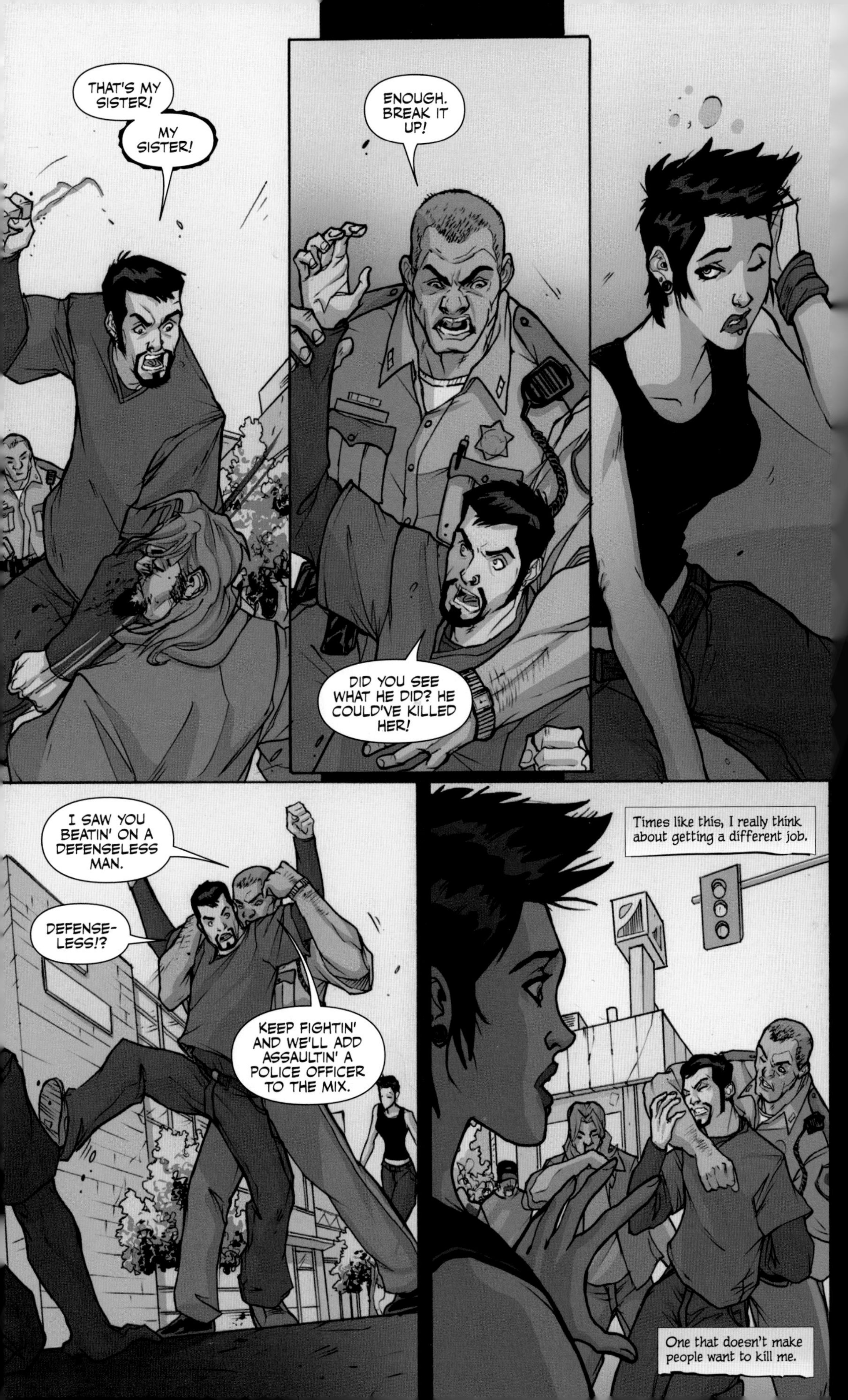
THAT'S MY SISTER!
MY SISTER!
ENOUGH. BREAK IT UP!
DID YOU SEE WHAT HE DID? HE COULD'VE KILLED HER!
I SAW YOU BEATIN' ON A DEFENSELESS MAN.
DEFENSE-LESS!?
KEEP FIGHTIN' AND WE'LL ADD ASSAULTIN' A POLICE OFFICER TO THE MIX.
Times like this, I really think about getting a different job.
One that doesn't make people want to kill me.

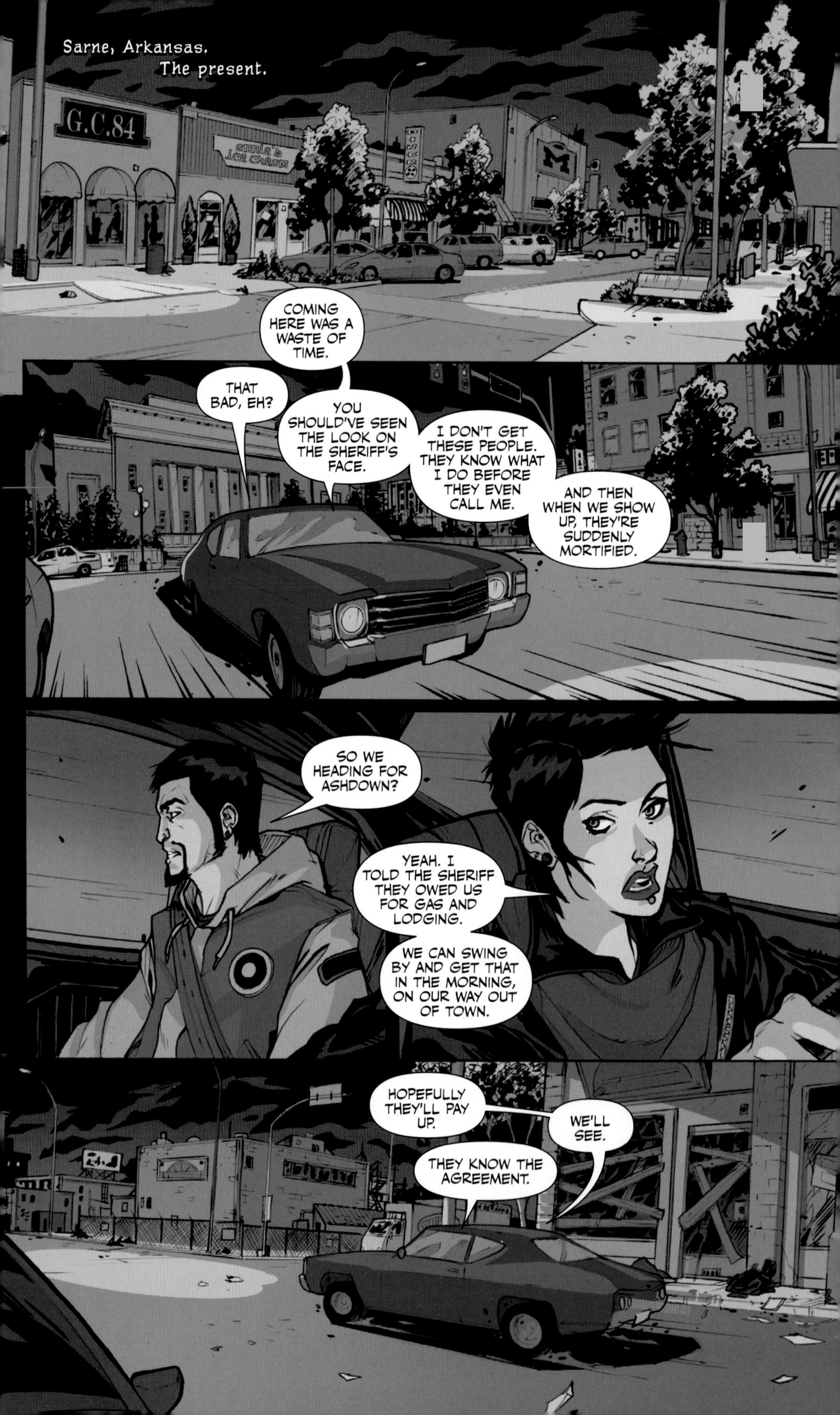
Sarne, Arkansas. The present.
G.C.84
COMING HERE WAS A WASTE OF TIME.
THAT BAD, EH?
YOU SHOULD'VE SEEN THE LOOK ON THE SHERIFF'S FACE.
I DON'T GET THESE PEOPLE. THEY KNOW WHAT I DO BEFORE THEY EVEN CALL ME.
AND THEN WHEN WE SHOW UP, THEY'RE SUDDENLY MORTIFIED.
SO WE HEADING FOR ASHDOWN?
YEAH. I TOLD THE SHERIFF THEY OWED US FOR GAS AND LODGING.
WE CAN SWING BY AND GET THAT IN THE MORNING, ON OUR WAY OUT OF TOWN.
HOPEFULLY THEY'LL PAY UP.
WE'LL SEE.
THEY KNOW THE AGREEMENT.

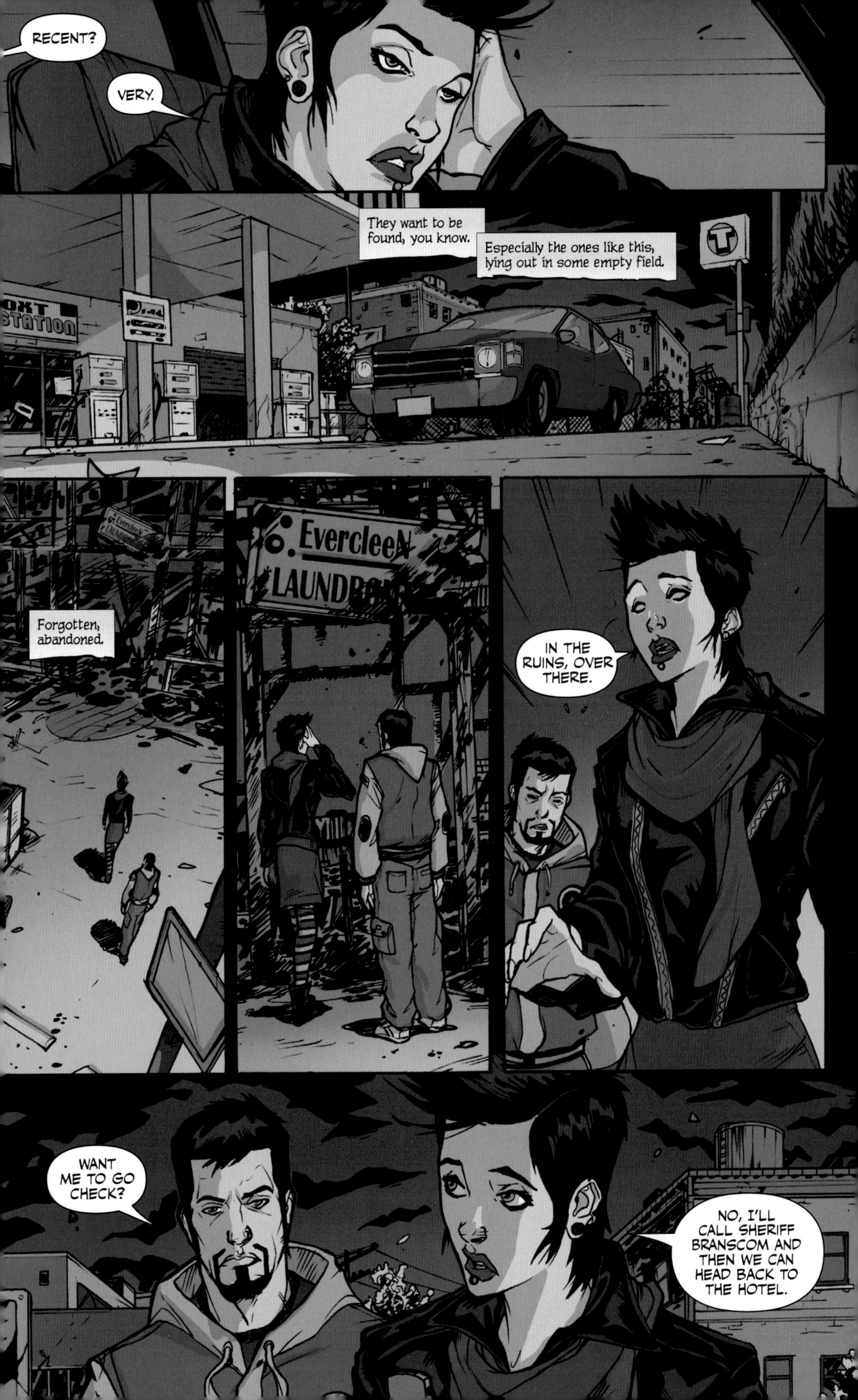
RECENT?
VERY.
They want to be found, you know.
Especially the ones like this, lying out in some empty field.
Forgotten, abandoned.
IN THE RUINS, OVER THERE.
WANT ME TO GO CHECK?
NO, I'LL CALL SHERIFF BRANSCOM AND THEN WE CAN HEAD BACK TO THE HOTEL.

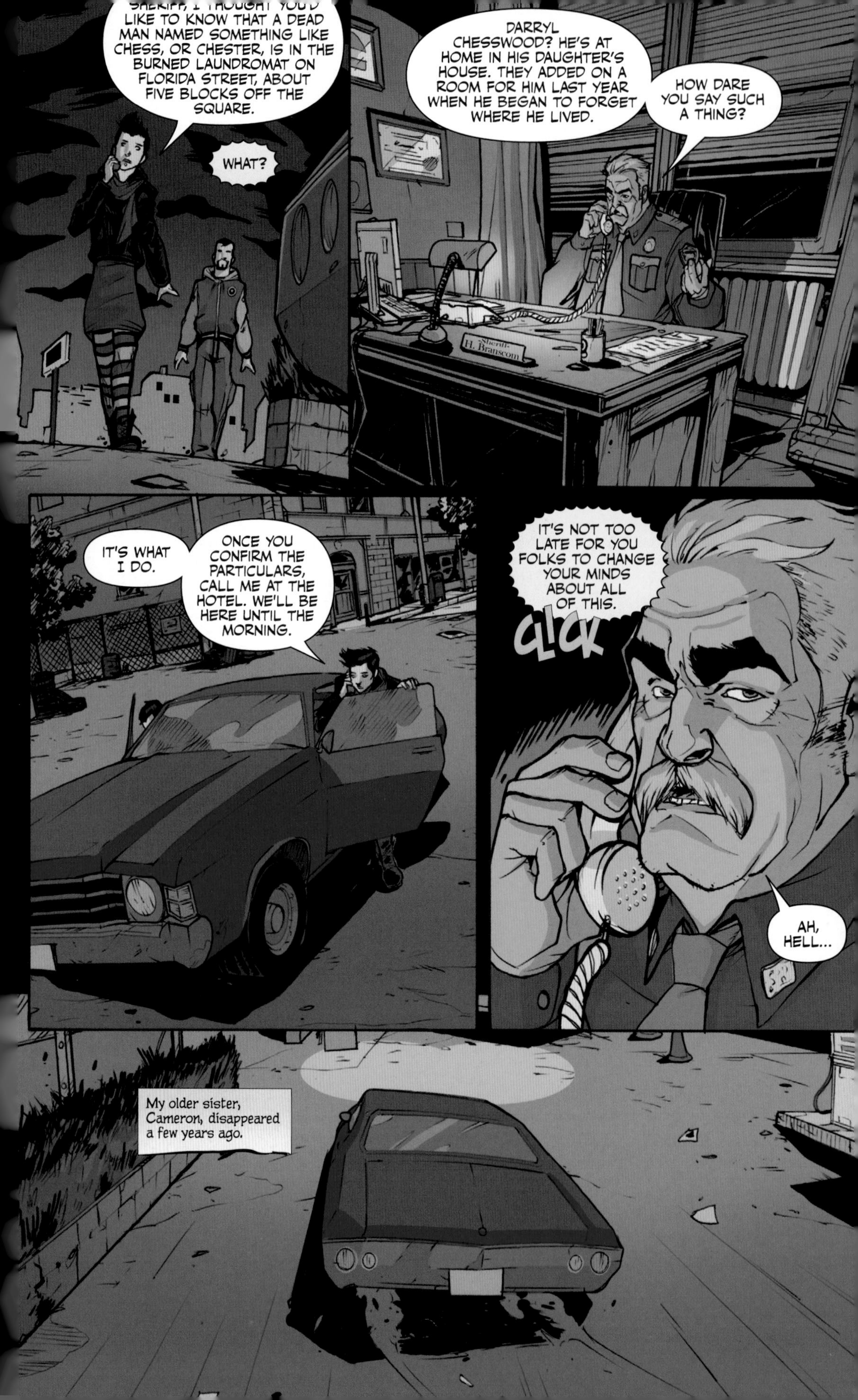
SHERIFF, I THOUGHT YOU'D LIKE TO KNOW THAT A DEAD MAN NAMED SOMETHING LIKE CHESS, OR CHESTER, IS IN THE BURNED LAUNDROMAT ON FLORIDA STREET, ABOUT FIVE BLOCKS OFF THE SQUARE.
WHAT?
DARRYL CHESSWOOD? HE'S AT HOME IN HIS DAUGHTER'S HOUSE. THEY ADDED ON A ROOM FOR HIM LAST YEAR WHEN HE BEGAN TO FORGET WHERE HE LIVED.
HOW DARE YOU SAY SUCH A THING?
-Sheriff- H. Branscom
IT'S WHAT I DO.
ONCE YOU CONFIRM THE PARTICULARS, CALL ME AT THE HOTEL. WE'LL BE HERE UNTIL THE MORNING.
IT'S NOT TOO LATE FOR YOU FOLKS TO CHANGE YOUR MINDS ABOUT ALL OF THIS.
CLICK
AH, HELL...
My older sister, Cameron, disappeared a few years ago.

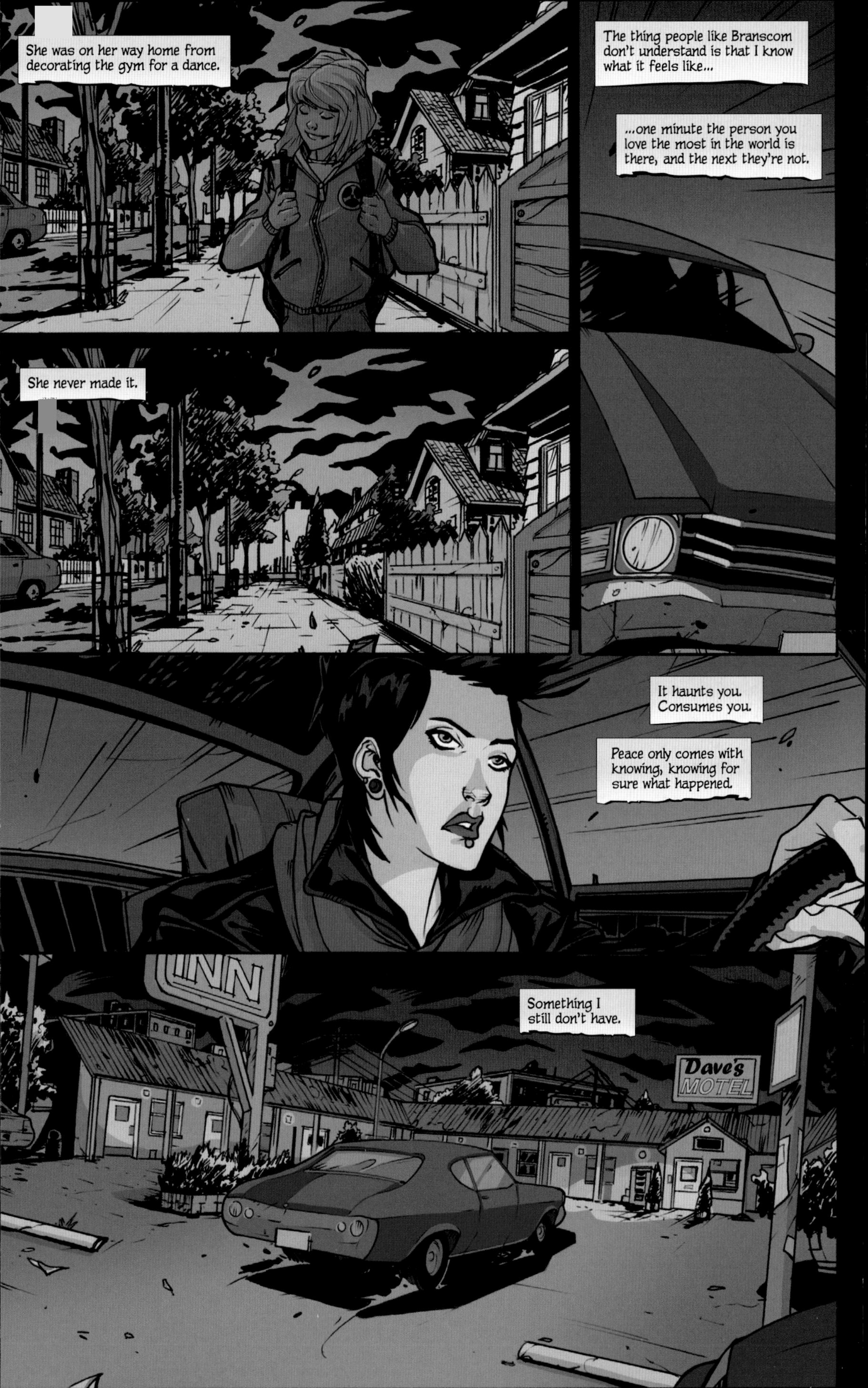
She was on her way home from decorating the gym for a dance.
She never made it.
The thing people like Branscom don't understand is that I know what it feels like...
...one minute the person you love the most in the world is there, and the next they're not.
It haunts you. Consumes you.
Peace only comes with knowing, knowing for sure what happened.
Something I still don't have.
INN
Dave's MOTEL

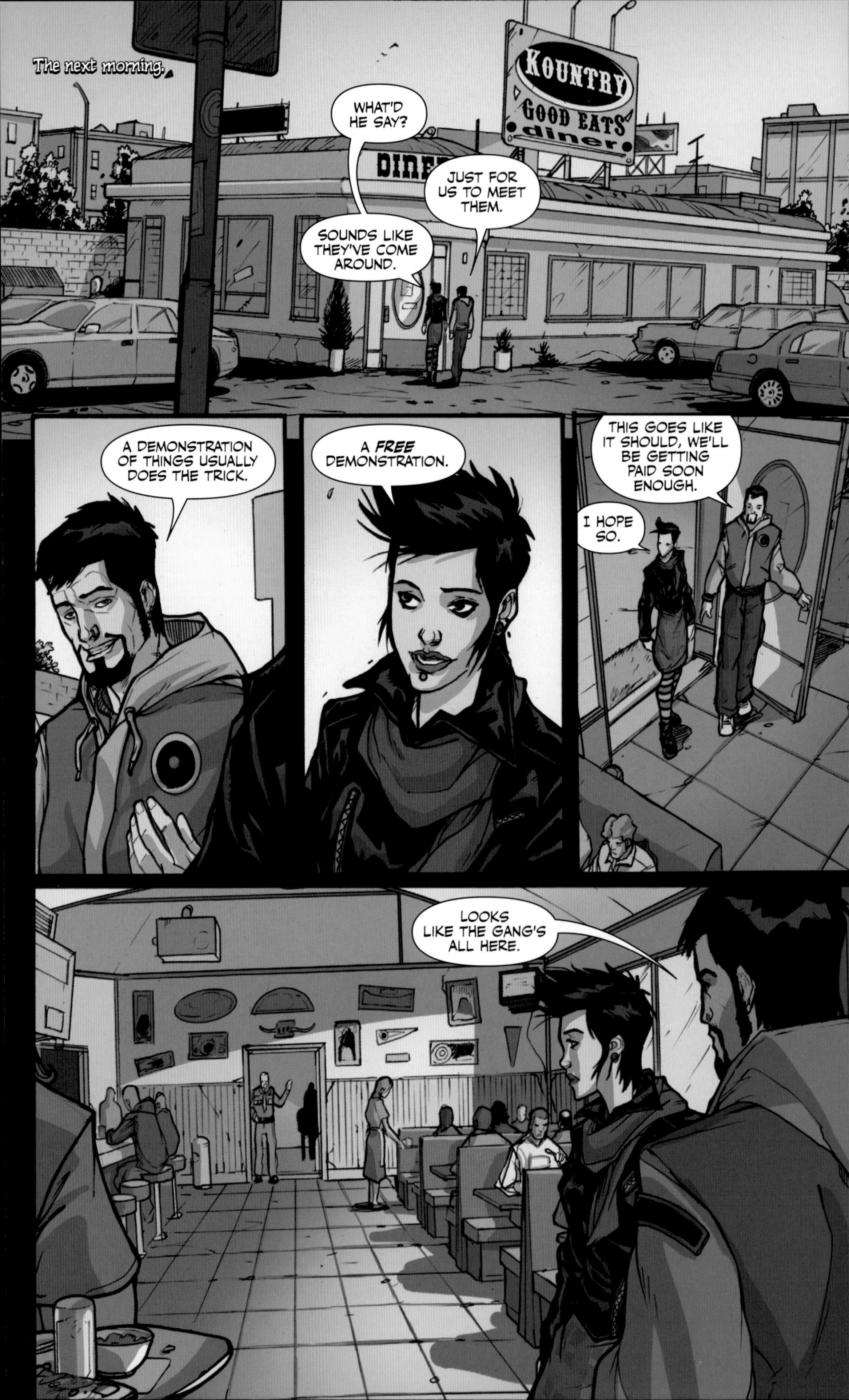
The next morning.
WHAT'D HE SAY?
JUST FOR US TO MEET THEM.
SOUNDS LIKE THEY'VE COME AROUND.
KOUNTRY GOOD EATS diner
DINE
A DEMONSTRATION OF THINGS USUALLY DOES THE TRICK.
A *FREE* DEMONSTRATION.
THIS GOES LIKE IT SHOULD, WE'LL BE GETTING PAID SOON ENOUGH.
I HOPE SO.
LOOKS LIKE THE GANG'S ALL HERE.

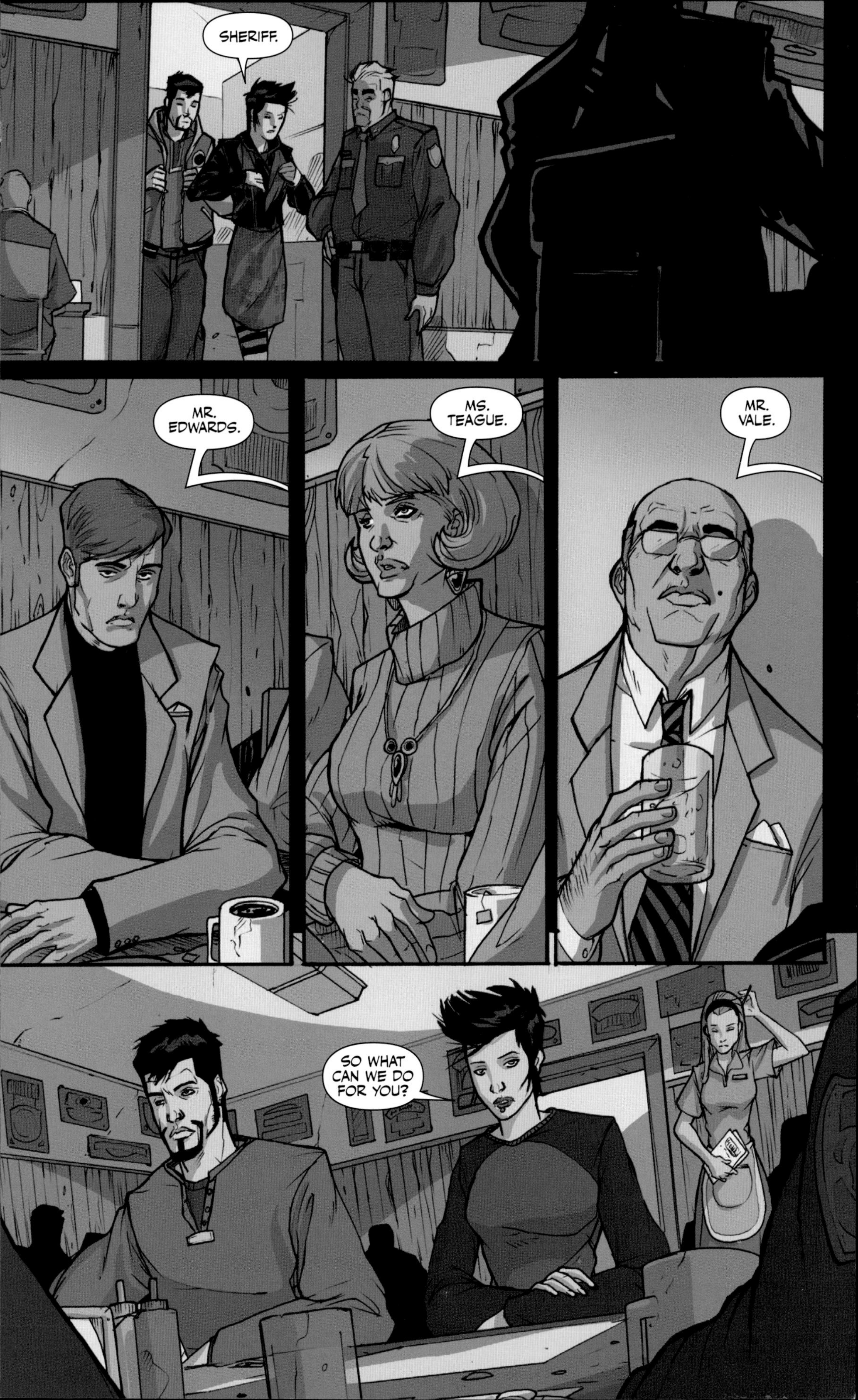
SHERIFF.
MR. EDWARDS.
MS. TEAGUE.
MR. VALE.
SO WHAT CAN WE DO FOR YOU?

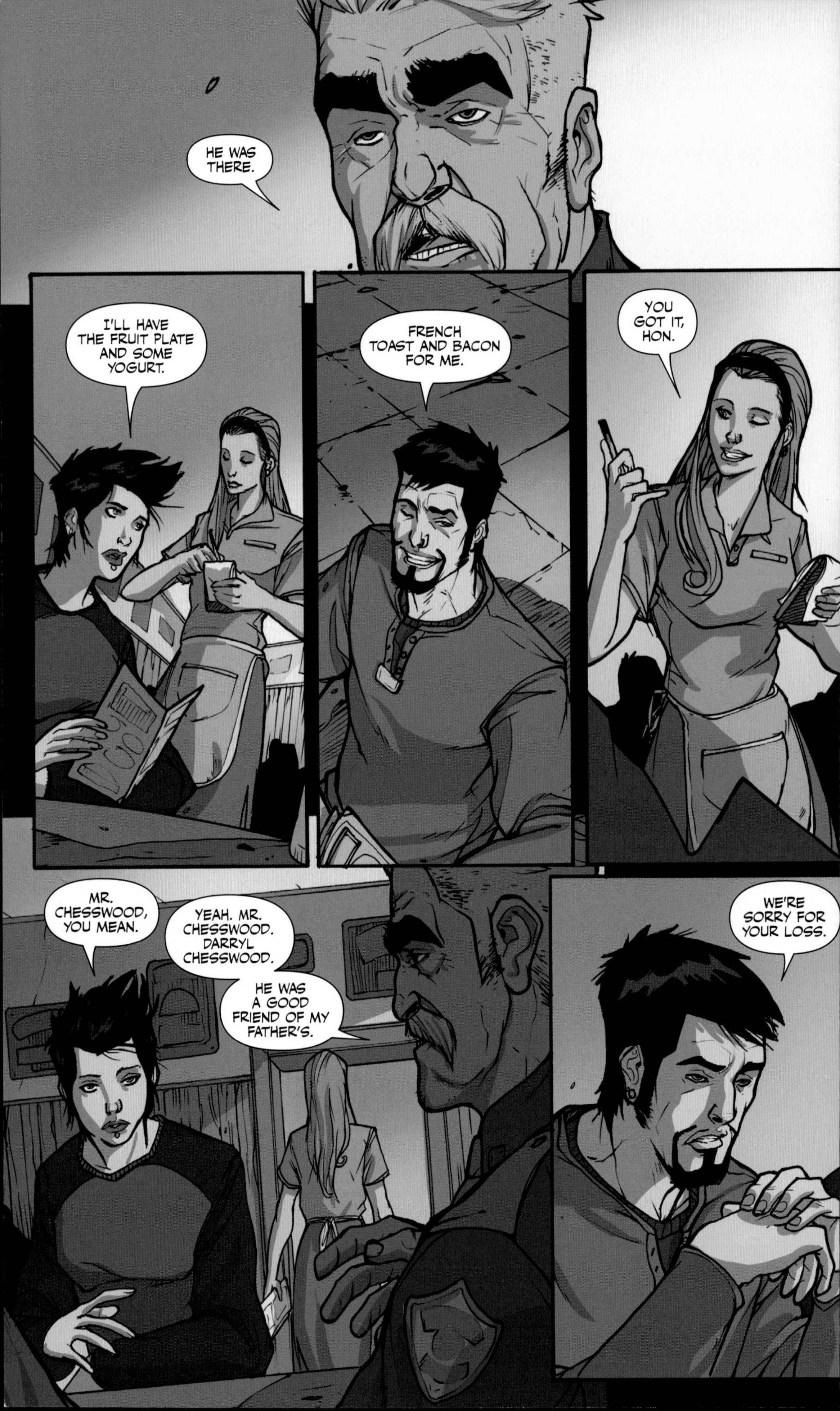
HE WAS THERE.
I'LL HAVE THE FRUIT PLATE AND SOME YOGURT.
FRENCH TOAST AND BACON FOR ME.
YOU GOT IT, HON.
MR. CHESSWOOD, YOU MEAN.
YEAH. MR. CHESSWOOD. DARRYL CHESSWOOD.
HE WAS A GOOD FRIEND OF MY FATHER'S.
WE'RE SORRY FOR YOUR LOSS.

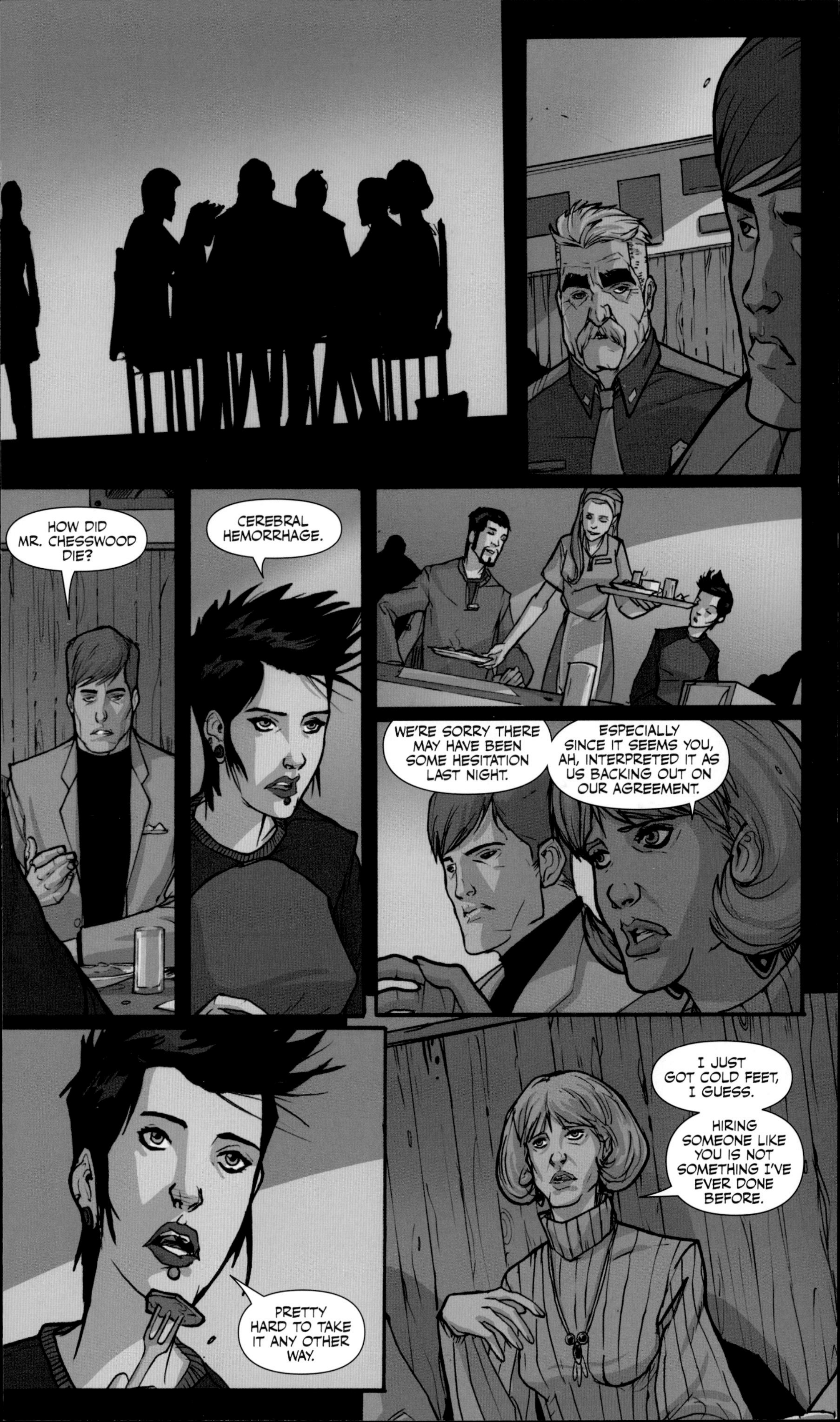

HOW DID MR. CHESSWOOD DIE?
CEREBRAL HEMORRHAGE.
WE'RE SORRY THERE MAY HAVE BEEN SOME HESITATION LAST NIGHT.
ESPECIALLY SINCE IT SEEMS YOU, AH, INTERPRETED IT AS US BACKING OUT ON OUR AGREEMENT.
PRETTY HARD TO TAKE IT ANY OTHER WAY.
I JUST GOT COLD FEET, I GUESS.
HIRING SOMEONE LIKE YOU IS NOT SOMETHING I'VE EVER DONE BEFORE.

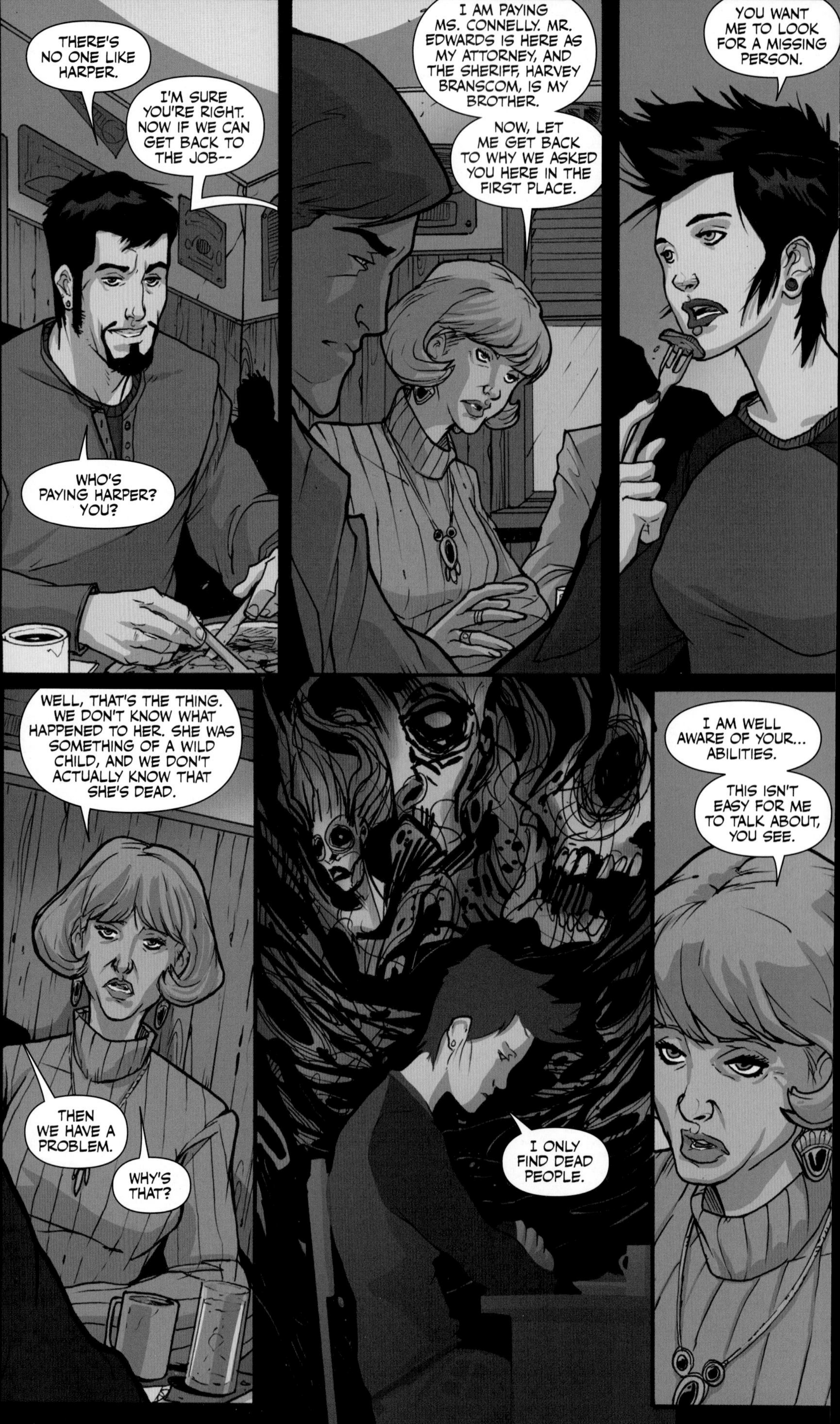
THERE'S NO ONE LIKE HARPER.
I'M SURE YOU'RE RIGHT. NOW IF WE CAN GET BACK TO THE JOB--
WHO'S PAYING HARPER? YOU?
I AM PAYING MS. CONNELLY. MR. EDWARDS IS HERE AS MY ATTORNEY, AND THE SHERIFF, HARVEY BRANSCOM, IS MY BROTHER.
NOW, LET ME GET BACK TO WHY WE ASKED YOU HERE IN THE FIRST PLACE.
YOU WANT ME TO LOOK FOR A MISSING PERSON.
WELL, THAT'S THE THING. WE DON'T KNOW WHAT HAPPENED TO HER. SHE WAS SOMETHING OF A WILD CHILD, AND WE DON'T ACTUALLY KNOW THAT SHE'S DEAD.
THEN WE HAVE A PROBLEM.
WHY'S THAT?
I ONLY FIND DEAD PEOPLE.
I AM WELL AWARE OF YOUR... ABILITIES.
THIS ISN'T EASY FOR ME TO TALK ABOUT, YOU SEE.

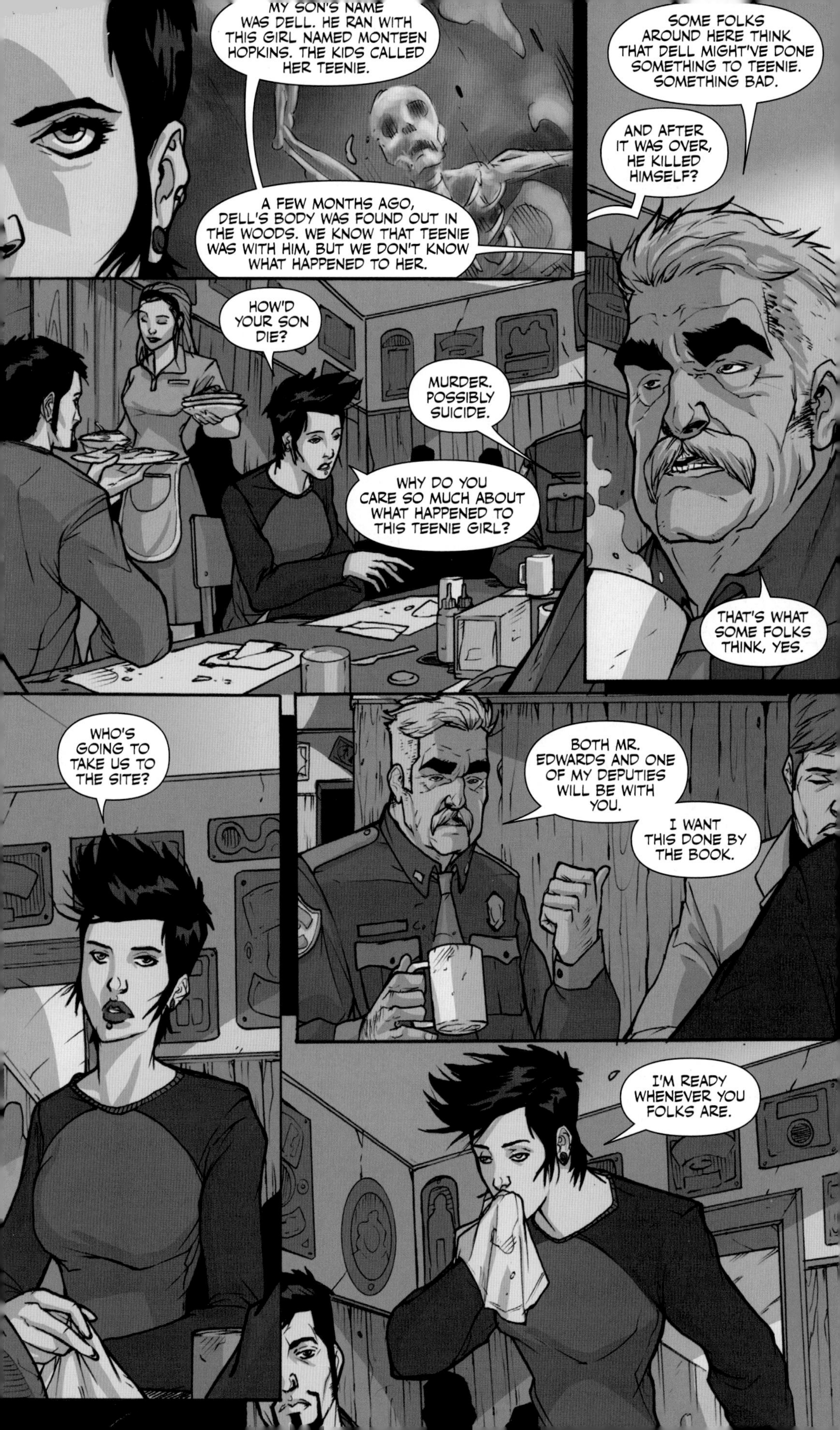
MY SON'S NAME WAS DELL. HE RAN WITH THIS GIRL NAMED MONTEEN HOPKINS. THE KIDS CALLED HER TEENIE.
A FEW MONTHS AGO, DELL'S BODY WAS FOUND OUT IN THE WOODS. WE KNOW THAT TEENIE WAS WITH HIM, BUT WE DON'T KNOW WHAT HAPPENED TO HER.
SOME FOLKS AROUND HERE THINK THAT DELL MIGHT'VE DONE SOMETHING TO TEENIE. SOMETHING BAD.
AND AFTER IT WAS OVER, HE KILLED HIMSELF?
HOW'D YOUR SON DIE?
MURDER. POSSIBLY SUICIDE.
WHY DO YOU CARE SO MUCH ABOUT WHAT HAPPENED TO THIS TEENIE GIRL?
THAT'S WHAT SOME FOLKS THINK, YES.
WHO'S GOING TO TAKE US TO THE SITE?
BOTH MR. EDWARDS AND ONE OF MY DEPUTIES WILL BE WITH YOU.
I WANT THIS DONE BY THE BOOK.
I'M READY WHENEVER YOU FOLKS ARE.

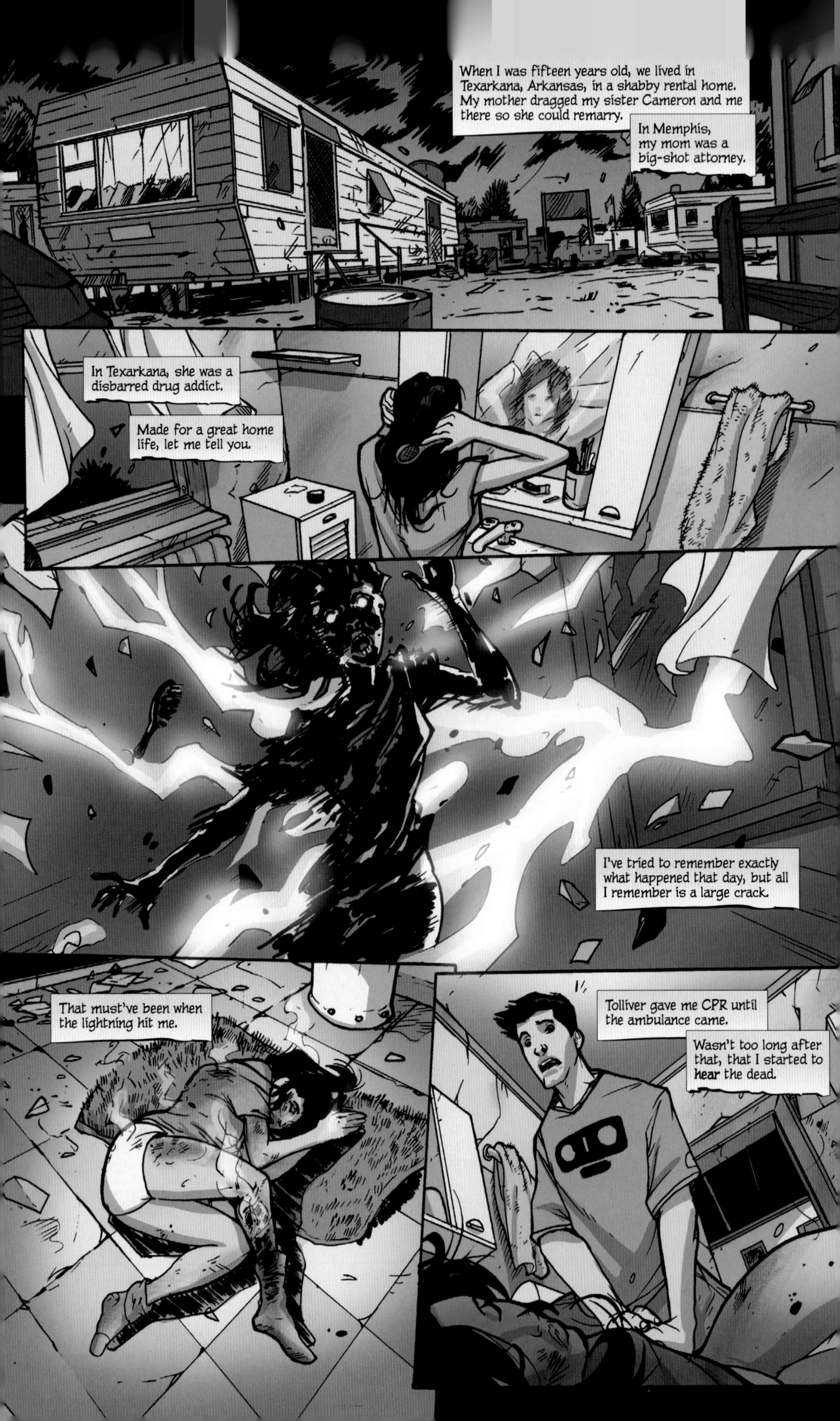
When I was fifteen years old, we lived in Texarkana, Arkansas, in a shabby rental home. My mother dragged my sister Cameron and me there so she could remarry.
In Memphis, my mom was a big-shot attorney.
In Texarkana, she was a disbarred drug addict.
Made for a great home life, let me tell you.
I've tried to remember exactly what happened that day, but all I remember is a large crack.
That must've been when the lightning hit me.
Tolliver gave me CPR until the ambulance came.
Wasn't too long after that, that I started to hear the dead.

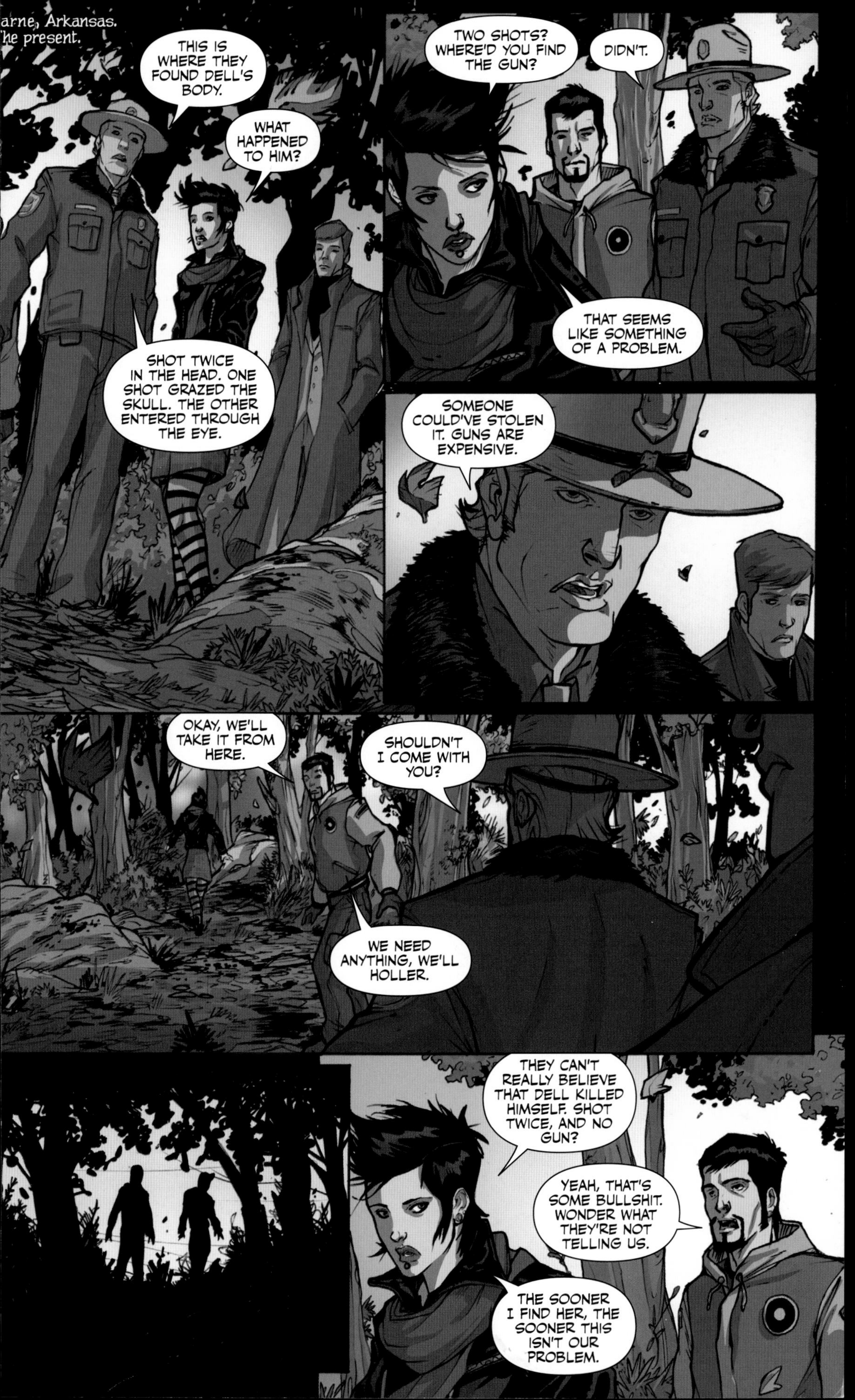
arne, Arkansas.
The present.
THIS IS WHERE THEY FOUND DELL'S BODY.
WHAT HAPPENED TO HIM?
SHOT TWICE IN THE HEAD. ONE SHOT GRAZED THE SKULL. THE OTHER ENTERED THROUGH THE EYE.
TWO SHOTS? WHERE'D YOU FIND THE GUN?
DIDN'T.
THAT SEEMS LIKE SOMETHING OF A PROBLEM.
SOMEONE COULD'VE STOLEN IT. GUNS ARE EXPENSIVE.
OKAY, WE'LL TAKE IT FROM HERE.
SHOULDN'T I COME WITH YOU?
WE NEED ANYTHING, WE'LL HOLLER.
THEY CAN'T REALLY BELIEVE THAT DELL KILLED HIMSELF. SHOT TWICE, AND NO GUN?
YEAH, THAT'S SOME BULLSHIT. WONDER WHAT THEY'RE NOT TELLING US.
THE SOONER I FIND HER, THE SOONER THIS ISN'T OUR PROBLEM.

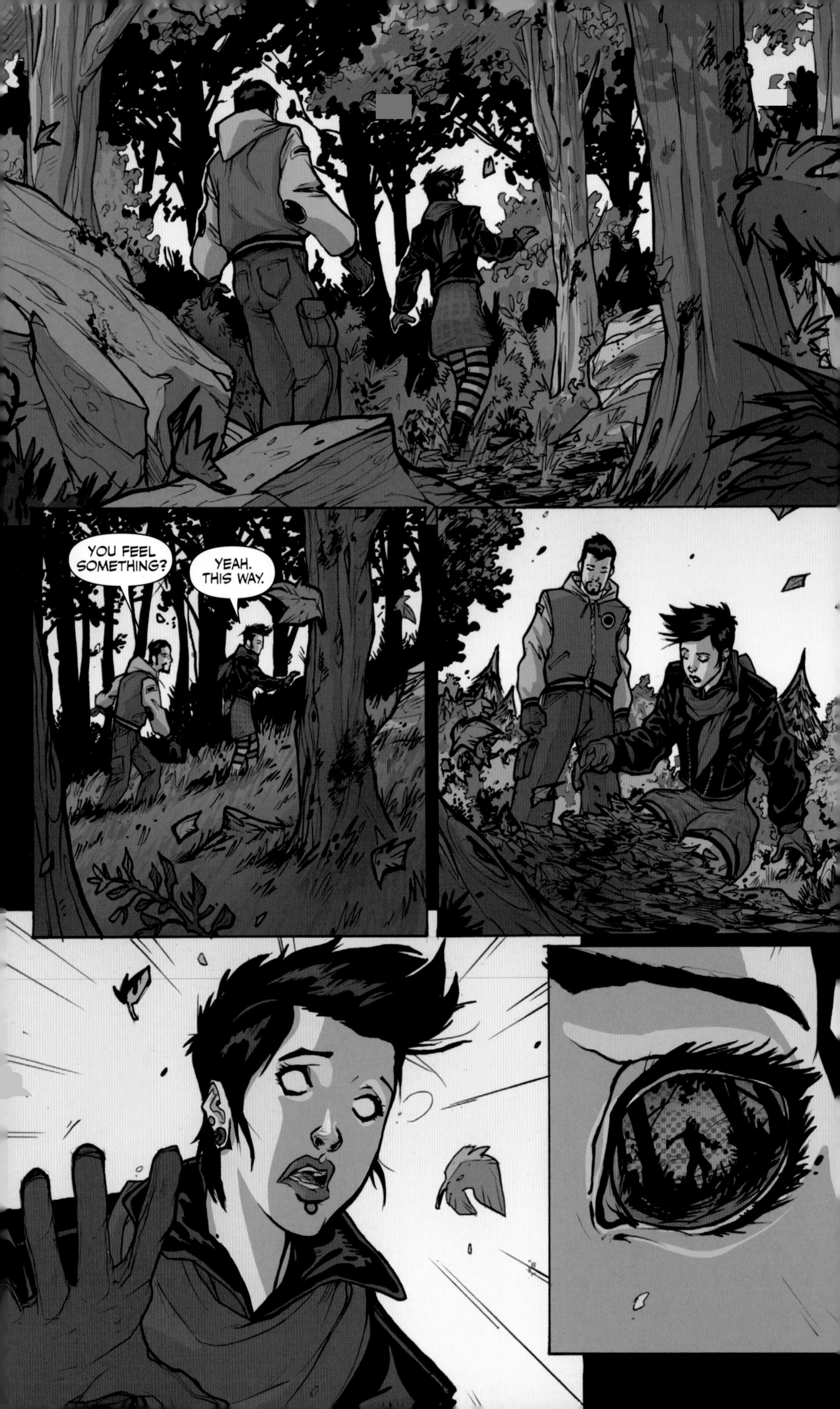

YOU FEEL SOMETHING?
YEAH. THIS WAY.

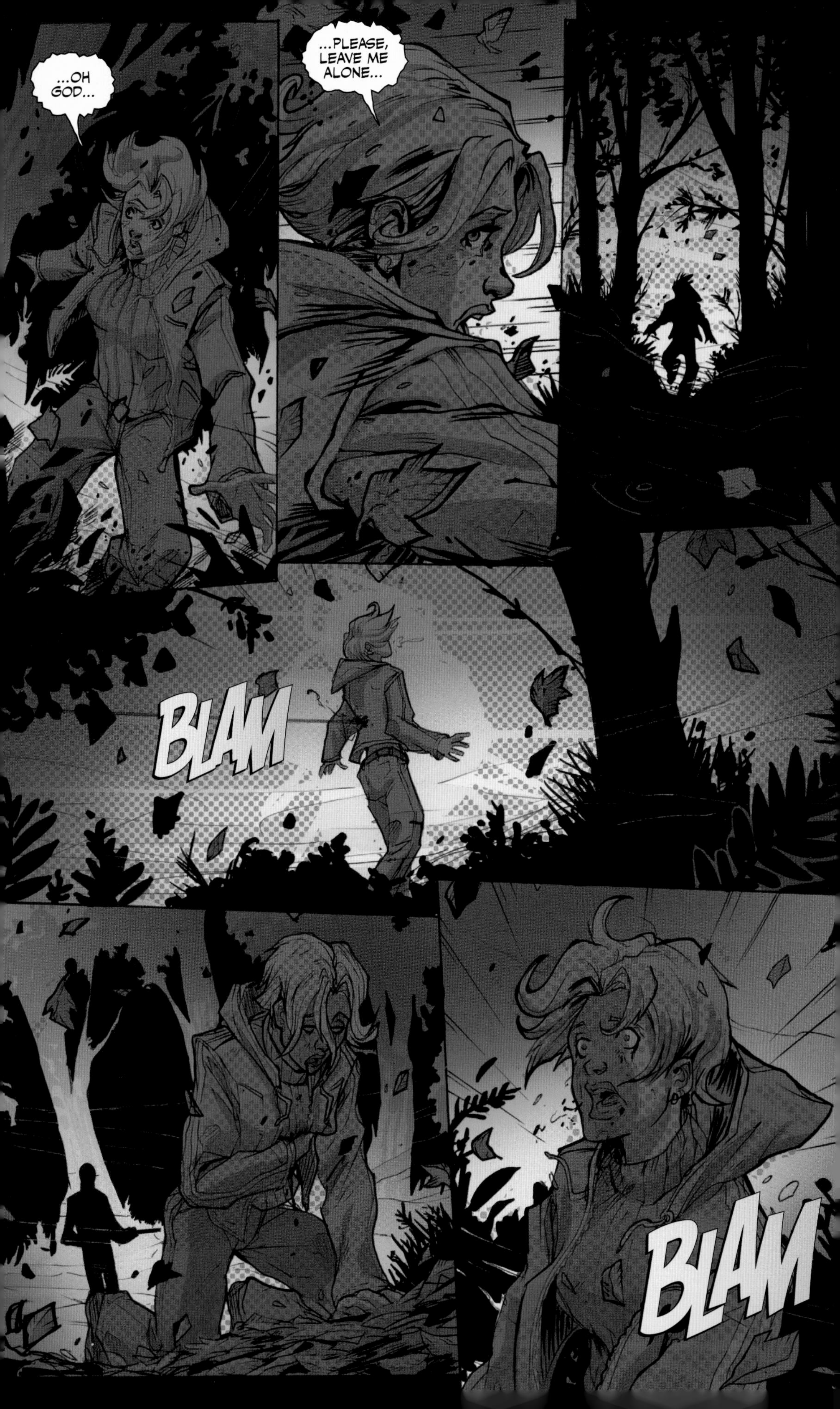
...OH GOD...
...PLEASE, LEAVE ME ALONE...
BLAM
BLAM

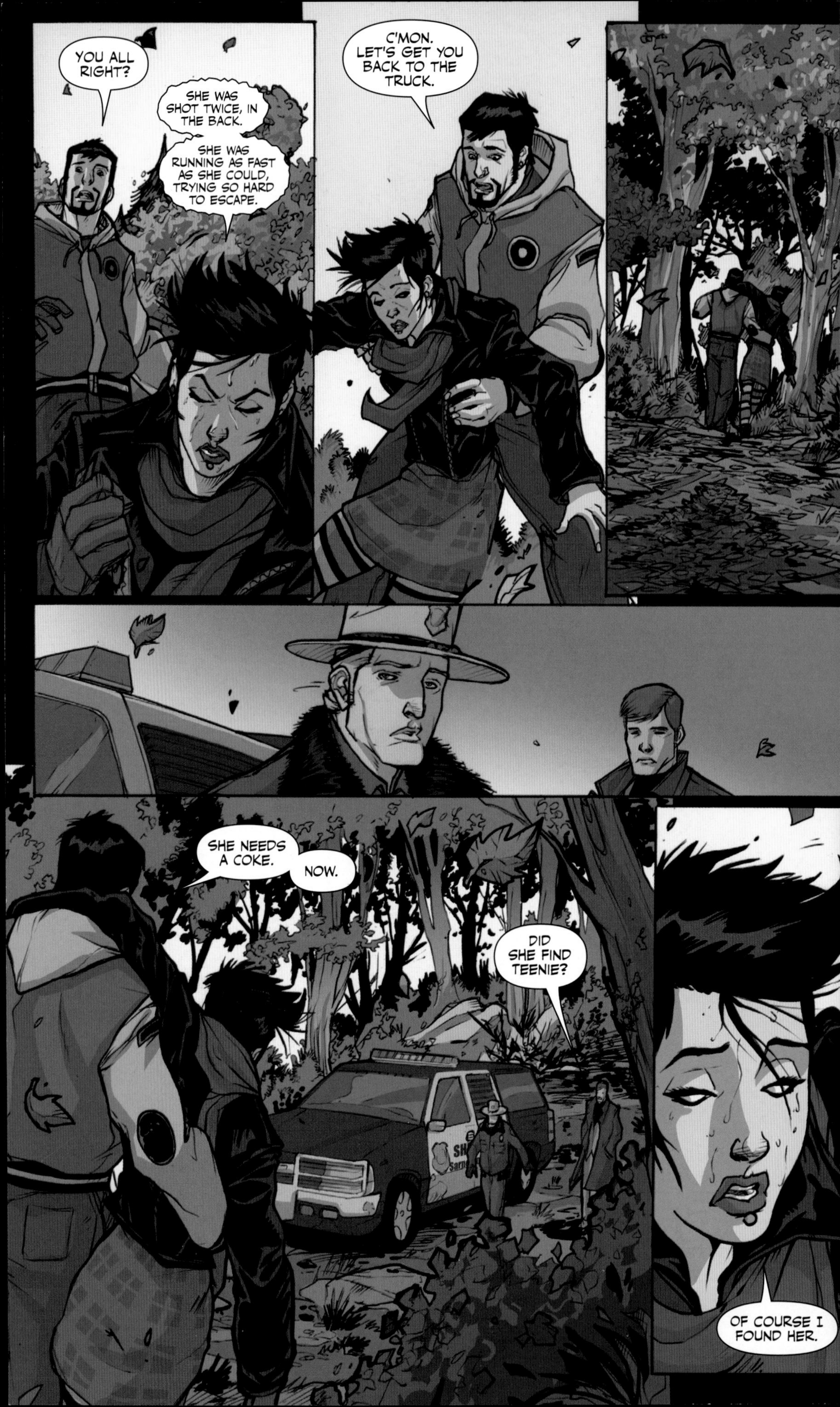

YOU ALL RIGHT?
SHE WAS SHOT TWICE, IN THE BACK.
SHE WAS RUNNING AS FAST AS SHE COULD, TRYING SO HARD TO ESCAPE.
C'MON. LET'S GET YOU BACK TO THE TRUCK.
SHE NEEDS A COKE.
NOW.
DID SHE FIND TEENIE?
OF COURSE I FOUND HER.

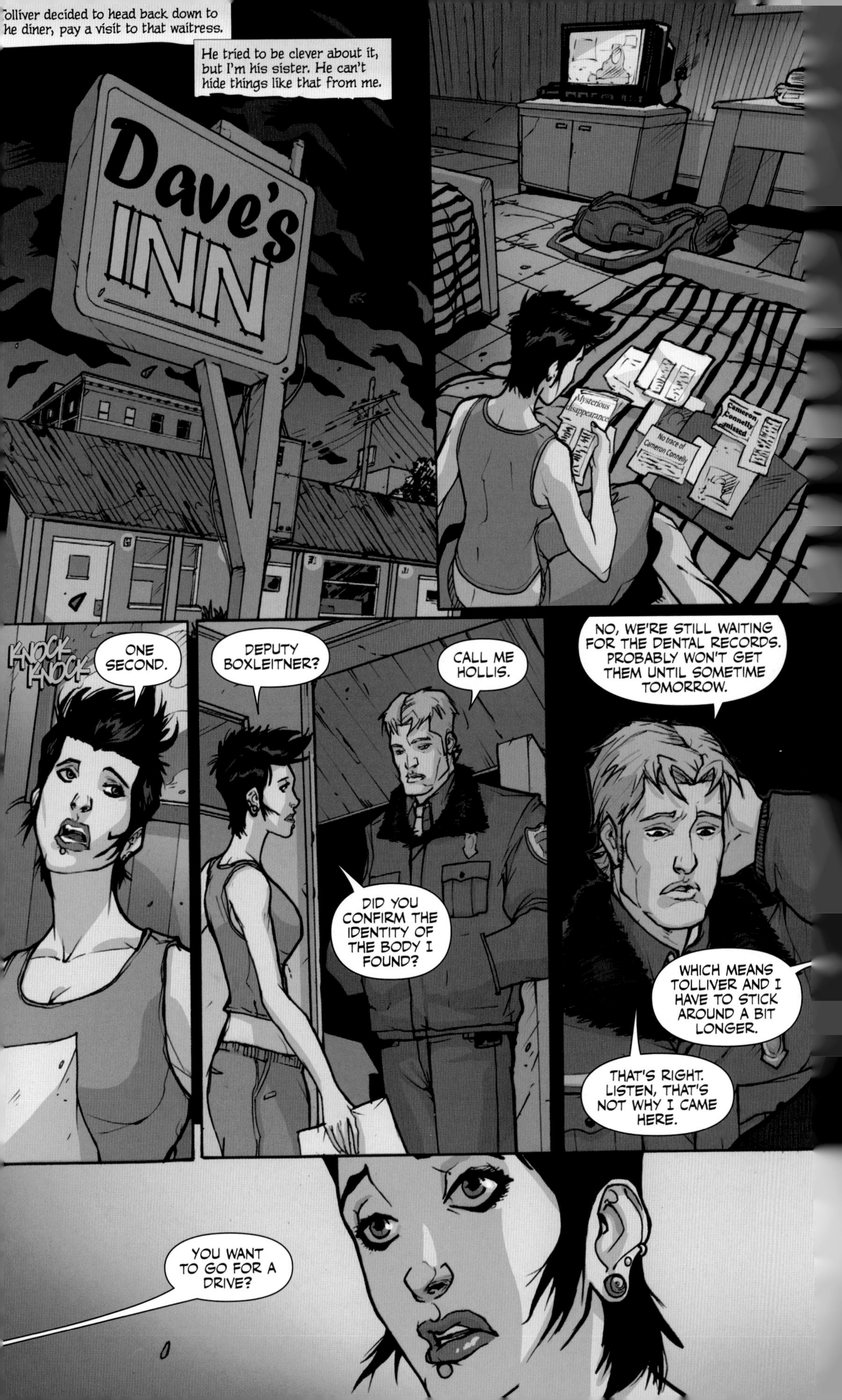
Tolliver decided to head back down to the diner, pay a visit to that waitress.
He tried to be clever about it, but I'm his sister. He can't hide things like that from me.
Dave's INN
Mysterious disappearance
No trace of Cameron Connelly
Cameron Connelly missed
KNOCK KNOCK
ONE SECOND.
DEPUTY BOXLEITNER?
CALL ME HOLLIS.
DID YOU CONFIRM THE IDENTITY OF THE BODY I FOUND?
NO, WE'RE STILL WAITING FOR THE DENTAL RECORDS. PROBABLY WON'T GET THEM UNTIL SOMETIME TOMORROW.
WHICH MEANS TOLLIVER AND I HAVE TO STICK AROUND A BIT LONGER.
THAT'S RIGHT. LISTEN, THAT'S NOT WHY I CAME HERE.
YOU WANT TO GO FOR A DRIVE?

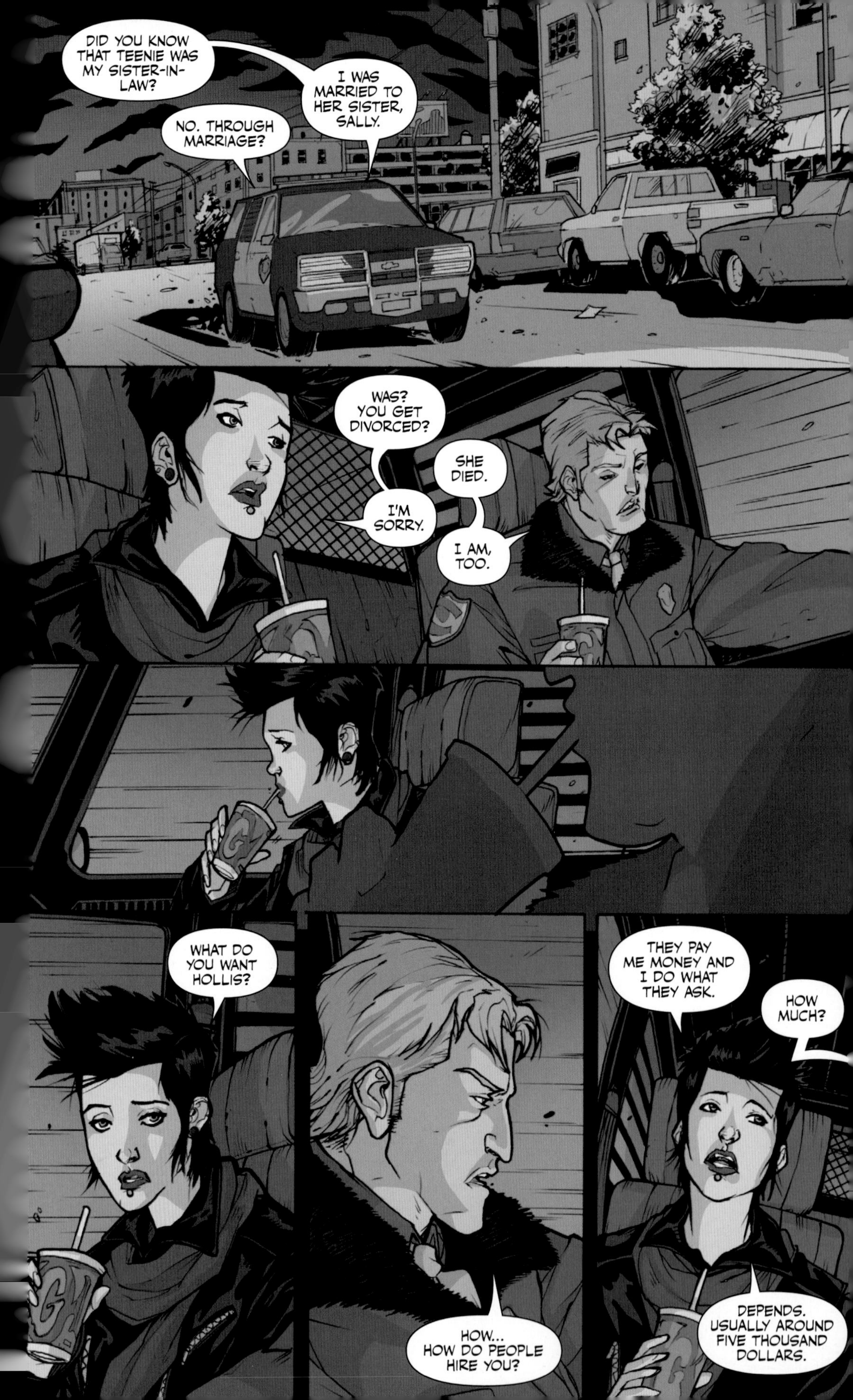
DID YOU KNOW THAT TEENIE WAS MY SISTER-IN-LAW?
NO. THROUGH MARRIAGE?
I WAS MARRIED TO HER SISTER, SALLY.
WAS? YOU GET DIVORCED?
SHE DIED.
I'M SORRY.
I AM, TOO.
WHAT DO YOU WANT HOLLIS?
HOW... HOW DO PEOPLE HIRE YOU?
THEY PAY ME MONEY AND I DO WHAT THEY ASK.
HOW MUCH?
DEPENDS. USUALLY AROUND FIVE THOUSAND DOLLARS.

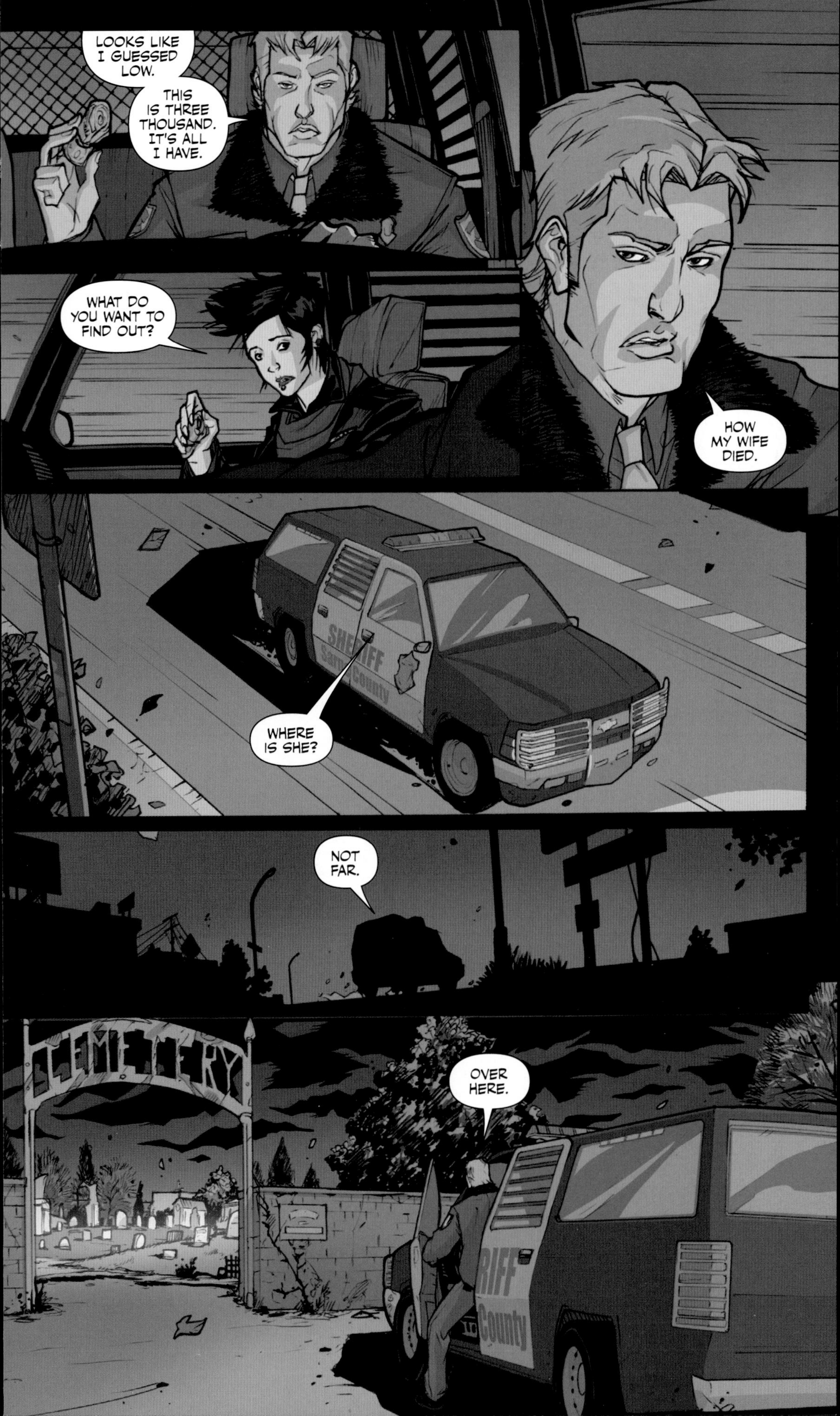
LOOKS LIKE I GUESSED LOW.
THIS IS THREE THOUSAND. IT'S ALL I HAVE.
WHAT DO YOU WANT TO FIND OUT?
HOW MY WIFE DIED.
SHERIFF
WHERE IS SHE?
NOT FAR.
CEMETERY
OVER HERE.

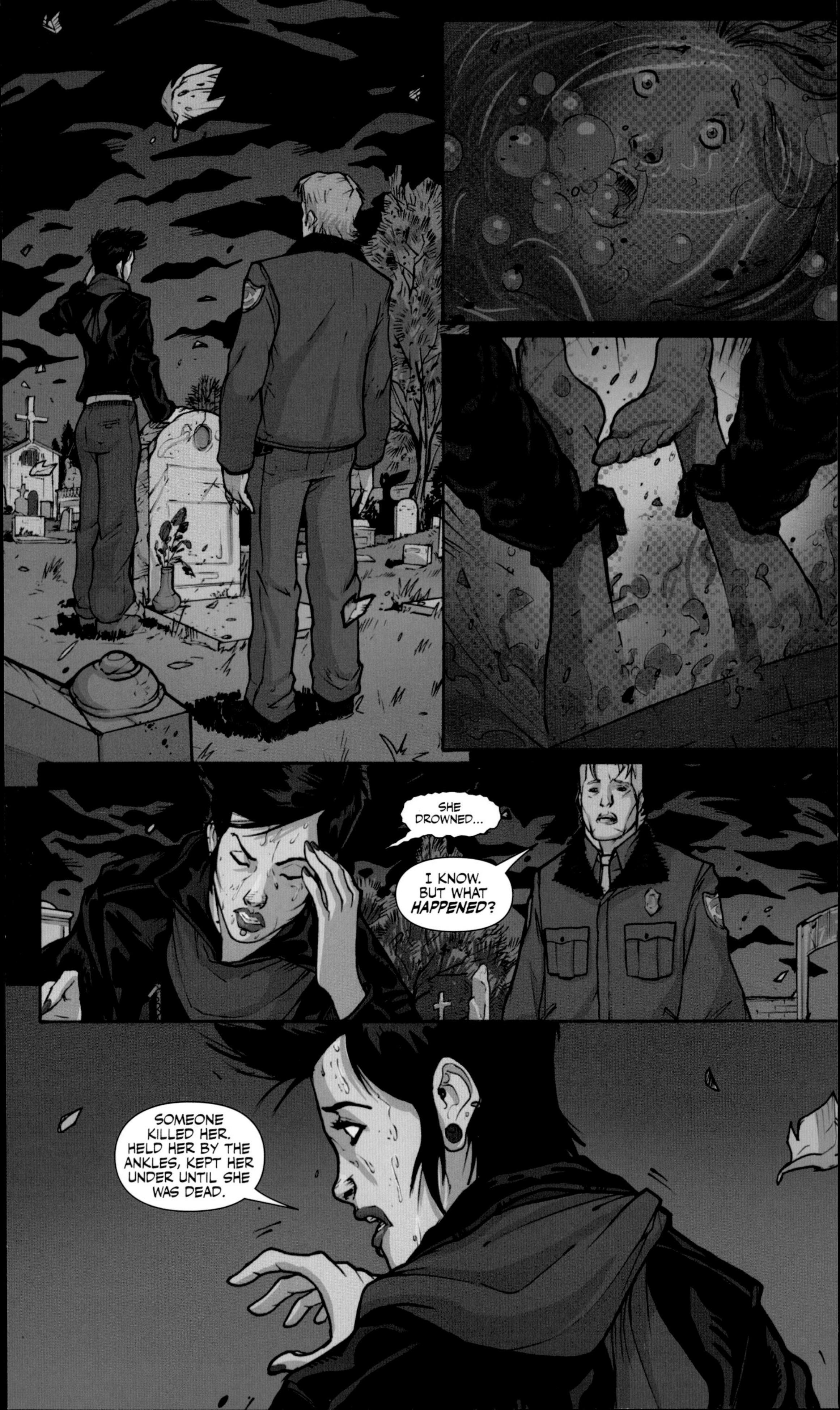
SHE DROWNED...
I KNOW. BUT WHAT HAPPENED?
SOMEONE KILLED HER. HELD HER BY THE ANKLES, KEPT HER UNDER UNTIL SHE WAS DEAD.

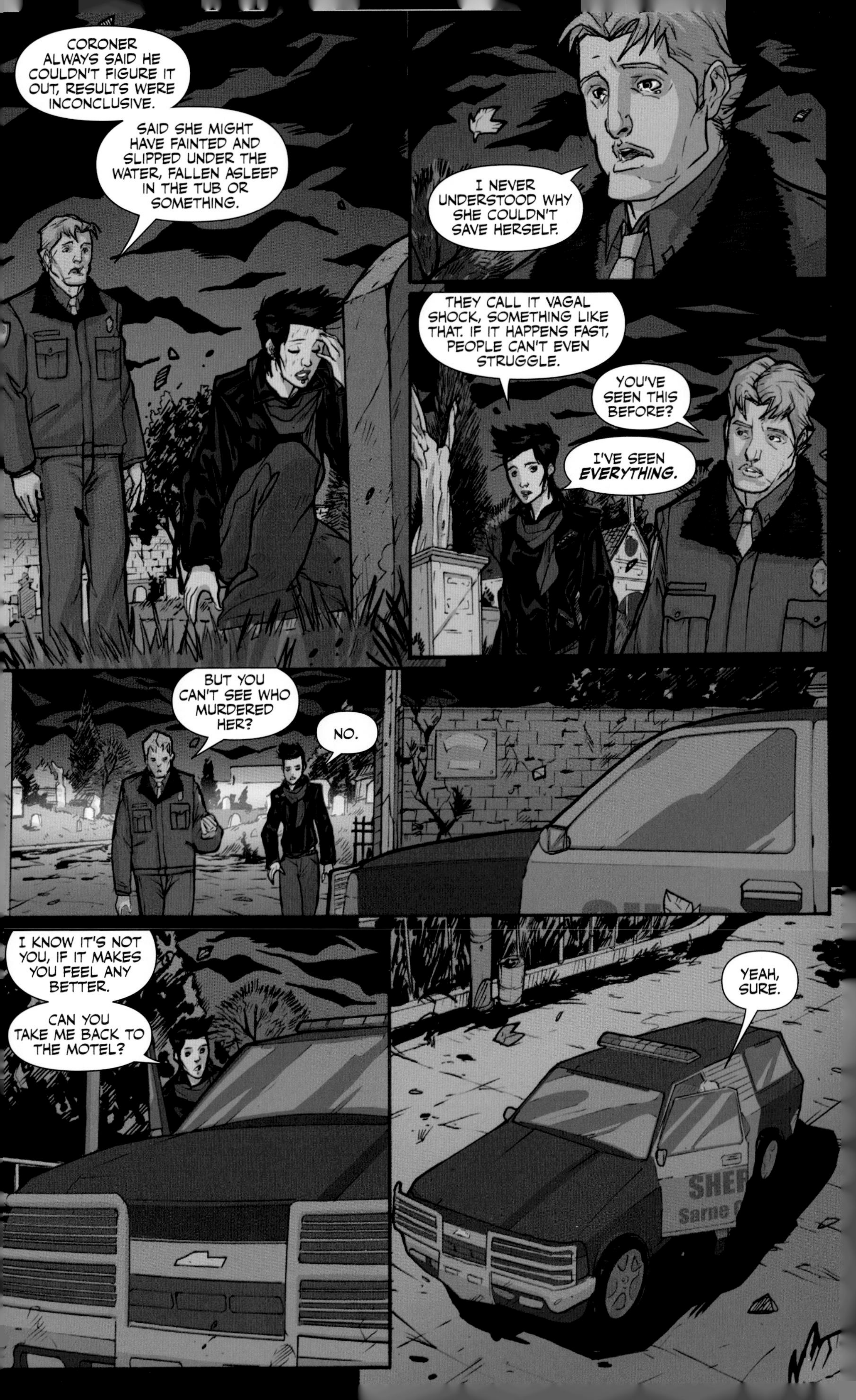
CORONER ALWAYS SAID HE COULDN'T FIGURE IT OUT, RESULTS WERE INCONCLUSIVE.
SAID SHE MIGHT HAVE FAINTED AND SLIPPED UNDER THE WATER, FALLEN ASLEEP IN THE TUB OR SOMETHING.
I NEVER UNDERSTOOD WHY SHE COULDN'T SAVE HERSELF.
THEY CALL IT VAGAL SHOCK, SOMETHING LIKE THAT. IF IT HAPPENS FAST, PEOPLE CAN'T EVEN STRUGGLE.
YOU'VE SEEN THIS BEFORE?
I'VE SEEN *EVERYTHING.*
BUT YOU CAN'T SEE WHO MURDERED HER?
NO.
I KNOW IT'S NOT YOU, IF IT MAKES YOU FEEL ANY BETTER.
CAN YOU TAKE ME BACK TO THE MOTEL?
YEAH, SURE.

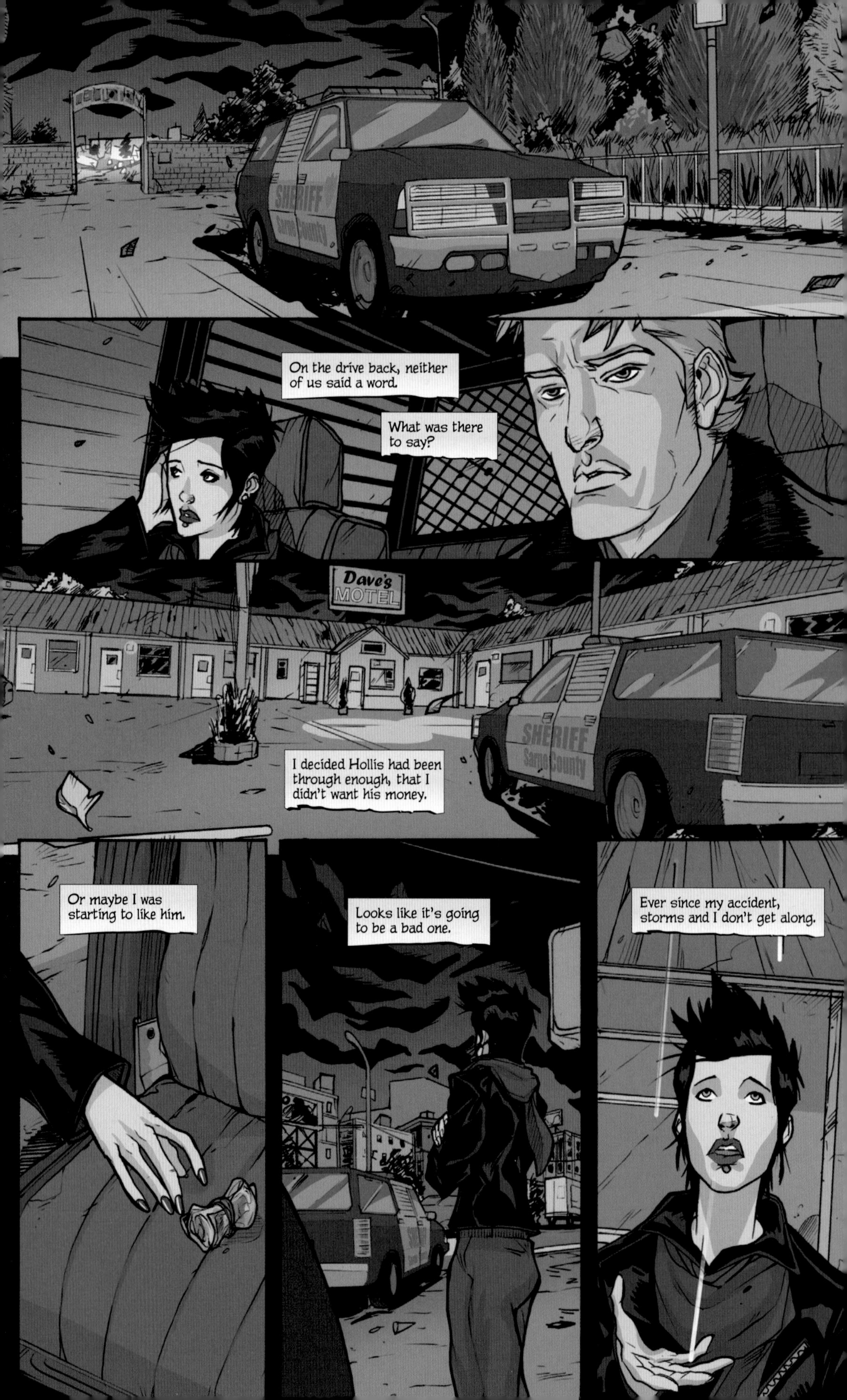
SHERIFF
Sarpe County
On the drive back, neither of us said a word.
What was there to say?
Dave's
MOTEL
SHERIFF
Sarpe County
I decided Hollis had been through enough, that I didn't want his money.
Or maybe I was starting to like him.
Looks like it's going to be a bad one.
Ever since my accident, storms and I don't get along.

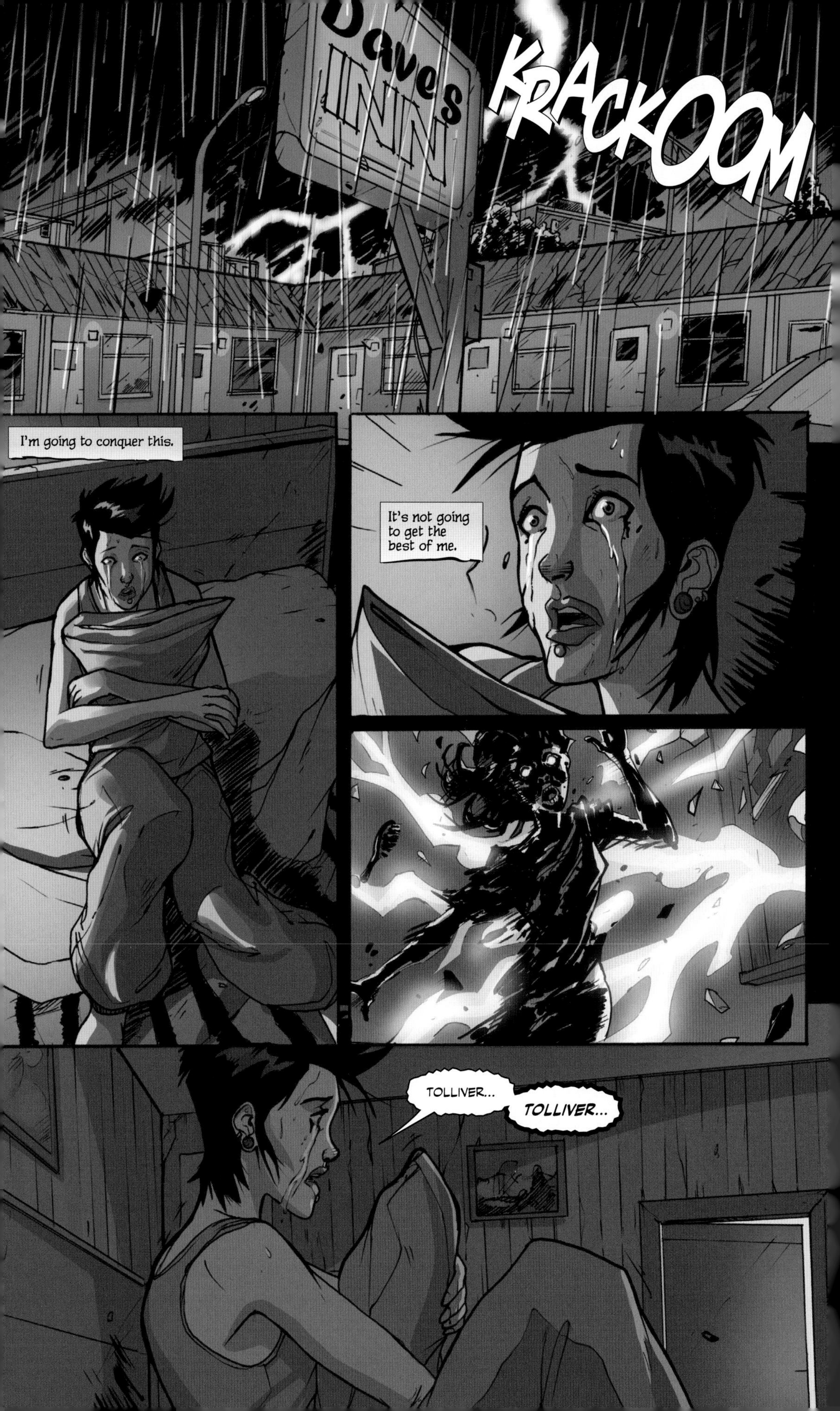
Daves INN
KRACKOOM
I'm going to conquer this.
It's not going to get the best of me.
TOLLIVER...
TOLLIVER...

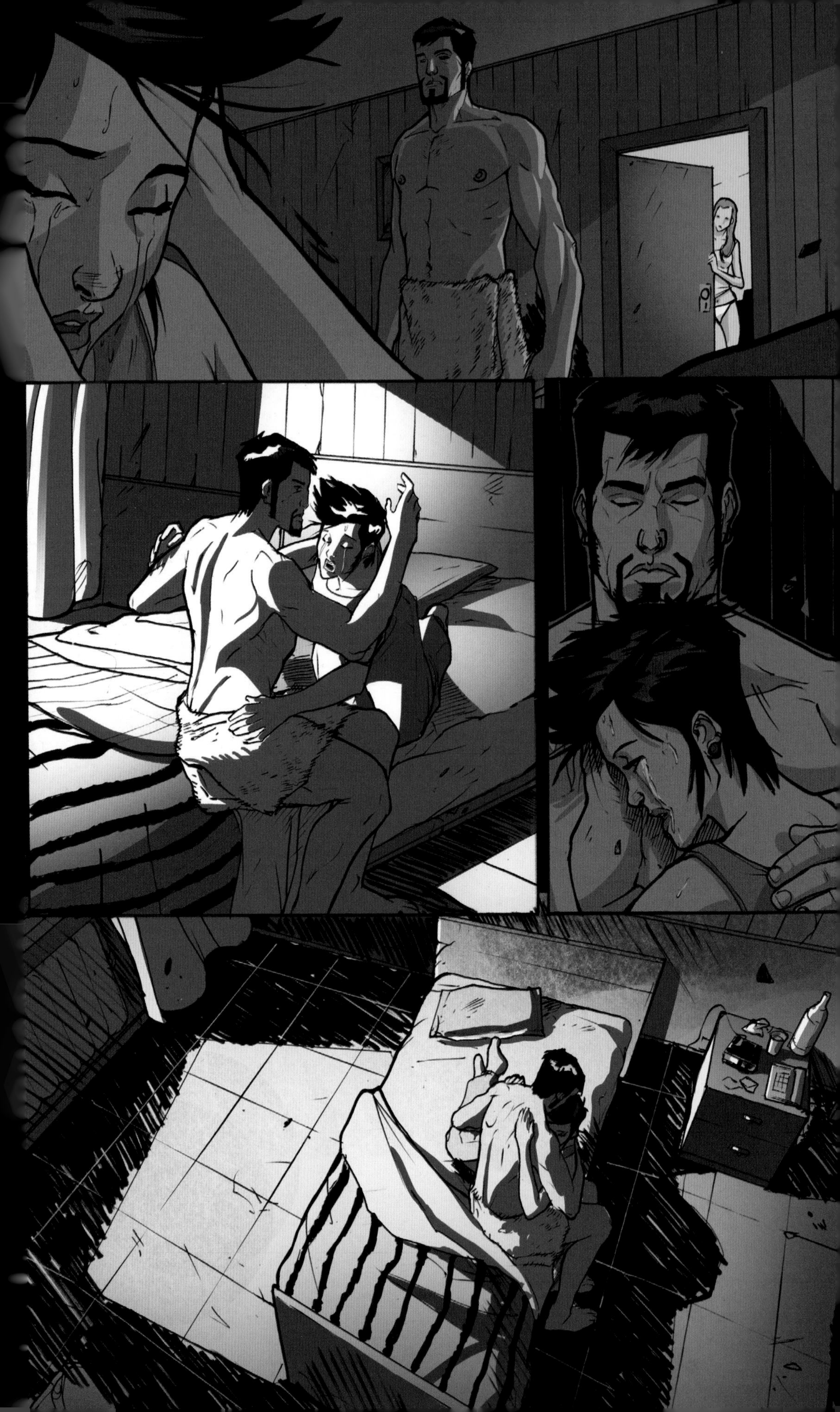

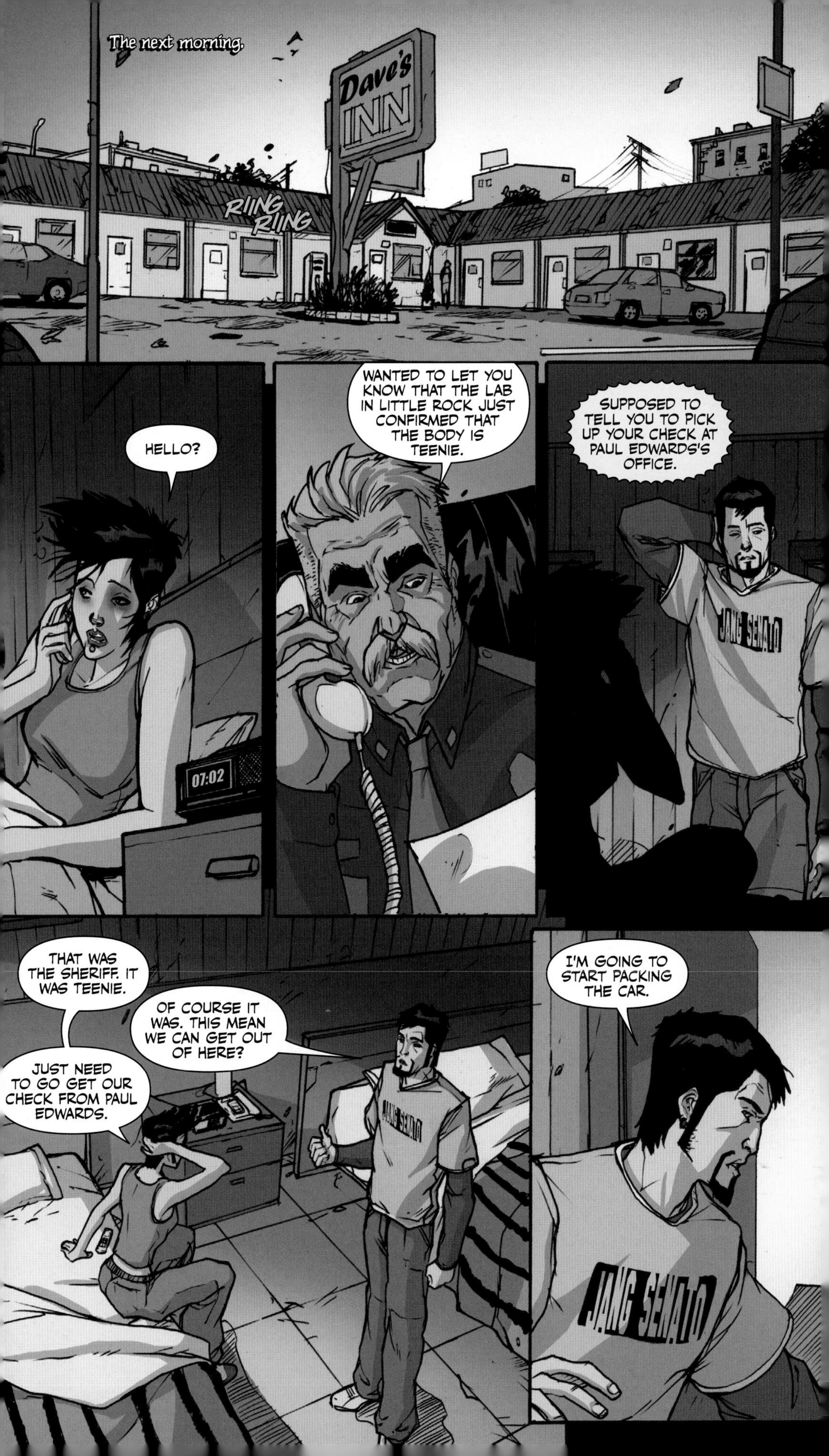
The next morning.
Dave's INN
RIING RIING
HELLO?
WANTED TO LET YOU KNOW THAT THE LAB IN LITTLE ROCK JUST CONFIRMED THAT THE BODY IS TEENIE.
07:02
SUPPOSED TO TELL YOU TO PICK UP YOUR CHECK AT PAUL EDWARDS'S OFFICE.
THAT WAS THE SHERIFF. IT WAS TEENIE.
OF COURSE IT WAS. THIS MEAN WE CAN GET OUT OF HERE?
JUST NEED TO GO GET OUR CHECK FROM PAUL EDWARDS.
I'M GOING TO START PACKING THE CAR.

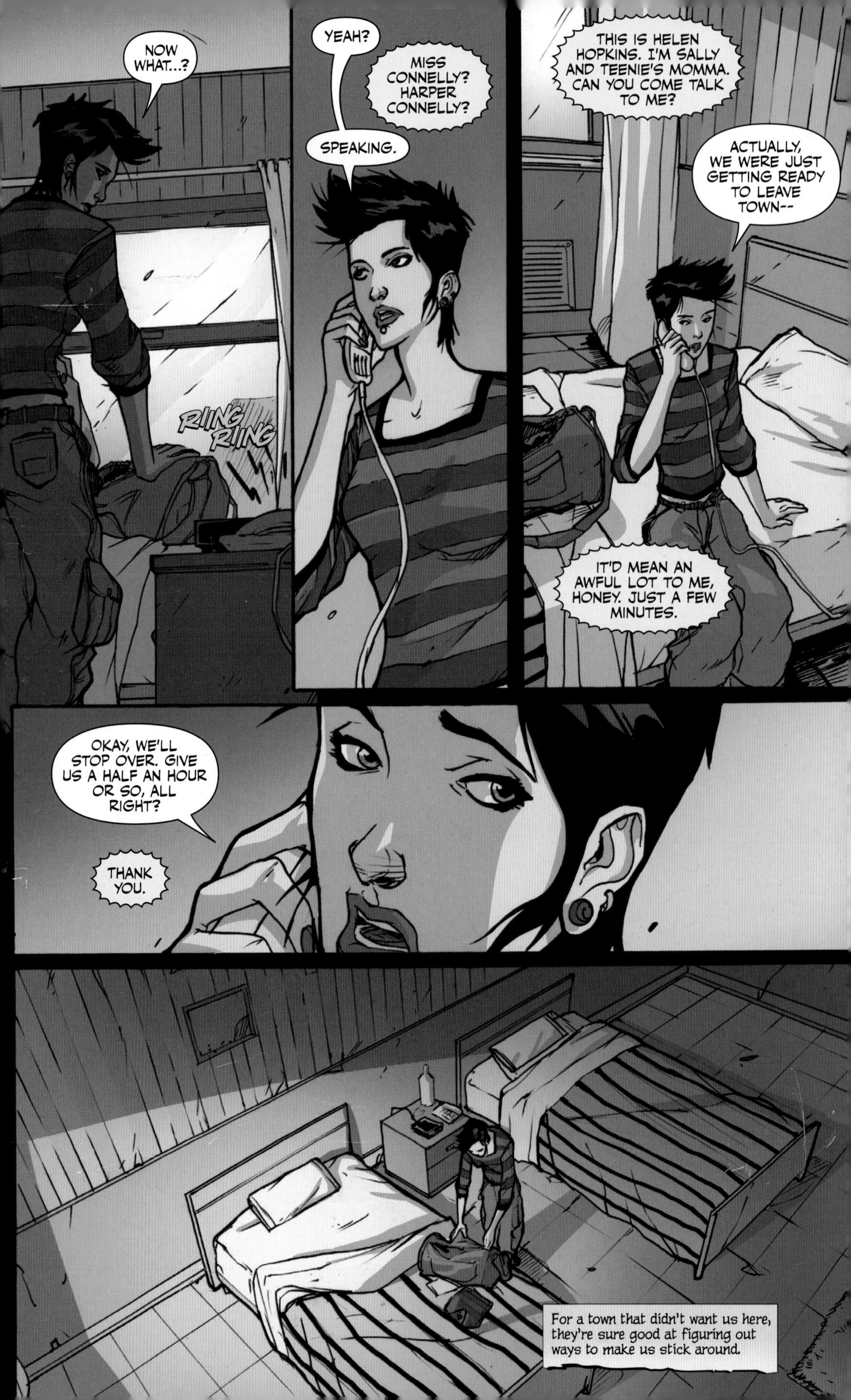
NOW WHAT...?
RIING RIING
YEAH?
MISS CONNELLY? HARPER CONNELLY?
SPEAKING.
THIS IS HELEN HOPKINS. I'M SALLY AND TEENIE'S MOMMA. CAN YOU COME TALK TO ME?
ACTUALLY, WE WERE JUST GETTING READY TO LEAVE TOWN--
IT'D MEAN AN AWFUL LOT TO ME, HONEY. JUST A FEW MINUTES.
OKAY, WE'LL STOP OVER. GIVE US A HALF AN HOUR OR SO, ALL RIGHT?
THANK YOU.
For a town that didn't want us here, they're sure good at figuring out ways to make us stick around.

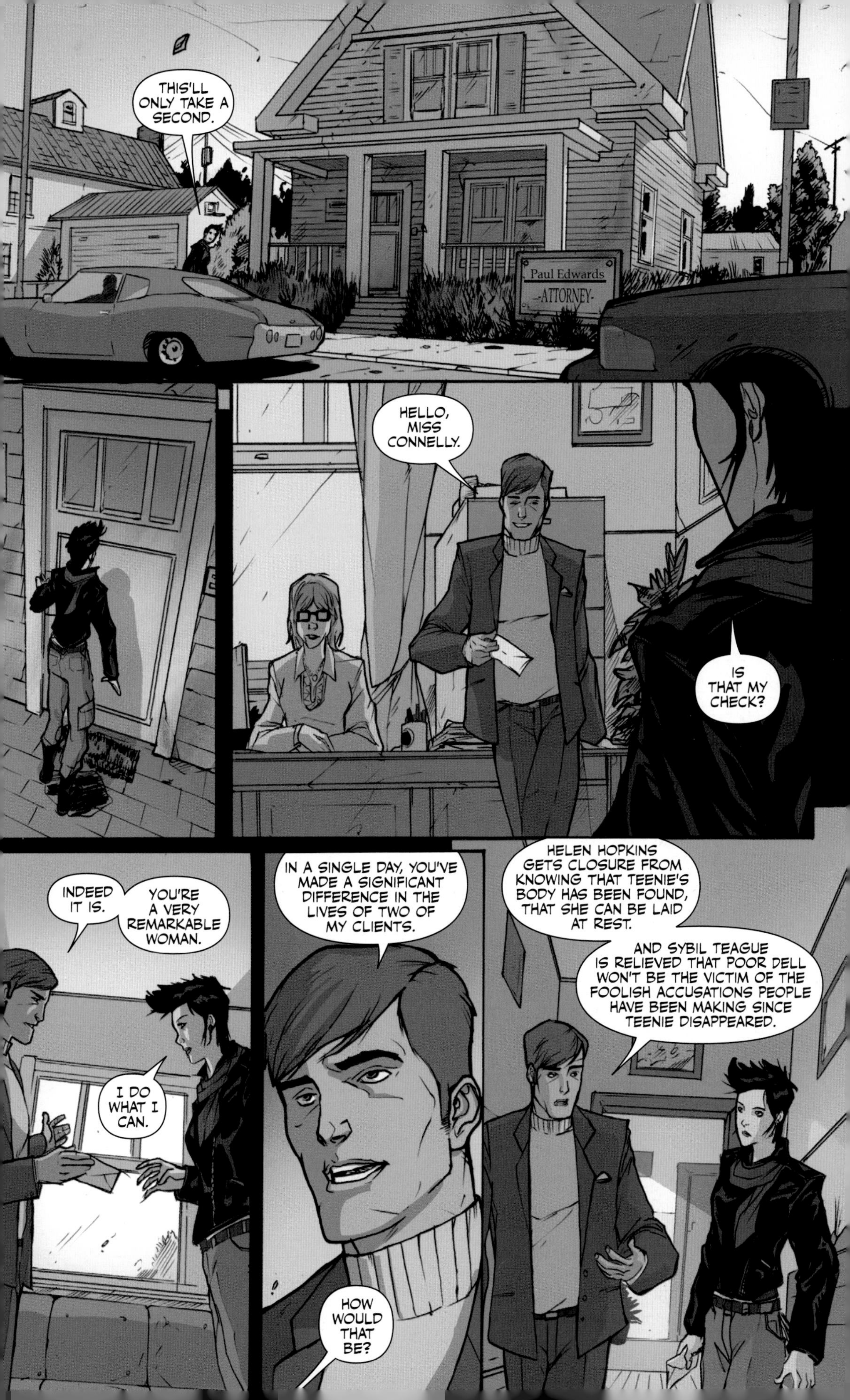
THIS'LL ONLY TAKE A SECOND.
Paul Edwards
-ATTORNEY-
HELLO, MISS CONNELLY.
IS THAT MY CHECK?
INDEED IT IS.
YOU'RE A VERY REMARKABLE WOMAN.
I DO WHAT I CAN.
IN A SINGLE DAY, YOU'VE MADE A SIGNIFICANT DIFFERENCE IN THE LIVES OF TWO OF MY CLIENTS.
HOW WOULD THAT BE?
HELEN HOPKINS GETS CLOSURE FROM KNOWING THAT TEENIE'S BODY HAS BEEN FOUND, THAT SHE CAN BE LAID AT REST.
AND SYBIL TEAGUE IS RELIEVED THAT POOR DELL WON'T BE THE VICTIM OF THE FOOLISH ACCUSATIONS PEOPLE HAVE BEEN MAKING SINCE TEENIE DISAPPEARED.

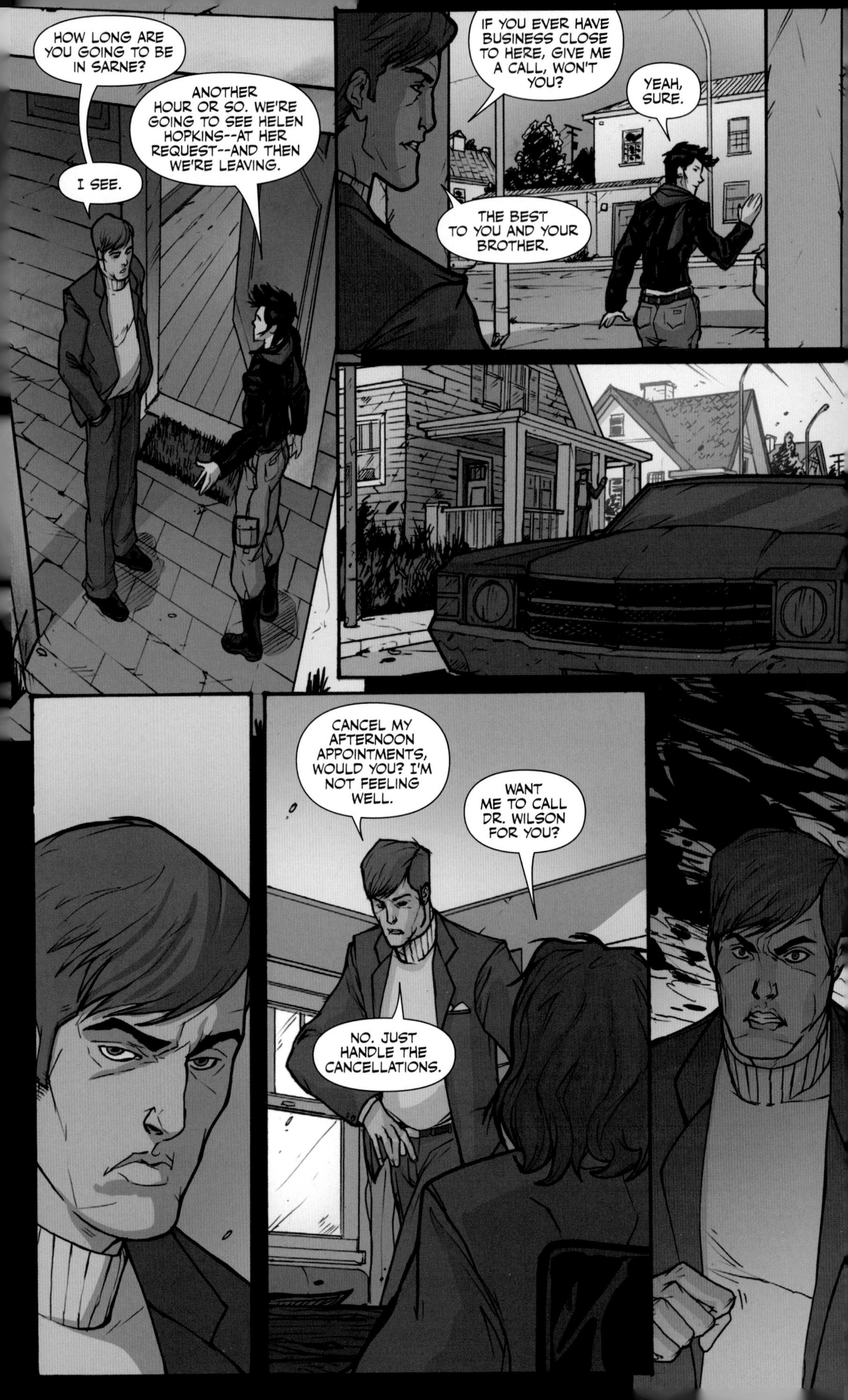
HOW LONG ARE YOU GOING TO BE IN SARNE?
ANOTHER HOUR OR SO. WE'RE GOING TO SEE HELEN HOPKINS--AT HER REQUEST--AND THEN WE'RE LEAVING.
I SEE.
IF YOU EVER HAVE BUSINESS CLOSE TO HERE, GIVE ME A CALL, WON'T YOU?
YEAH, SURE.
THE BEST TO YOU AND YOUR BROTHER.
CANCEL MY AFTERNOON APPOINTMENTS, WOULD YOU? I'M NOT FEELING WELL.
WANT ME TO CALL DR. WILSON FOR YOU?
NO. JUST HANDLE THE CANCELLATIONS.

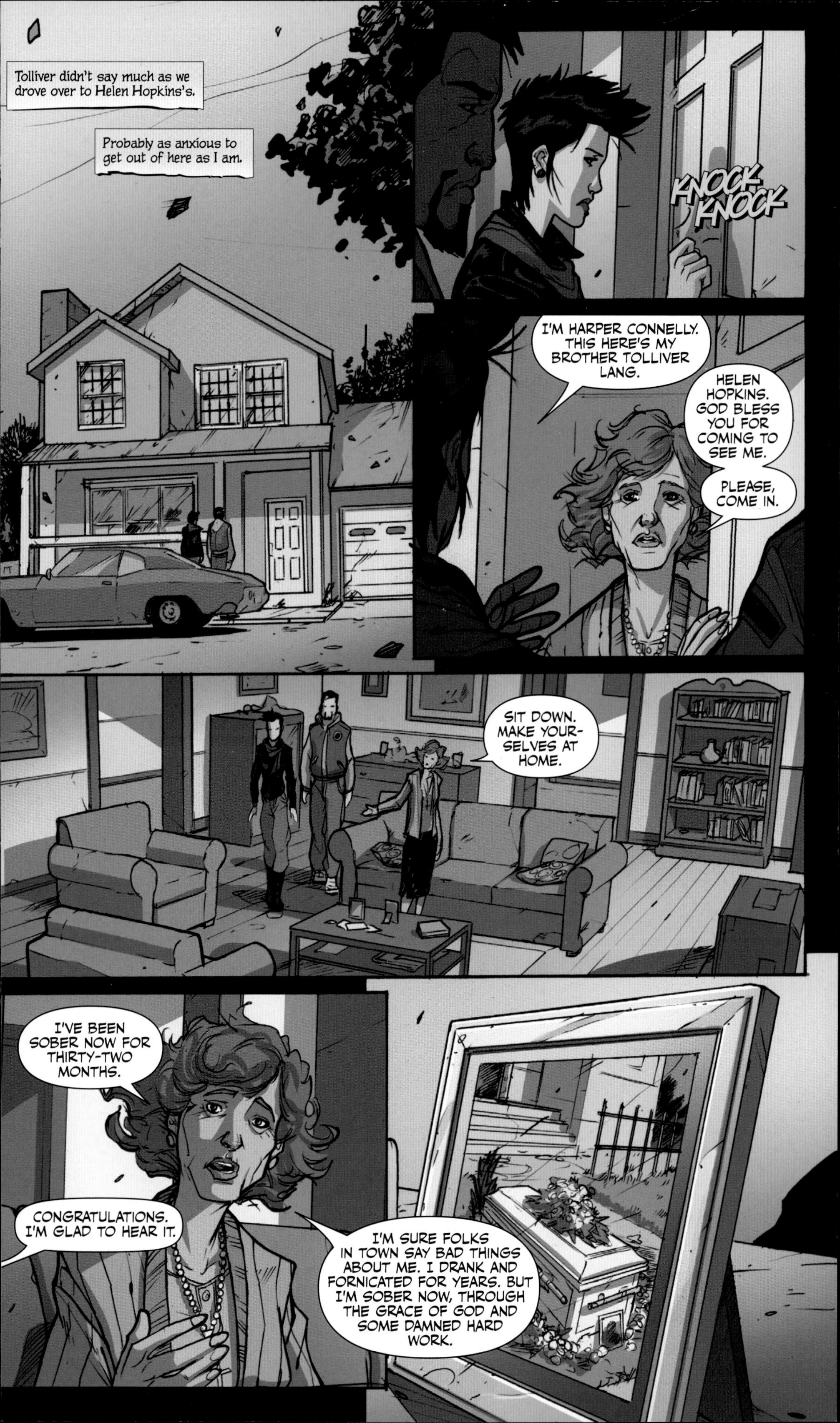
Tolliver didn't say much as we drove over to Helen Hopkins's.
Probably as anxious to get out of here as I am.
KNOCK KNOCK
I'M HARPER CONNELLY. THIS HERE'S MY BROTHER TOLLIVER LANG.
HELEN HOPKINS. GOD BLESS YOU FOR COMING TO SEE ME.
PLEASE, COME IN.
SIT DOWN. MAKE YOUR-SELVES AT HOME.
I'VE BEEN SOBER NOW FOR THIRTY-TWO MONTHS.
CONGRATULATIONS. I'M GLAD TO HEAR IT.
I'M SURE FOLKS IN TOWN SAY BAD THINGS ABOUT ME. I DRANK AND FORNICATED FOR YEARS. BUT I'M SOBER NOW, THROUGH THE GRACE OF GOD AND SOME DAMNED HARD WORK.

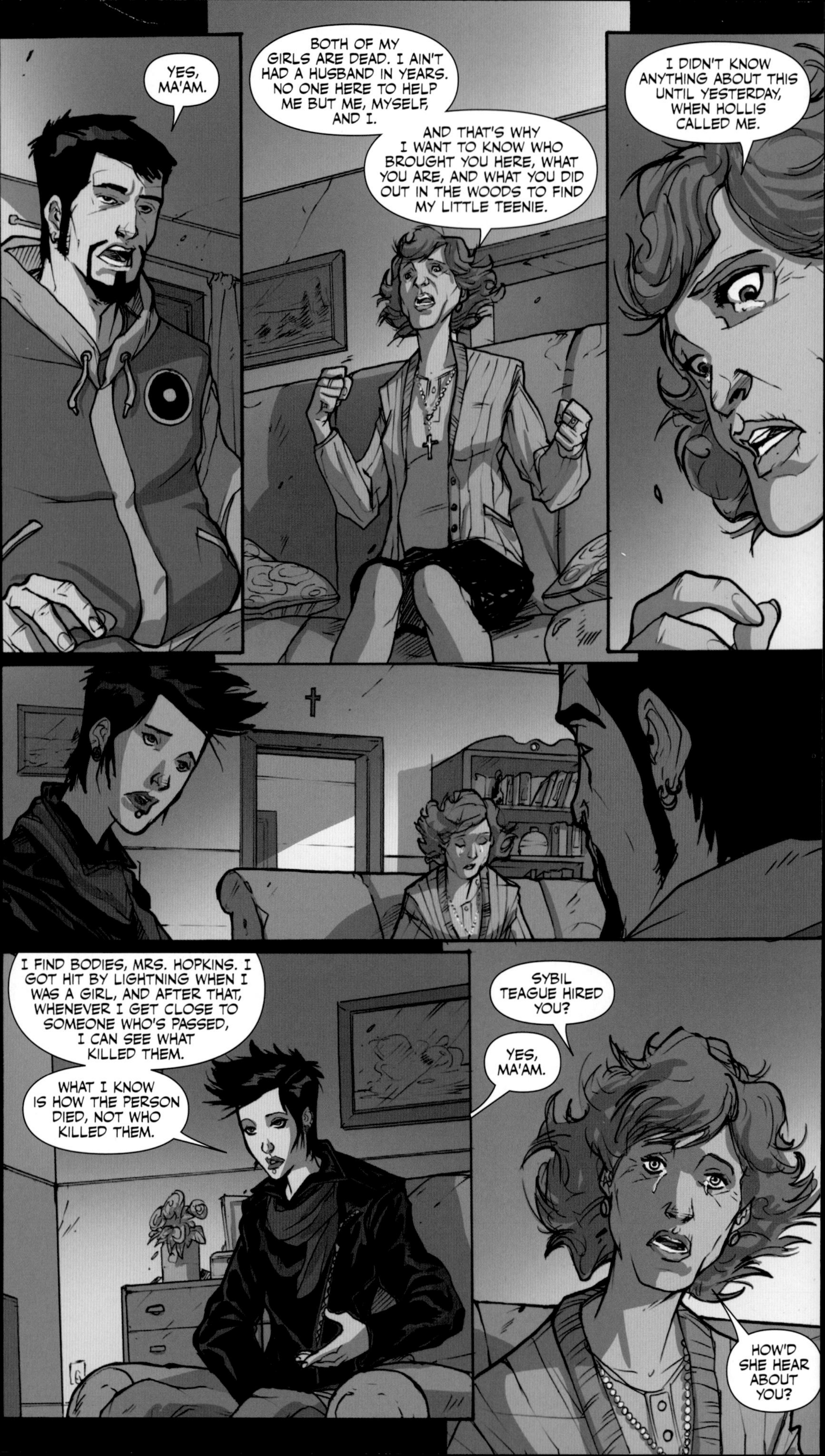
YES, MA'AM.
BOTH OF MY GIRLS ARE DEAD. I AIN'T HAD A HUSBAND IN YEARS. NO ONE HERE TO HELP ME BUT ME, MYSELF, AND I.
AND THAT'S WHY I WANT TO KNOW WHO BROUGHT YOU HERE, WHAT YOU ARE, AND WHAT YOU DID OUT IN THE WOODS TO FIND MY LITTLE TEENIE.
I DIDN'T KNOW ANYTHING ABOUT THIS UNTIL YESTERDAY, WHEN HOLLIS CALLED ME.
I FIND BODIES, MRS. HOPKINS. I GOT HIT BY LIGHTNING WHEN I WAS A GIRL, AND AFTER THAT, WHENEVER I GET CLOSE TO SOMEONE WHO'S PASSED, I CAN SEE WHAT KILLED THEM.
WHAT I KNOW IS HOW THE PERSON DIED, NOT WHO KILLED THEM.
SYBIL TEAGUE HIRED YOU?
YES, MA'AM.
HOW'D SHE HEAR ABOUT YOU?

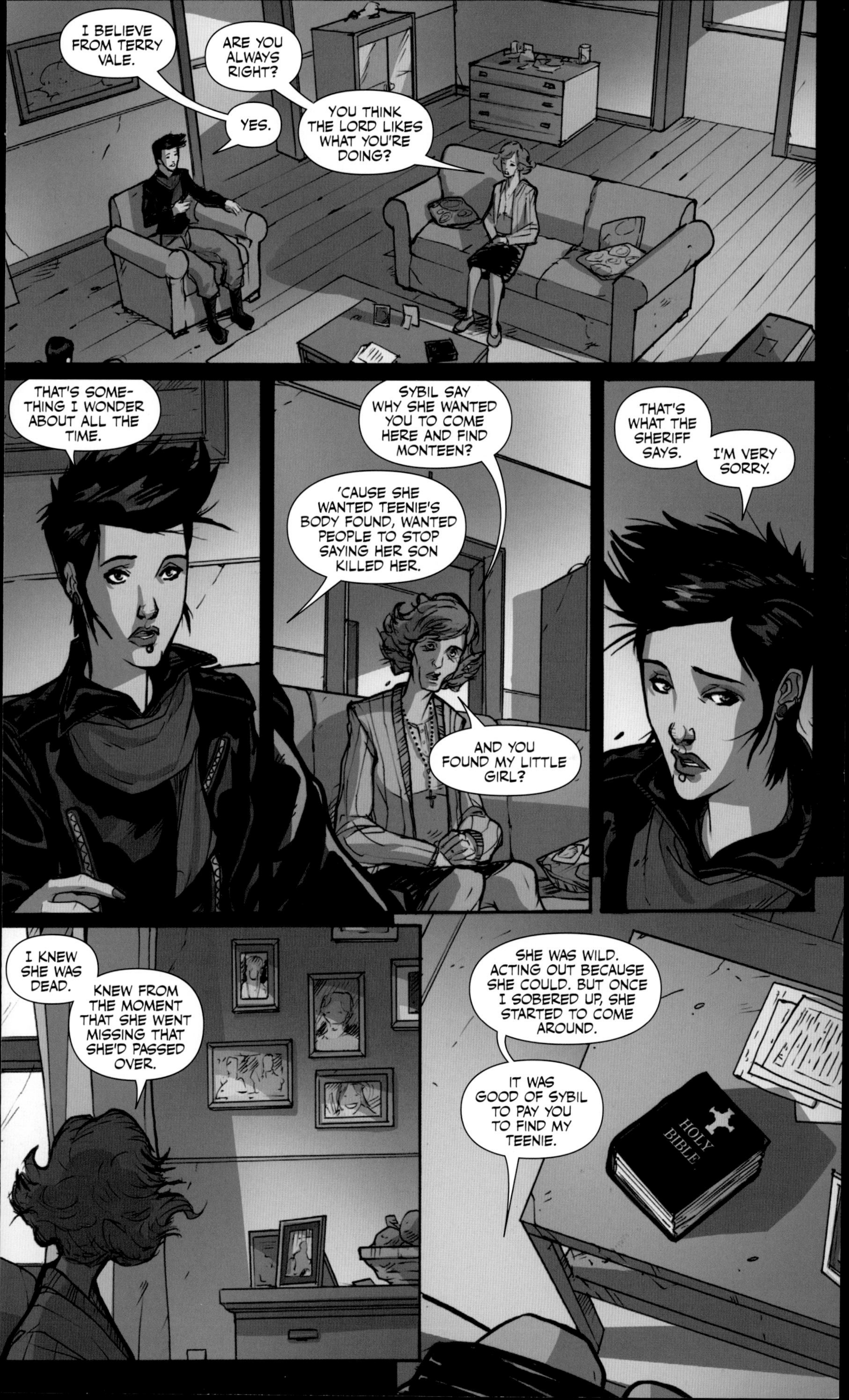
I BELIEVE FROM TERRY VALE.
ARE YOU ALWAYS RIGHT?
YES.
YOU THINK THE LORD LIKES WHAT YOU'RE DOING?
THAT'S SOME-THING I WONDER ABOUT ALL THE TIME.
SYBIL SAY WHY SHE WANTED YOU TO COME HERE AND FIND MONTEEN?
'CAUSE SHE WANTED TEENIE'S BODY FOUND, WANTED PEOPLE TO STOP SAYING HER SON KILLED HER.
AND YOU FOUND MY LITTLE GIRL?
THAT'S WHAT THE SHERIFF SAYS.
I'M VERY SORRY.
I KNEW SHE WAS DEAD.
KNEW FROM THE MOMENT THAT SHE WENT MISSING THAT SHE'D PASSED OVER.
SHE WAS WILD. ACTING OUT BECAUSE SHE COULD. BUT ONCE I SOBERED UP, SHE STARTED TO COME AROUND.
IT WAS GOOD OF SYBIL TO PAY YOU TO FIND MY TEENIE.
HOLY BIBLE

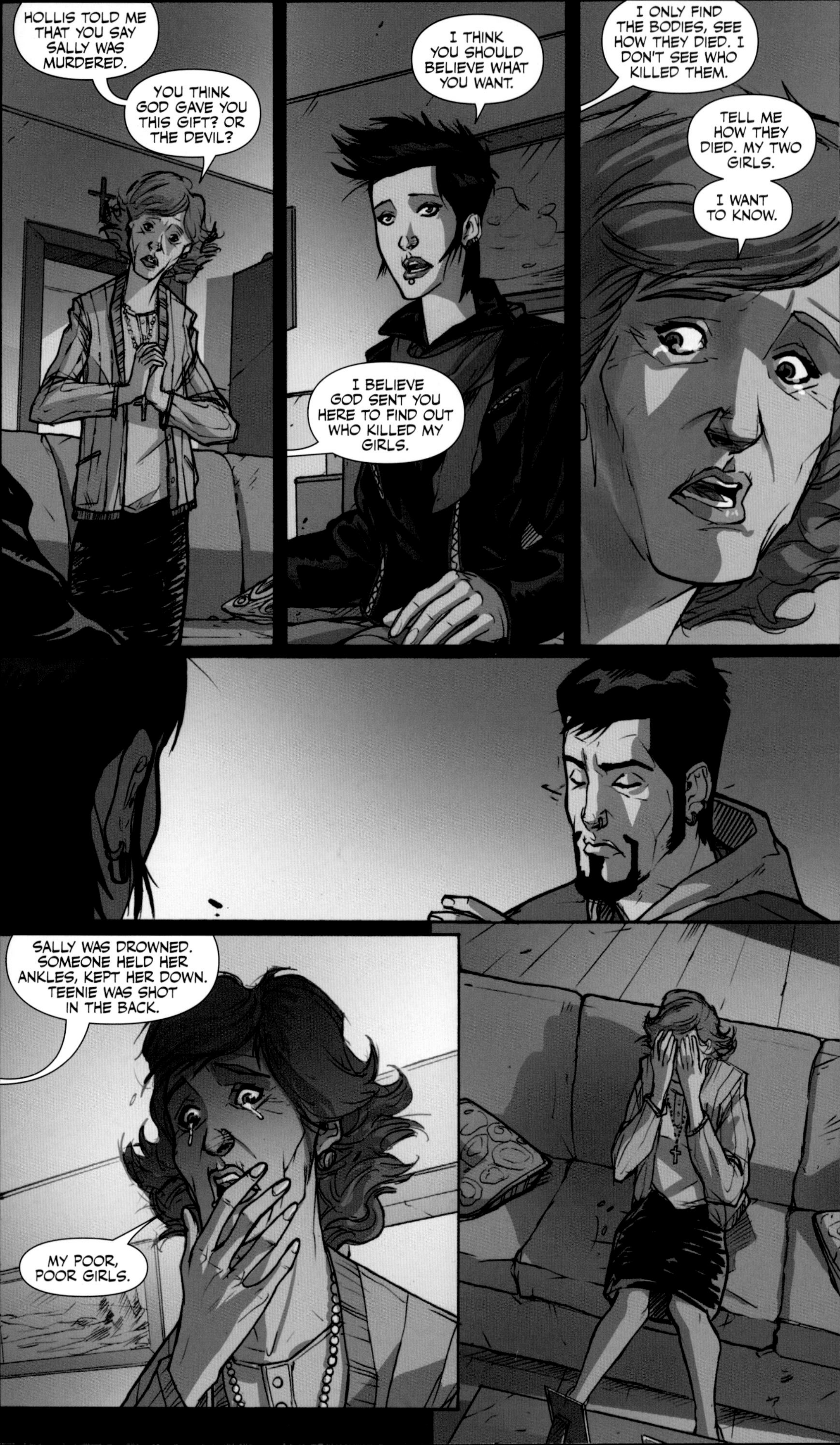
HOLLIS TOLD ME THAT YOU SAY SALLY WAS MURDERED.
YOU THINK GOD GAVE YOU THIS GIFT? OR THE DEVIL?
I THINK YOU SHOULD BELIEVE WHAT YOU WANT.
I BELIEVE GOD SENT YOU HERE TO FIND OUT WHO KILLED MY GIRLS.
I ONLY FIND THE BODIES, SEE HOW THEY DIED. I DON'T SEE WHO KILLED THEM.
TELL ME HOW THEY DIED. MY TWO GIRLS.
I WANT TO KNOW.
SALLY WAS DROWNED. SOMEONE HELD HER ANKLES, KEPT HER DOWN. TEENIE WAS SHOT IN THE BACK.
MY POOR, POOR GIRLS.

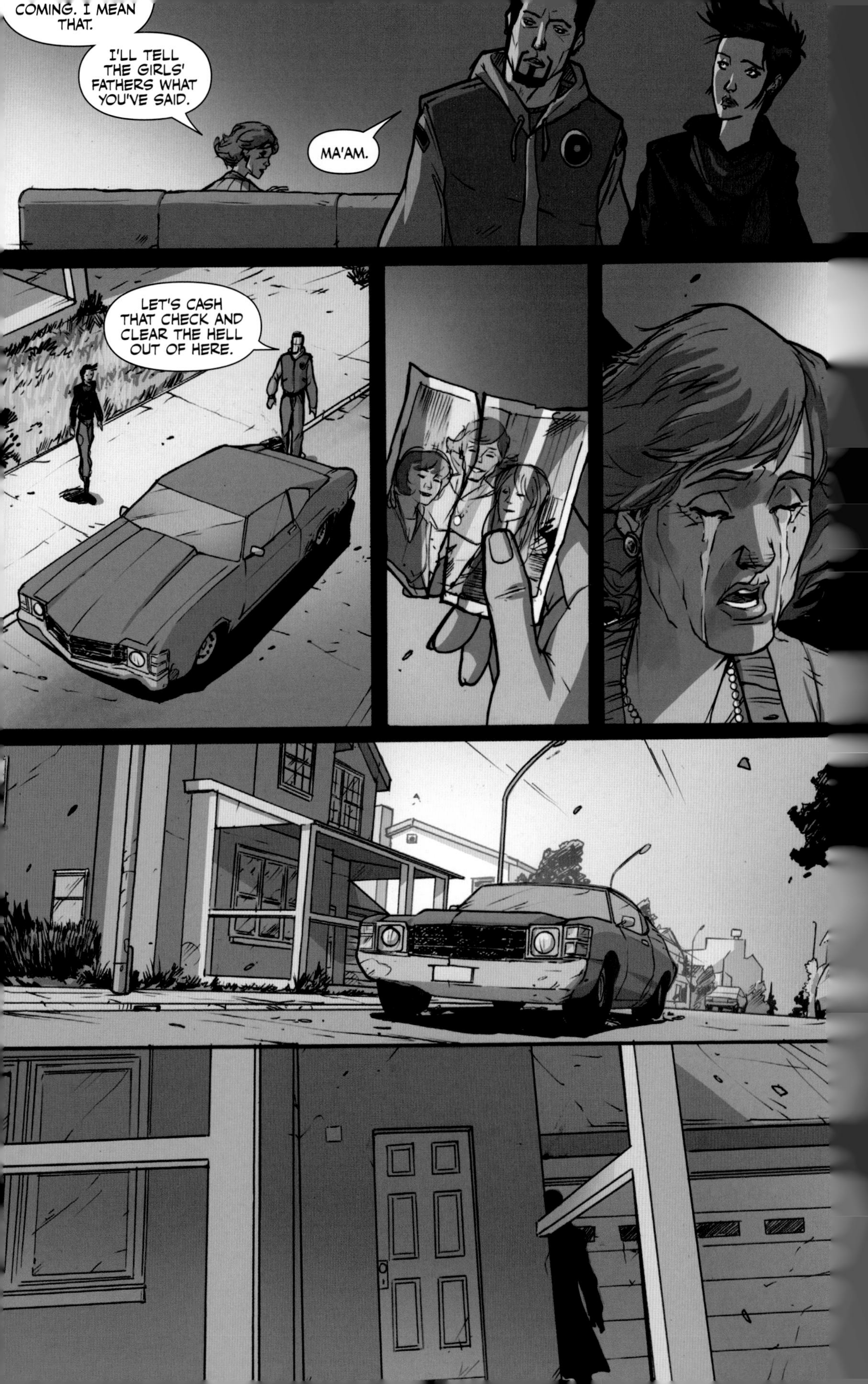
COMING. I MEAN THAT.
I'LL TELL THE GIRLS' FATHERS WHAT YOU'VE SAID.
MA'AM.
LET'S CASH THAT CHECK AND CLEAR THE HELL OUT OF HERE.

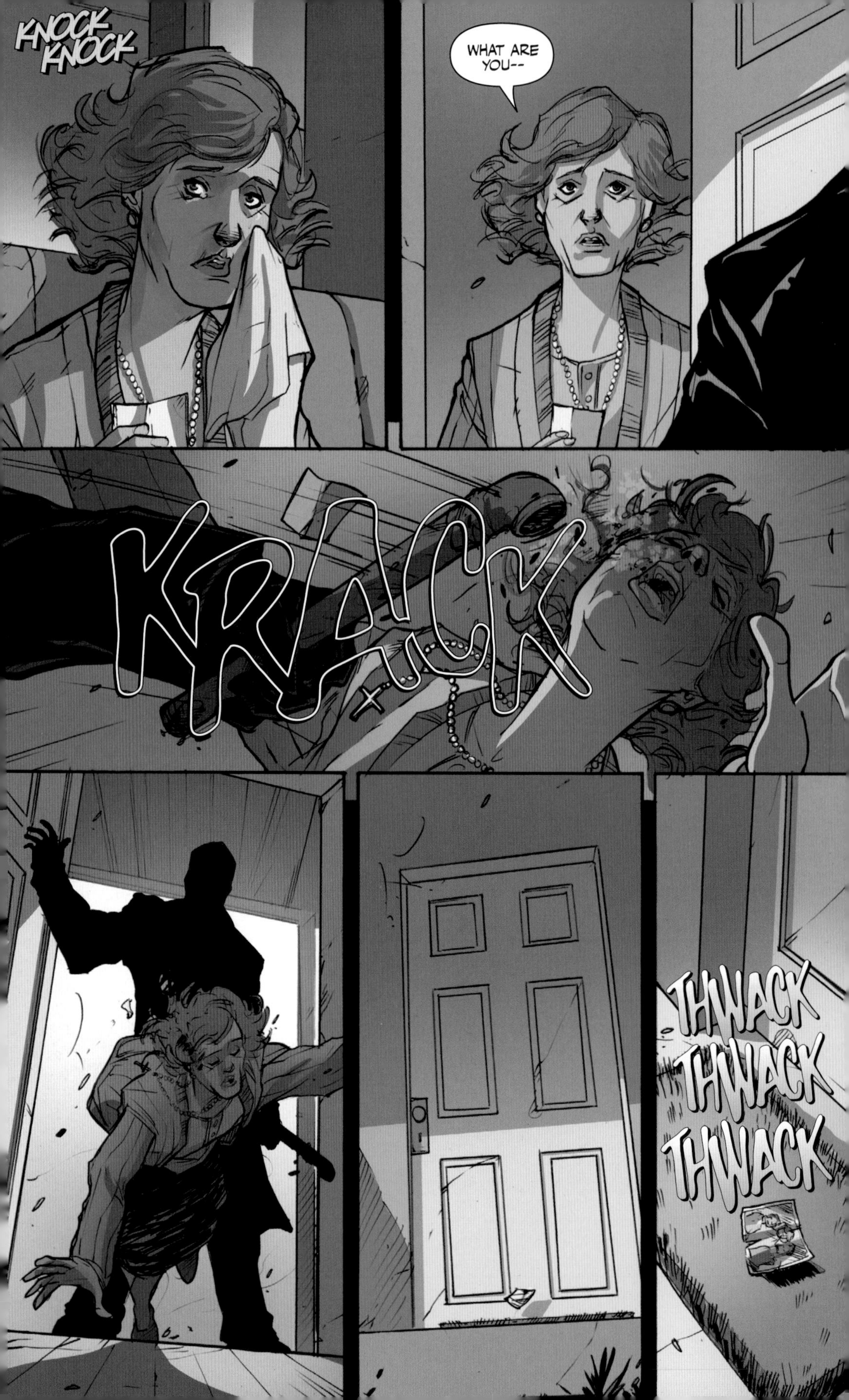
KNOCK KNOCK
WHAT ARE YOU--
KRACK
THWACK
THWACK
THWACK

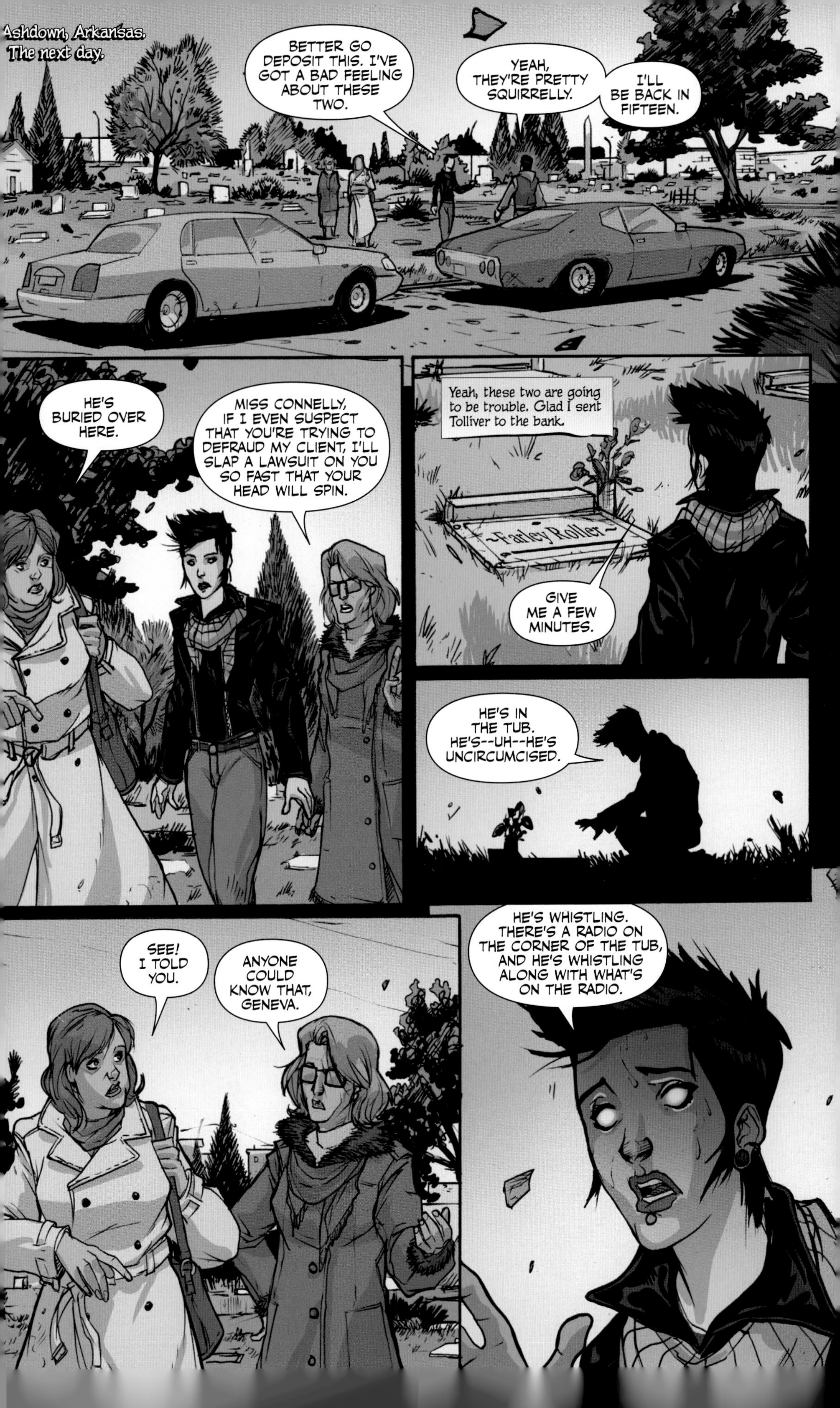

Ashdown, Arkansas. The next day.
BETTER GO DEPOSIT THIS. I'VE GOT A BAD FEELING ABOUT THESE TWO.
YEAH, THEY'RE PRETTY SQUIRRELLY.
I'LL BE BACK IN FIFTEEN.
HE'S BURIED OVER HERE.
MISS CONNELLY, IF I EVEN SUSPECT THAT YOU'RE TRYING TO DEFRAUD MY CLIENT, I'LL SLAP A LAWSUIT ON YOU SO FAST THAT YOUR HEAD WILL SPIN.
Yeah, these two are going to be trouble. Glad I sent Tolliver to the bank.
~Farley Roller~
GIVE ME A FEW MINUTES.
HE'S IN THE TUB. HE'S--UH--HE'S UNCIRCUMCISED.
SEE! I TOLD YOU.
ANYONE COULD KNOW THAT, GENEVA.
HE'S WHISTLING. THERE'S A RADIO ON THE CORNER OF THE TUB, AND HE'S WHISTLING ALONG WITH WHAT'S ON THE RADIO.

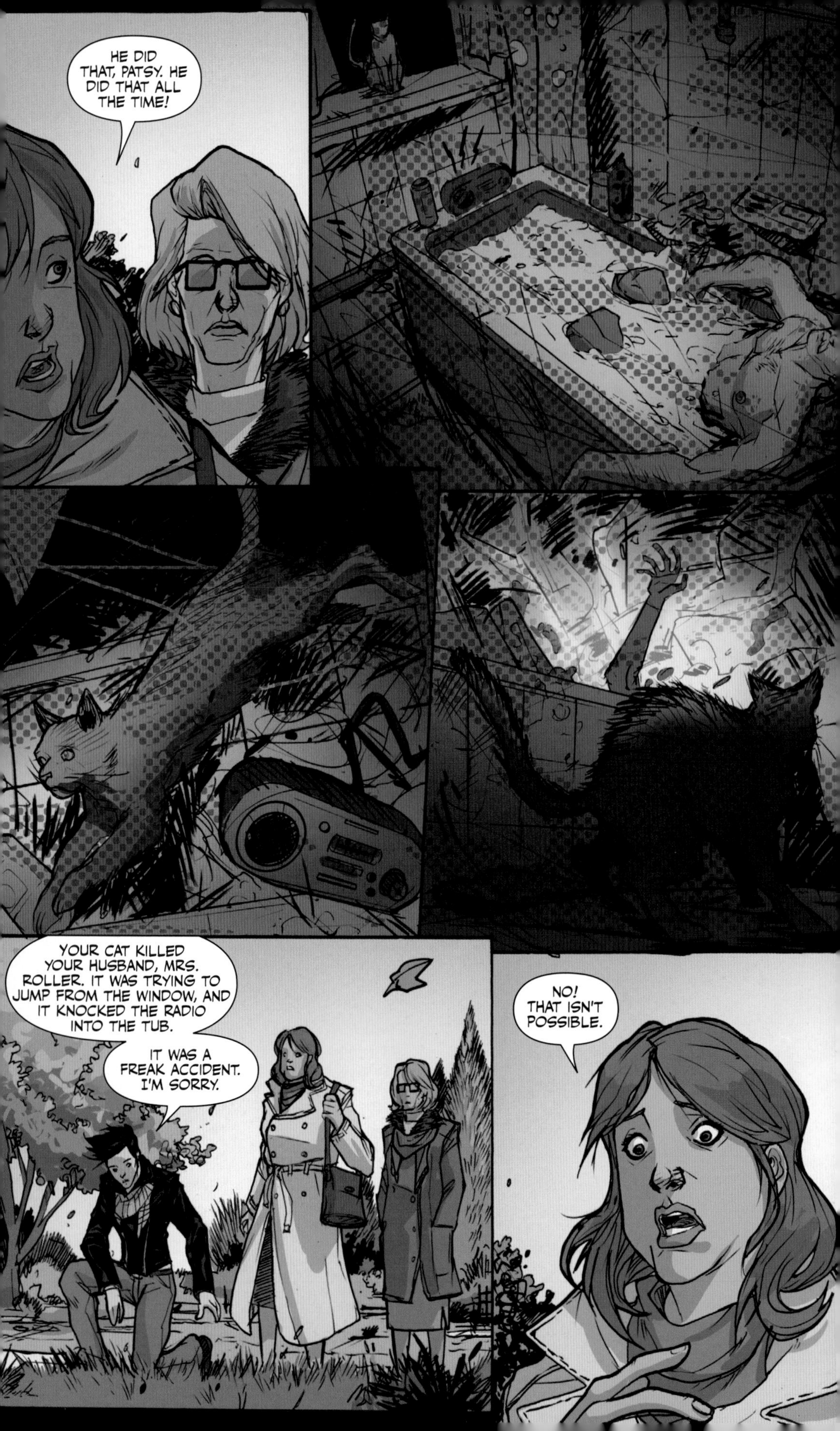
HE DID THAT, PATSY. HE DID THAT ALL THE TIME!
YOUR CAT KILLED YOUR HUSBAND, MRS. ROLLER. IT WAS TRYING TO JUMP FROM THE WINDOW, AND IT KNOCKED THE RADIO INTO THE TUB.
IT WAS A FREAK ACCIDENT. I'M SORRY.
NO! THAT ISN'T POSSIBLE.

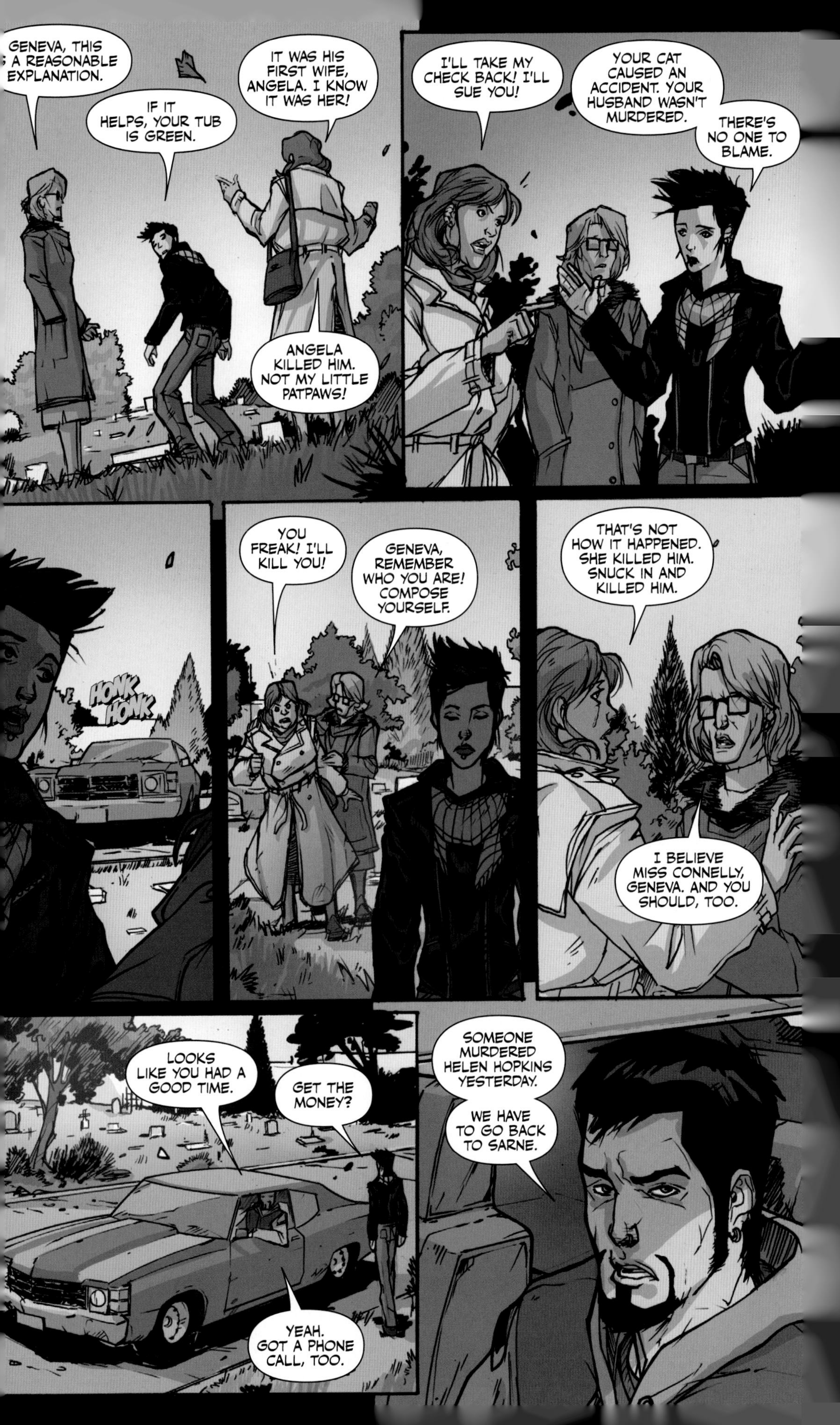
GENEVA, THIS IS A REASONABLE EXPLANATION.
IF IT HELPS, YOUR TUB IS GREEN.
IT WAS HIS FIRST WIFE, ANGELA. I KNOW IT WAS HER!
ANGELA KILLED HIM. NOT MY LITTLE PATPAWS!
I'LL TAKE MY CHECK BACK! I'LL SUE YOU!
YOUR CAT CAUSED AN ACCIDENT. YOUR HUSBAND WASN'T MURDERED.
THERE'S NO ONE TO BLAME.
HONK HONK
YOU FREAK! I'LL KILL YOU!
GENEVA, REMEMBER WHO YOU ARE! COMPOSE YOURSELF.
THAT'S NOT HOW IT HAPPENED. SHE KILLED HIM. SNUCK IN AND KILLED HIM.
I BELIEVE MISS CONNELLY, GENEVA. AND YOU SHOULD, TOO.
LOOKS LIKE YOU HAD A GOOD TIME.
GET THE MONEY?
YEAH. GOT A PHONE CALL, TOO.
SOMEONE MURDERED HELEN HOPKINS YESTERDAY.
WE HAVE TO GO BACK TO SARNE.

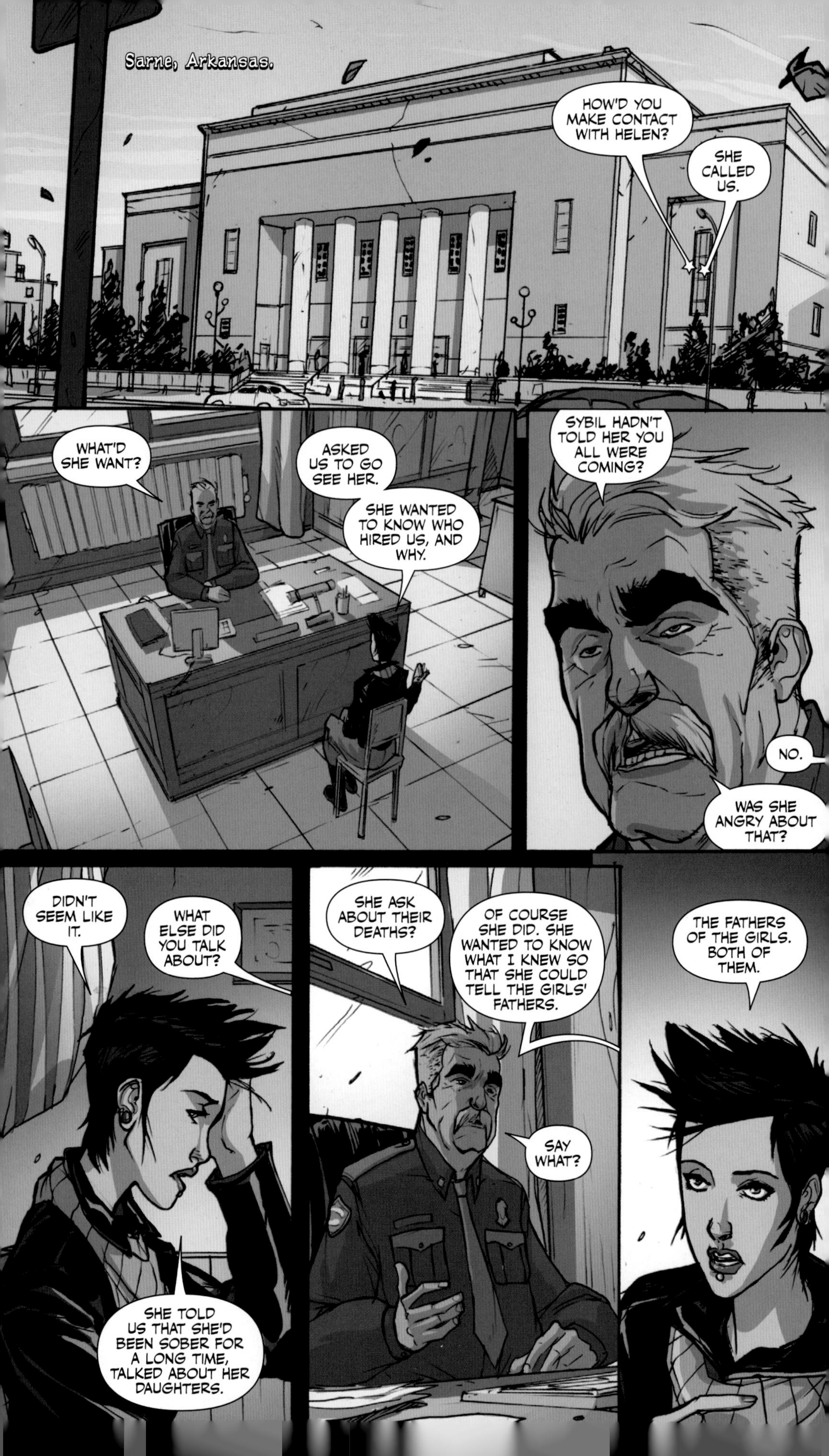
Sarne, Arkansas.
HOW'D YOU MAKE CONTACT WITH HELEN?
SHE CALLED US.
WHAT'D SHE WANT?
ASKED US TO GO SEE HER.
SHE WANTED TO KNOW WHO HIRED US, AND WHY.
SYBIL HADN'T TOLD HER YOU ALL WERE COMING?
NO.
WAS SHE ANGRY ABOUT THAT?
DIDN'T SEEM LIKE IT.
WHAT ELSE DID YOU TALK ABOUT?
SHE TOLD US THAT SHE'D BEEN SOBER FOR A LONG TIME, TALKED ABOUT HER DAUGHTERS.
SHE ASK ABOUT THEIR DEATHS?
OF COURSE SHE DID. SHE WANTED TO KNOW WHAT I KNEW SO THAT SHE COULD TELL THE GIRLS' FATHERS.
SAY WHAT?
THE FATHERS OF THE GIRLS. BOTH OF THEM.

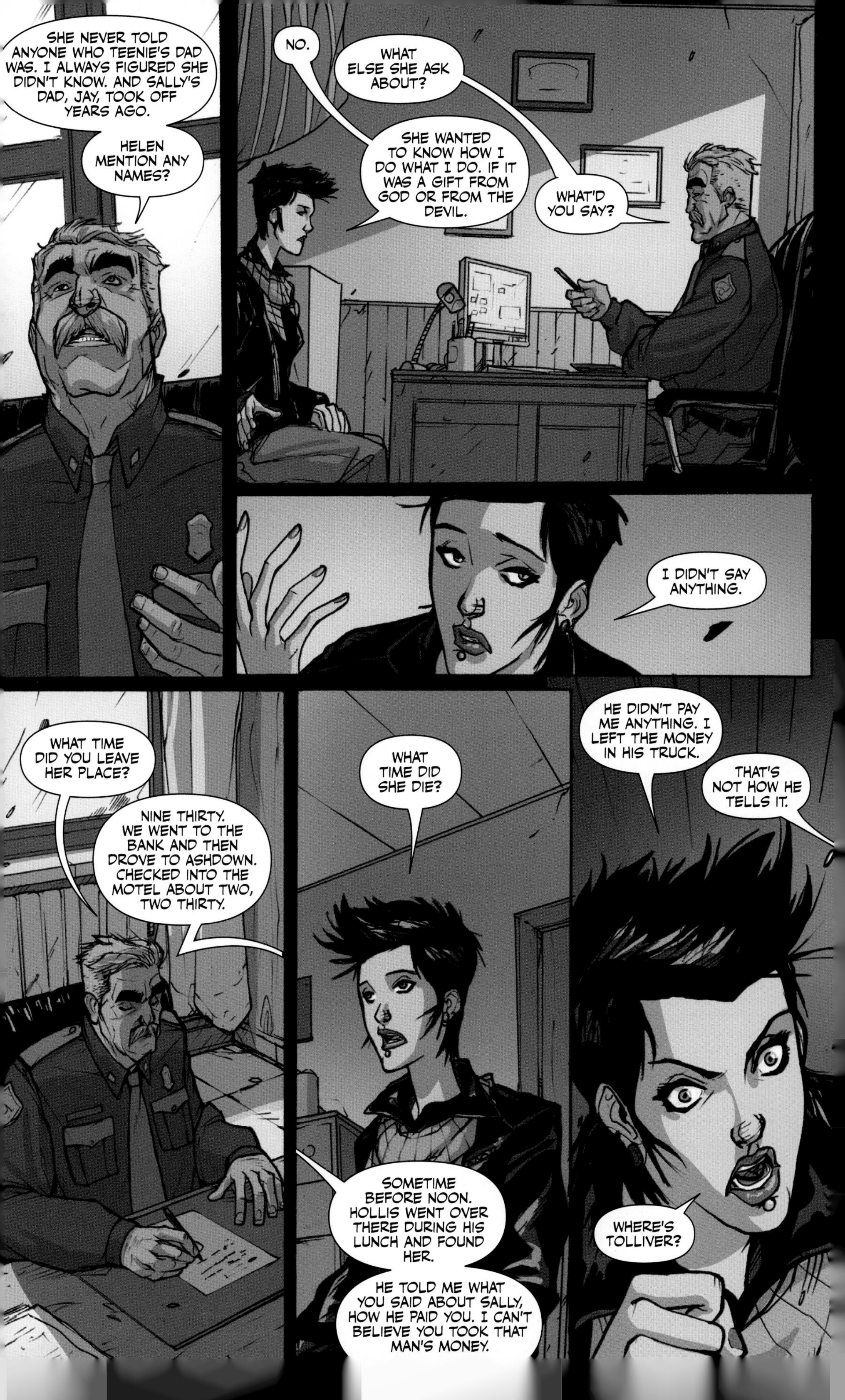
SHE NEVER TOLD ANYONE WHO TEENIE'S DAD WAS. I ALWAYS FIGURED SHE DIDN'T KNOW. AND SALLY'S DAD, JAY, TOOK OFF YEARS AGO.
HELEN MENTION ANY NAMES?
NO.
WHAT ELSE SHE ASK ABOUT?
SHE WANTED TO KNOW HOW I DO WHAT I DO. IF IT WAS A GIFT FROM GOD OR FROM THE DEVIL.
WHAT'D YOU SAY?
I DIDN'T SAY ANYTHING.
WHAT TIME DID YOU LEAVE HER PLACE?
NINE THIRTY. WE WENT TO THE BANK AND THEN DROVE TO ASHDOWN. CHECKED INTO THE MOTEL ABOUT TWO, TWO THIRTY.
WHAT TIME DID SHE DIE?
SOMETIME BEFORE NOON. HOLLIS WENT OVER THERE DURING HIS LUNCH AND FOUND HER.
HE TOLD ME WHAT YOU SAID ABOUT SALLY, HOW HE PAID YOU. I CAN'T BELIEVE YOU TOOK THAT MAN'S MONEY.
HE DIDN'T PAY ME ANYTHING. I LEFT THE MONEY IN HIS TRUCK.
THAT'S NOT HOW HE TELLS IT.
WHERE'S TOLLIVER?

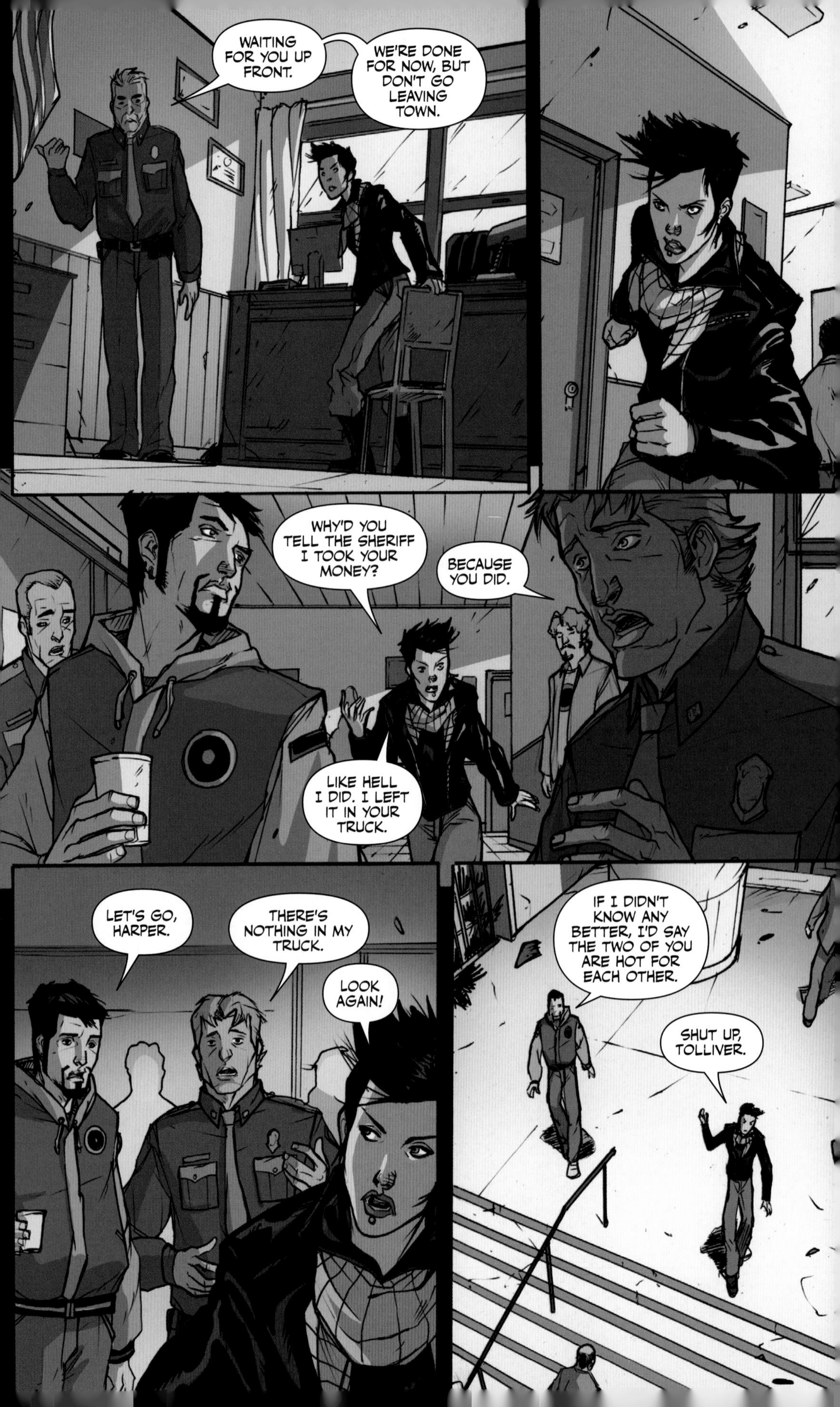
WAITING FOR YOU UP FRONT.
WE'RE DONE FOR NOW, BUT DON'T GO LEAVING TOWN.
WHY'D YOU TELL THE SHERIFF I TOOK YOUR MONEY?
BECAUSE YOU DID.
LIKE HELL I DID. I LEFT IT IN YOUR TRUCK.
LET'S GO, HARPER.
THERE'S NOTHING IN MY TRUCK.
LOOK AGAIN!
IF I DIDN'T KNOW ANY BETTER, I'D SAY THE TWO OF YOU ARE HOT FOR EACH OTHER.
SHUT UP, TOLLIVER.

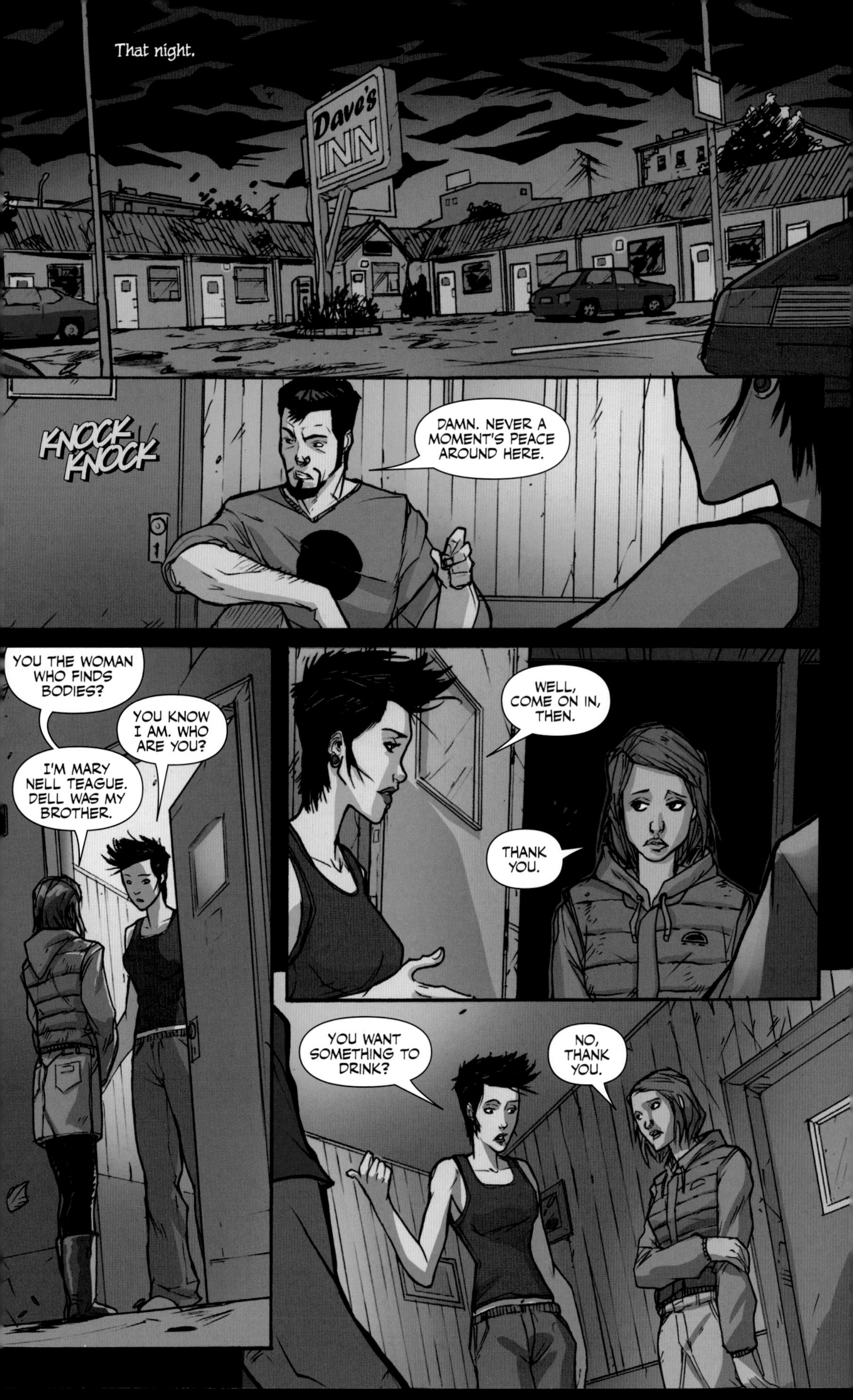
That night.
Dave's INN
KNOCK KNOCK
DAMN. NEVER A MOMENT'S PEACE AROUND HERE.
YOU THE WOMAN WHO FINDS BODIES?
YOU KNOW I AM. WHO ARE YOU?
I'M MARY NELL TEAGUE. DELL WAS MY BROTHER.
WELL, COME ON IN, THEN.
THANK YOU.
YOU WANT SOMETHING TO DRINK?
NO, THANK YOU.

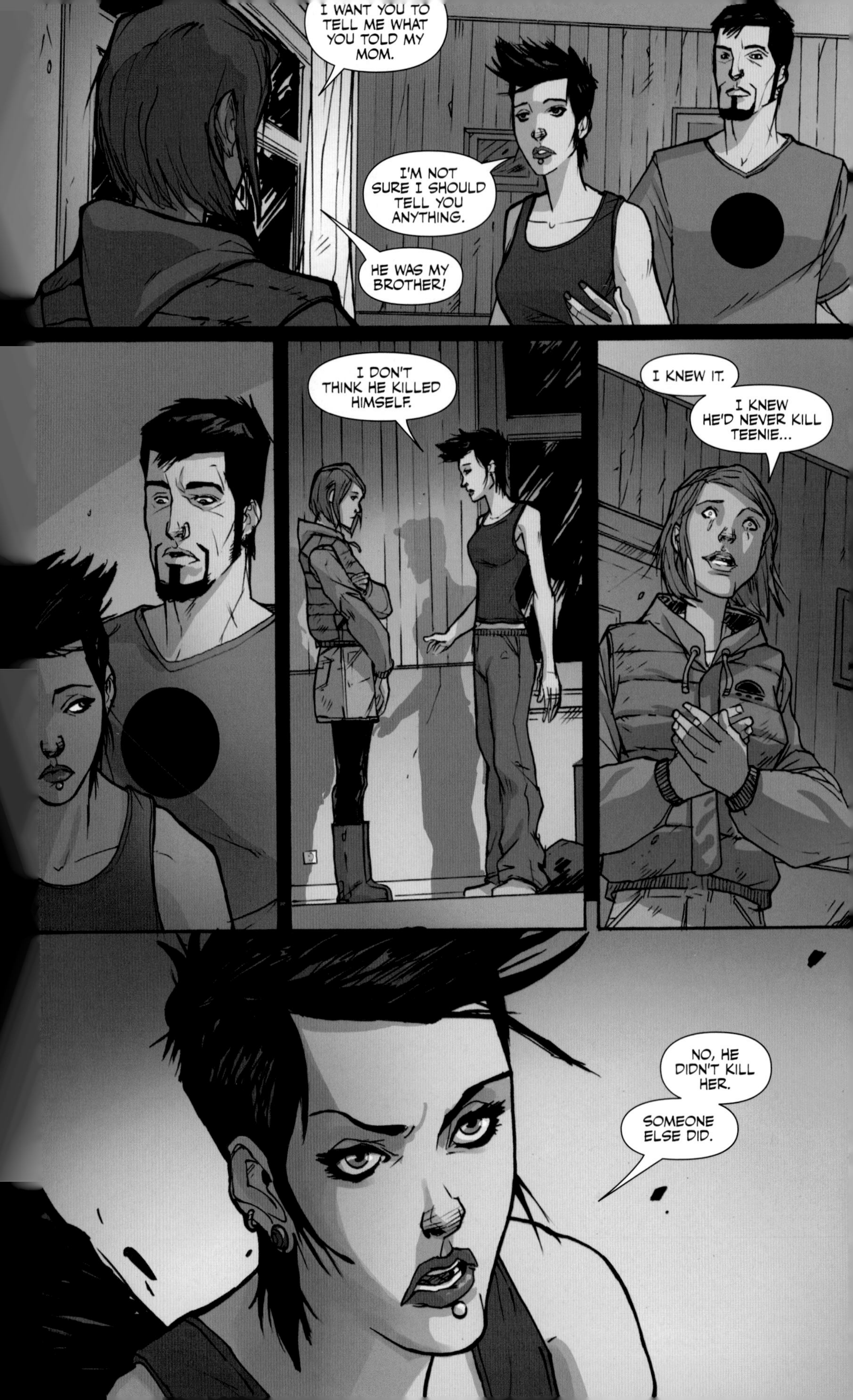
I WANT YOU TO TELL ME WHAT YOU TOLD MY MOM.
I'M NOT SURE I SHOULD TELL YOU ANYTHING.
HE WAS MY BROTHER!
I DON'T THINK HE KILLED HIMSELF.
I KNEW IT.
I KNEW HE'D NEVER KILL TEENIE...
NO, HE DIDN'T KILL HER.
SOMEONE ELSE DID.

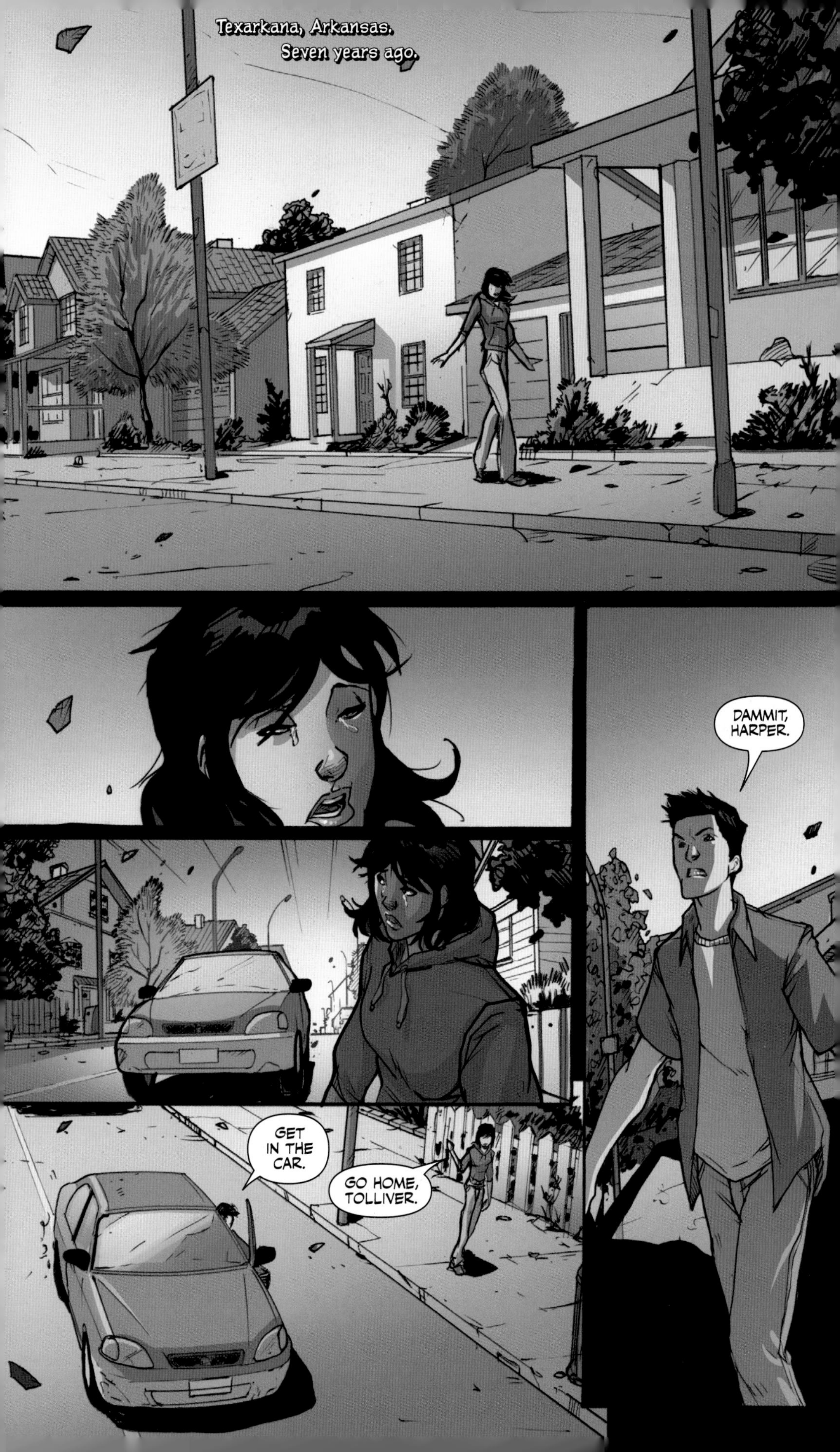
Texarkana, Arkansas.
Seven years ago.
DAMMIT, HARPER.
GET IN THE CAR.
GO HOME, TOLLIVER.

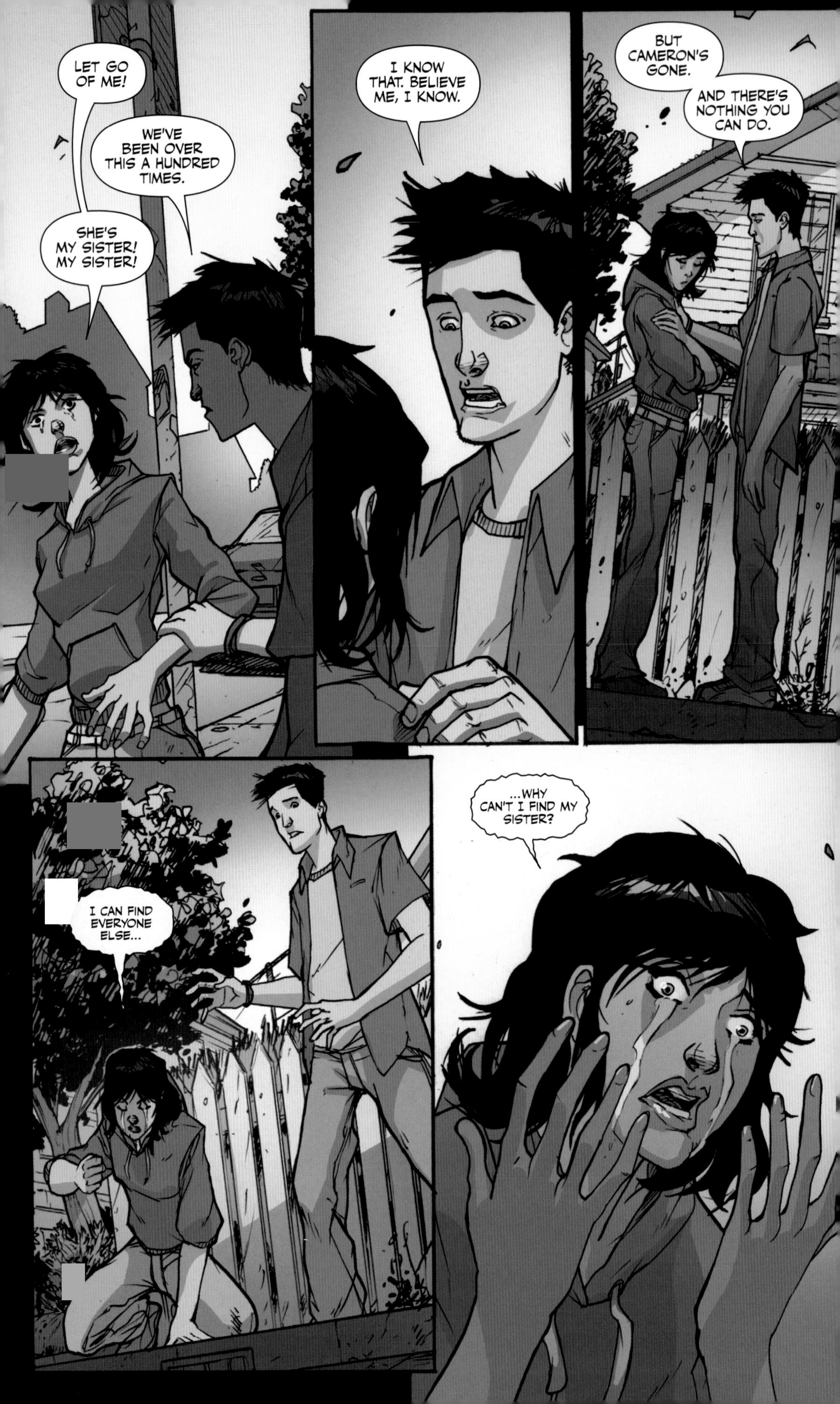

LET GO OF ME!
WE'VE BEEN OVER THIS A HUNDRED TIMES.
SHE'S MY SISTER! MY SISTER!
I KNOW THAT. BELIEVE ME, I KNOW.
BUT CAMERON'S GONE.
AND THERE'S NOTHING YOU CAN DO.
I CAN FIND EVERYONE ELSE...
...WHY CAN'T I FIND MY SISTER?

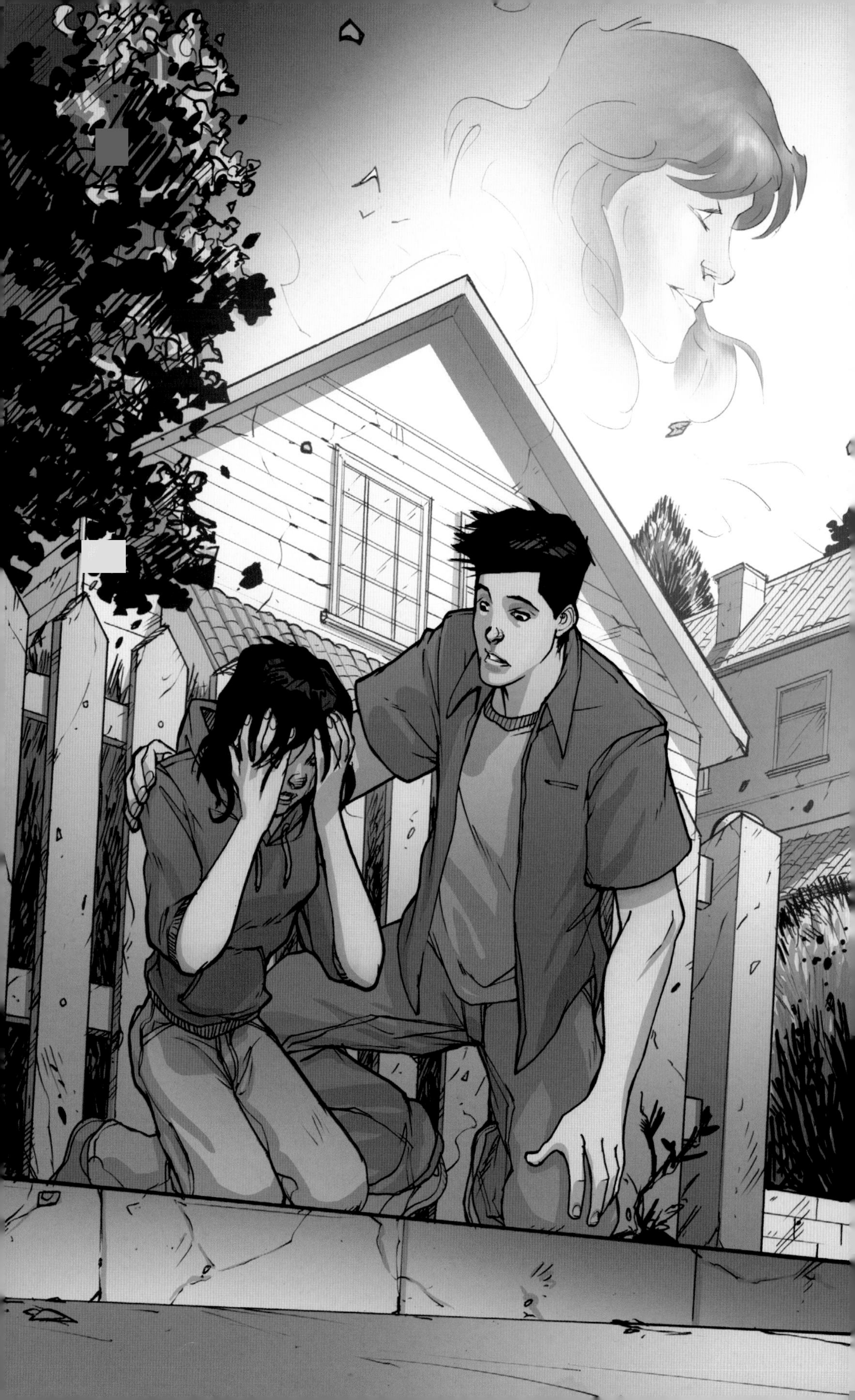

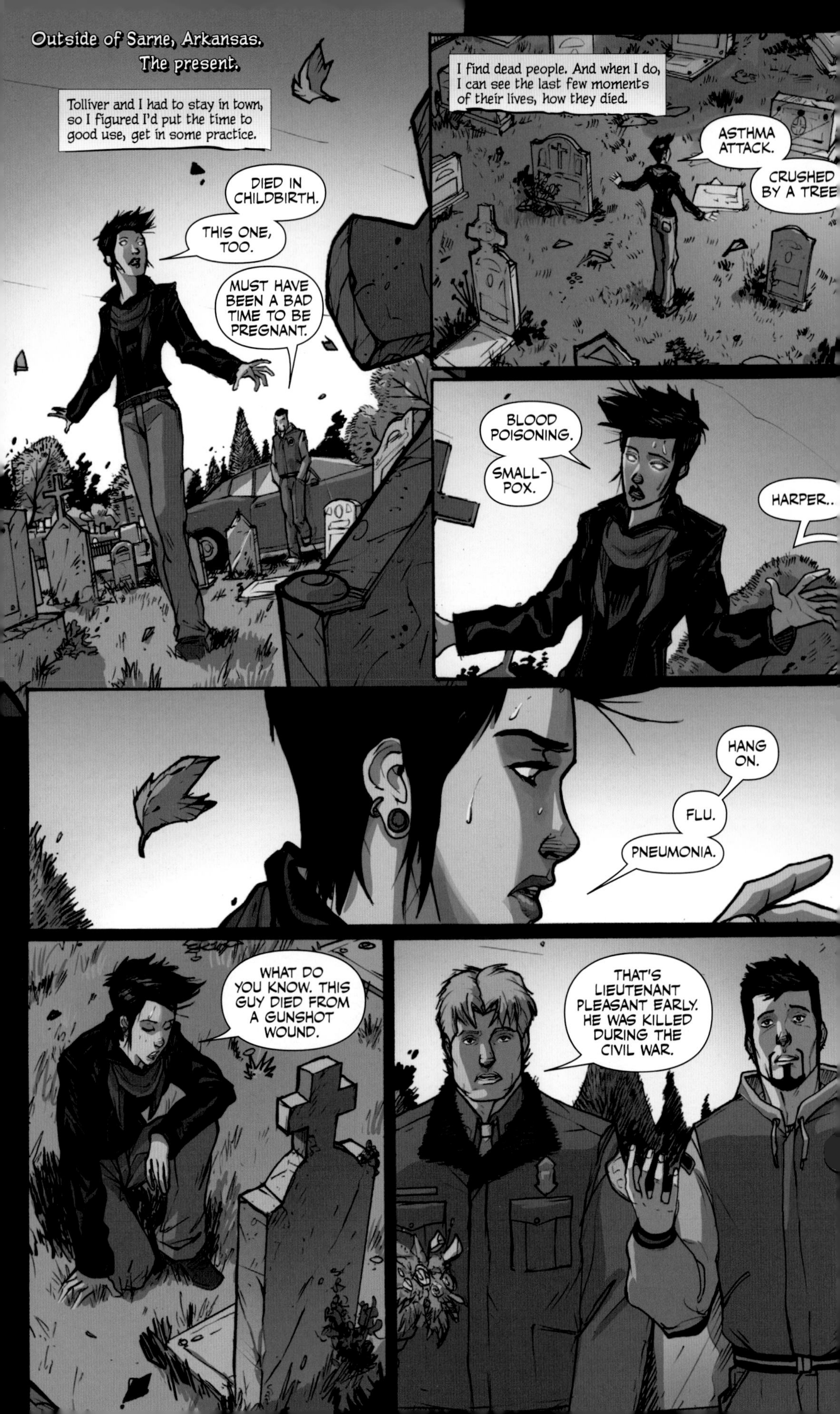
Outside of Sarne, Arkansas. The present.
Tolliver and I had to stay in town, so I figured I'd put the time to good use, get in some practice.
DIED IN CHILDBIRTH.
THIS ONE, TOO.
MUST HAVE BEEN A BAD TIME TO BE PREGNANT.
I find dead people. And when I do, I can see the last few moments of their lives, how they died.
ASTHMA ATTACK.
CRUSHED BY A TREE
BLOOD POISONING.
SMALL-POX.
HARPER..
HANG ON.
FLU.
PNEUMONIA.
WHAT DO YOU KNOW. THIS GUY DIED FROM A GUNSHOT WOUND.
THAT'S LIEUTENANT PLEASANT EARLY. HE WAS KILLED DURING THE CIVIL WAR.

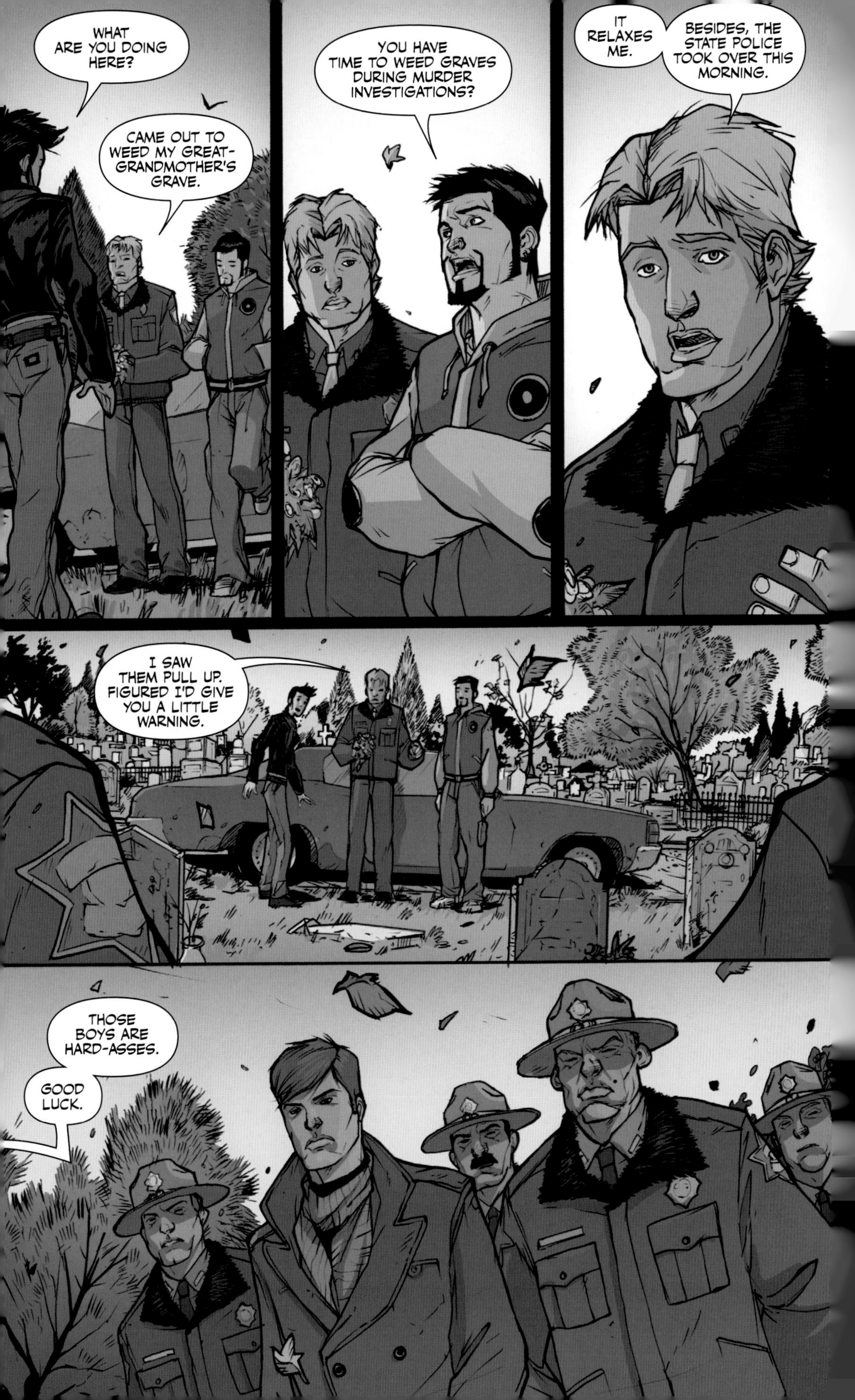
WHAT ARE YOU DOING HERE?
CAME OUT TO WEED MY GREAT-GRANDMOTHER'S GRAVE.
YOU HAVE TIME TO WEED GRAVES DURING MURDER INVESTIGATIONS?
IT RELAXES ME.
BESIDES, THE STATE POLICE TOOK OVER THIS MORNING.
I SAW THEM PULL UP. FIGURED I'D GIVE YOU A LITTLE WARNING.
THOSE BOYS ARE HARD-ASSES.
GOOD LUCK.

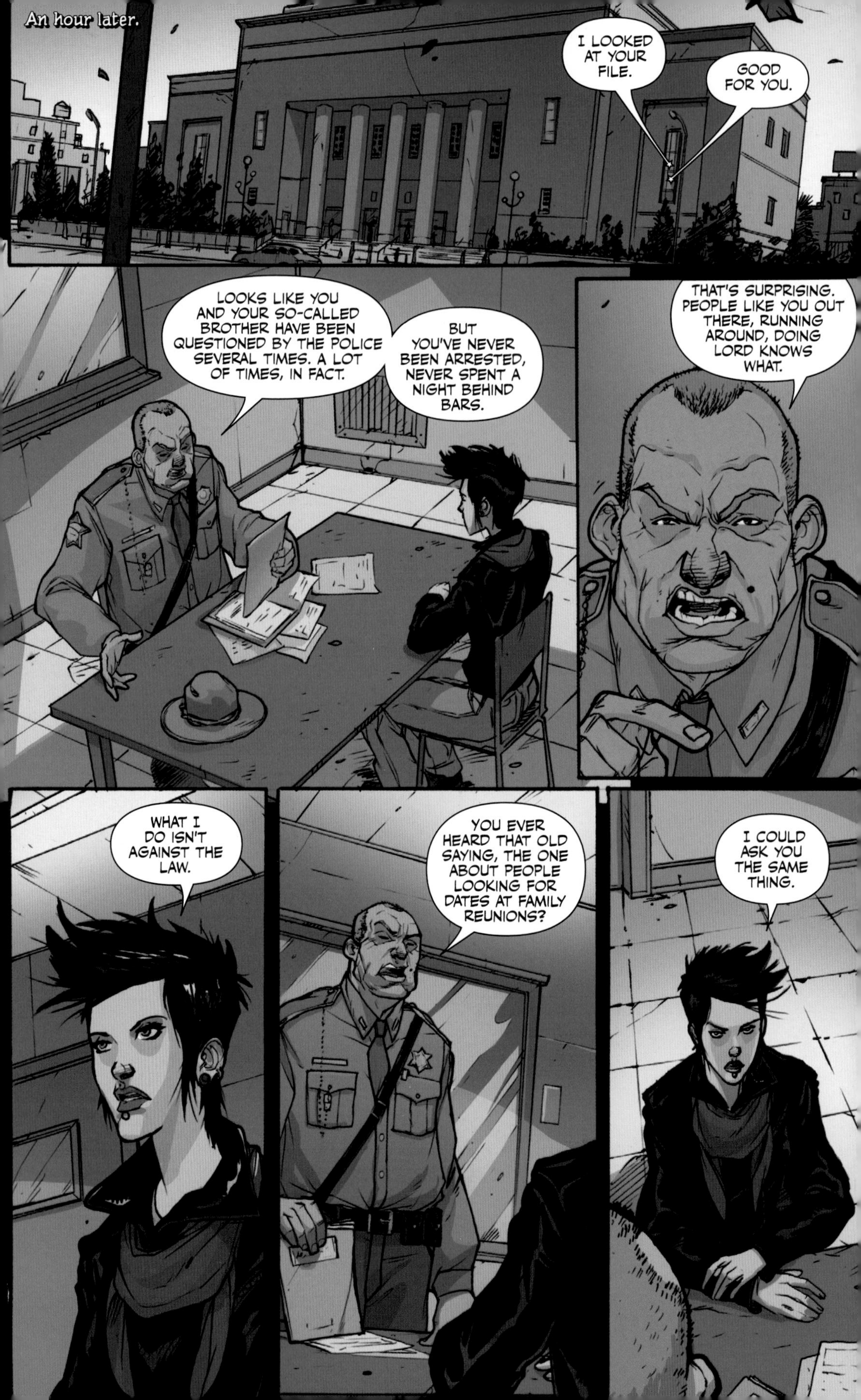

An hour later.
I LOOKED AT YOUR FILE.
GOOD FOR YOU.
LOOKS LIKE YOU AND YOUR SO-CALLED BROTHER HAVE BEEN QUESTIONED BY THE POLICE SEVERAL TIMES. A LOT OF TIMES, IN FACT.
BUT YOU'VE NEVER BEEN ARRESTED, NEVER SPENT A NIGHT BEHIND BARS.
THAT'S SURPRISING. PEOPLE LIKE YOU OUT THERE, RUNNING AROUND, DOING LORD KNOWS WHAT.
WHAT I DO ISN'T AGAINST THE LAW.
YOU EVER HEARD THAT OLD SAYING, THE ONE ABOUT PEOPLE LOOKING FOR DATES AT FAMILY REUNIONS?
I COULD ASK YOU THE SAME THING.

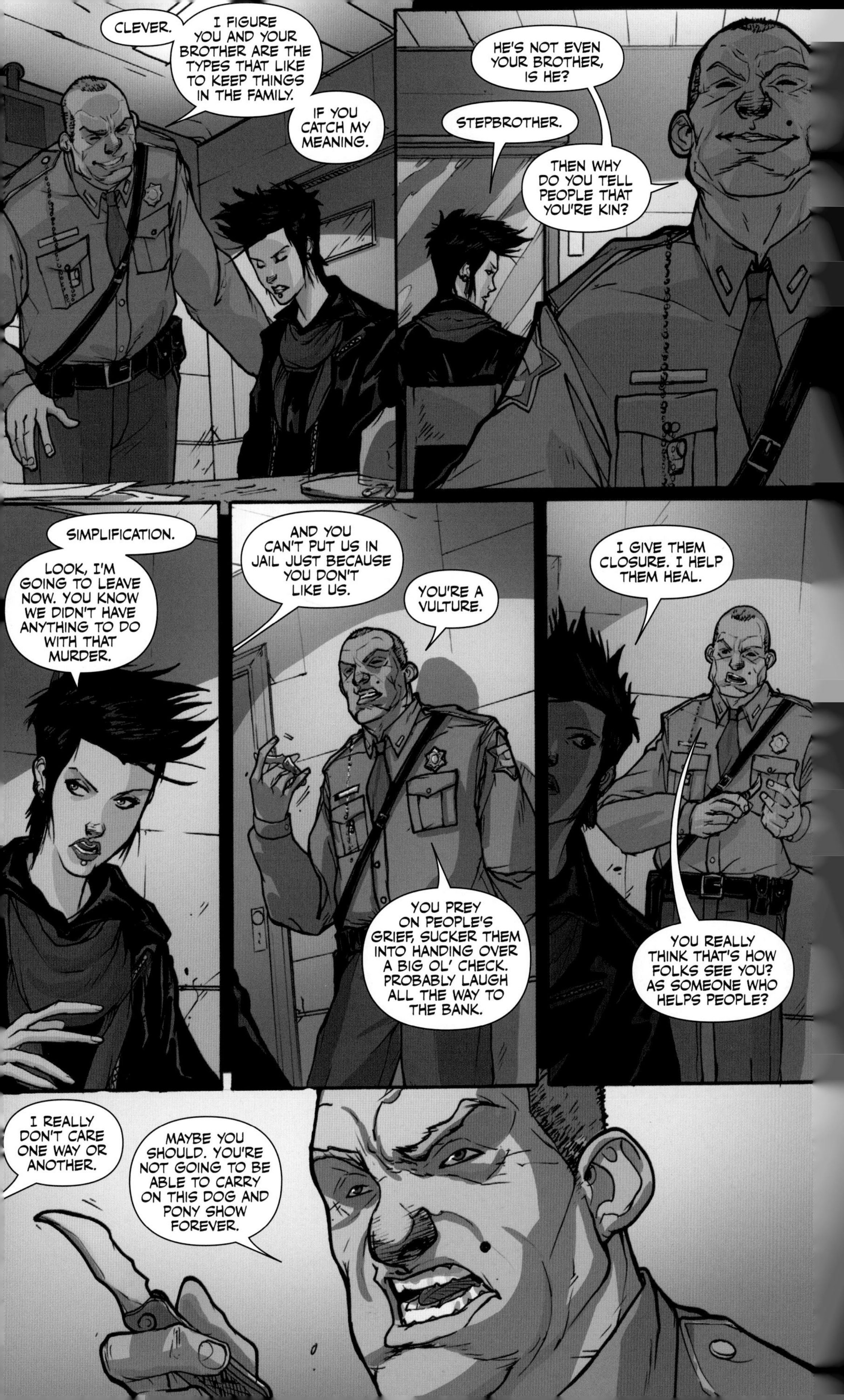
CLEVER.
I FIGURE YOU AND YOUR BROTHER ARE THE TYPES THAT LIKE TO KEEP THINGS IN THE FAMILY.
IF YOU CATCH MY MEANING.
HE'S NOT EVEN YOUR BROTHER, IS HE?
STEPBROTHER.
THEN WHY DO YOU TELL PEOPLE THAT YOU'RE KIN?
SIMPLIFICATION.
LOOK, I'M GOING TO LEAVE NOW. YOU KNOW WE DIDN'T HAVE ANYTHING TO DO WITH THAT MURDER.
AND YOU CAN'T PUT US IN JAIL JUST BECAUSE YOU DON'T LIKE US.
YOU'RE A VULTURE.
YOU PREY ON PEOPLE'S GRIEF, SUCKER THEM INTO HANDING OVER A BIG OL' CHECK. PROBABLY LAUGH ALL THE WAY TO THE BANK.
I GIVE THEM CLOSURE. I HELP THEM HEAL.
YOU REALLY THINK THAT'S HOW FOLKS SEE YOU? AS SOMEONE WHO HELPS PEOPLE?
I REALLY DON'T CARE ONE WAY OR ANOTHER.
MAYBE YOU SHOULD. YOU'RE NOT GOING TO BE ABLE TO CARRY ON THIS DOG AND PONY SHOW FOREVER.

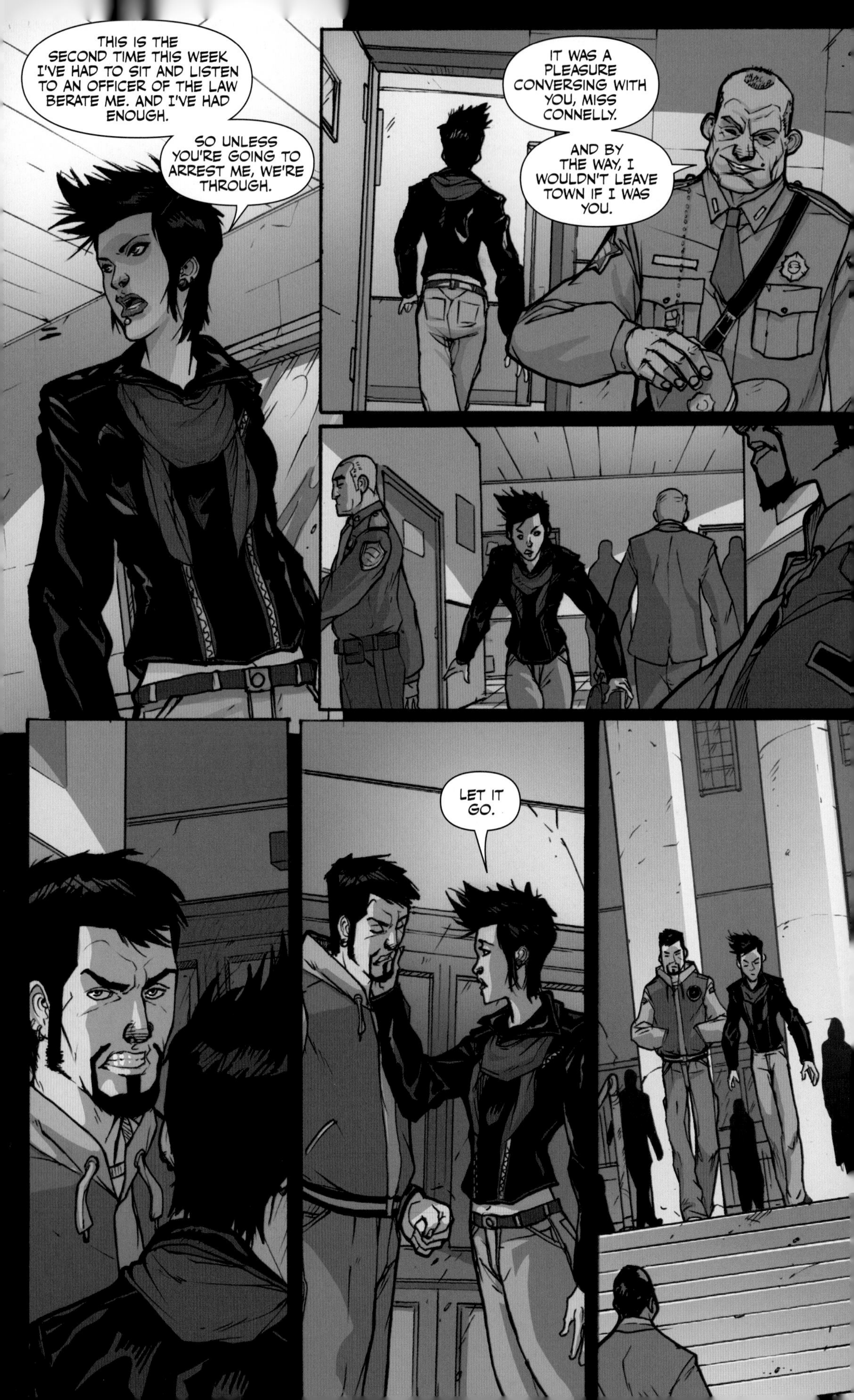
THIS IS THE SECOND TIME THIS WEEK I'VE HAD TO SIT AND LISTEN TO AN OFFICER OF THE LAW BERATE ME. AND I'VE HAD ENOUGH.
SO UNLESS YOU'RE GOING TO ARREST ME, WE'RE THROUGH.
IT WAS A PLEASURE CONVERSING WITH YOU, MISS CONNELLY.
AND BY THE WAY, I WOULDN'T LEAVE TOWN IF I WAS YOU.
LET IT GO.

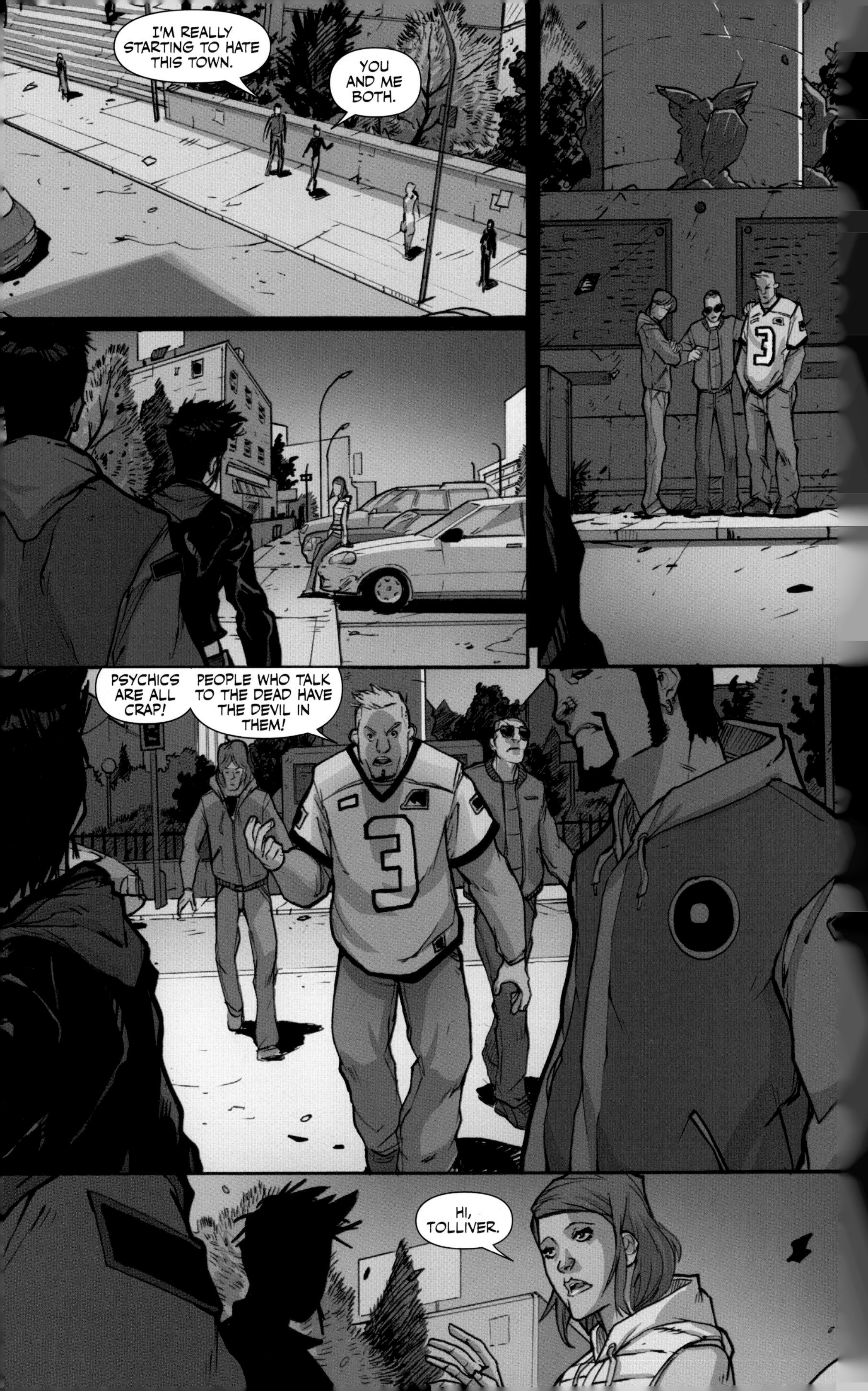
I'M REALLY STARTING TO HATE THIS TOWN.
YOU AND ME BOTH.
PSYCHICS ARE ALL CRAP!
PEOPLE WHO TALK TO THE DEAD HAVE THE DEVIL IN THEM!
HI, TOLLIVER.

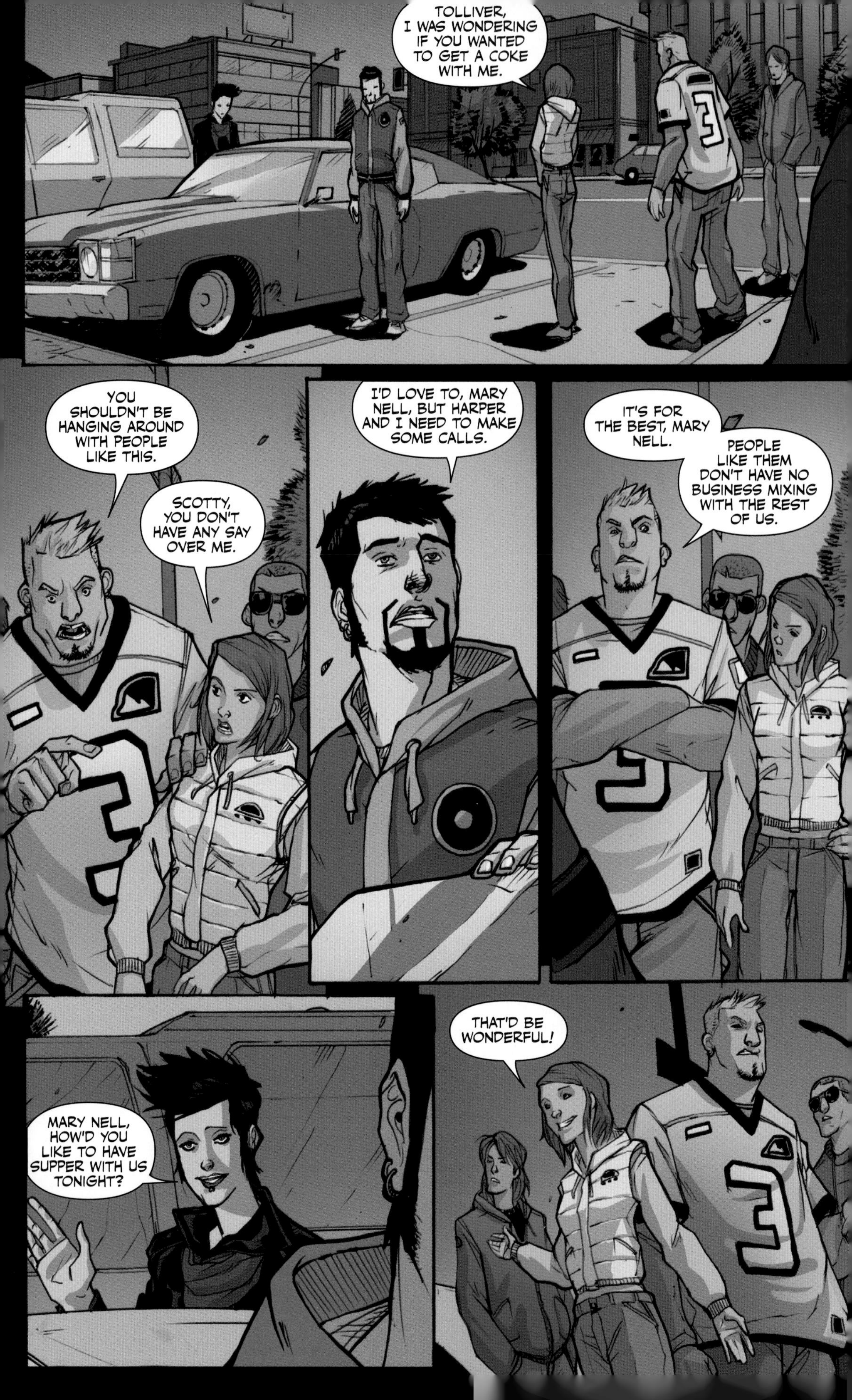
TOLLIVER, I WAS WONDERING IF YOU WANTED TO GET A COKE WITH ME.
YOU SHOULDN'T BE HANGING AROUND WITH PEOPLE LIKE THIS.
SCOTTY, YOU DON'T HAVE ANY SAY OVER ME.
I'D LOVE TO, MARY NELL, BUT HARPER AND I NEED TO MAKE SOME CALLS.
IT'S FOR THE BEST, MARY NELL.
PEOPLE LIKE THEM DON'T HAVE NO BUSINESS MIXING WITH THE REST OF US.
MARY NELL, HOW'D YOU LIKE TO HAVE SUPPER WITH US TONIGHT?
THAT'D BE WONDERFUL!

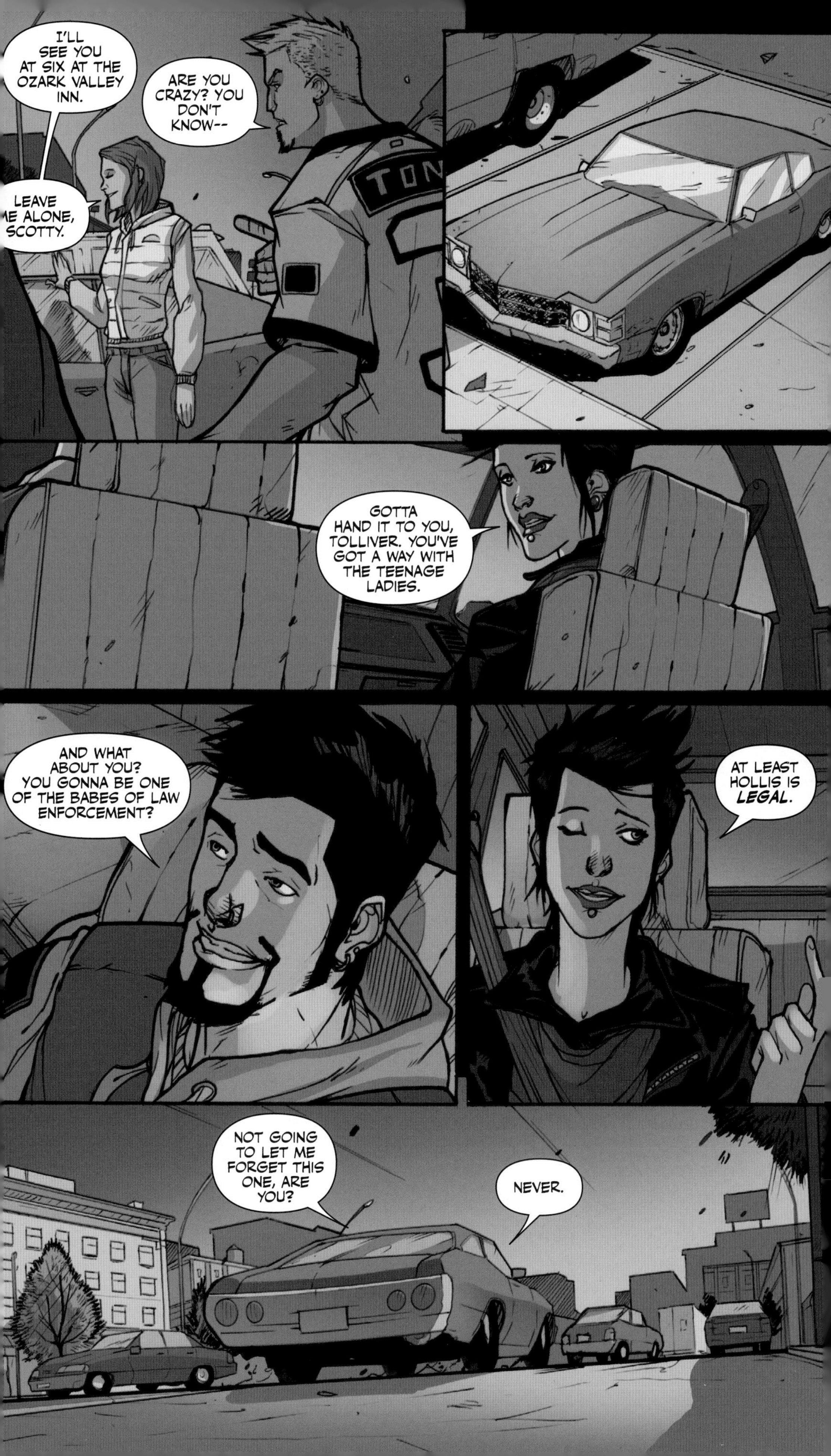
I'LL SEE YOU AT SIX AT THE OZARK VALLEY INN.
ARE YOU CRAZY? YOU DON'T KNOW--
LEAVE ME ALONE, SCOTTY.
GOTTA HAND IT TO YOU, TOLLIVER. YOU'VE GOT A WAY WITH THE TEENAGE LADIES.
AND WHAT ABOUT YOU? YOU GONNA BE ONE OF THE BABES OF LAW ENFORCEMENT?
AT LEAST HOLLIS IS LEGAL.
NOT GOING TO LET ME FORGET THIS ONE, ARE YOU?
NEVER.

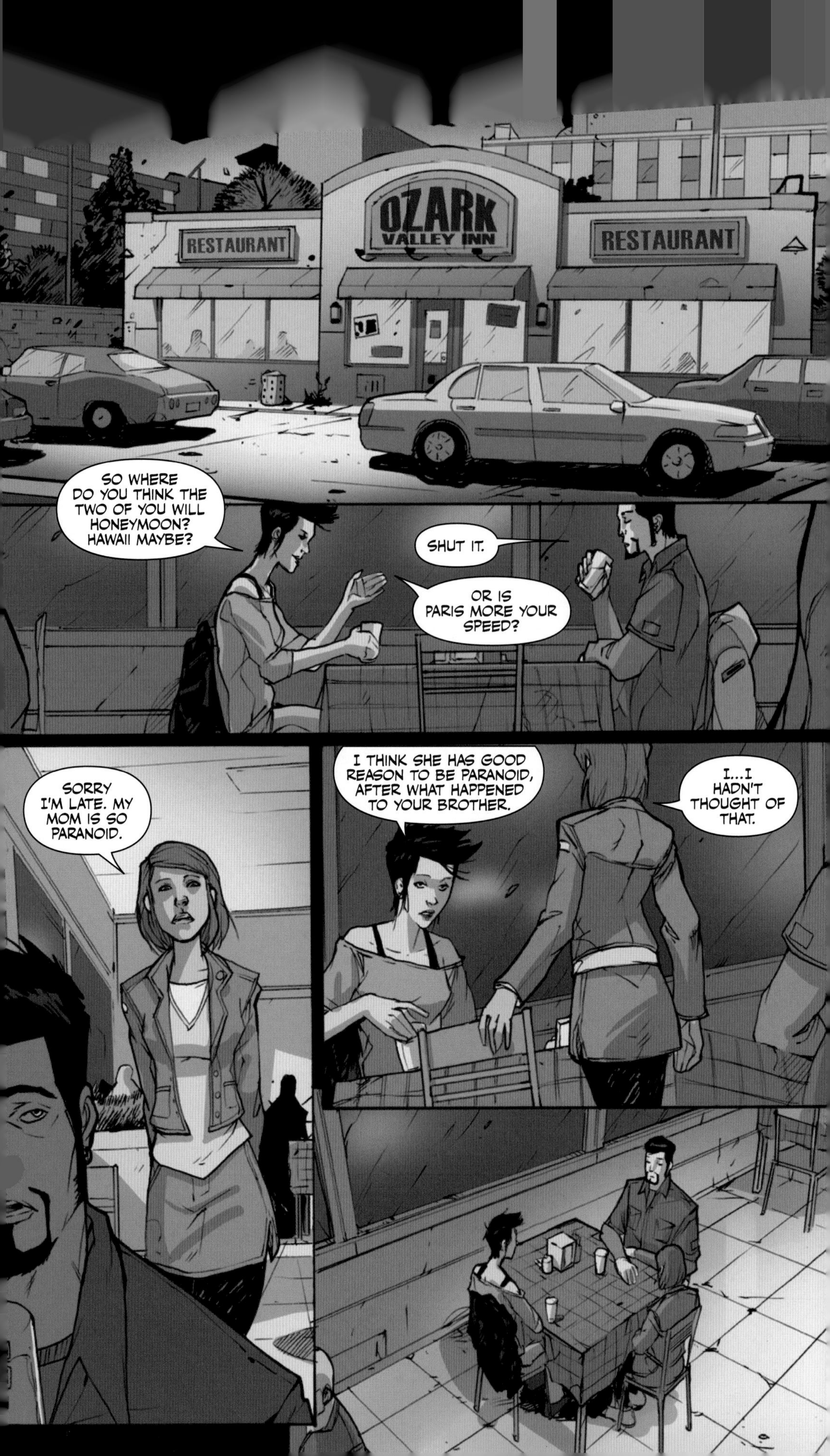
OZARK VALLEY INN
RESTAURANT
RESTAURANT
SO WHERE DO YOU THINK THE TWO OF YOU WILL HONEYMOON? HAWAII MAYBE?
SHUT IT.
OR IS PARIS MORE YOUR SPEED?
SORRY I'M LATE. MY MOM IS SO PARANOID.
I THINK SHE HAS GOOD REASON TO BE PARANOID, AFTER WHAT HAPPENED TO YOUR BROTHER.
I...I HADN'T THOUGHT OF THAT.

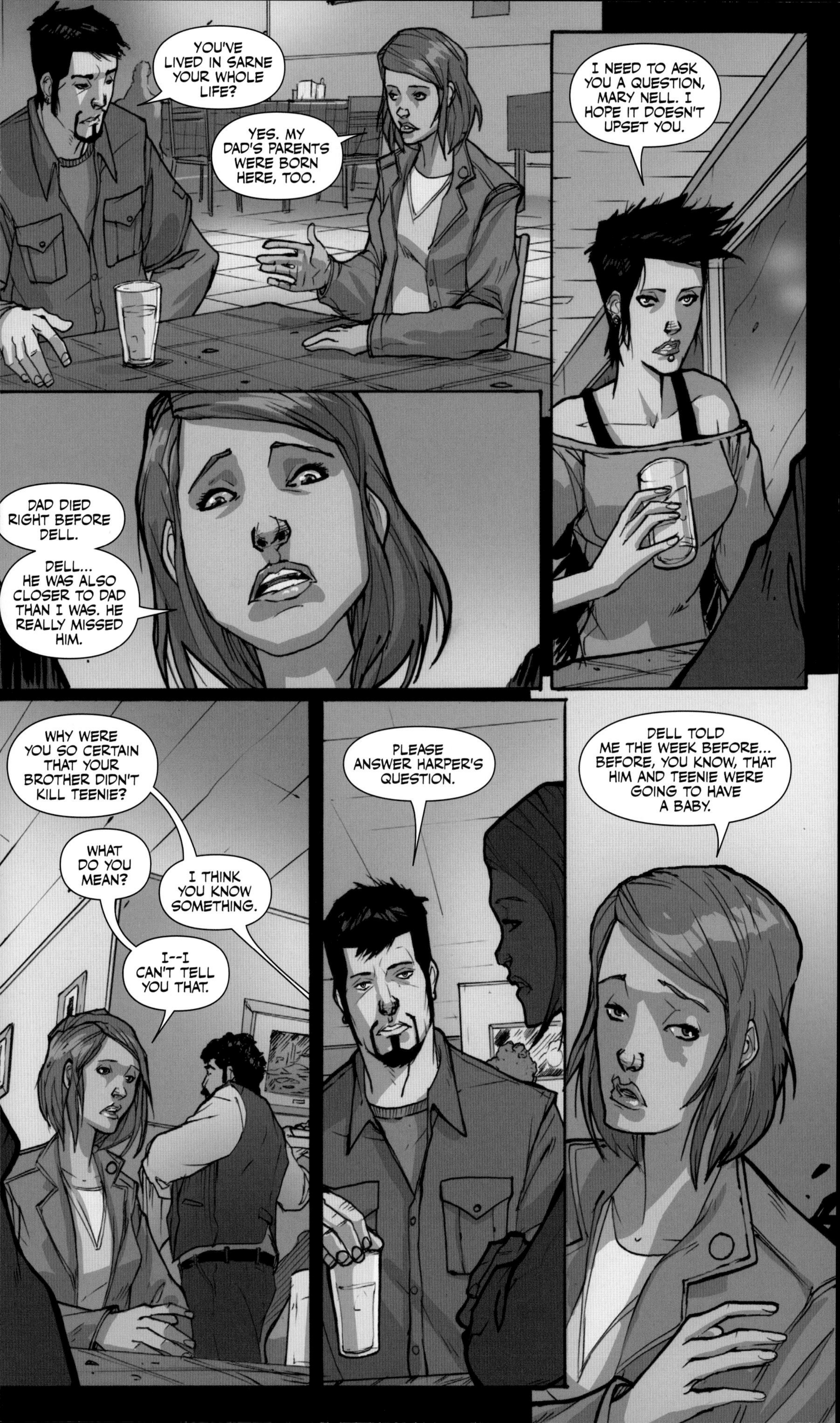
YOU'VE LIVED IN SARNE YOUR WHOLE LIFE?
YES. MY DAD'S PARENTS WERE BORN HERE, TOO.
I NEED TO ASK YOU A QUESTION, MARY NELL. I HOPE IT DOESN'T UPSET YOU.
DAD DIED RIGHT BEFORE DELL.
DELL... HE WAS ALSO CLOSER TO DAD THAN I WAS. HE REALLY MISSED HIM.
WHY WERE YOU SO CERTAIN THAT YOUR BROTHER DIDN'T KILL TEENIE?
WHAT DO YOU MEAN?
I THINK YOU KNOW SOMETHING.
I--I CAN'T TELL YOU THAT.
PLEASE ANSWER HARPER'S QUESTION.
DELL TOLD ME THE WEEK BEFORE... BEFORE, YOU KNOW, THAT HIM AND TEENIE WERE GOING TO HAVE A BABY.

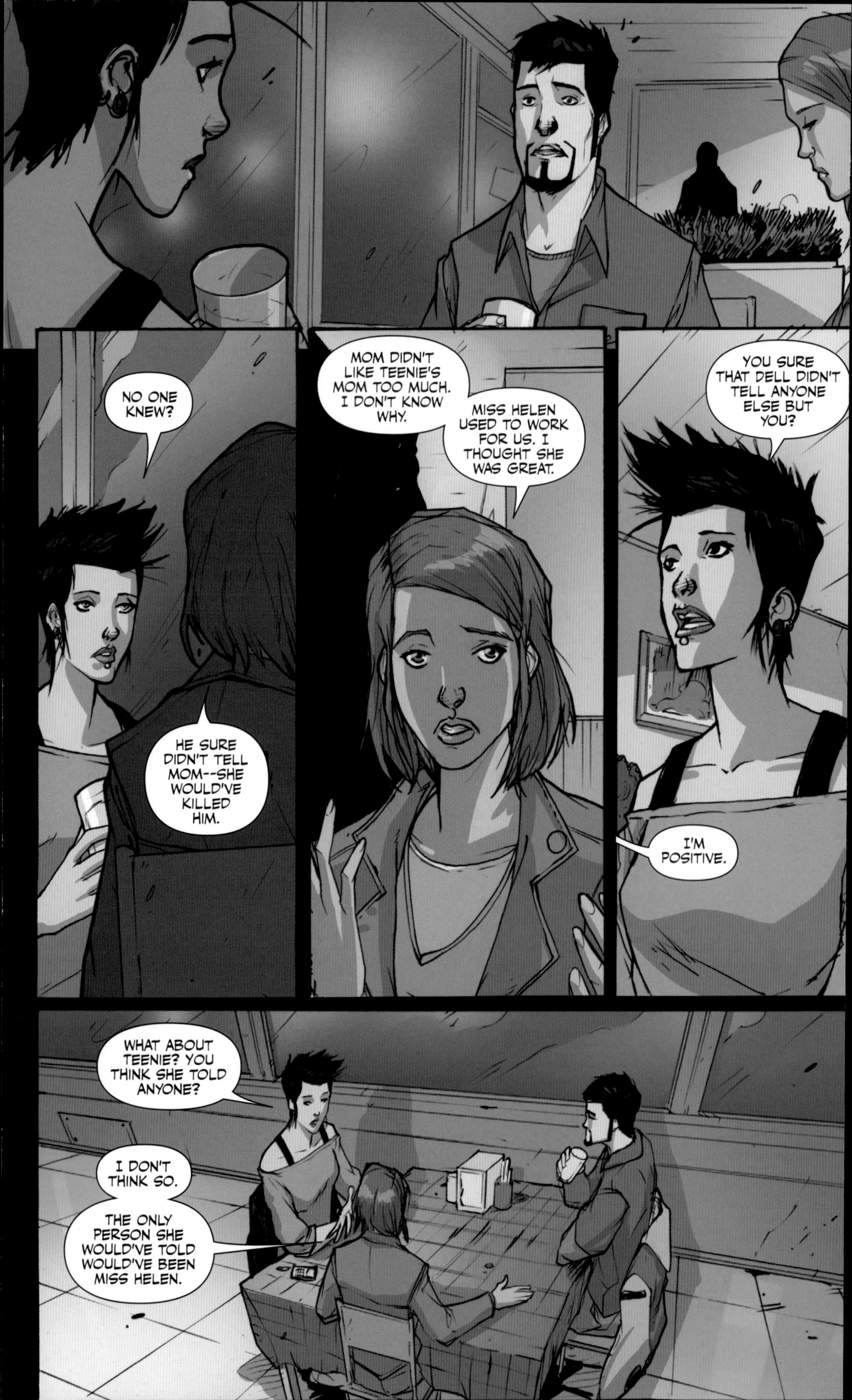
NO ONE KNEW?
HE SURE DIDN'T TELL MOM--SHE WOULD'VE KILLED HIM.
MOM DIDN'T LIKE TEENIE'S MOM TOO MUCH. I DON'T KNOW WHY.
MISS HELEN USED TO WORK FOR US. I THOUGHT SHE WAS GREAT.
YOU SURE THAT DELL DIDN'T TELL ANYONE ELSE BUT YOU?
I'M POSITIVE.
WHAT ABOUT TEENIE? YOU THINK SHE TOLD ANYONE?
I DON'T THINK SO.
THE ONLY PERSON SHE WOULD'VE TOLD WOULD'VE BEEN MISS HELEN.

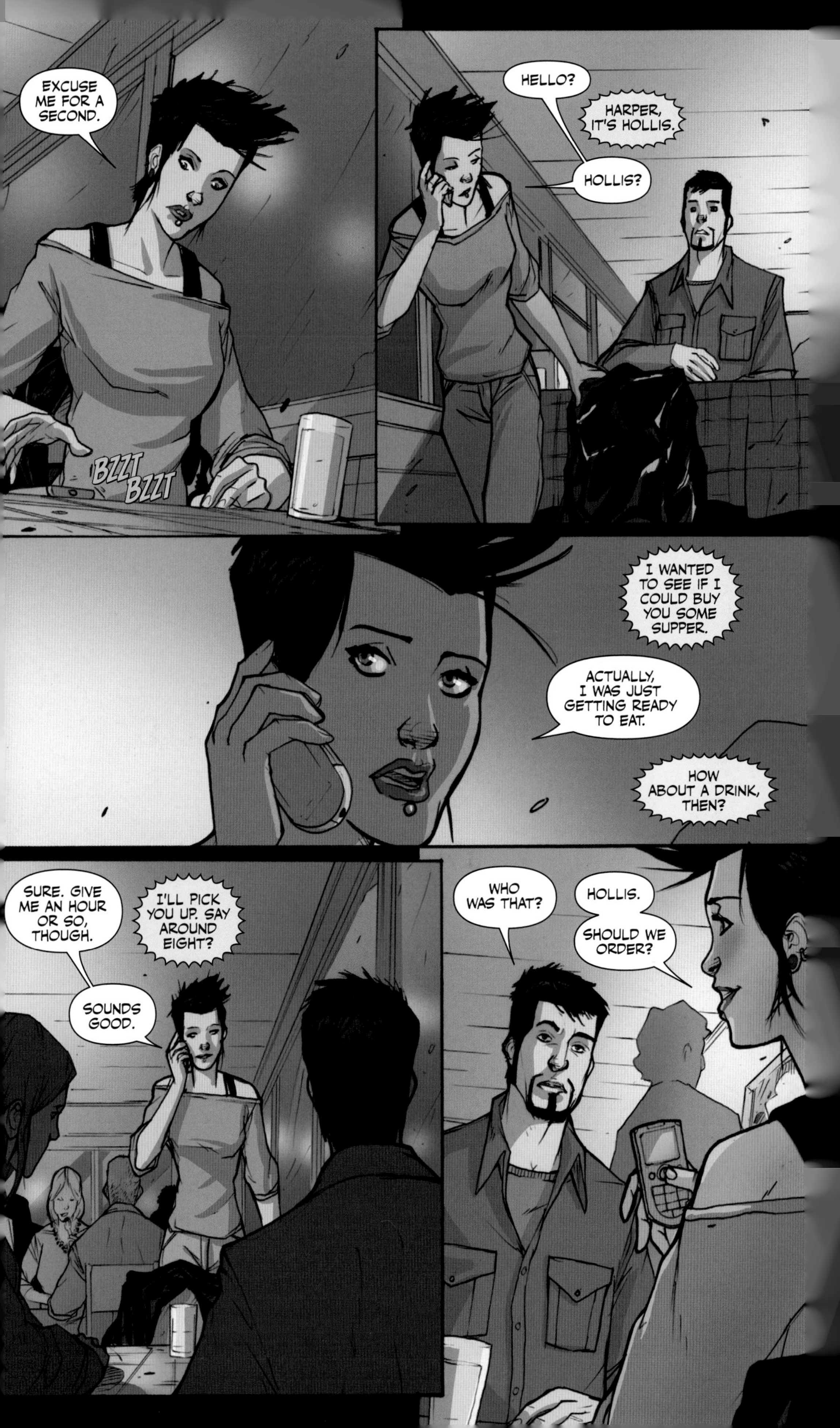
EXCUSE ME FOR A SECOND.
BZZT BZZT
HELLO?
HARPER, IT'S HOLLIS.
HOLLIS?
I WANTED TO SEE IF I COULD BUY YOU SOME SUPPER.
ACTUALLY, I WAS JUST GETTING READY TO EAT.
HOW ABOUT A DRINK, THEN?
SURE. GIVE ME AN HOUR OR SO, THOUGH.
I'LL PICK YOU UP. SAY AROUND EIGHT?
SOUNDS GOOD.
WHO WAS THAT?
HOLLIS.
SHOULD WE ORDER?

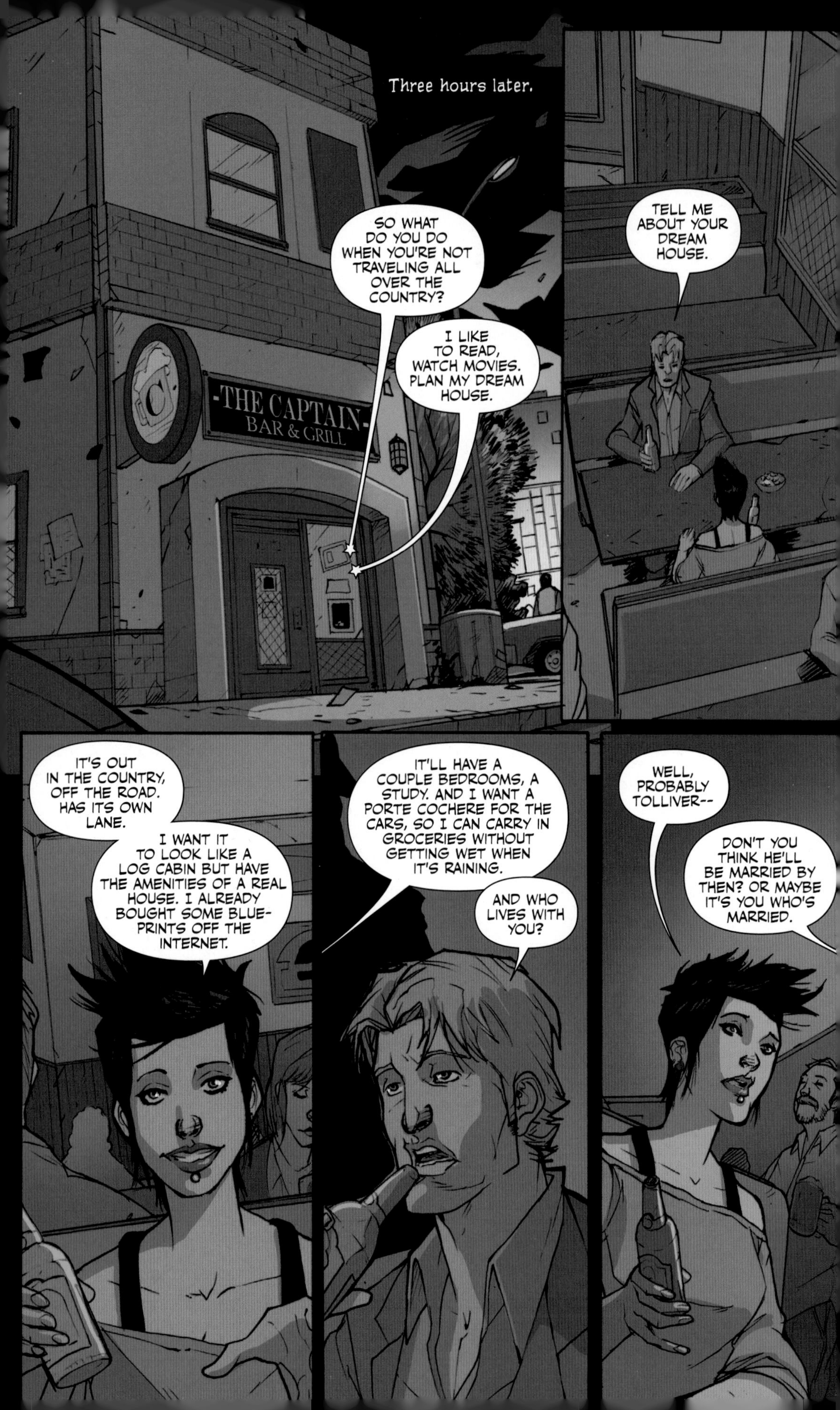
Three hours later.
SO WHAT DO YOU DO WHEN YOU'RE NOT TRAVELING ALL OVER THE COUNTRY?
I LIKE TO READ, WATCH MOVIES. PLAN MY DREAM HOUSE.
-THE CAPTAIN- BAR & GRILL
TELL ME ABOUT YOUR DREAM HOUSE.
IT'S OUT IN THE COUNTRY, OFF THE ROAD. HAS ITS OWN LANE.
I WANT IT TO LOOK LIKE A LOG CABIN BUT HAVE THE AMENITIES OF A REAL HOUSE. I ALREADY BOUGHT SOME BLUE-PRINTS OFF THE INTERNET.
IT'LL HAVE A COUPLE BEDROOMS, A STUDY. AND I WANT A PORTE COCHERE FOR THE CARS, SO I CAN CARRY IN GROCERIES WITHOUT GETTING WET WHEN IT'S RAINING.
AND WHO LIVES WITH YOU?
WELL, PROBABLY TOLLIVER--
DON'T YOU THINK HE'LL BE MARRIED BY THEN? OR MAYBE IT'S YOU WHO'S MARRIED.

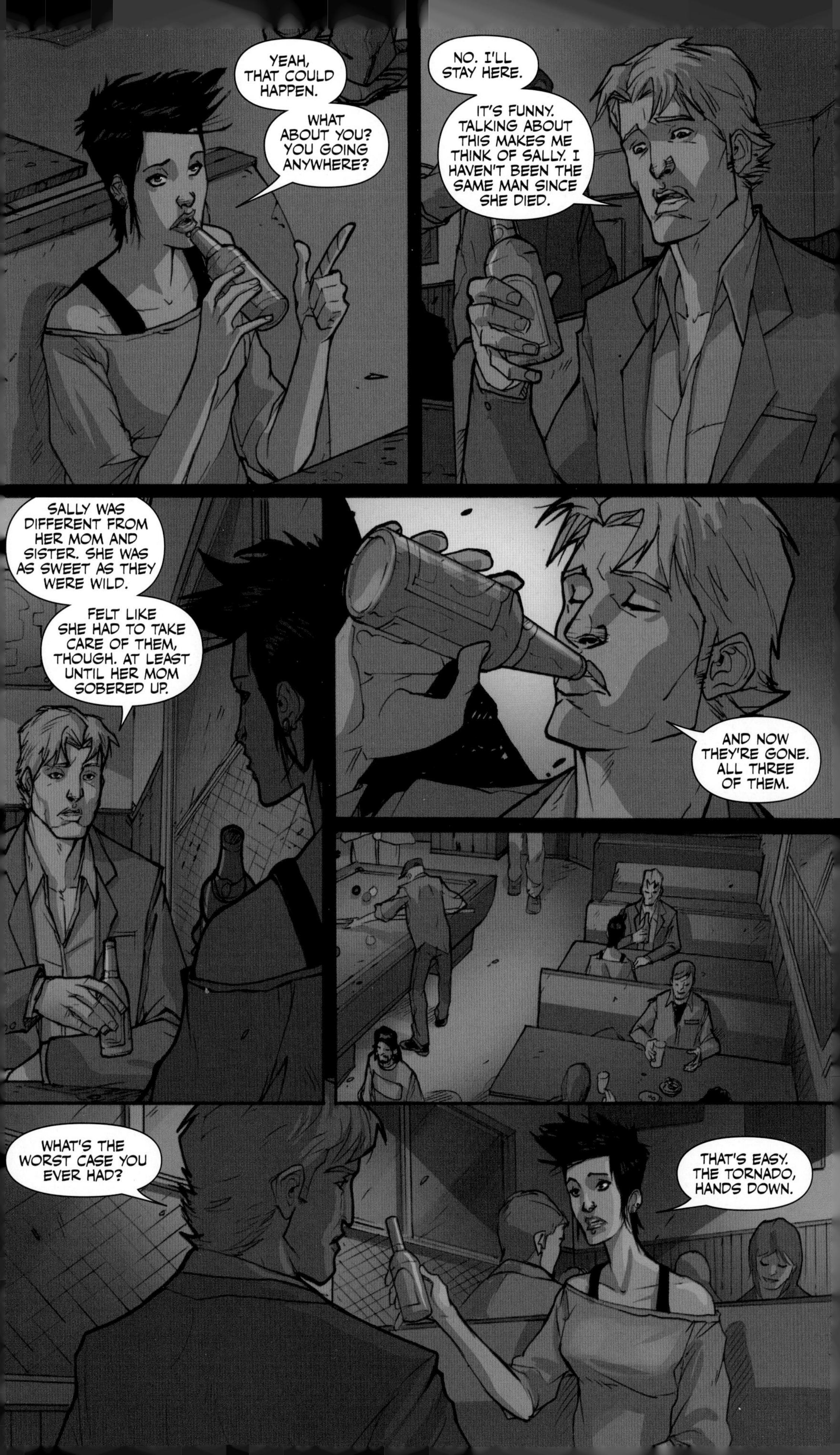
YEAH, THAT COULD HAPPEN.
WHAT ABOUT YOU? YOU GOING ANYWHERE?
NO. I'LL STAY HERE.
IT'S FUNNY. TALKING ABOUT THIS MAKES ME THINK OF SALLY. I HAVEN'T BEEN THE SAME MAN SINCE SHE DIED.
SALLY WAS DIFFERENT FROM HER MOM AND SISTER. SHE WAS AS SWEET AS THEY WERE WILD.
FELT LIKE SHE HAD TO TAKE CARE OF THEM, THOUGH. AT LEAST UNTIL HER MOM SOBERED UP.
AND NOW THEY'RE GONE. ALL THREE OF THEM.
WHAT'S THE WORST CASE YOU EVER HAD?
THAT'S EASY. THE TORNADO, HANDS DOWN.

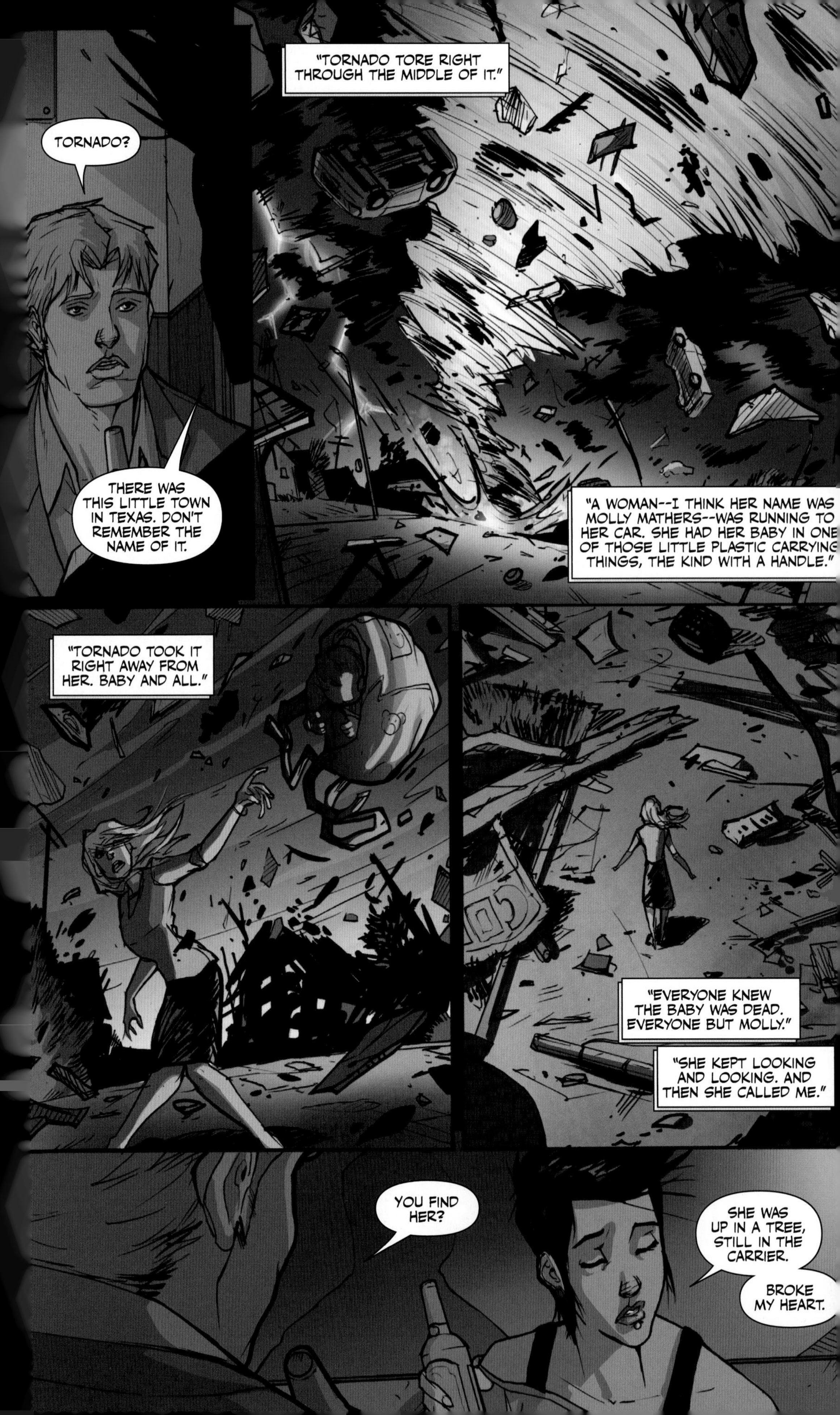

TORNADO?
"TORNADO TORE RIGHT THROUGH THE MIDDLE OF IT."
THERE WAS THIS LITTLE TOWN IN TEXAS. DON'T REMEMBER THE NAME OF IT.
"A WOMAN--I THINK HER NAME WAS MOLLY MATHERS--WAS RUNNING TO HER CAR. SHE HAD HER BABY IN ONE OF THOSE LITTLE PLASTIC CARRYING THINGS, THE KIND WITH A HANDLE."
"TORNADO TOOK IT RIGHT AWAY FROM HER. BABY AND ALL."
"EVERYONE KNEW THE BABY WAS DEAD. EVERYONE BUT MOLLY."
"SHE KEPT LOOKING AND LOOKING. AND THEN SHE CALLED ME."
YOU FIND HER?
SHE WAS UP IN A TREE, STILL IN THE CARRIER.
BROKE MY HEART.

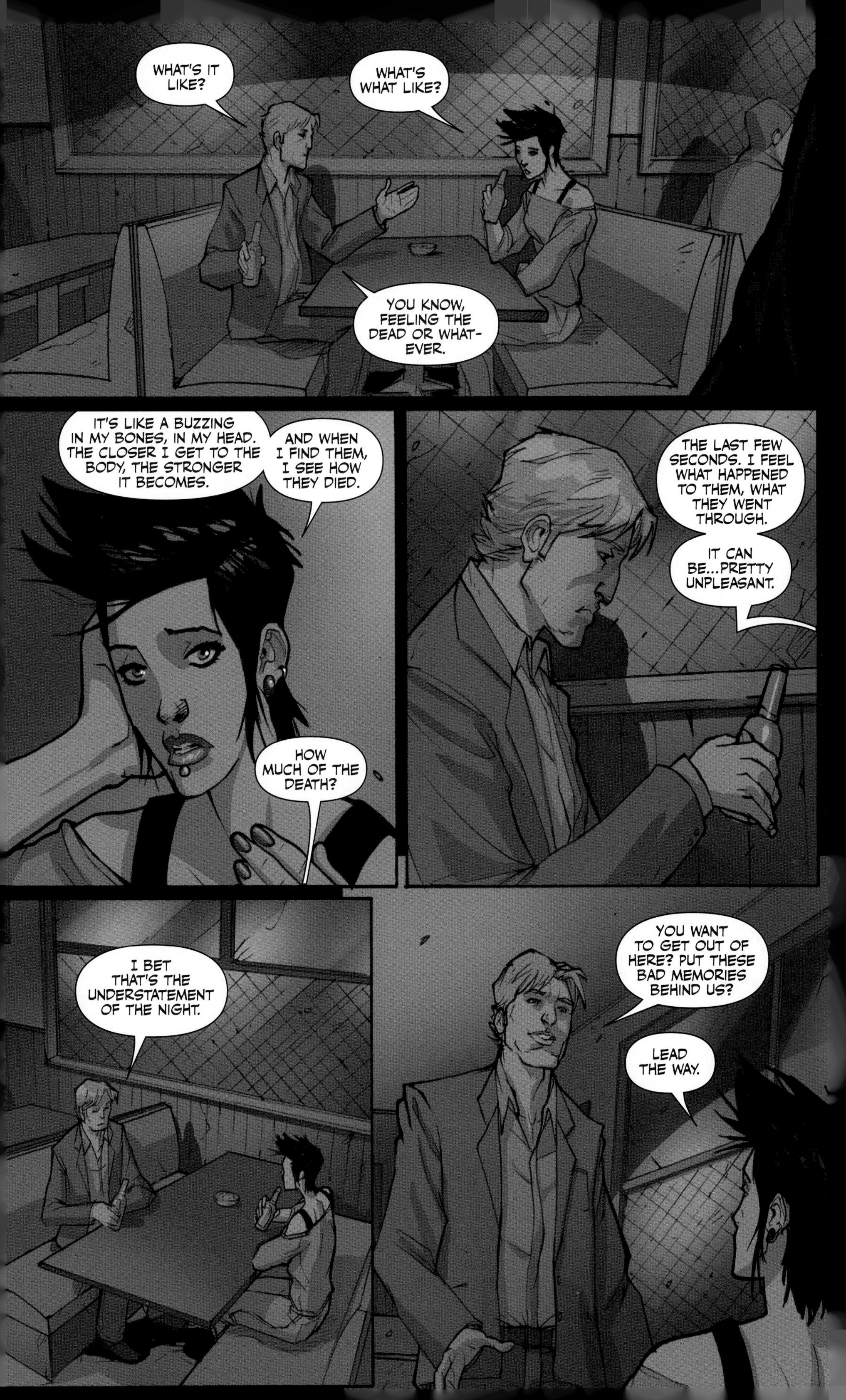
WHAT'S IT LIKE?
WHAT'S WHAT LIKE?
YOU KNOW, FEELING THE DEAD OR WHAT-EVER.
IT'S LIKE A BUZZING IN MY BONES, IN MY HEAD. THE CLOSER I GET TO THE BODY, THE STRONGER IT BECOMES.
AND WHEN I FIND THEM, I SEE HOW THEY DIED.
HOW MUCH OF THE DEATH?
THE LAST FEW SECONDS. I FEEL WHAT HAPPENED TO THEM, WHAT THEY WENT THROUGH.
IT CAN BE...PRETTY UNPLEASANT.
I BET THAT'S THE UNDERSTATEMENT OF THE NIGHT.
YOU WANT TO GET OUT OF HERE? PUT THESE BAD MEMORIES BEHIND US?
LEAD THE WAY.

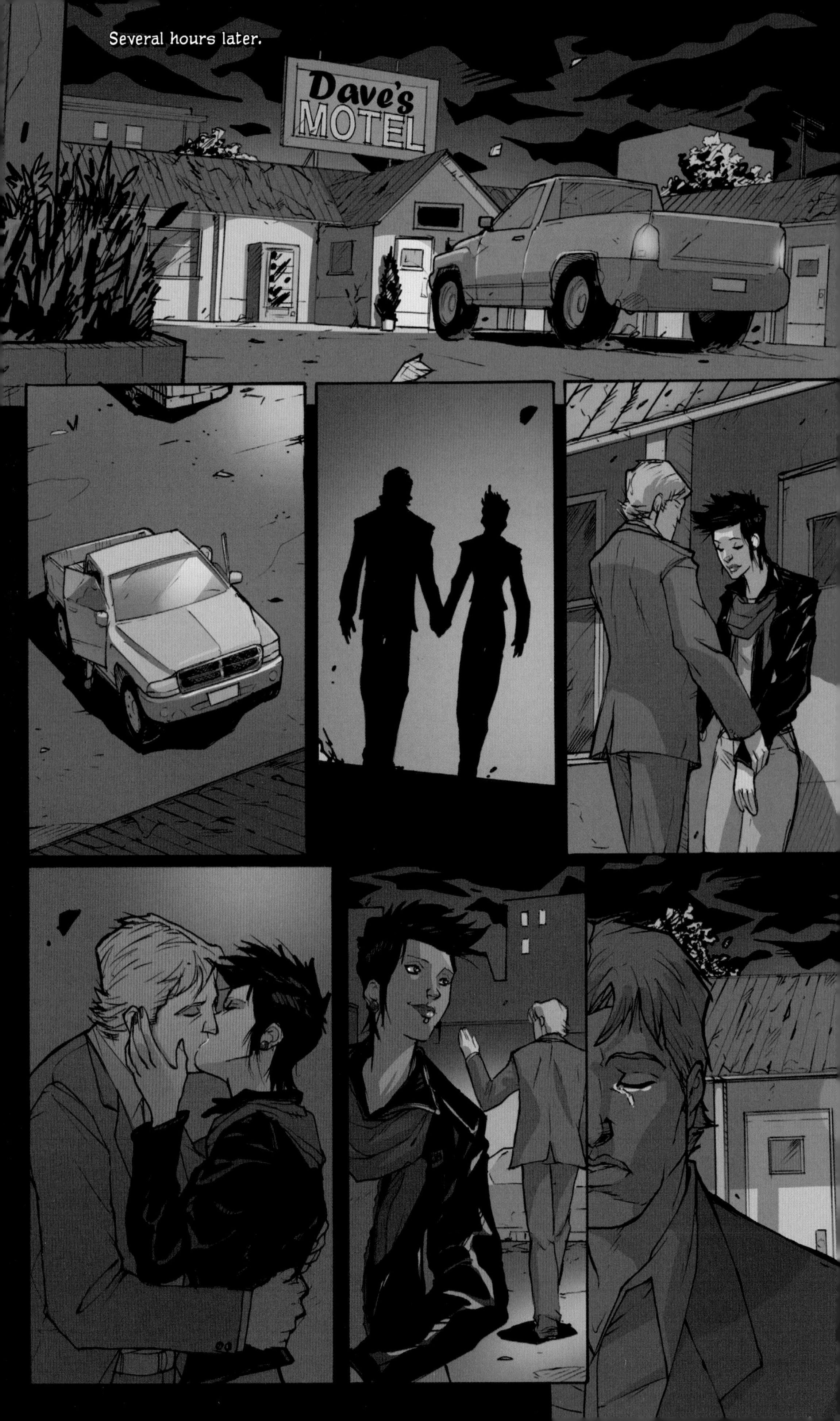
Several hours later.
Dave's
MOTEL

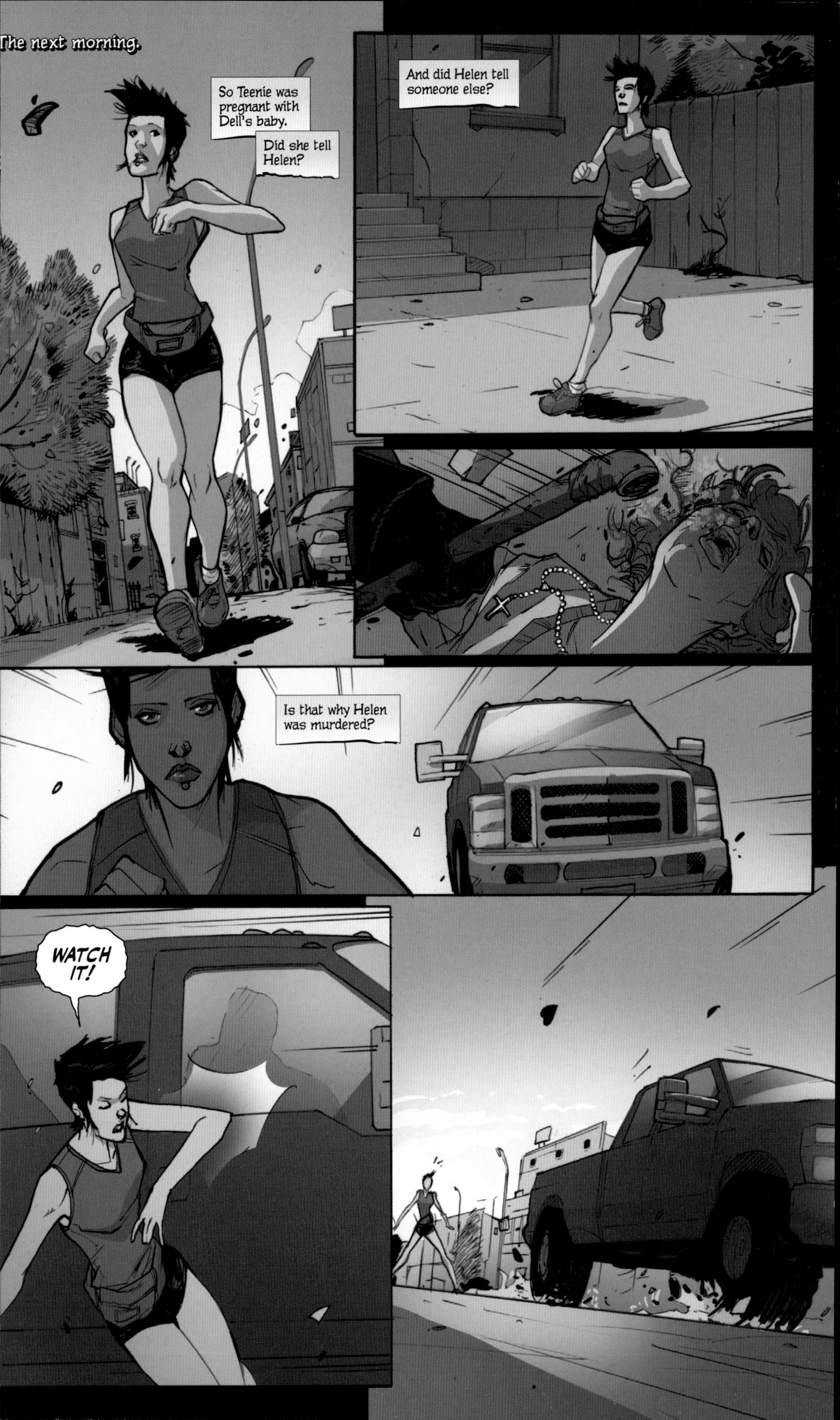
The next morning.
So Teenie was pregnant with Dell's baby.
Did she tell Helen?
And did Helen tell someone else?
Is that why Helen was murdered?
WATCH IT!

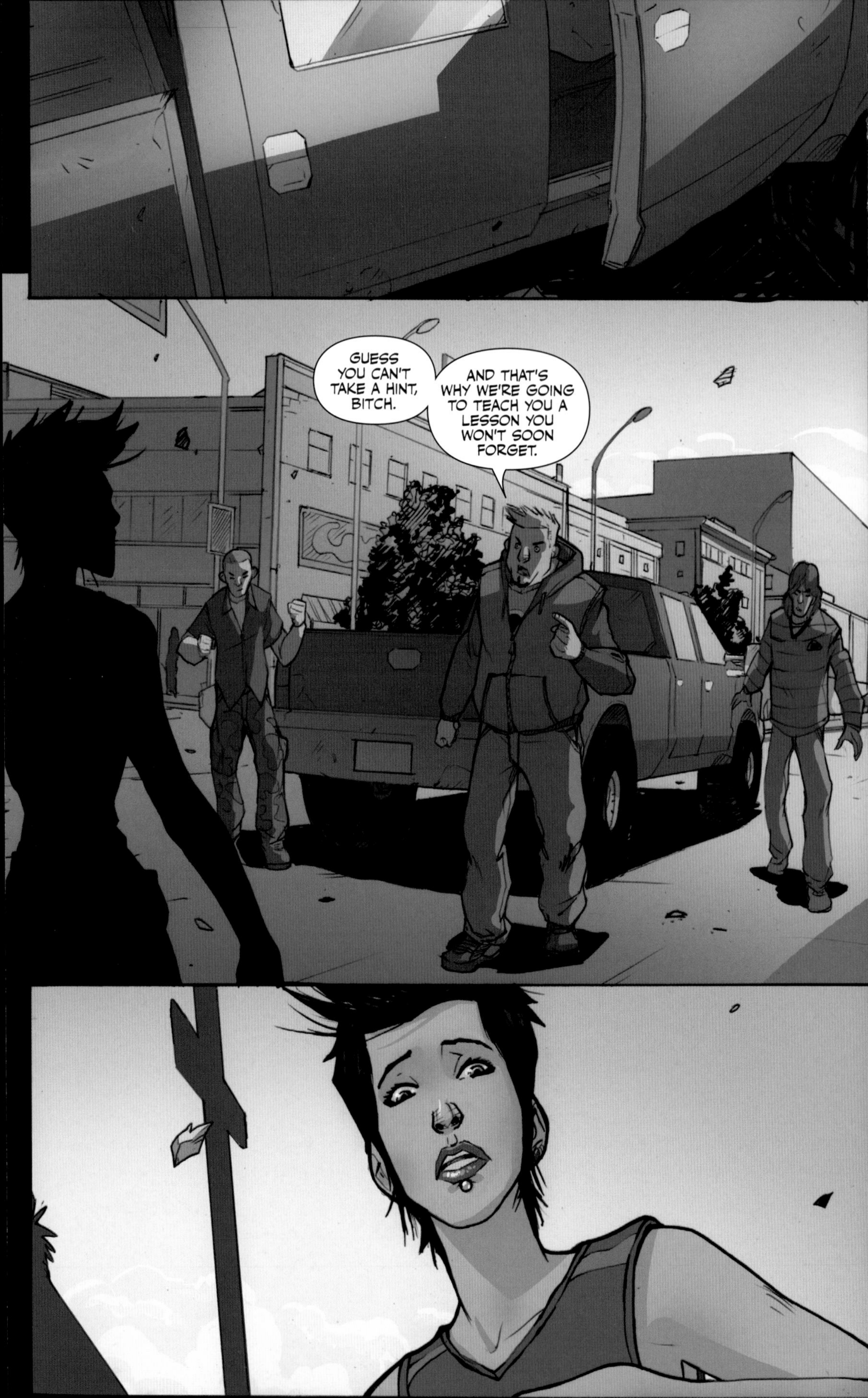
GUESS YOU CAN'T TAKE A HINT, BITCH.
AND THAT'S WHY WE'RE GOING TO TEACH YOU A LESSON YOU WON'T SOON FORGET.

CHAPTER FOUR

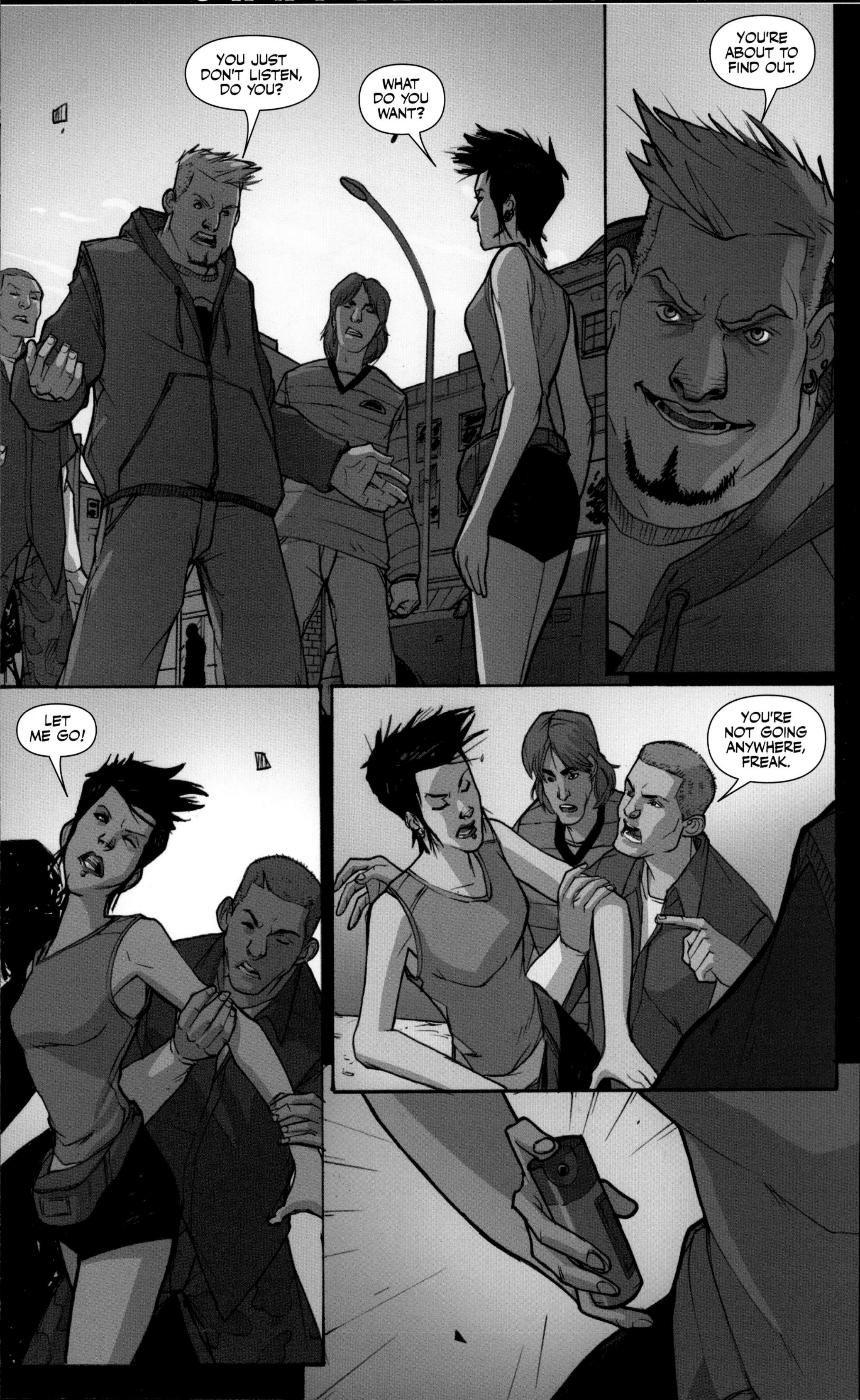

YOU JUST DON'T LISTEN, DO YOU?
WHAT DO YOU WANT?
YOU'RE ABOUT TO FIND OUT.
LET ME GO!
YOU'RE NOT GOING ANYWHERE, FREAK.

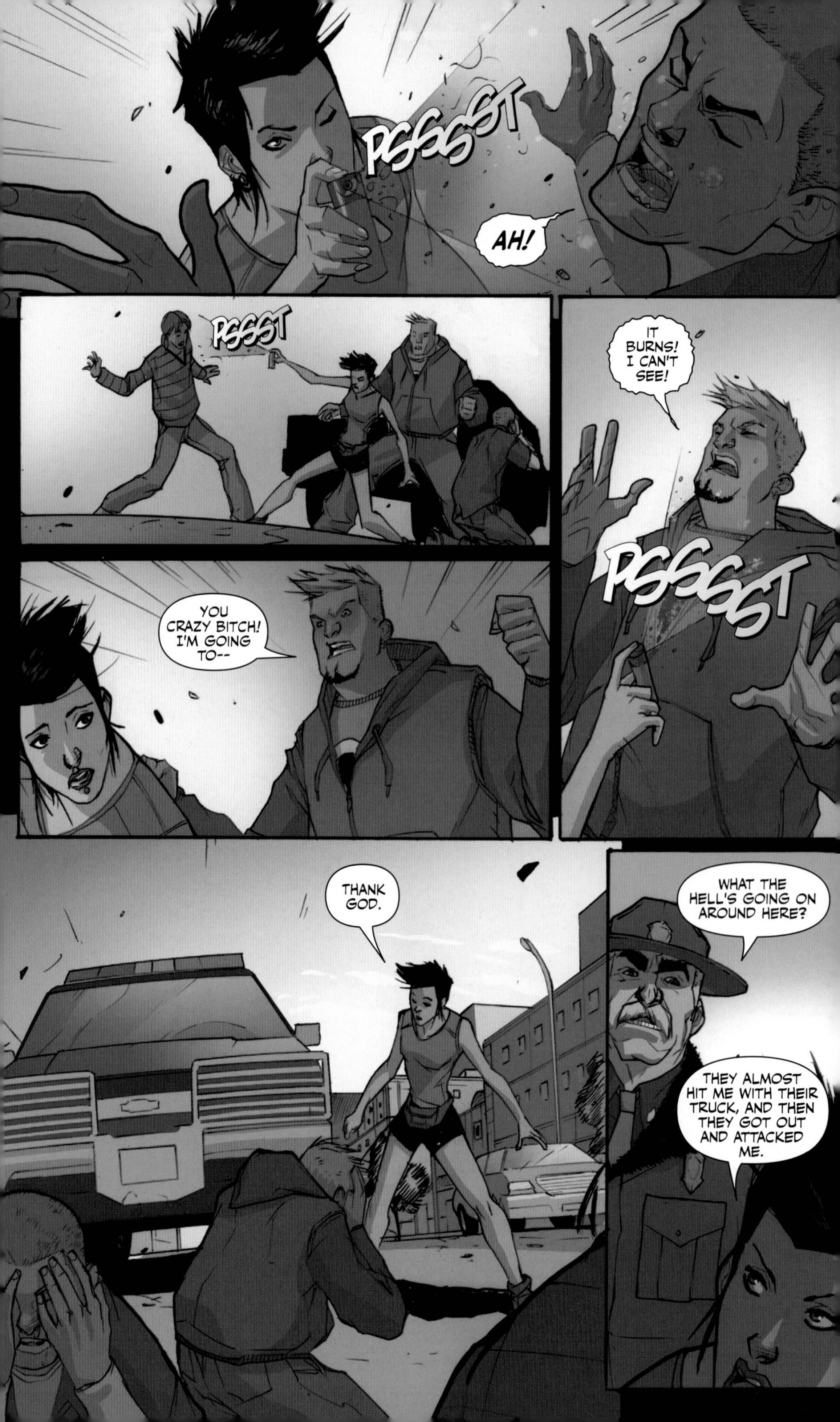
PSSSST
AH!
PSSST
IT BURNS! I CAN'T SEE!
PSSSST
YOU CRAZY BITCH! I'M GOING TO--
THANK GOD.
WHAT THE HELL'S GOING ON AROUND HERE?
THEY ALMOST HIT ME WITH THEIR TRUCK, AND THEN THEY GOT OUT AND ATTACKED ME.

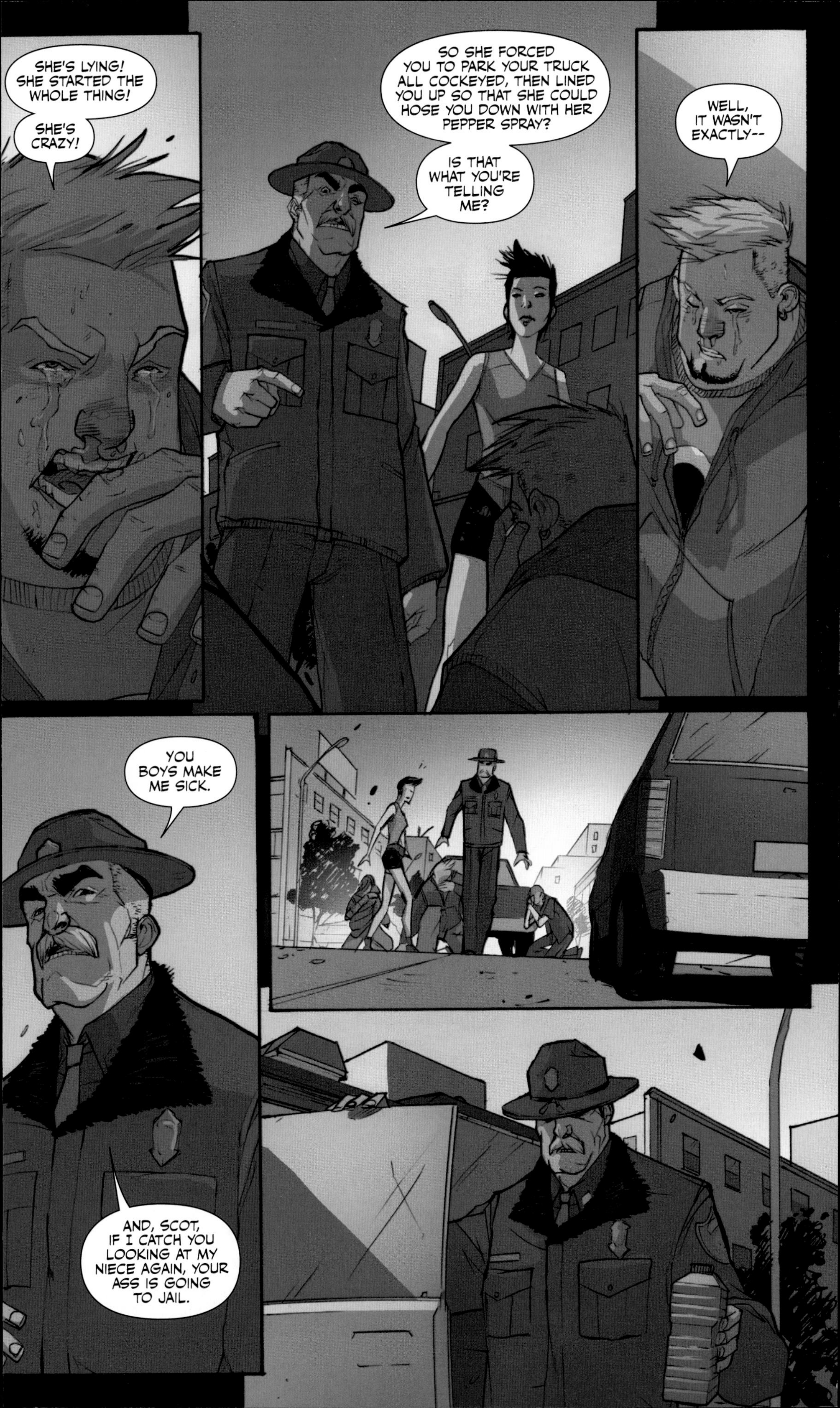
SHE'S LYING! SHE STARTED THE WHOLE THING!
SHE'S CRAZY!
SO SHE FORCED YOU TO PARK YOUR TRUCK ALL COCKEYED, THEN LINED YOU UP SO THAT SHE COULD HOSE YOU DOWN WITH HER PEPPER SPRAY?
IS THAT WHAT YOU'RE TELLING ME?
WELL, IT WASN'T EXACTLY--
YOU BOYS MAKE ME SICK.
AND, SCOT, IF I CATCH YOU LOOKING AT MY NIECE AGAIN, YOUR ASS IS GOING TO JAIL.

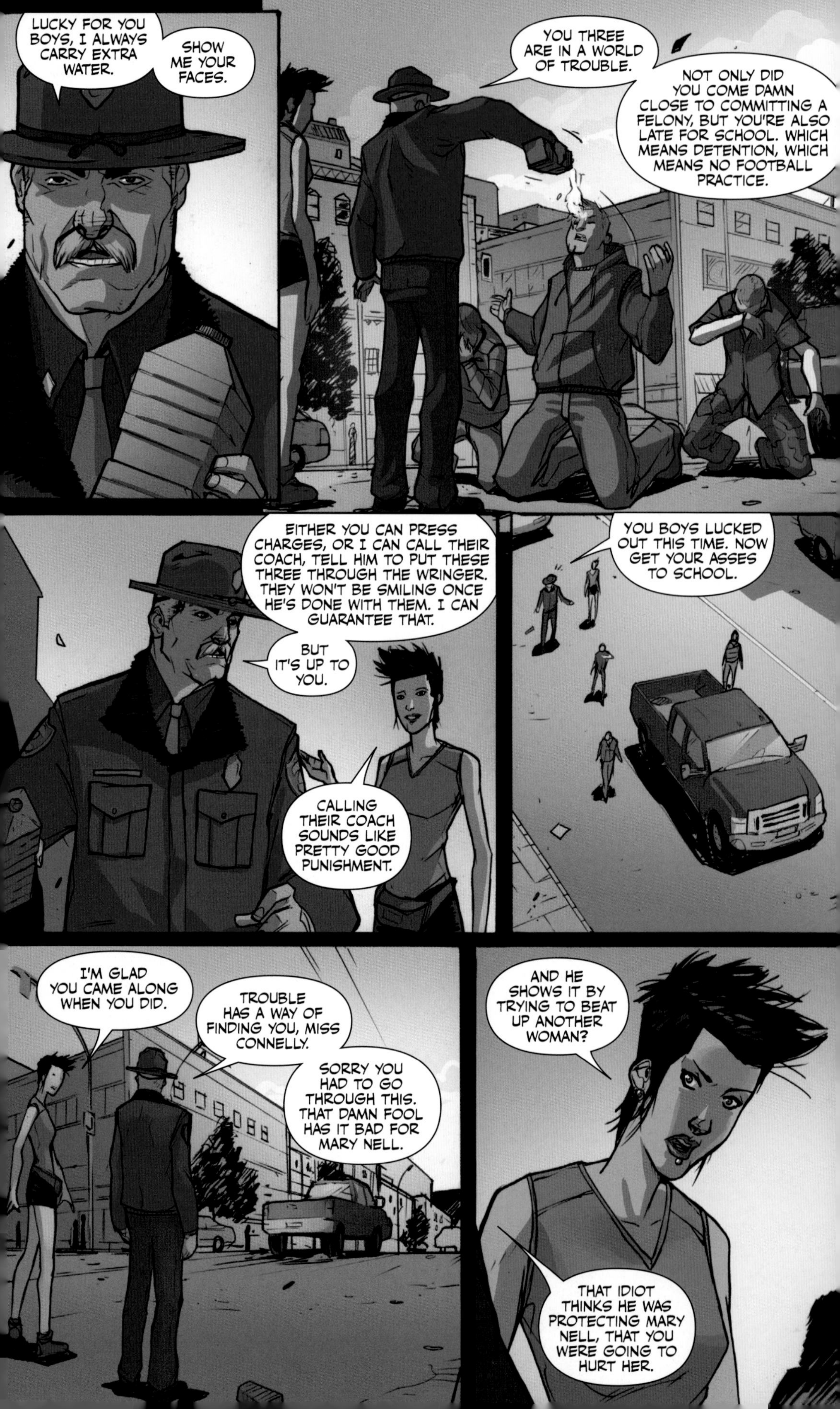
LUCKY FOR YOU BOYS, I ALWAYS CARRY EXTRA WATER.
SHOW ME YOUR FACES.
YOU THREE ARE IN A WORLD OF TROUBLE.
NOT ONLY DID YOU COME DAMN CLOSE TO COMMITTING A FELONY, BUT YOU'RE ALSO LATE FOR SCHOOL. WHICH MEANS DETENTION, WHICH MEANS NO FOOTBALL PRACTICE.
EITHER YOU CAN PRESS CHARGES, OR I CAN CALL THEIR COACH, TELL HIM TO PUT THESE THREE THROUGH THE WRINGER. THEY WON'T BE SMILING ONCE HE'S DONE WITH THEM. I CAN GUARANTEE THAT.
BUT IT'S UP TO YOU.
CALLING THEIR COACH SOUNDS LIKE PRETTY GOOD PUNISHMENT.
YOU BOYS LUCKED OUT THIS TIME. NOW GET YOUR ASSES TO SCHOOL.
I'M GLAD YOU CAME ALONG WHEN YOU DID.
TROUBLE HAS A WAY OF FINDING YOU, MISS CONNELLY.
SORRY YOU HAD TO GO THROUGH THIS. THAT DAMN FOOL HAS IT BAD FOR MARY NELL.
AND HE SHOWS IT BY TRYING TO BEAT UP ANOTHER WOMAN?
THAT IDIOT THINKS HE WAS PROTECTING MARY NELL, THAT YOU WERE GOING TO HURT HER.

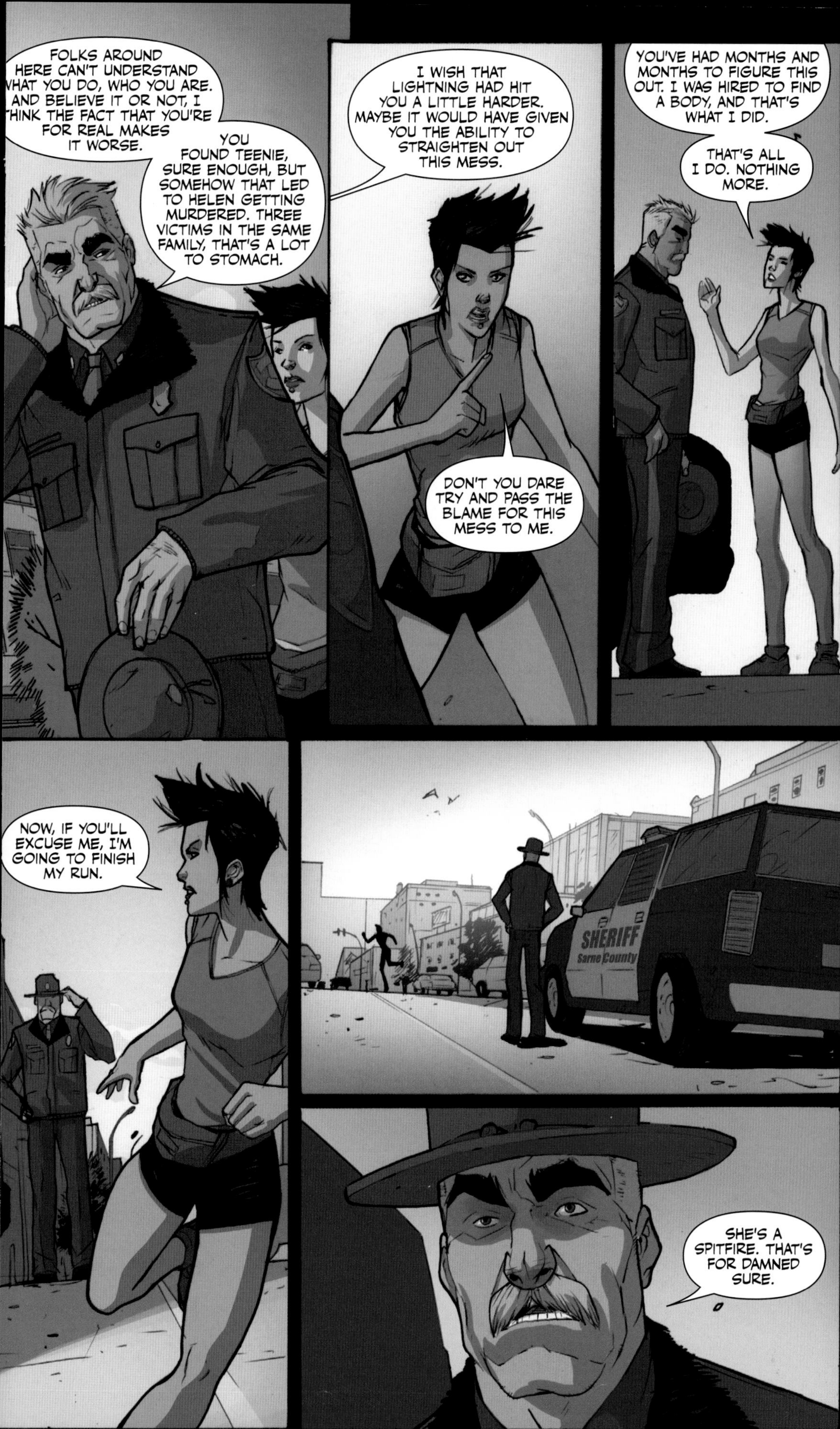
FOLKS AROUND HERE CAN'T UNDERSTAND WHAT YOU DO, WHO YOU ARE. AND BELIEVE IT OR NOT, I THINK THE FACT THAT YOU'RE FOR REAL MAKES IT WORSE.
YOU FOUND TEENIE, SURE ENOUGH, BUT SOMEHOW THAT LED TO HELEN GETTING MURDERED. THREE VICTIMS IN THE SAME FAMILY, THAT'S A LOT TO STOMACH.
I WISH THAT LIGHTNING HAD HIT YOU A LITTLE HARDER. MAYBE IT WOULD HAVE GIVEN YOU THE ABILITY TO STRAIGHTEN OUT THIS MESS.
DON'T YOU DARE TRY AND PASS THE BLAME FOR THIS MESS TO ME.
YOU'VE HAD MONTHS AND MONTHS TO FIGURE THIS OUT. I WAS HIRED TO FIND A BODY, AND THAT'S WHAT I DID.
THAT'S ALL I DO. NOTHING MORE.
NOW, IF YOU'LL EXCUSE ME, I'M GOING TO FINISH MY RUN.
SHERIFF
Sarne County
SHE'S A SPITFIRE. THAT'S FOR DAMNED SURE.

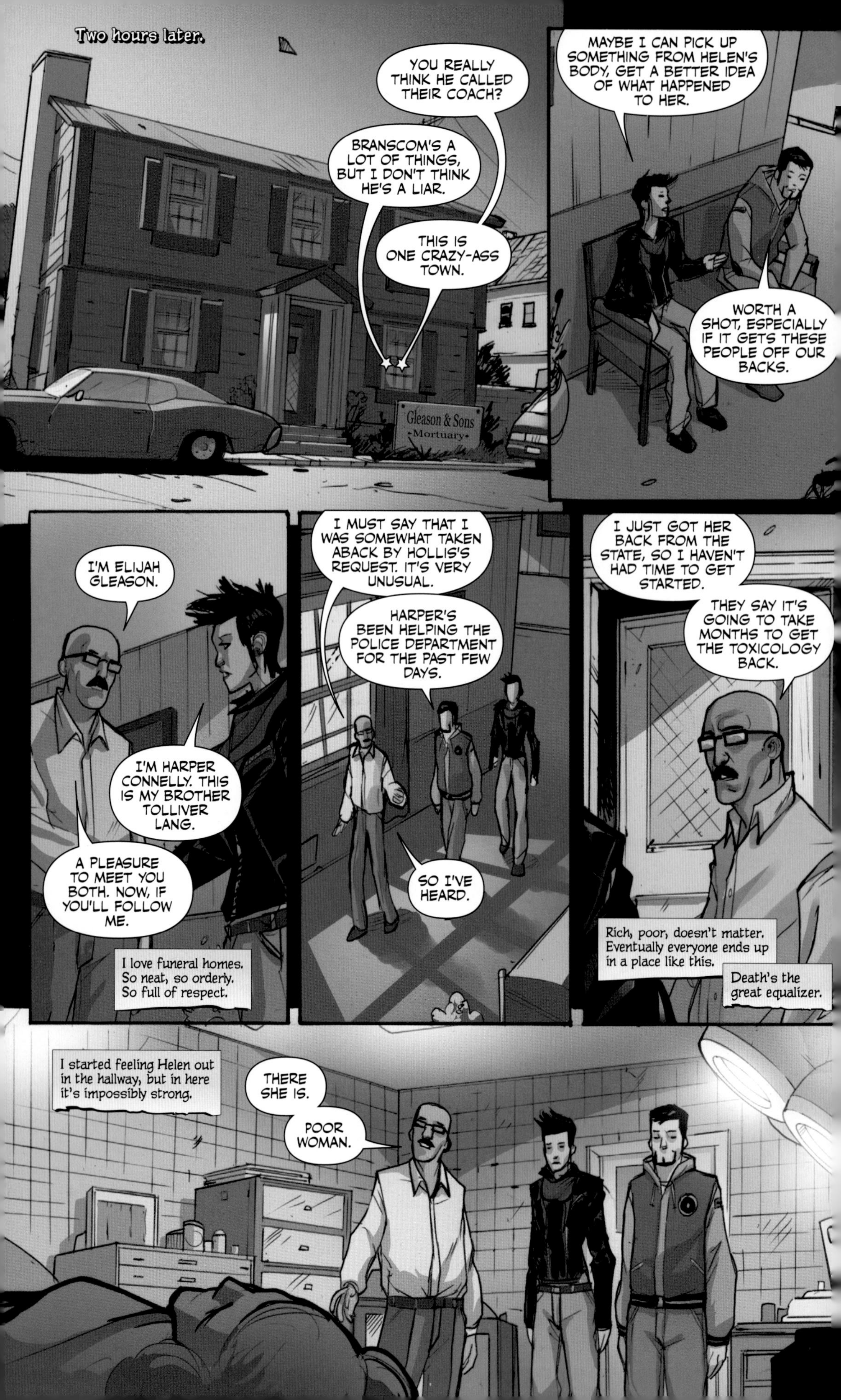
Two hours later.
YOU REALLY THINK HE CALLED THEIR COACH?
BRANSCOM'S A LOT OF THINGS, BUT I DON'T THINK HE'S A LIAR.
THIS IS ONE CRAZY-ASS TOWN.
Gleason & Sons
Mortuary
MAYBE I CAN PICK UP SOMETHING FROM HELEN'S BODY, GET A BETTER IDEA OF WHAT HAPPENED TO HER.
WORTH A SHOT, ESPECIALLY IF IT GETS THESE PEOPLE OFF OUR BACKS.
I'M ELIJAH GLEASON.
I'M HARPER CONNELLY. THIS IS MY BROTHER TOLLIVER LANG.
A PLEASURE TO MEET YOU BOTH. NOW, IF YOU'LL FOLLOW ME.
I love funeral homes. So neat, so orderly. So full of respect.
I MUST SAY THAT I WAS SOMEWHAT TAKEN ABACK BY HOLLIS'S REQUEST. IT'S VERY UNUSUAL.
HARPER'S BEEN HELPING THE POLICE DEPARTMENT FOR THE PAST FEW DAYS.
SO I'VE HEARD.
I JUST GOT HER BACK FROM THE STATE, SO I HAVEN'T HAD TIME TO GET STARTED.
THEY SAY IT'S GOING TO TAKE MONTHS TO GET THE TOXICOLOGY BACK.
Rich, poor, doesn't matter. Eventually everyone ends up in a place like this.
Death's the great equalizer.
I started feeling Helen out in the hallway, but in here it's impossibly strong.
THERE SHE IS.
POOR WOMAN.

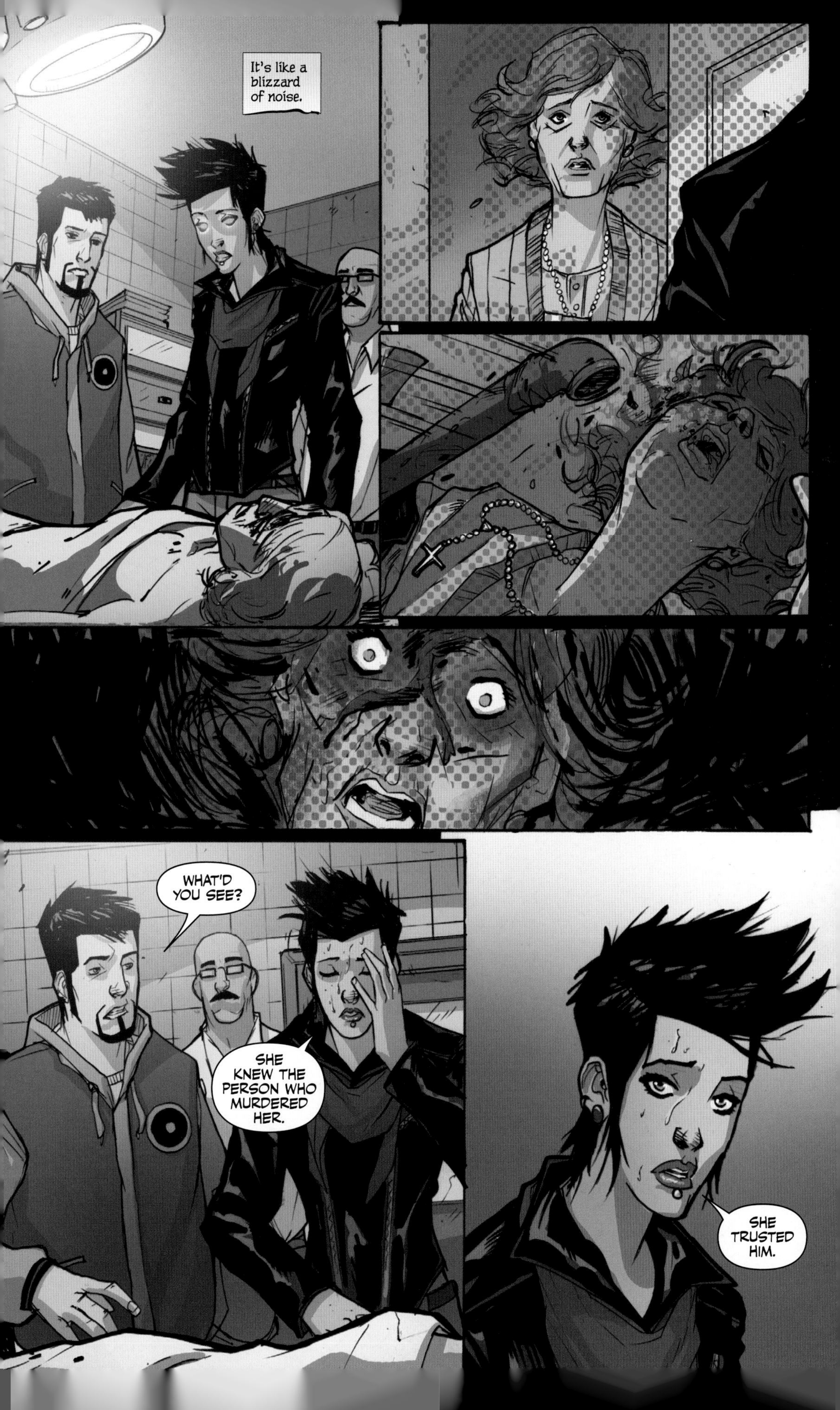
It's like a blizzard of noise.
WHAT'D YOU SEE?
SHE KNEW THE PERSON WHO MURDERED HER.
SHE TRUSTED HIM.

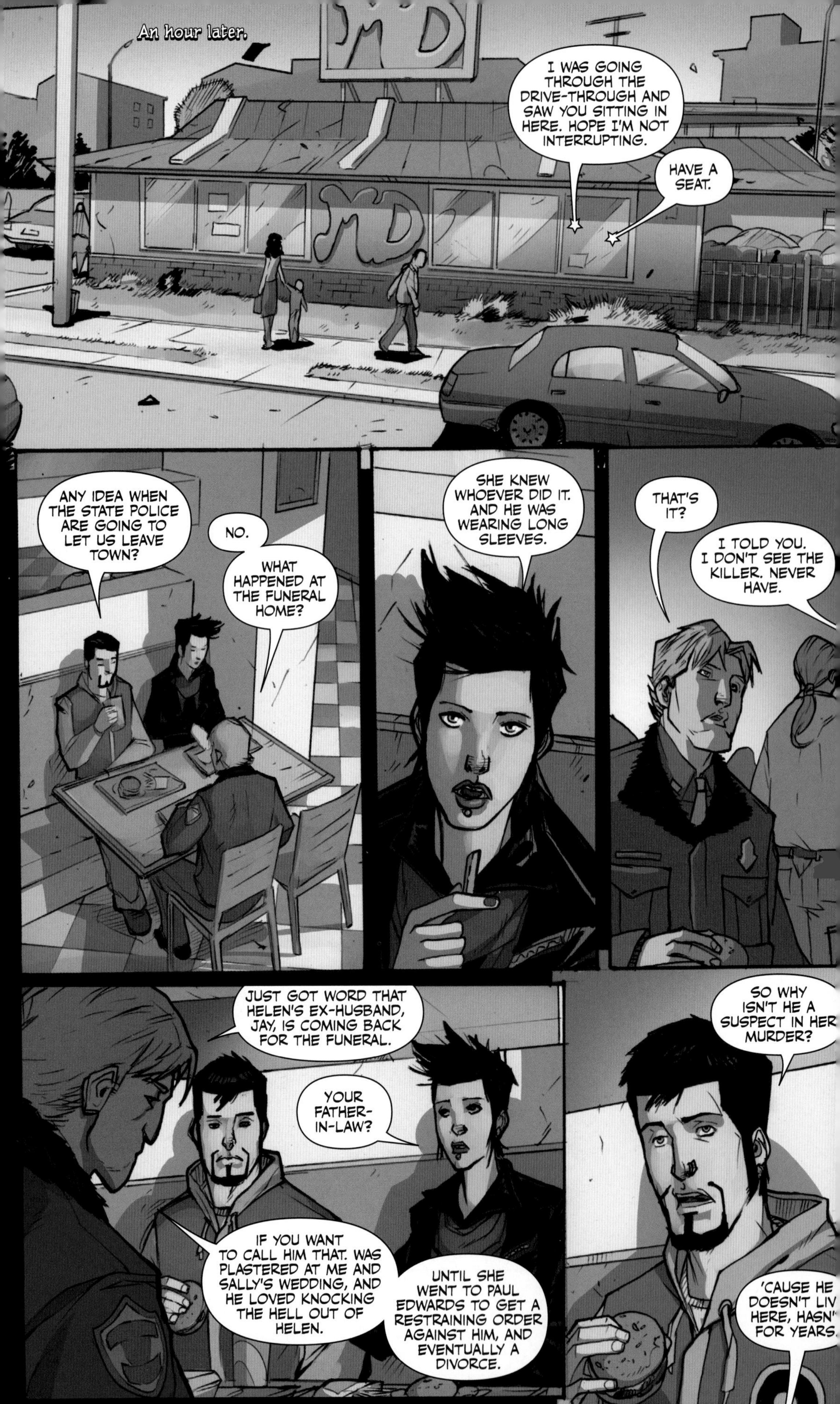
An hour later.
I WAS GOING THROUGH THE DRIVE-THROUGH AND SAW YOU SITTING IN HERE. HOPE I'M NOT INTERRUPTING.
HAVE A SEAT.
ANY IDEA WHEN THE STATE POLICE ARE GOING TO LET US LEAVE TOWN?
NO.
WHAT HAPPENED AT THE FUNERAL HOME?
SHE KNEW WHOEVER DID IT. AND HE WAS WEARING LONG SLEEVES.
THAT'S IT?
I TOLD YOU. I DON'T SEE THE KILLER. NEVER HAVE.
JUST GOT WORD THAT HELEN'S EX-HUSBAND, JAY, IS COMING BACK FOR THE FUNERAL.
YOUR FATHER-IN-LAW?
IF YOU WANT TO CALL HIM THAT. WAS PLASTERED AT ME AND SALLY'S WEDDING, AND HE LOVED KNOCKING THE HELL OUT OF HELEN.
UNTIL SHE WENT TO PAUL EDWARDS TO GET A RESTRAINING ORDER AGAINST HIM, AND EVENTUALLY A DIVORCE.
SO WHY ISN'T HE A SUSPECT IN HER MURDER?

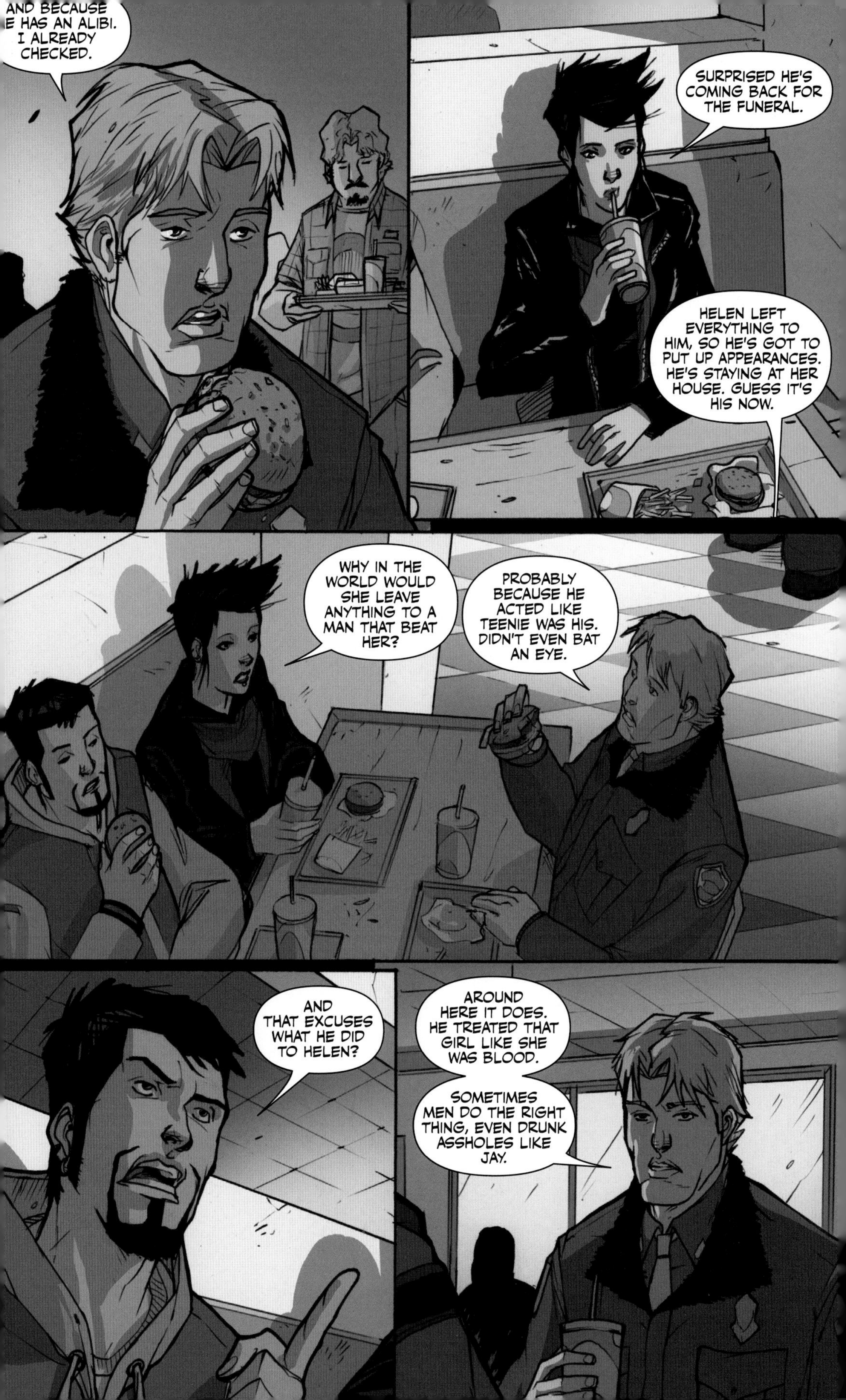

AND BECAUSE E HAS AN ALIBI. I ALREADY CHECKED.
SURPRISED HE'S COMING BACK FOR THE FUNERAL.
HELEN LEFT EVERYTHING TO HIM, SO HE'S GOT TO PUT UP APPEARANCES. HE'S STAYING AT HER HOUSE. GUESS IT'S HIS NOW.
WHY IN THE WORLD WOULD SHE LEAVE ANYTHING TO A MAN THAT BEAT HER?
PROBABLY BECAUSE HE ACTED LIKE TEENIE WAS HIS. DIDN'T EVEN BAT AN EYE.
AND THAT EXCUSES WHAT HE DID TO HELEN?
AROUND HERE IT DOES. HE TREATED THAT GIRL LIKE SHE WAS BLOOD.
SOMETIMES MEN DO THE RIGHT THING, EVEN DRUNK ASSHOLES LIKE JAY.

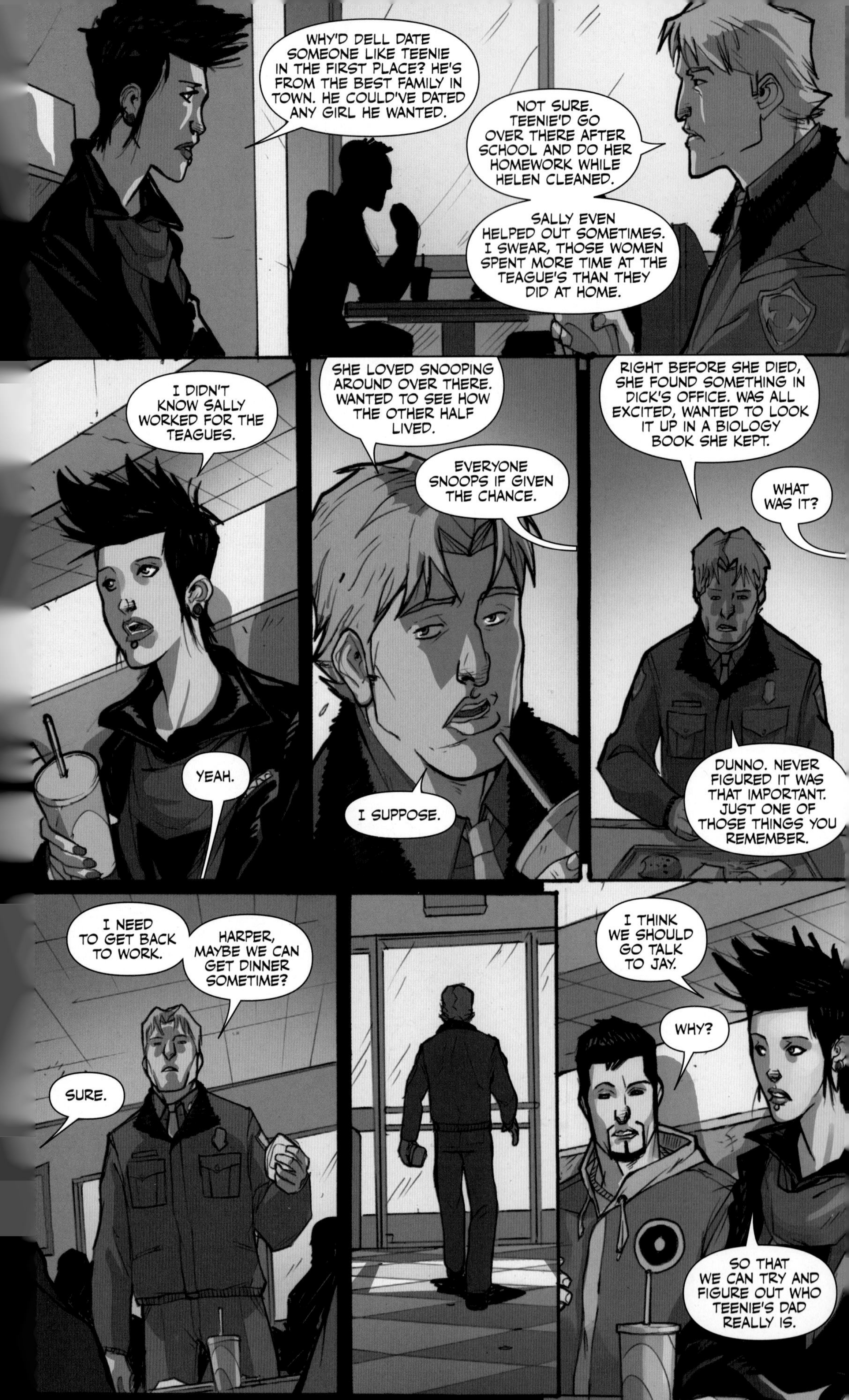
WHY'D DELL DATE SOMEONE LIKE TEENIE IN THE FIRST PLACE? HE'S FROM THE BEST FAMILY IN TOWN. HE COULD'VE DATED ANY GIRL HE WANTED.
NOT SURE. TEENIE'D GO OVER THERE AFTER SCHOOL AND DO HER HOMEWORK WHILE HELEN CLEANED.
SALLY EVEN HELPED OUT SOMETIMES. I SWEAR, THOSE WOMEN SPENT MORE TIME AT THE TEAGUE'S THAN THEY DID AT HOME.
I DIDN'T KNOW SALLY WORKED FOR THE TEAGUES.
YEAH.
SHE LOVED SNOOPING AROUND OVER THERE. WANTED TO SEE HOW THE OTHER HALF LIVED.
EVERYONE SNOOPS IF GIVEN THE CHANCE.
I SUPPOSE.
RIGHT BEFORE SHE DIED, SHE FOUND SOMETHING IN DICK'S OFFICE. WAS ALL EXCITED, WANTED TO LOOK IT UP IN A BIOLOGY BOOK SHE KEPT.
WHAT WAS IT?
DUNNO. NEVER FIGURED IT WAS THAT IMPORTANT. JUST ONE OF THOSE THINGS YOU REMEMBER.
I NEED TO GET BACK TO WORK.
HARPER, MAYBE WE CAN GET DINNER SOMETIME?
SURE.
I THINK WE SHOULD GO TALK TO JAY.
WHY?
SO THAT WE CAN TRY AND FIGURE OUT WHO TEENIE'S DAD REALLY IS.

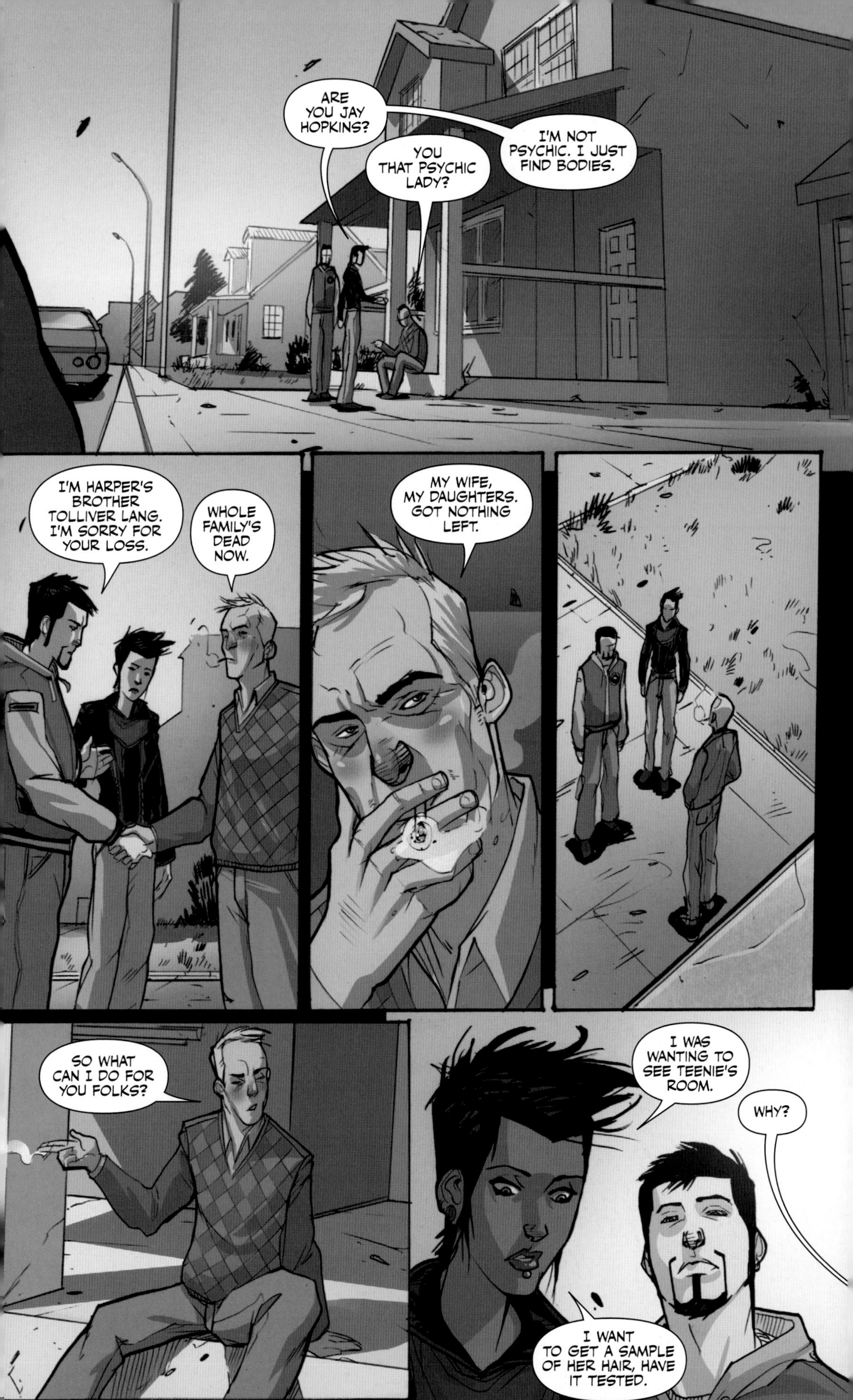
ARE YOU JAY HOPKINS?
YOU THAT PSYCHIC LADY?
I'M NOT PSYCHIC. I JUST FIND BODIES.
I'M HARPER'S BROTHER TOLLIVER LANG. I'M SORRY FOR YOUR LOSS.
WHOLE FAMILY'S DEAD NOW.
MY WIFE, MY DAUGHTERS. GOT NOTHING LEFT.
SO WHAT CAN I DO FOR YOU FOLKS?
I WAS WANTING TO SEE TEENIE'S ROOM.
WHY?
I WANT TO GET A SAMPLE OF HER HAIR, HAVE IT TESTED.

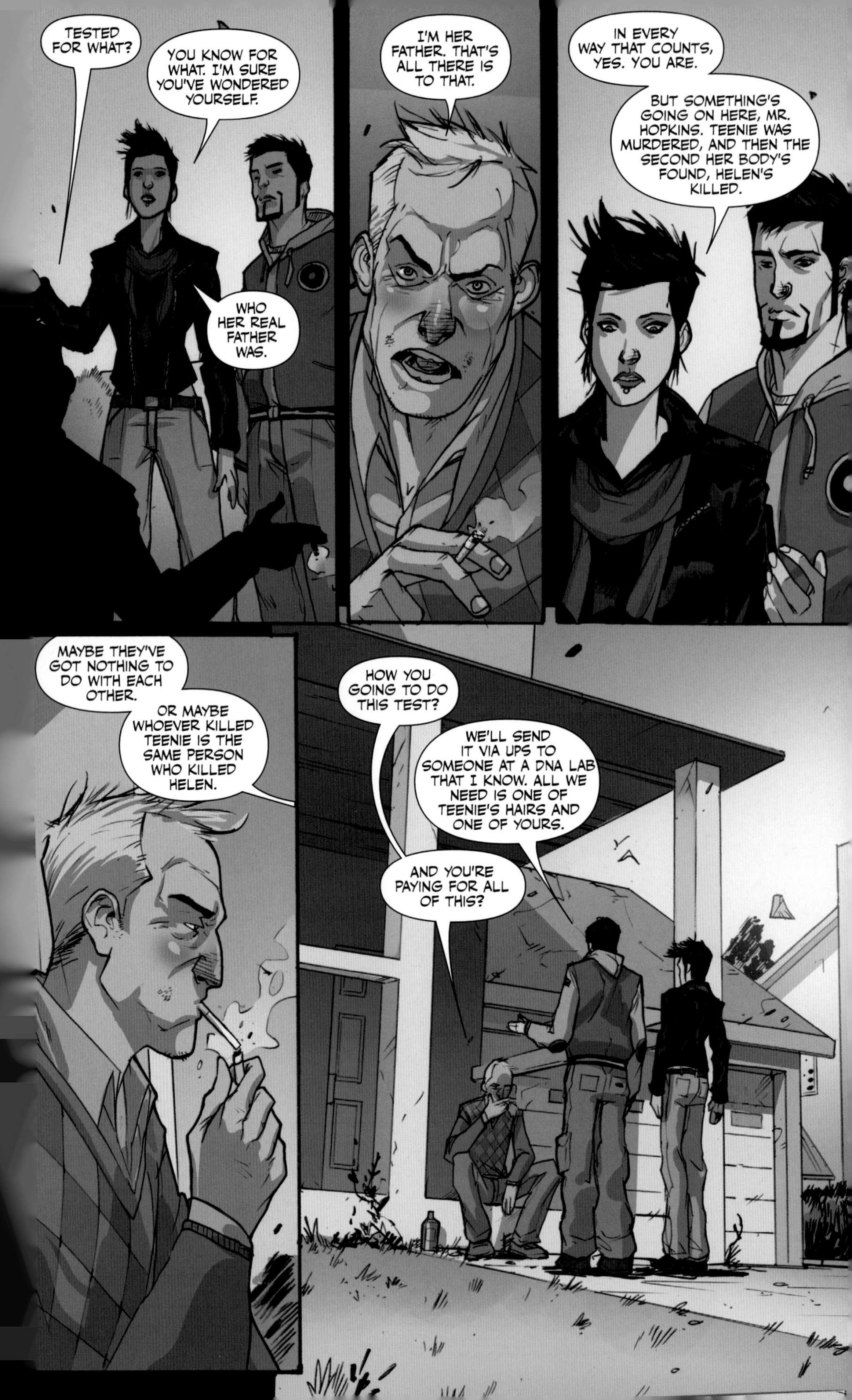
TESTED FOR WHAT?
YOU KNOW FOR WHAT. I'M SURE YOU'VE WONDERED YOURSELF.
WHO HER REAL FATHER WAS.
I'M HER FATHER. THAT'S ALL THERE IS TO THAT.
IN EVERY WAY THAT COUNTS, YES. YOU ARE.
BUT SOMETHING'S GOING ON HERE, MR. HOPKINS. TEENIE WAS MURDERED, AND THEN THE SECOND HER BODY'S FOUND, HELEN'S KILLED.
MAYBE THEY'VE GOT NOTHING TO DO WITH EACH OTHER.
OR MAYBE WHOEVER KILLED TEENIE IS THE SAME PERSON WHO KILLED HELEN.
HOW YOU GOING TO DO THIS TEST?
WE'LL SEND IT VIA UPS TO SOMEONE AT A DNA LAB THAT I KNOW. ALL WE NEED IS ONE OF TEENIE'S HAIRS AND ONE OF YOURS.
AND YOU'RE PAYING FOR ALL OF THIS?

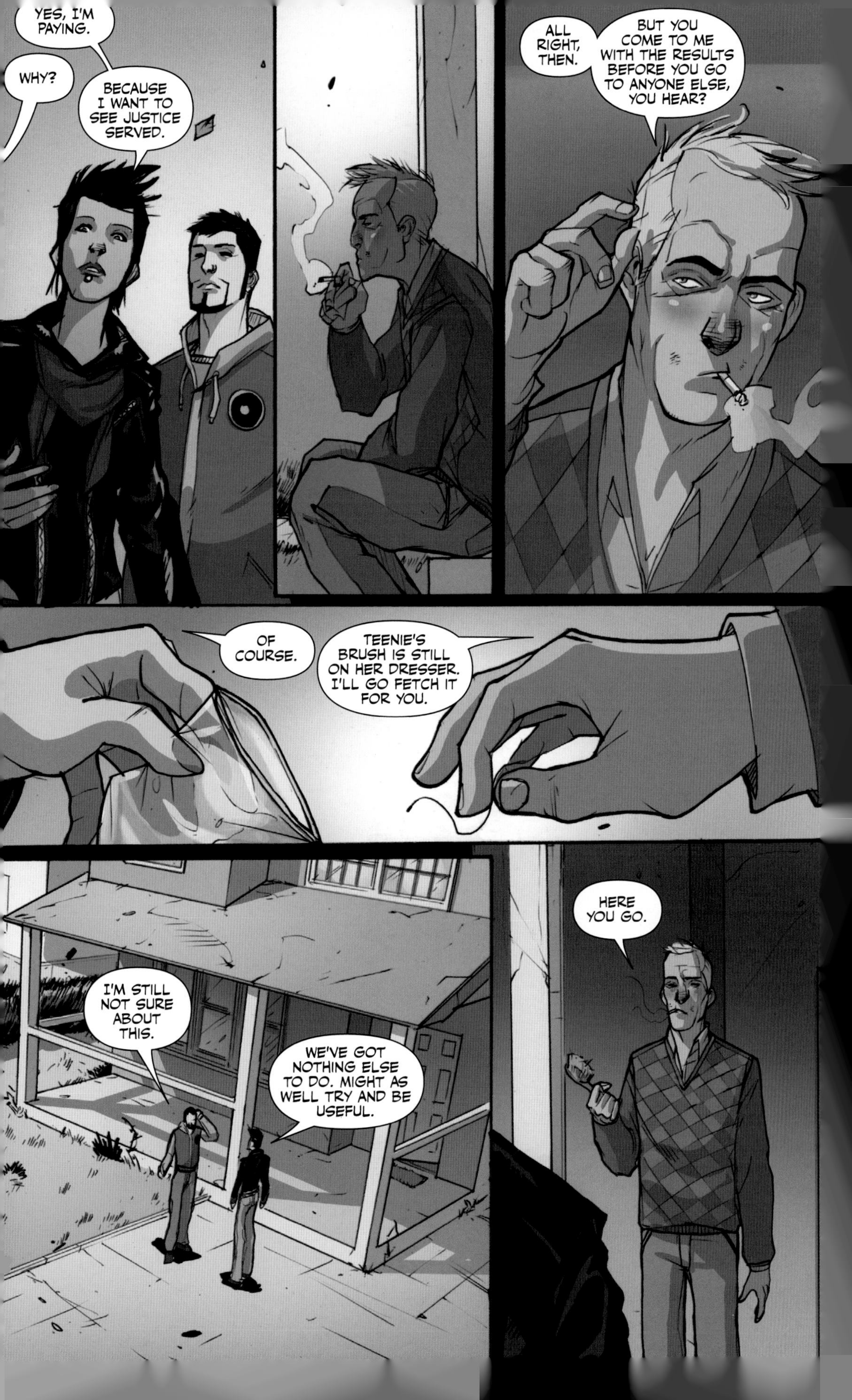
YES, I'M PAYING.
WHY?
BECAUSE I WANT TO SEE JUSTICE SERVED.
ALL RIGHT, THEN.
BUT YOU COME TO ME WITH THE RESULTS BEFORE YOU GO TO ANYONE ELSE, YOU HEAR?
OF COURSE.
TEENIE'S BRUSH IS STILL ON HER DRESSER. I'LL GO FETCH IT FOR YOU.
I'M STILL NOT SURE ABOUT THIS.
WE'VE GOT NOTHING ELSE TO DO. MIGHT AS WELL TRY AND BE USEFUL.
HERE YOU GO.

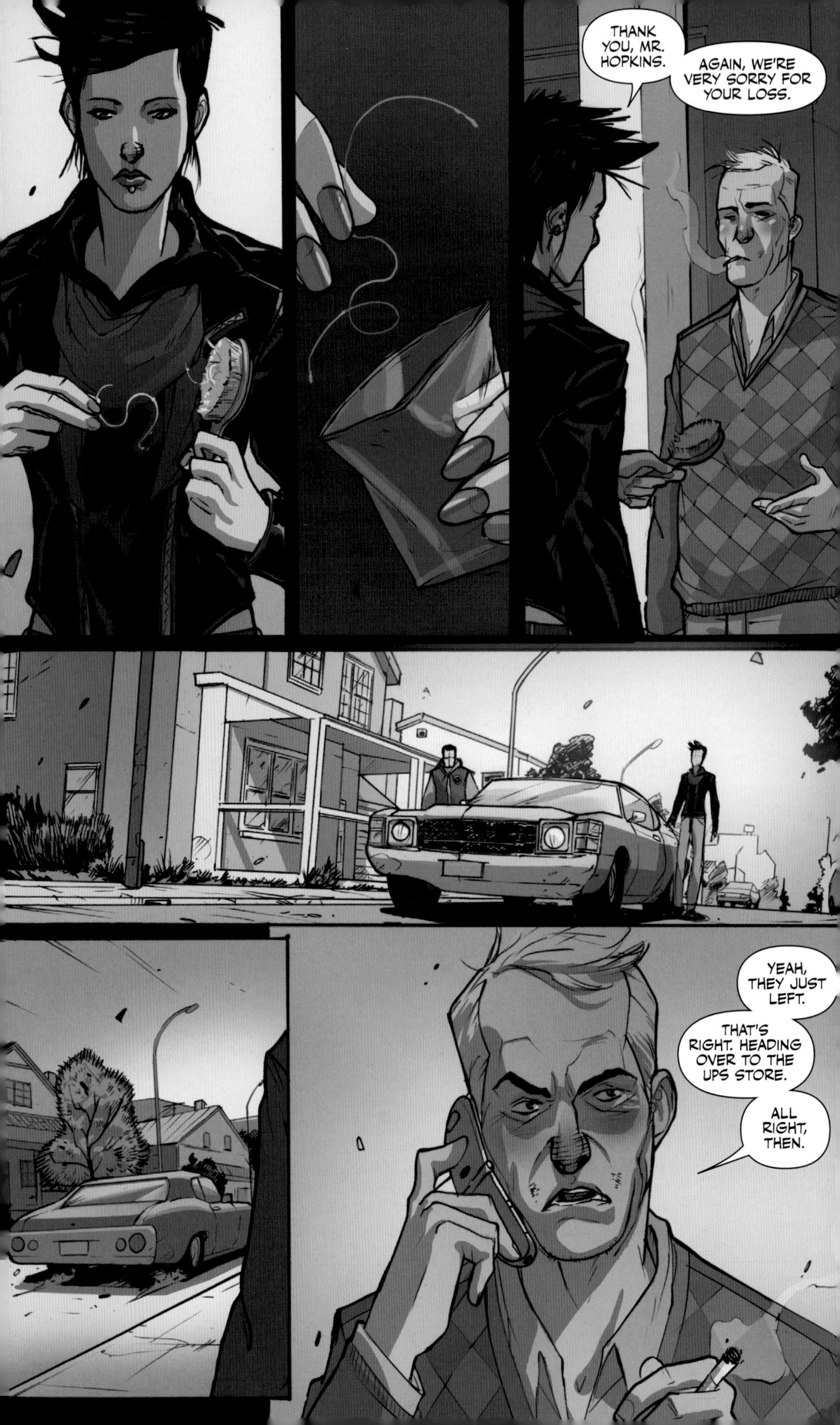
THANK YOU, MR. HOPKINS.
AGAIN, WE'RE VERY SORRY FOR YOUR LOSS.
YEAH, THEY JUST LEFT.
THAT'S RIGHT. HEADING OVER TO THE UPS STORE.
ALL RIGHT, THEN.

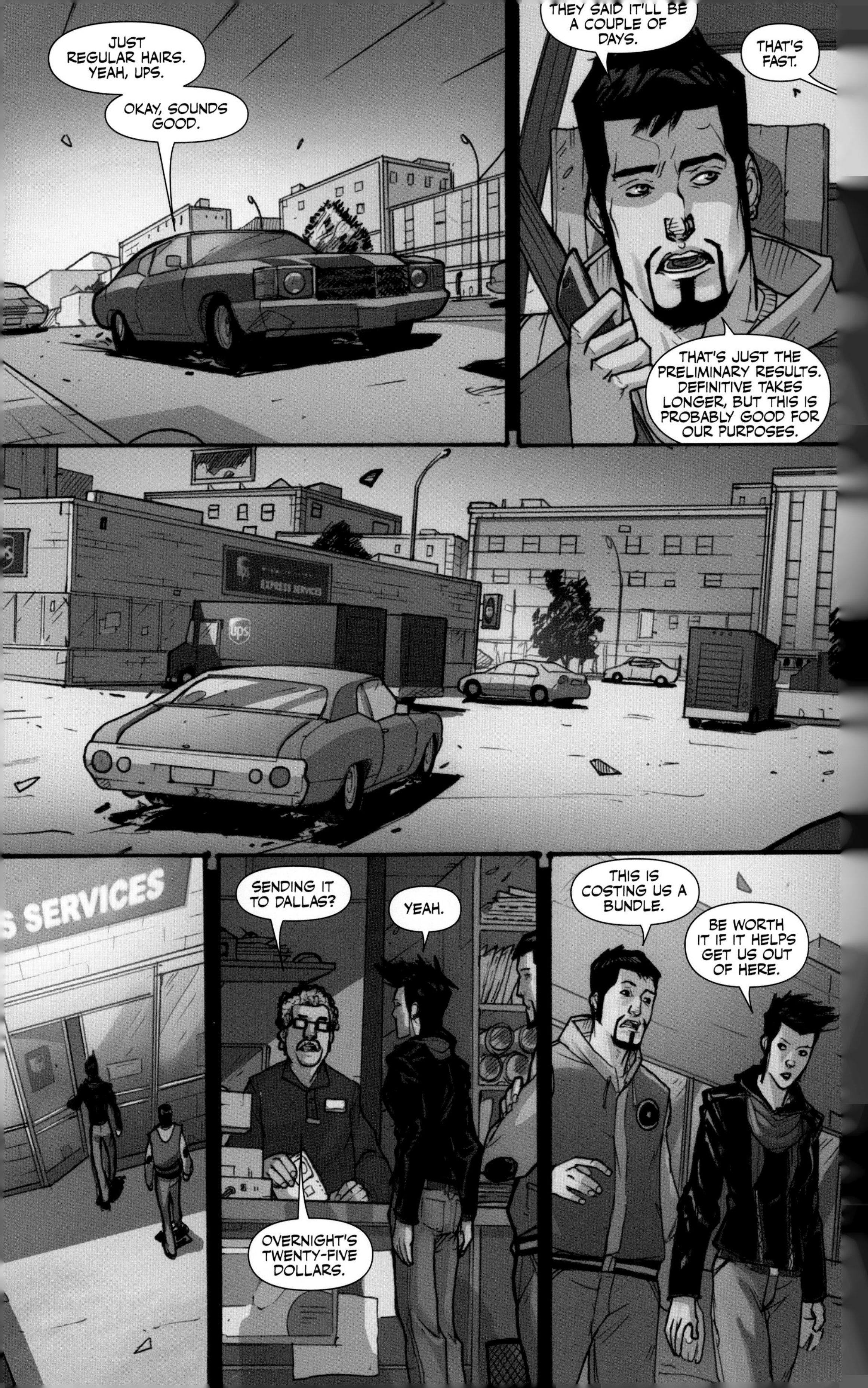
JUST REGULAR HAIRS. YEAH, UPS.
OKAY, SOUNDS GOOD.
THEY SAID IT'LL BE A COUPLE OF DAYS.
THAT'S FAST.
THAT'S JUST THE PRELIMINARY RESULTS. DEFINITIVE TAKES LONGER, BUT THIS IS PROBABLY GOOD FOR OUR PURPOSES.
EXPRESS SERVICES
UPS
S SERVICES
SENDING IT TO DALLAS?
YEAH.
OVERNIGHT'S TWENTY-FIVE DOLLARS.
THIS IS COSTING US A BUNDLE.
BE WORTH IT IF IT HELPS GET US OUT OF HERE.

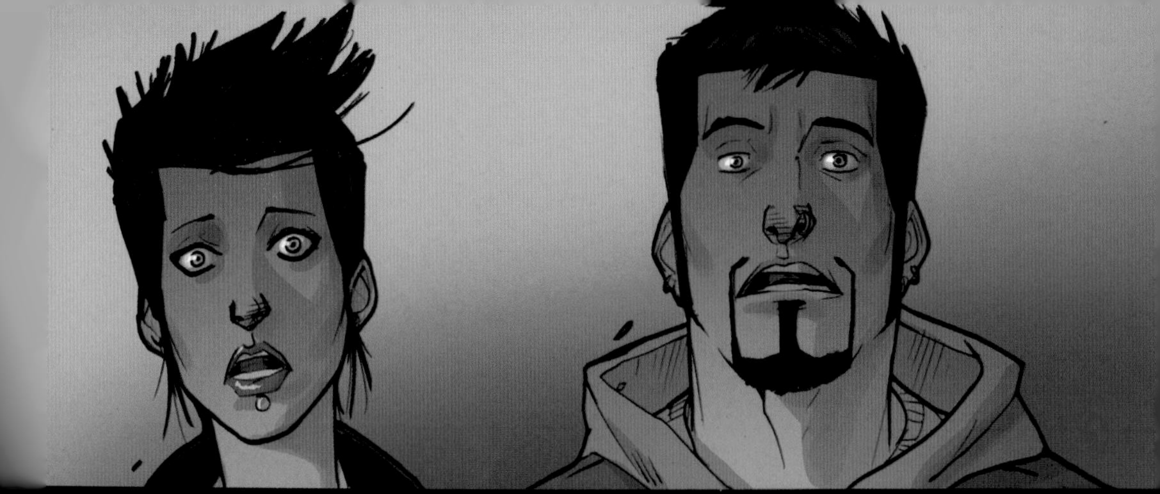

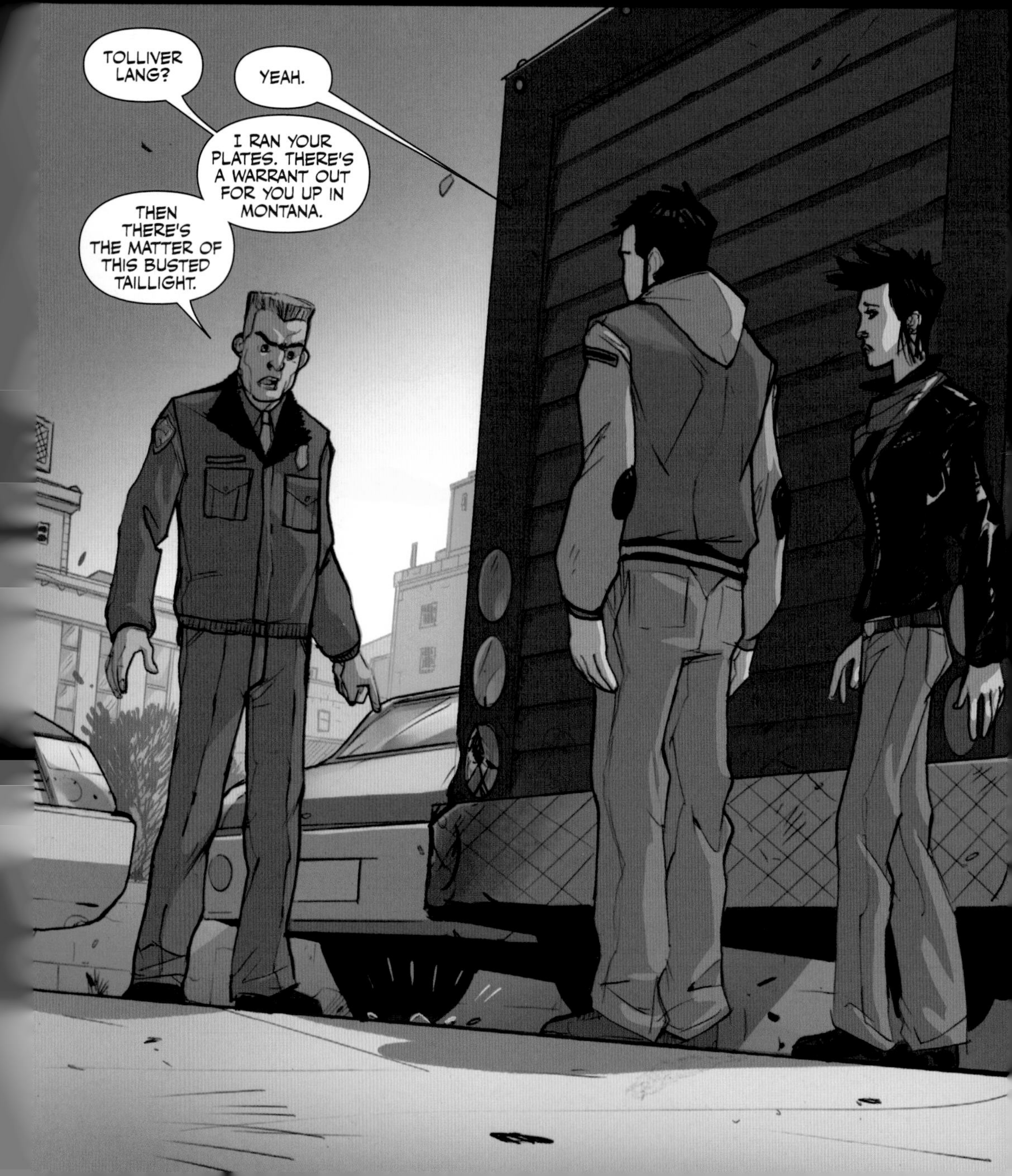
TOLLIVER LANG?
YEAH.
I RAN YOUR PLATES. THERE'S A WARRANT OUT FOR YOU UP IN MONTANA.
THEN THERE'S THE MATTER OF THIS BUSTED TAILLIGHT.

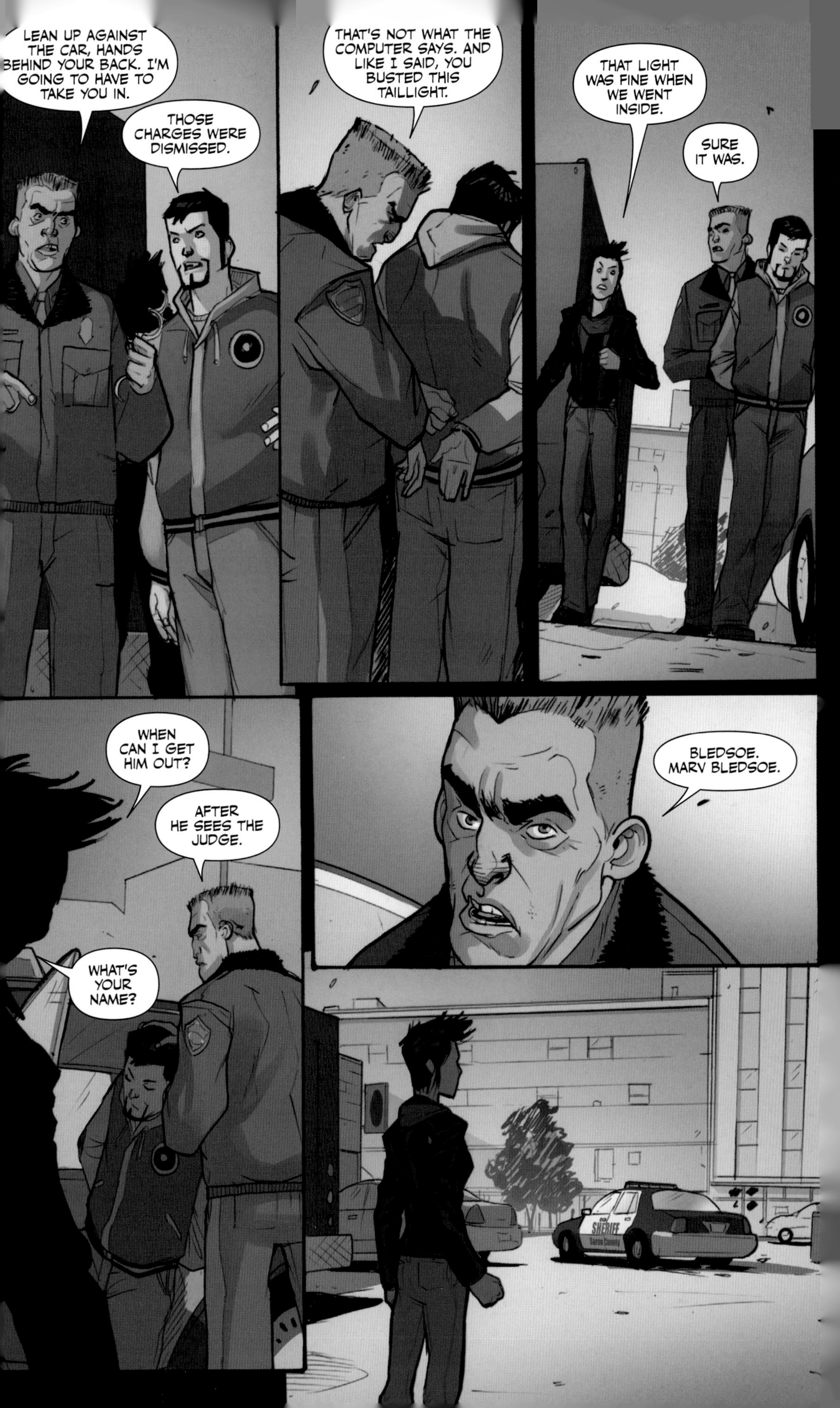
LEAN UP AGAINST THE CAR, HANDS BEHIND YOUR BACK. I'M GOING TO HAVE TO TAKE YOU IN.
THOSE CHARGES WERE DISMISSED.
THAT'S NOT WHAT THE COMPUTER SAYS. AND LIKE I SAID, YOU BUSTED THIS TAILLIGHT.
THAT LIGHT WAS FINE WHEN WE WENT INSIDE.
SURE IT WAS.
WHEN CAN I GET HIM OUT?
AFTER HE SEES THE JUDGE.
WHAT'S YOUR NAME?
BLEDSOE. MARV BLEDSOE.
SHERIFF

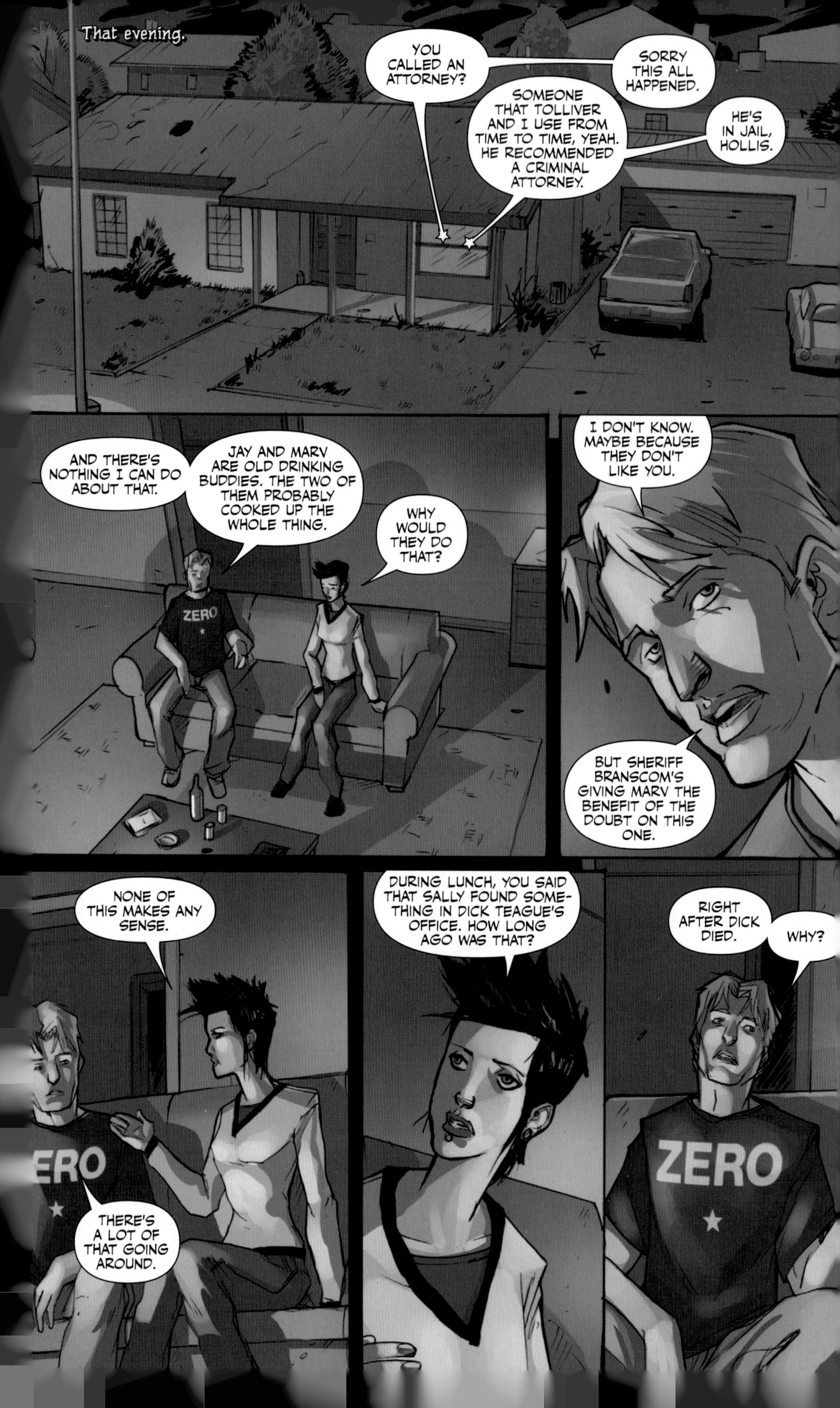
That evening.
YOU CALLED AN ATTORNEY?
SORRY THIS ALL HAPPENED.
SOMEONE THAT TOLLIVER AND I USE FROM TIME TO TIME, YEAH. HE RECOMMENDED A CRIMINAL ATTORNEY.
HE'S IN JAIL, HOLLIS.
AND THERE'S NOTHING I CAN DO ABOUT THAT.
JAY AND MARV ARE OLD DRINKING BUDDIES. THE TWO OF THEM PROBABLY COOKED UP THE WHOLE THING.
WHY WOULD THEY DO THAT?
ZERO
I DON'T KNOW. MAYBE BECAUSE THEY DON'T LIKE YOU.
BUT SHERIFF BRANSCOM'S GIVING MARV THE BENEFIT OF THE DOUBT ON THIS ONE.
NONE OF THIS MAKES ANY SENSE.
THERE'S A LOT OF THAT GOING AROUND.
DURING LUNCH, YOU SAID THAT SALLY FOUND SOMETHING IN DICK TEAGUE'S OFFICE. HOW LONG AGO WAS THAT?
RIGHT AFTER DICK DIED.
WHY?
ZERO

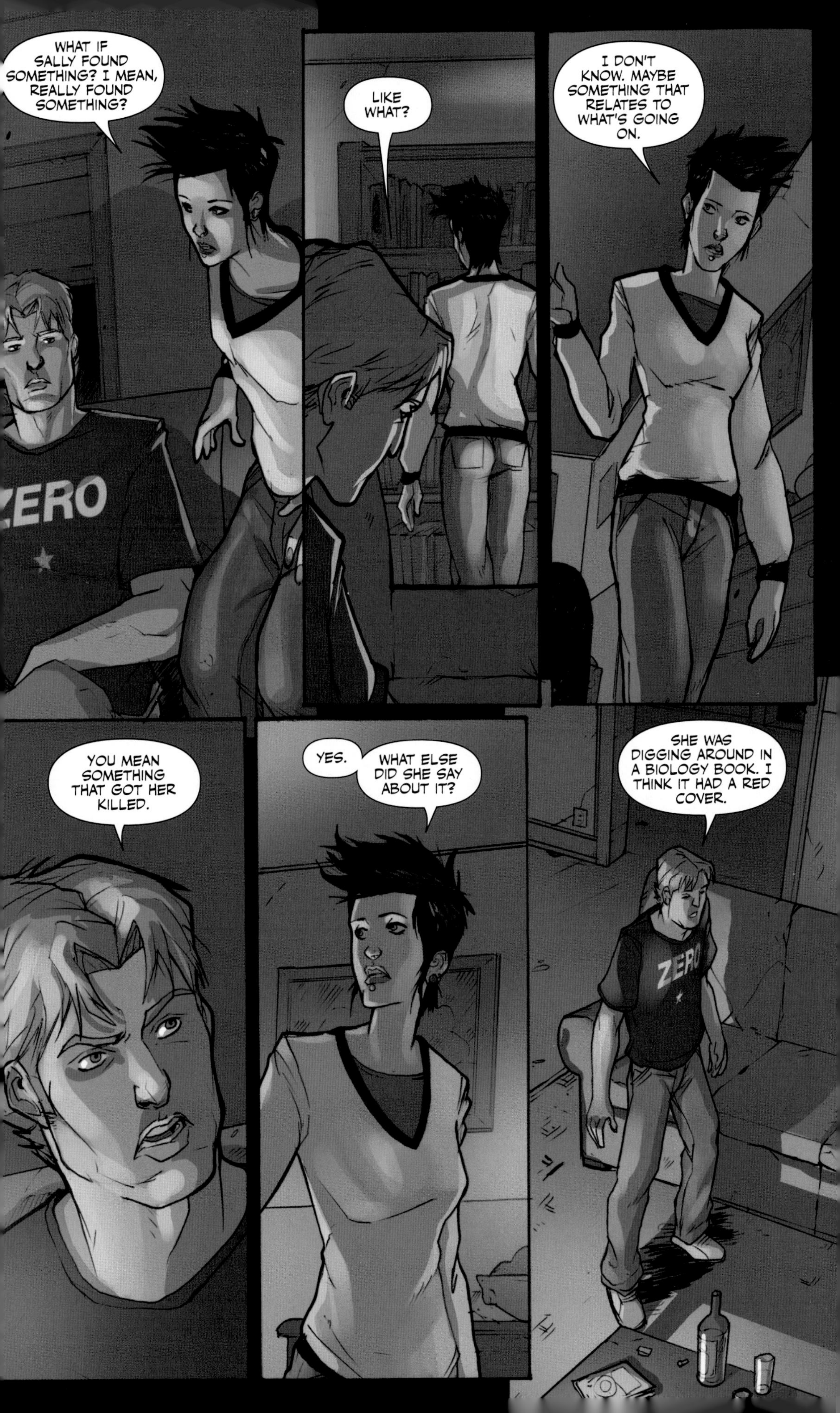
WHAT IF SALLY FOUND SOMETHING? I MEAN, REALLY FOUND SOMETHING?
ZERO
LIKE WHAT?
I DON'T KNOW. MAYBE SOMETHING THAT RELATES TO WHAT'S GOING ON.
YOU MEAN SOMETHING THAT GOT HER KILLED.
YES.
WHAT ELSE DID SHE SAY ABOUT IT?
SHE WAS DIGGING AROUND IN A BIOLOGY BOOK. I THINK IT HAD A RED COVER.
ZERO

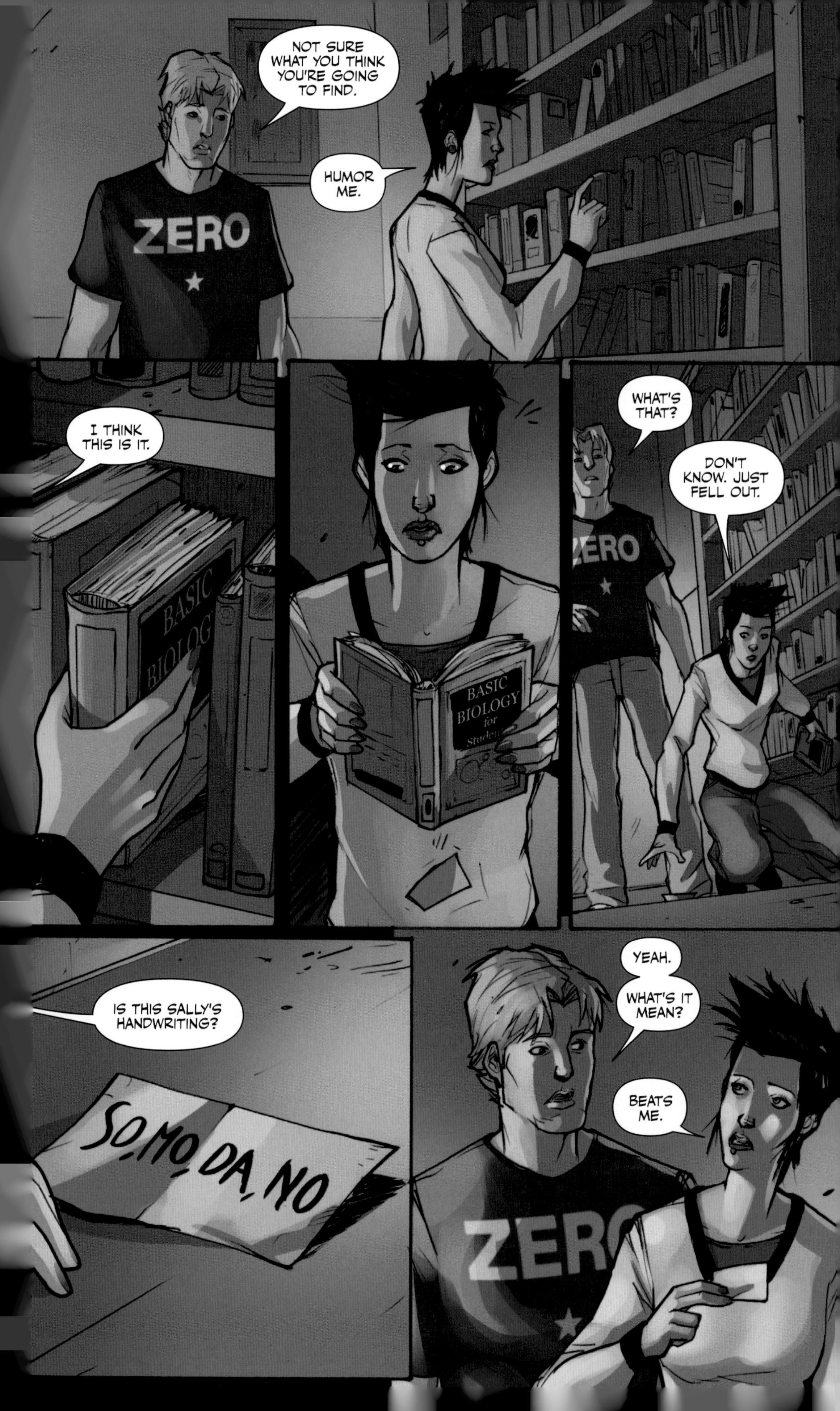

NOT SURE WHAT YOU THINK YOU'RE GOING TO FIND.
HUMOR ME.
ZERO
I THINK THIS IS IT.
BASIC BIOLOGY
BASIC BIOLOGY for
WHAT'S THAT?
DON'T KNOW. JUST FELL OUT.
ZERO
IS THIS SALLY'S HANDWRITING?
SO MO DA NO
YEAH.
WHAT'S IT MEAN?
BEATS ME.
ZERO

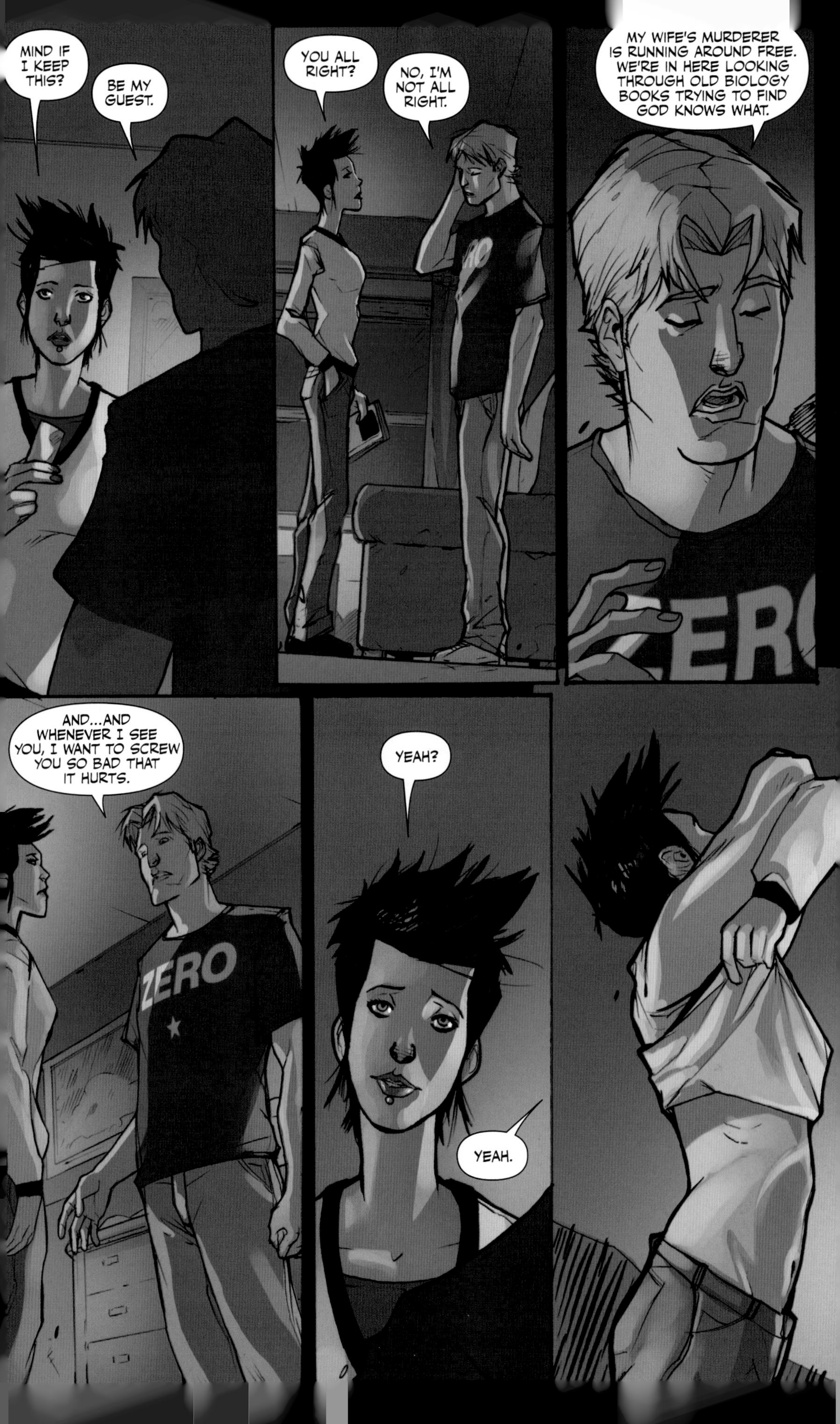
MIND IF I KEEP THIS?
BE MY GUEST.
YOU ALL RIGHT?
NO, I'M NOT ALL RIGHT.
MY WIFE'S MURDERER IS RUNNING AROUND FREE. WE'RE IN HERE LOOKING THROUGH OLD BIOLOGY BOOKS TRYING TO FIND GOD KNOWS WHAT.
ZERO
AND...AND WHENEVER I SEE YOU, I WANT TO SCREW YOU SO BAD THAT IT HURTS.
ZERO
YEAH?
YEAH.

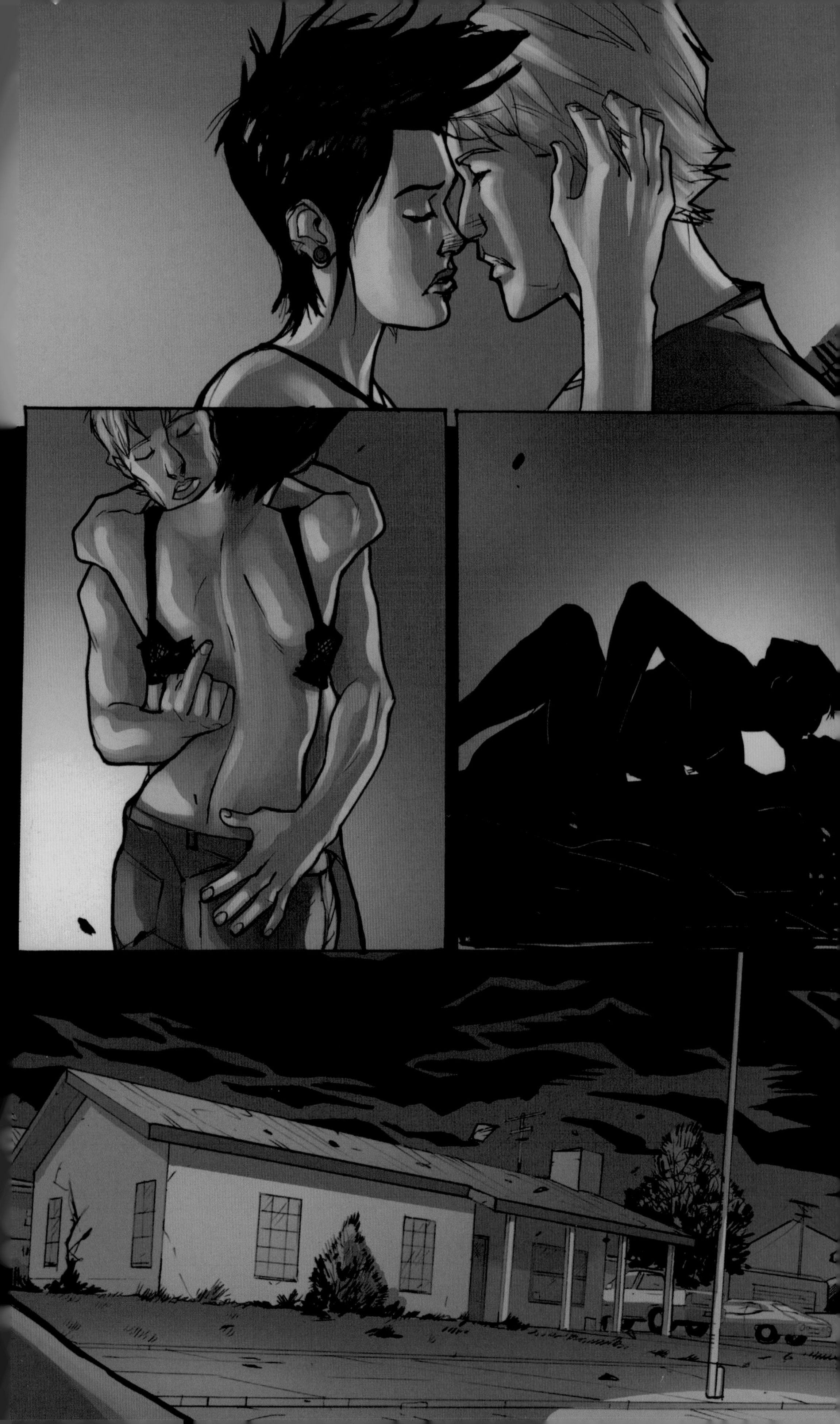

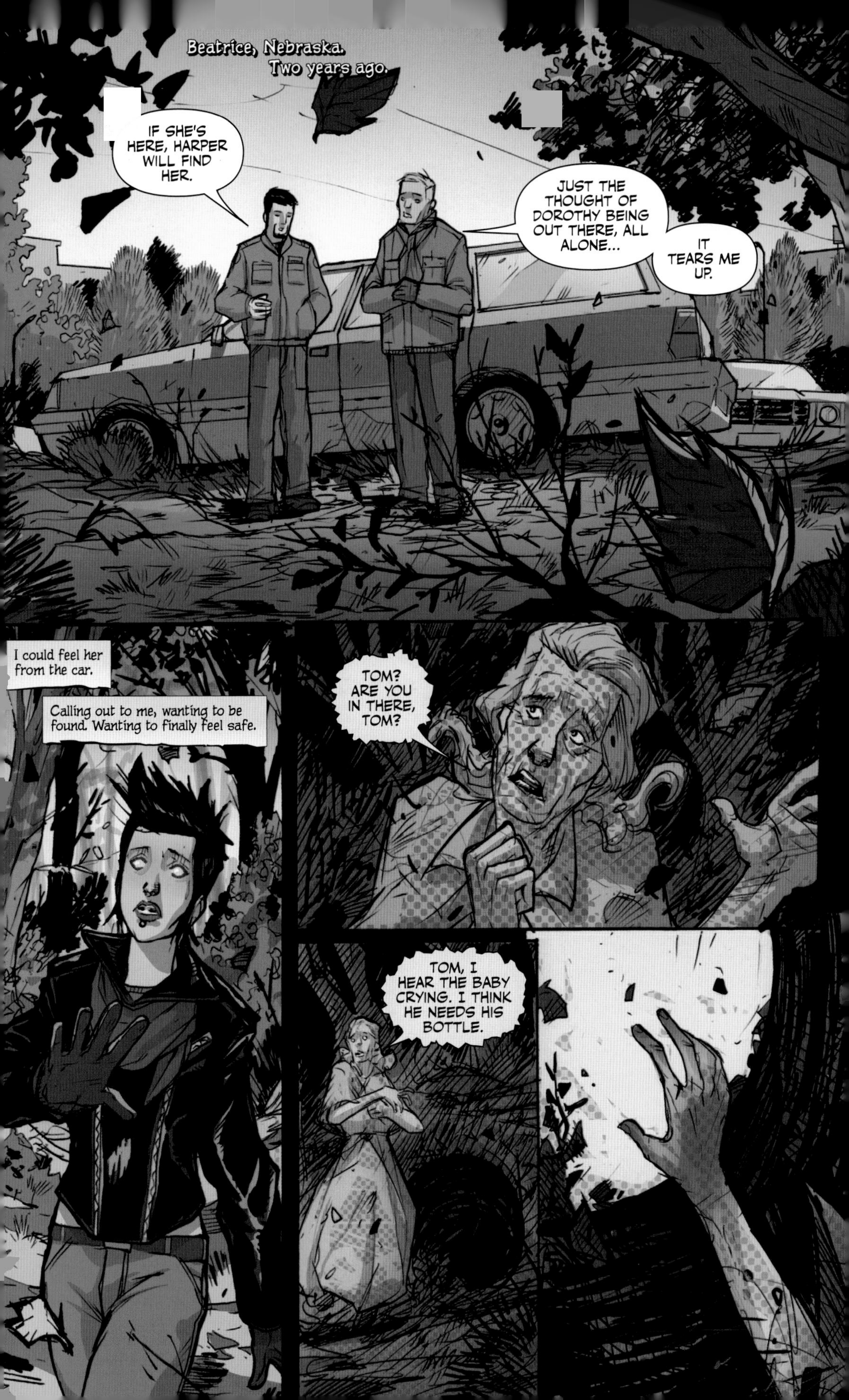
Beatrice, Nebraska.
Two years ago.
IF SHE'S HERE, HARPER WILL FIND HER.
JUST THE THOUGHT OF DOROTHY BEING OUT THERE, ALL ALONE...
IT TEARS ME UP.
I could feel her from the car.
Calling out to me, wanting to be found. Wanting to finally feel safe.
TOM? ARE YOU IN THERE, TOM?
TOM, I HEAR THE BABY CRYING. I THINK HE NEEDS HIS BOTTLE.

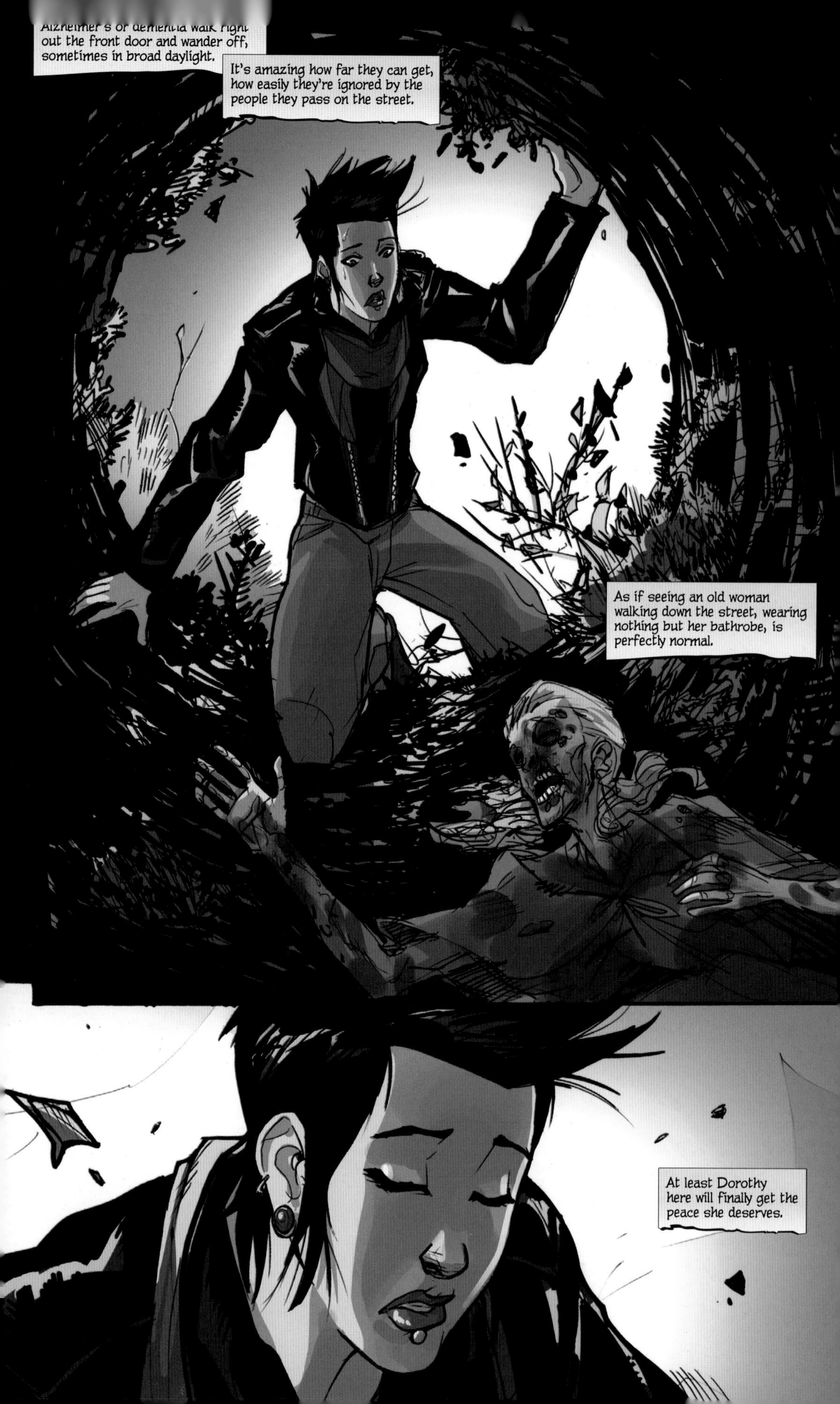
Alzheimer's or dementia walk right out the front door and wander off, sometimes in broad daylight.
It's amazing how far they can get, how easily they're ignored by the people they pass on the street.
As if seeing an old woman walking down the street, wearing nothing but her bathrobe, is perfectly normal.
At least Dorothy here will finally get the peace she deserves.

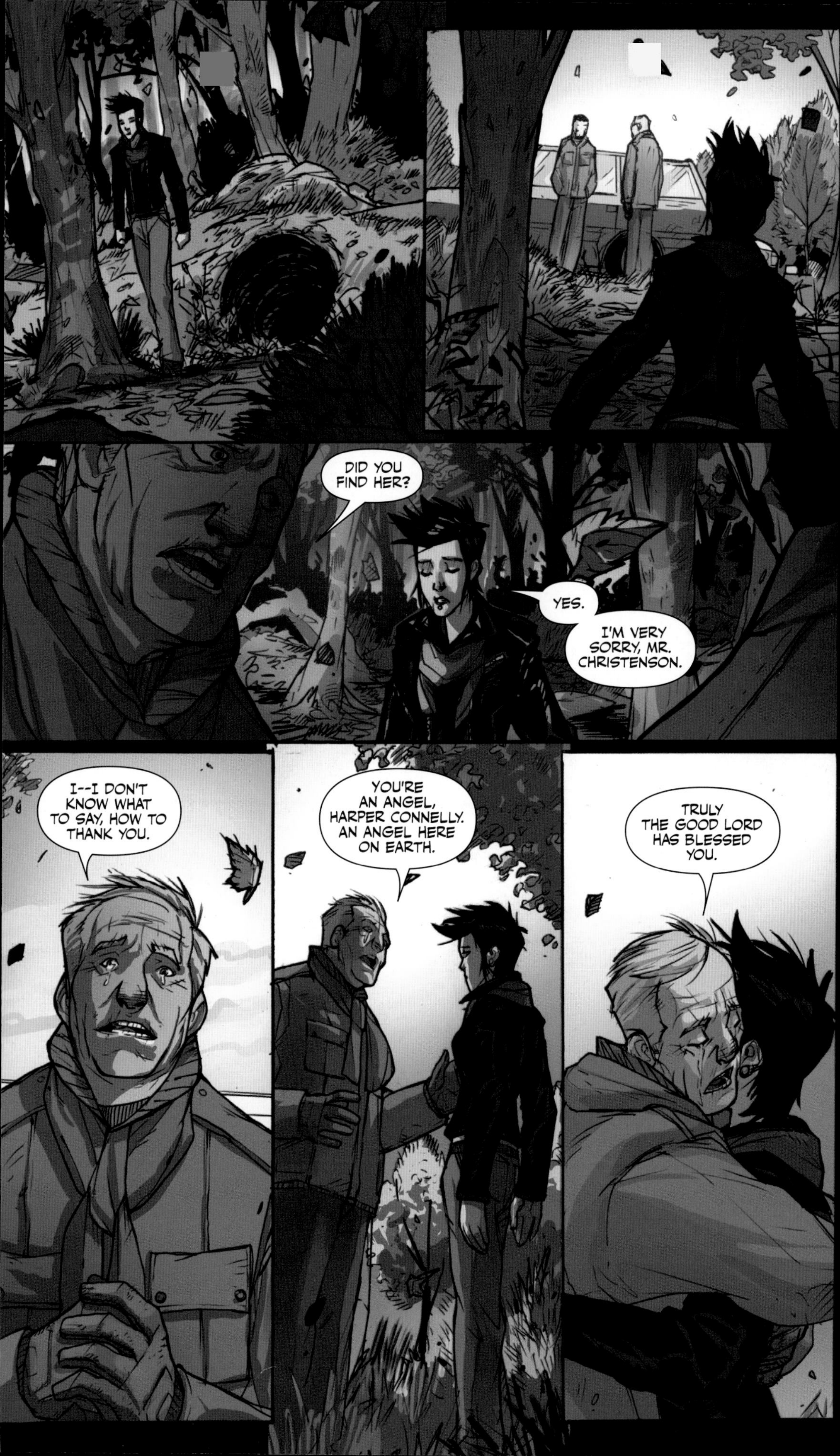
DID YOU FIND HER?
YES.
I'M VERY SORRY, MR. CHRISTENSON.
I--I DON'T KNOW WHAT TO SAY, HOW TO THANK YOU.
YOU'RE AN ANGEL, HARPER CONNELLY. AN ANGEL HERE ON EARTH.
TRULY THE GOOD LORD HAS BLESSED YOU.

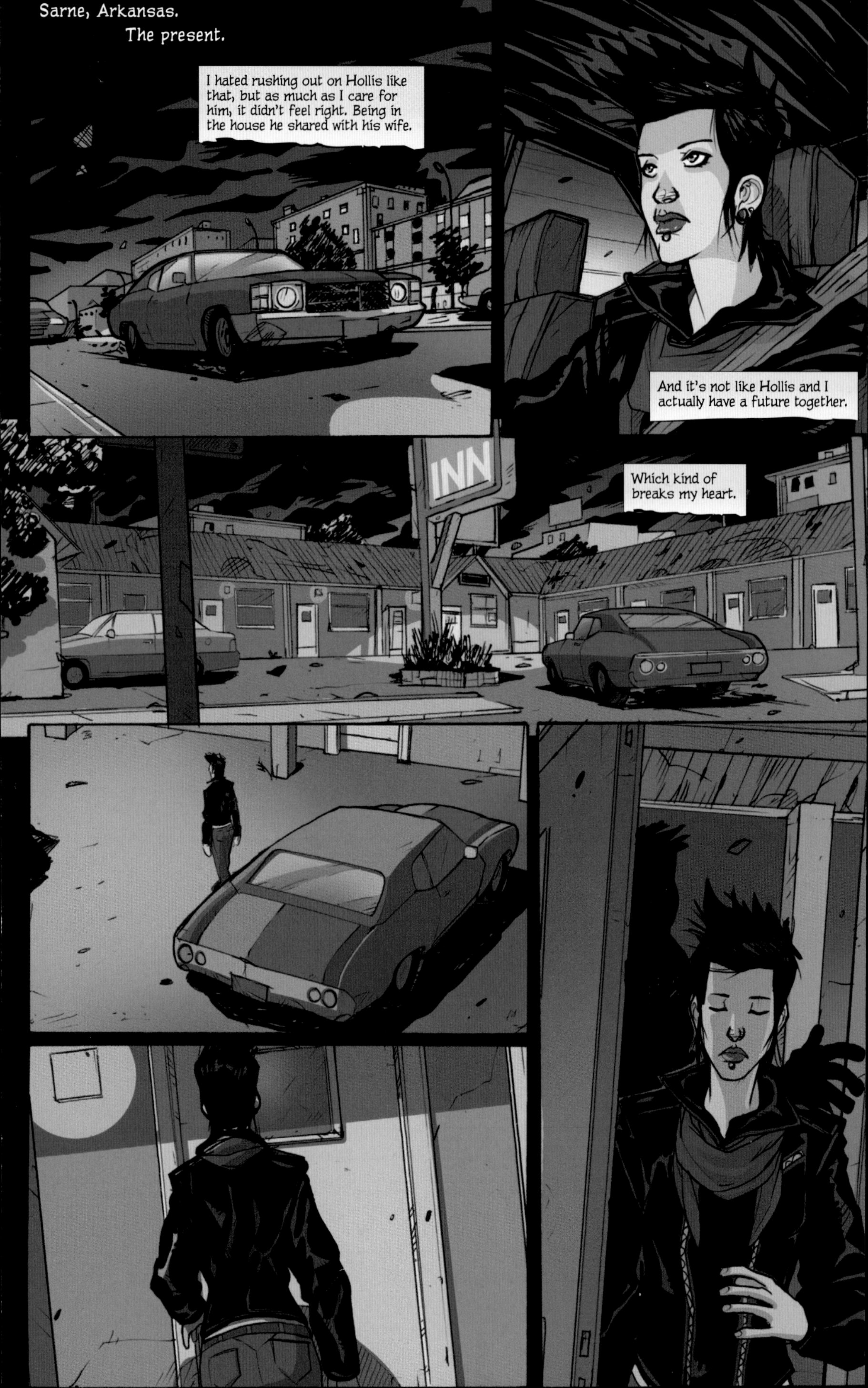

Sarne, Arkansas.
The present.
I hated rushing out on Hollis like that, but as much as I care for him, it didn't feel right. Being in the house he shared with his wife.
And it's not like Hollis and I actually have a future together.
INN
Which kind of breaks my heart.

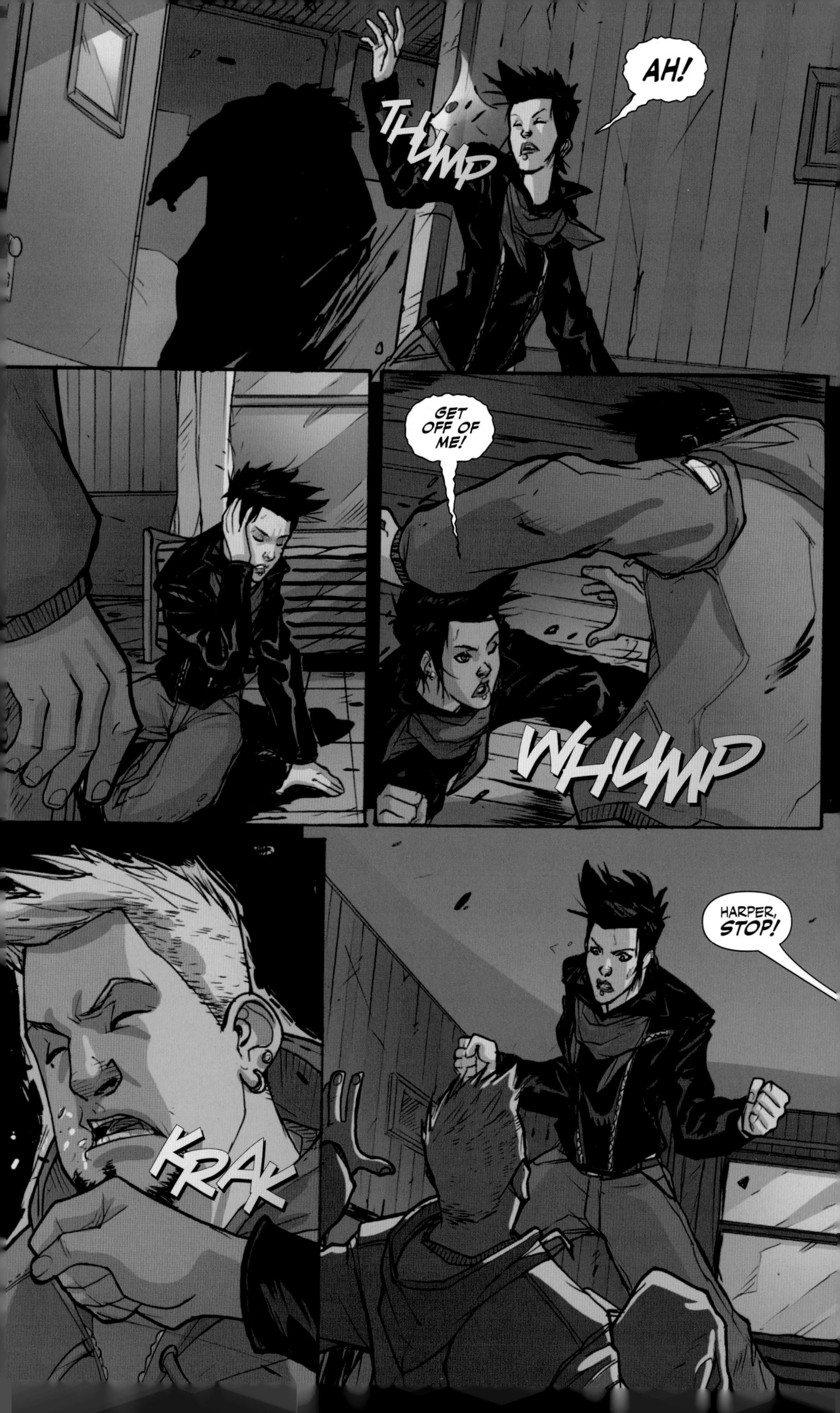
THUMP
AH!
GET OFF OF ME!
WHUMP
KRAK
HARPER, STOP!

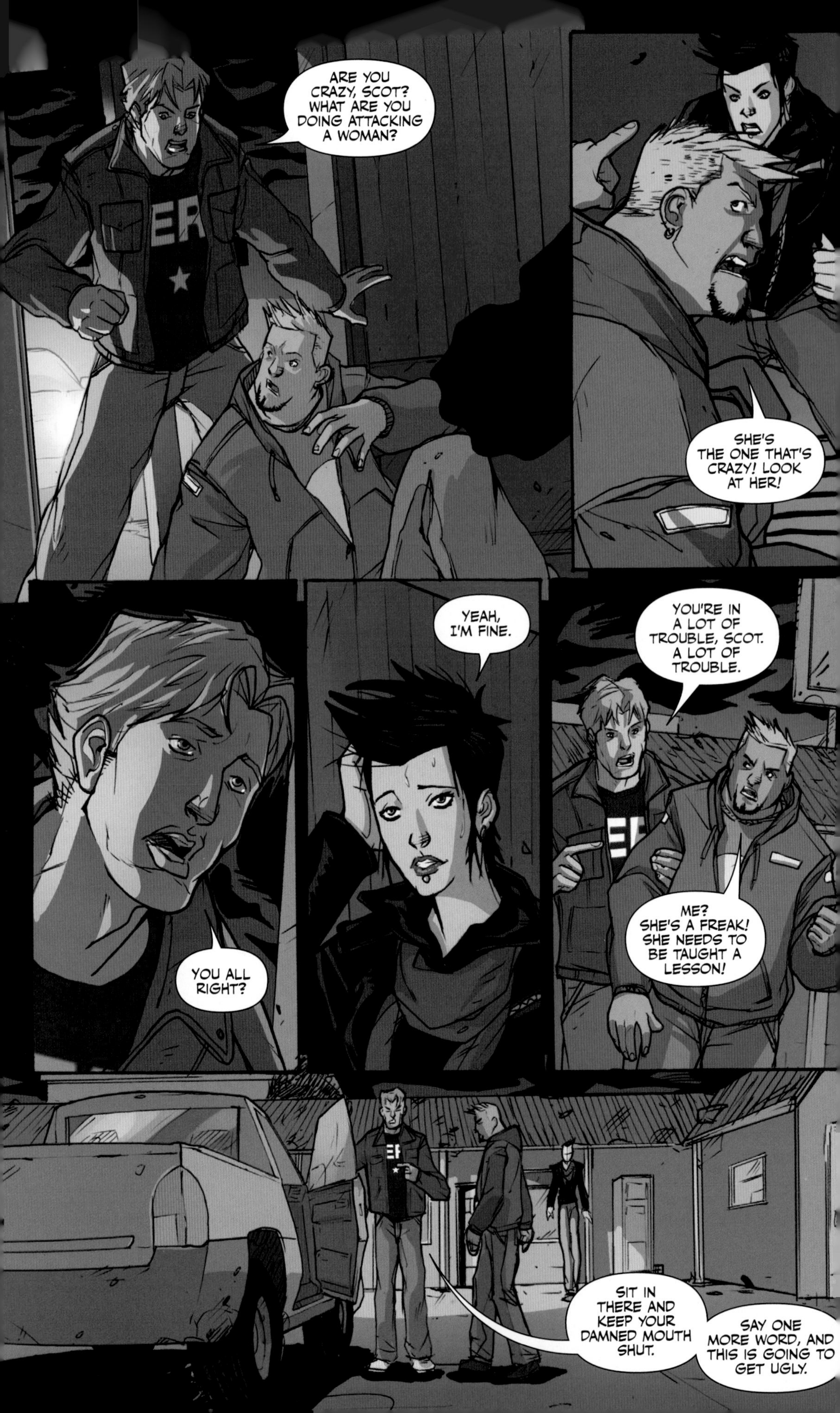
ARE YOU CRAZY, SCOT? WHAT ARE YOU DOING ATTACKING A WOMAN?
SHE'S THE ONE THAT'S CRAZY! LOOK AT HER!
YOU ALL RIGHT?
YEAH, I'M FINE.
YOU'RE IN A LOT OF TROUBLE, SCOT. A LOT OF TROUBLE.
ME? SHE'S A FREAK! SHE NEEDS TO BE TAUGHT A LESSON!
SIT IN THERE AND KEEP YOUR DAMNED MOUTH SHUT.
SAY ONE MORE WORD, AND THIS IS GOING TO GET UGLY.

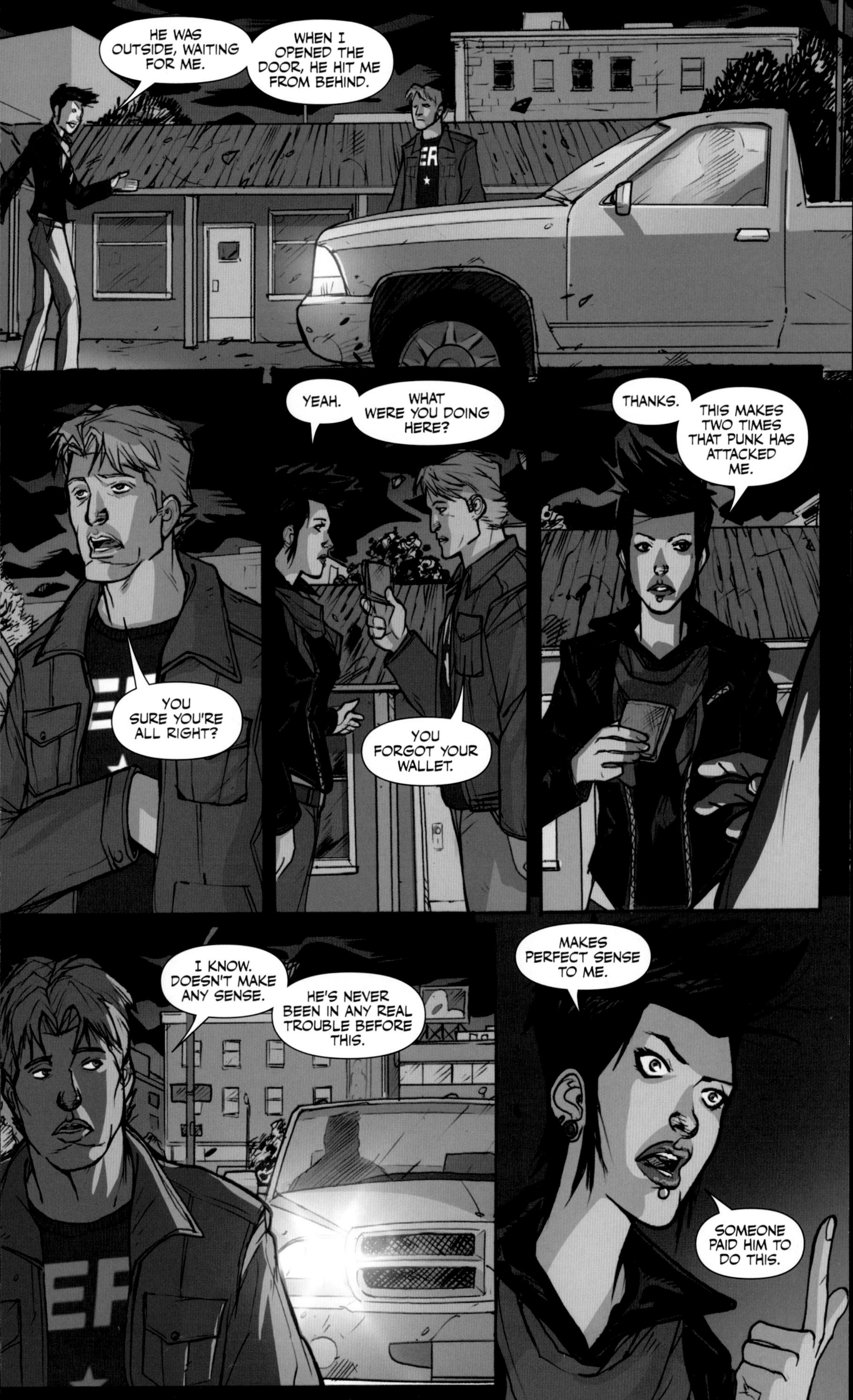
HE WAS OUTSIDE, WAITING FOR ME.
WHEN I OPENED THE DOOR, HE HIT ME FROM BEHIND.
YOU SURE YOU'RE ALL RIGHT?
YEAH.
WHAT WERE YOU DOING HERE?
YOU FORGOT YOUR WALLET.
THANKS.
THIS MAKES TWO TIMES THAT PUNK HAS ATTACKED ME.
I KNOW. DOESN'T MAKE ANY SENSE.
HE'S NEVER BEEN IN ANY REAL TROUBLE BEFORE THIS.
MAKES PERFECT SENSE TO ME.
SOMEONE PAID HIM TO DO THIS.

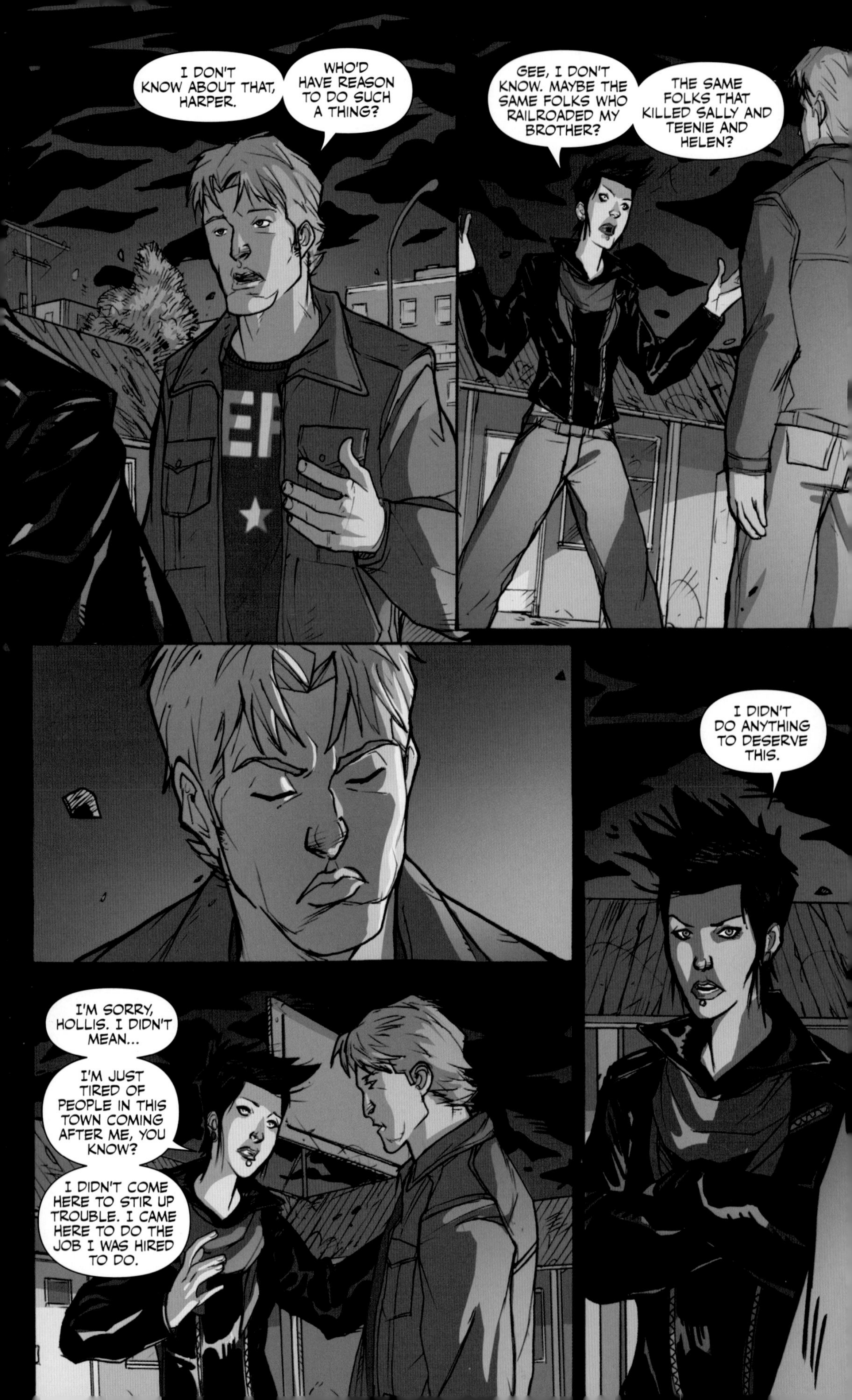
I DON'T KNOW ABOUT THAT, HARPER.
WHO'D HAVE REASON TO DO SUCH A THING?
GEE, I DON'T KNOW. MAYBE THE SAME FOLKS WHO RAILROADED MY BROTHER?
THE SAME FOLKS THAT KILLED SALLY AND TEENIE AND HELEN?
I DIDN'T DO ANYTHING TO DESERVE THIS.
I'M SORRY, HOLLIS. I DIDN'T MEAN...
I'M JUST TIRED OF PEOPLE IN THIS TOWN COMING AFTER ME, YOU KNOW?
I DIDN'T COME HERE TO STIR UP TROUBLE. I CAME HERE TO DO THE JOB I WAS HIRED TO DO.

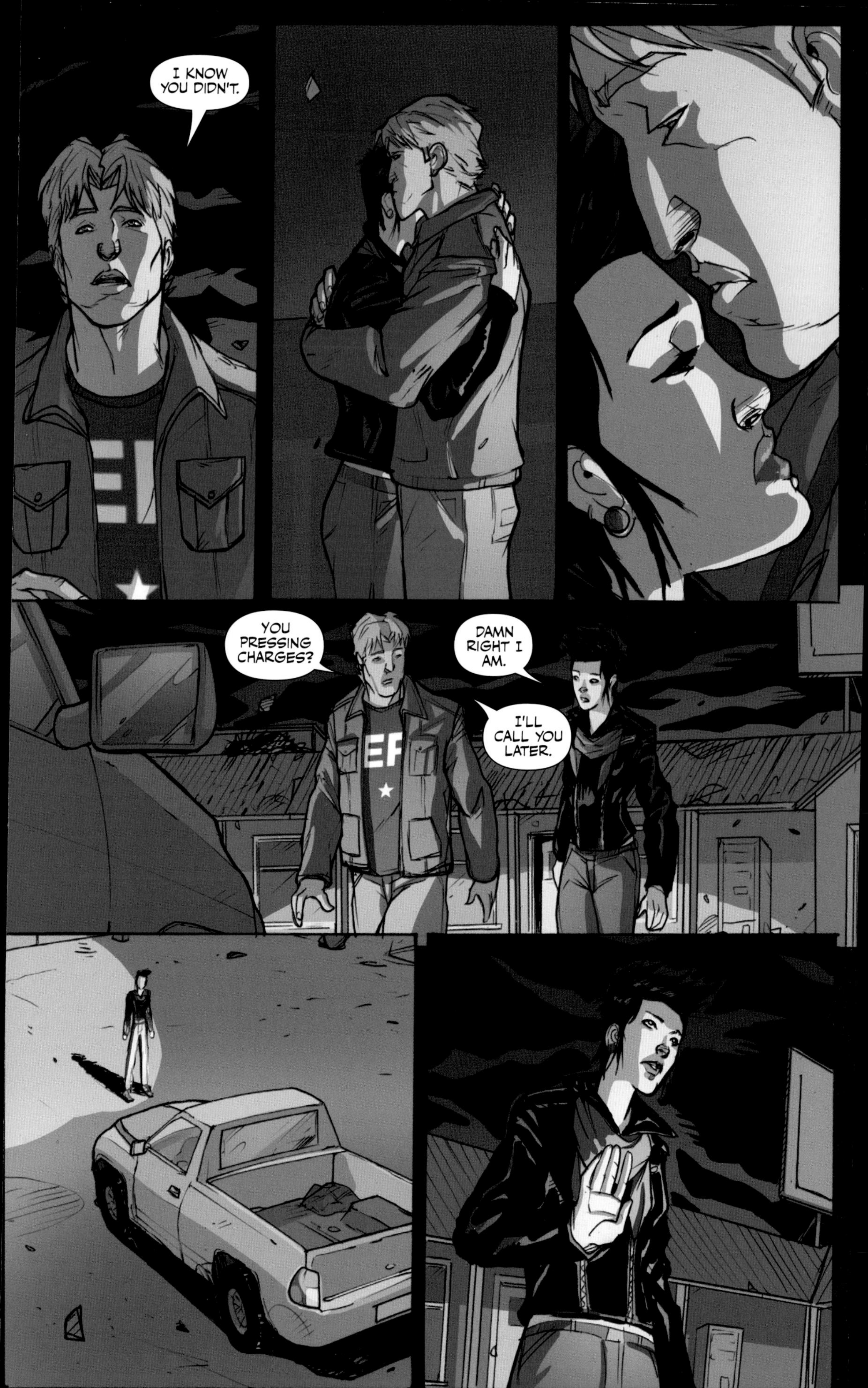
I KNOW YOU DIDN'T.
YOU PRESSING CHARGES?
DAMN RIGHT I AM.
I'LL CALL YOU LATER.

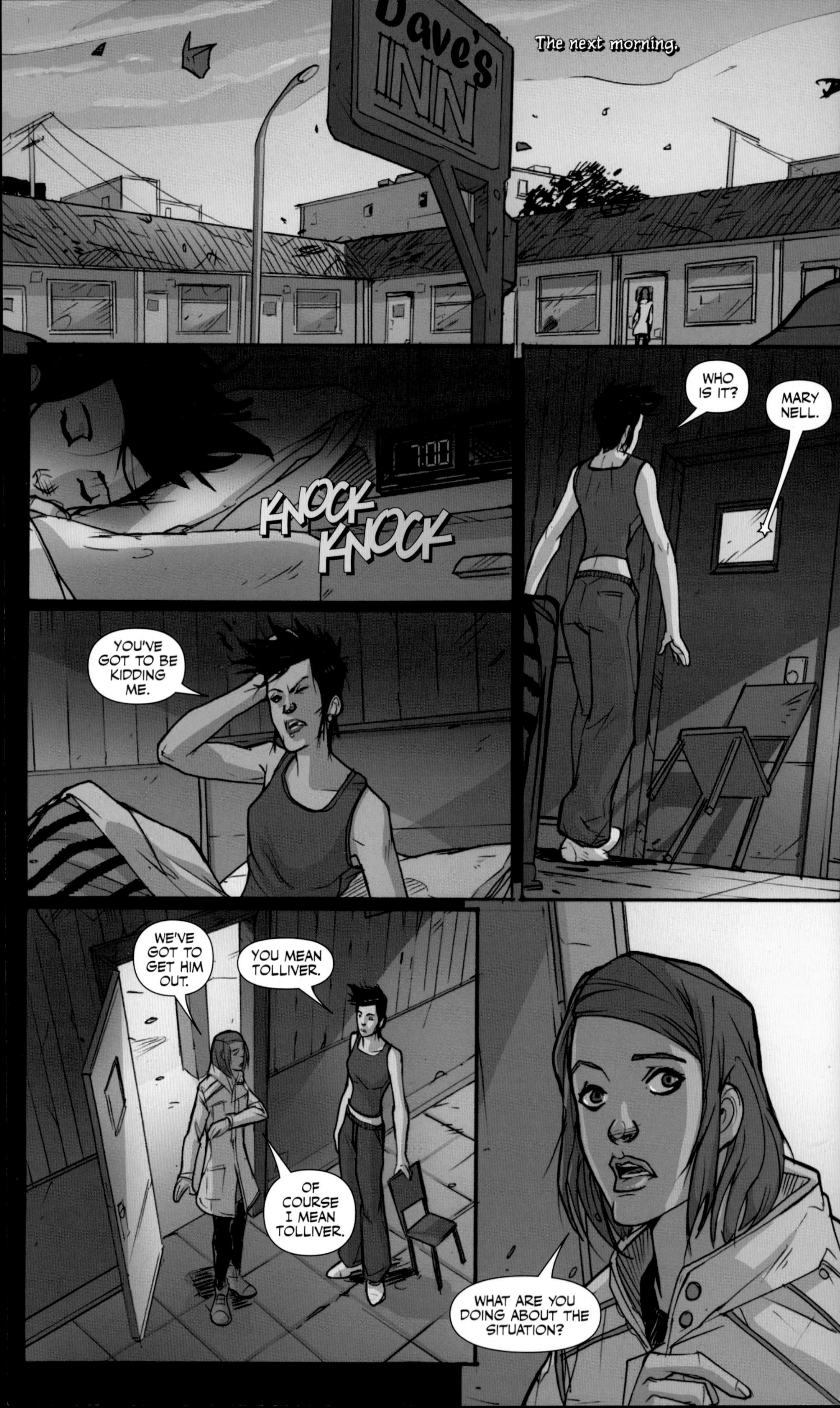
Dave's INN
The next morning.
7:00
KNOCK KNOCK
WHO IS IT?
MARY NELL.
YOU'VE GOT TO BE KIDDING ME.
WE'VE GOT TO GET HIM OUT.
YOU MEAN TOLLIVER.
OF COURSE I MEAN TOLLIVER.
WHAT ARE YOU DOING ABOUT THE SITUATION?

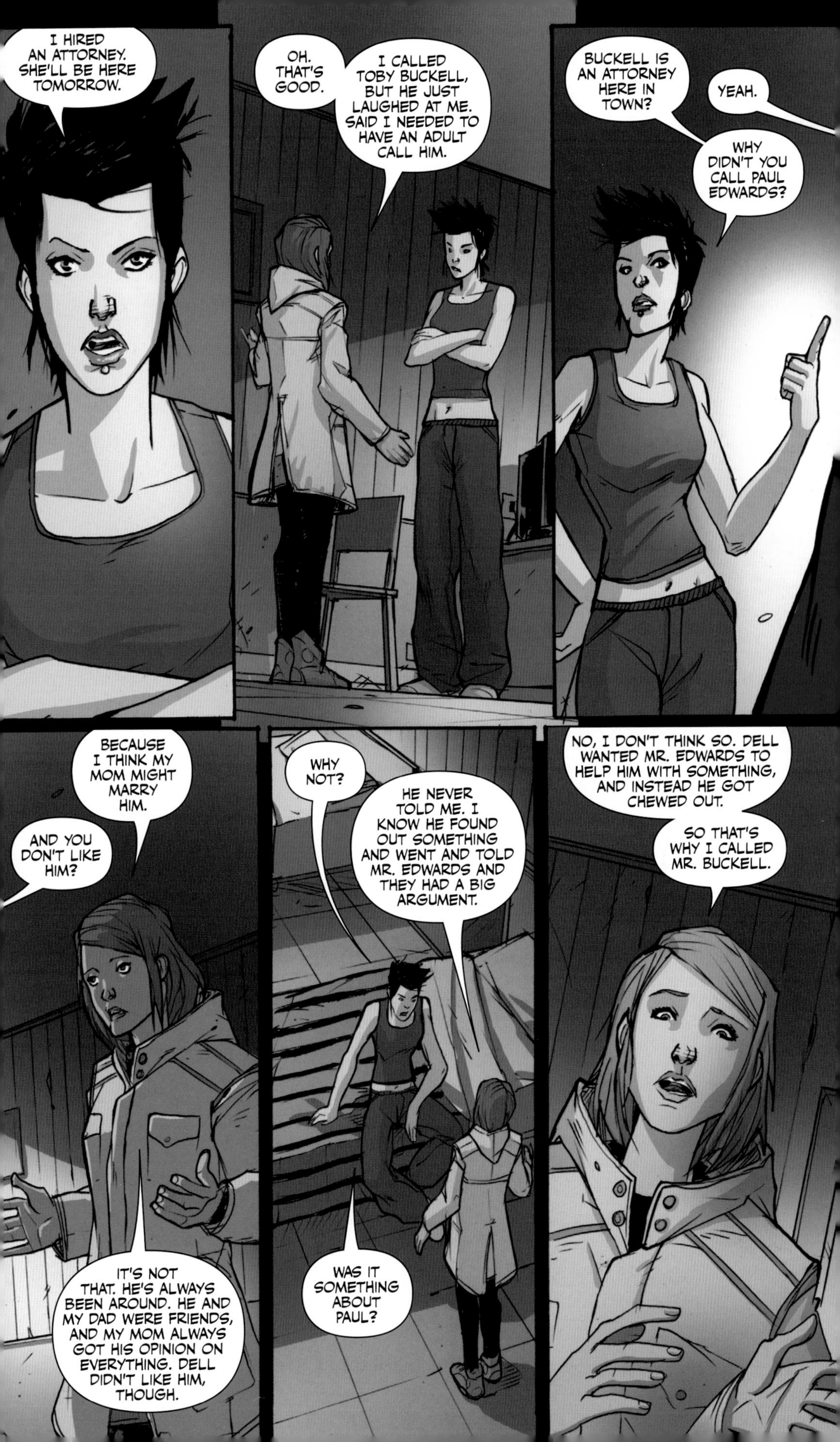

I HIRED AN ATTORNEY. SHE'LL BE HERE TOMORROW.
OH. THAT'S GOOD.
I CALLED TOBY BUCKELL, BUT HE JUST LAUGHED AT ME. SAID I NEEDED TO HAVE AN ADULT CALL HIM.
BUCKELL IS AN ATTORNEY HERE IN TOWN?
YEAH.
WHY DIDN'T YOU CALL PAUL EDWARDS?
BECAUSE I THINK MY MOM MIGHT MARRY HIM.
AND YOU DON'T LIKE HIM?
IT'S NOT THAT. HE'S ALWAYS BEEN AROUND. HE AND MY DAD WERE FRIENDS, AND MY MOM ALWAYS GOT HIS OPINION ON EVERYTHING. DELL DIDN'T LIKE HIM, THOUGH.
WHY NOT?
HE NEVER TOLD ME. I KNOW HE FOUND OUT SOMETHING AND WENT AND TOLD MR. EDWARDS AND THEY HAD A BIG ARGUMENT.
WAS IT SOMETHING ABOUT PAUL?
NO, I DON'T THINK SO. DELL WANTED MR. EDWARDS TO HELP HIM WITH SOMETHING, AND INSTEAD HE GOT CHEWED OUT.
SO THAT'S WHY I CALLED MR. BUCKELL.

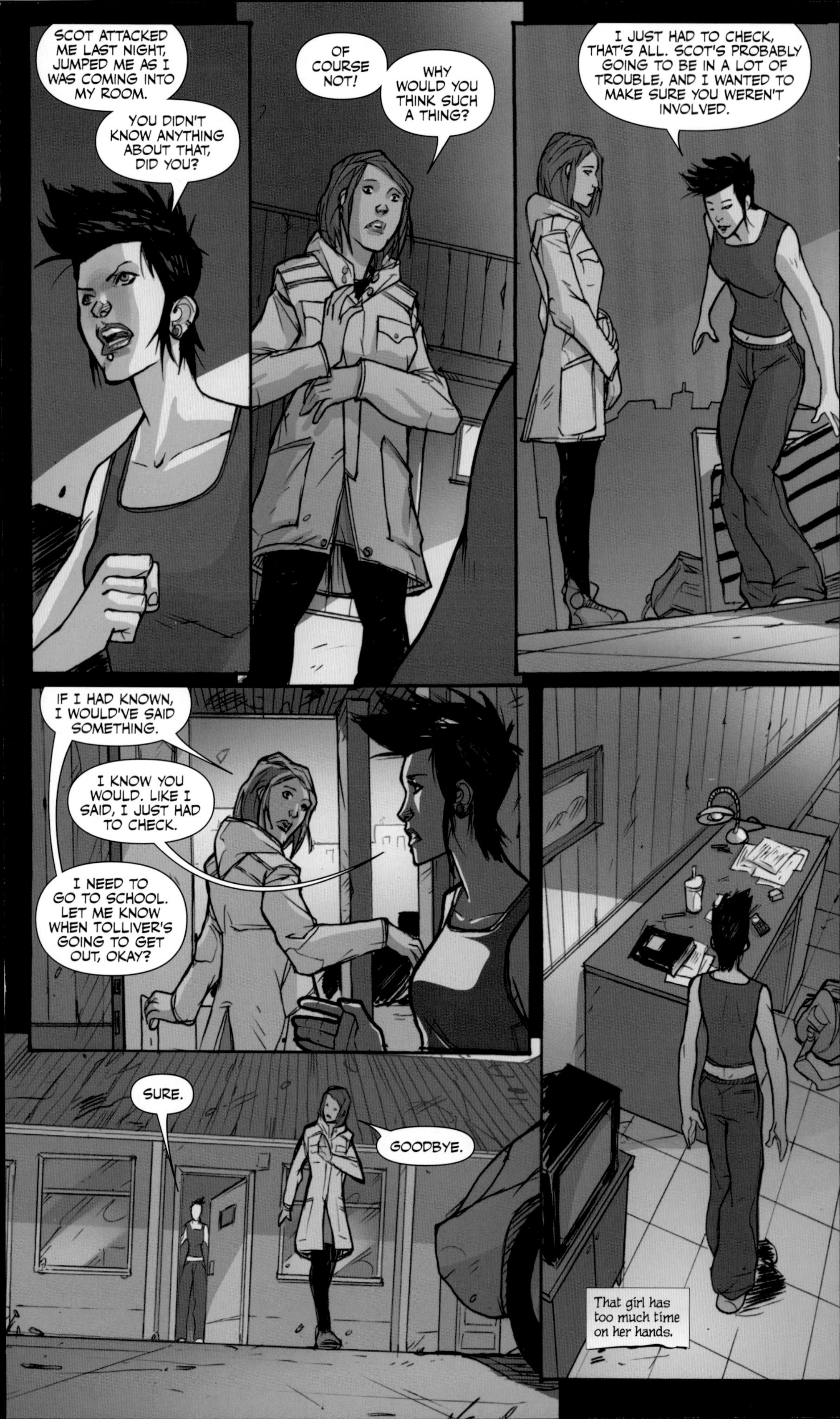

SCOT ATTACKED ME LAST NIGHT, JUMPED ME AS I WAS COMING INTO MY ROOM.
YOU DIDN'T KNOW ANYTHING ABOUT THAT, DID YOU?
OF COURSE NOT!
WHY WOULD YOU THINK SUCH A THING?
I JUST HAD TO CHECK, THAT'S ALL. SCOT'S PROBABLY GOING TO BE IN A LOT OF TROUBLE, AND I WANTED TO MAKE SURE YOU WEREN'T INVOLVED.
IF I HAD KNOWN, I WOULD'VE SAID SOMETHING.
I KNOW YOU WOULD. LIKE I SAID, I JUST HAD TO CHECK.
I NEED TO GO TO SCHOOL. LET ME KNOW WHEN TOLLIVER'S GOING TO GET OUT, OKAY?
SURE.
GOODBYE.
That girl has too much time on her hands.

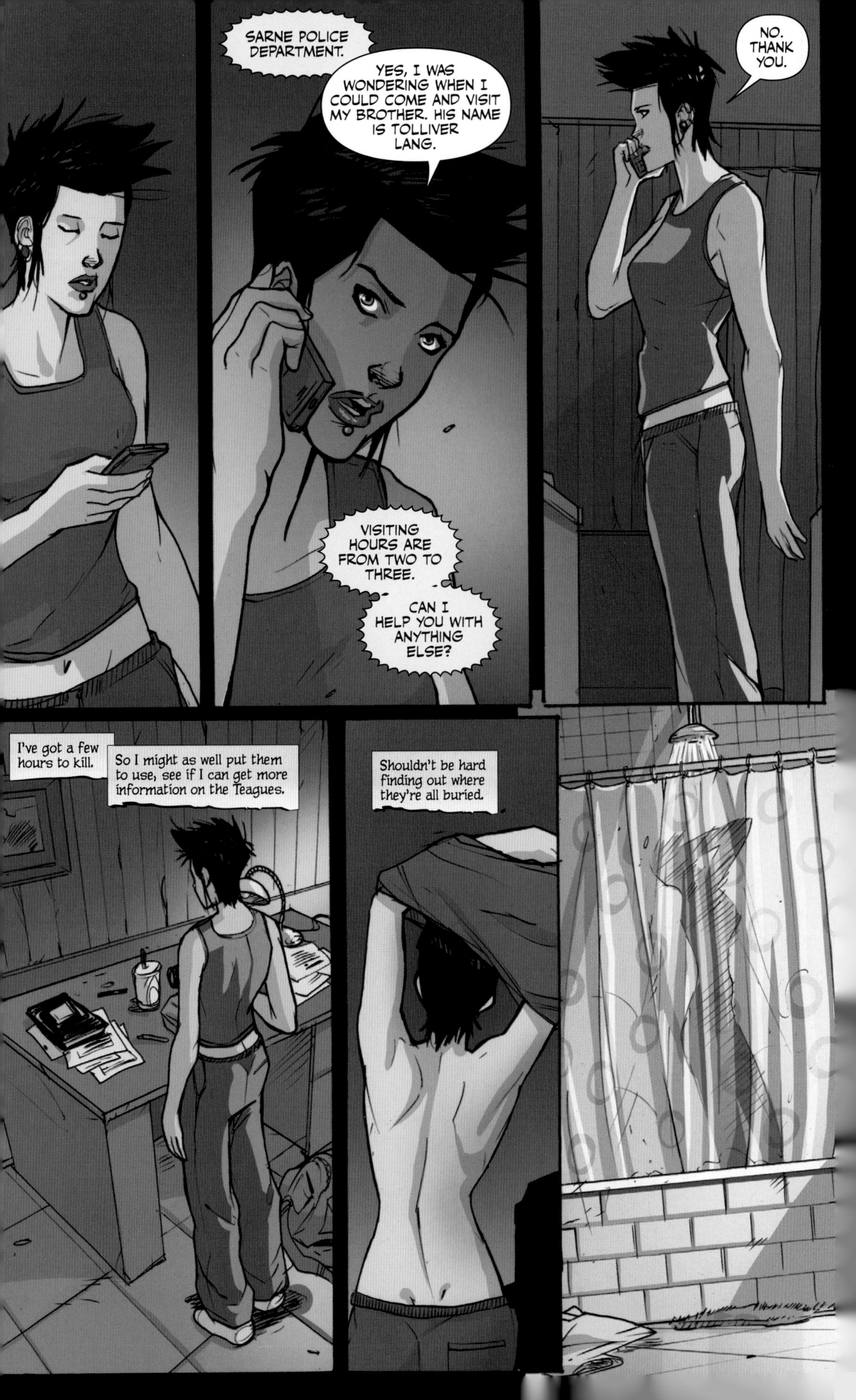
SARNE POLICE DEPARTMENT.
YES, I WAS WONDERING WHEN I COULD COME AND VISIT MY BROTHER. HIS NAME IS TOLLIVER LANG.
VISITING HOURS ARE FROM TWO TO THREE.
CAN I HELP YOU WITH ANYTHING ELSE?
NO. THANK YOU.
I've got a few hours to kill.
So I might as well put them to use, see if I can get more information on the Teagues.
Shouldn't be hard finding out where they're all buried.

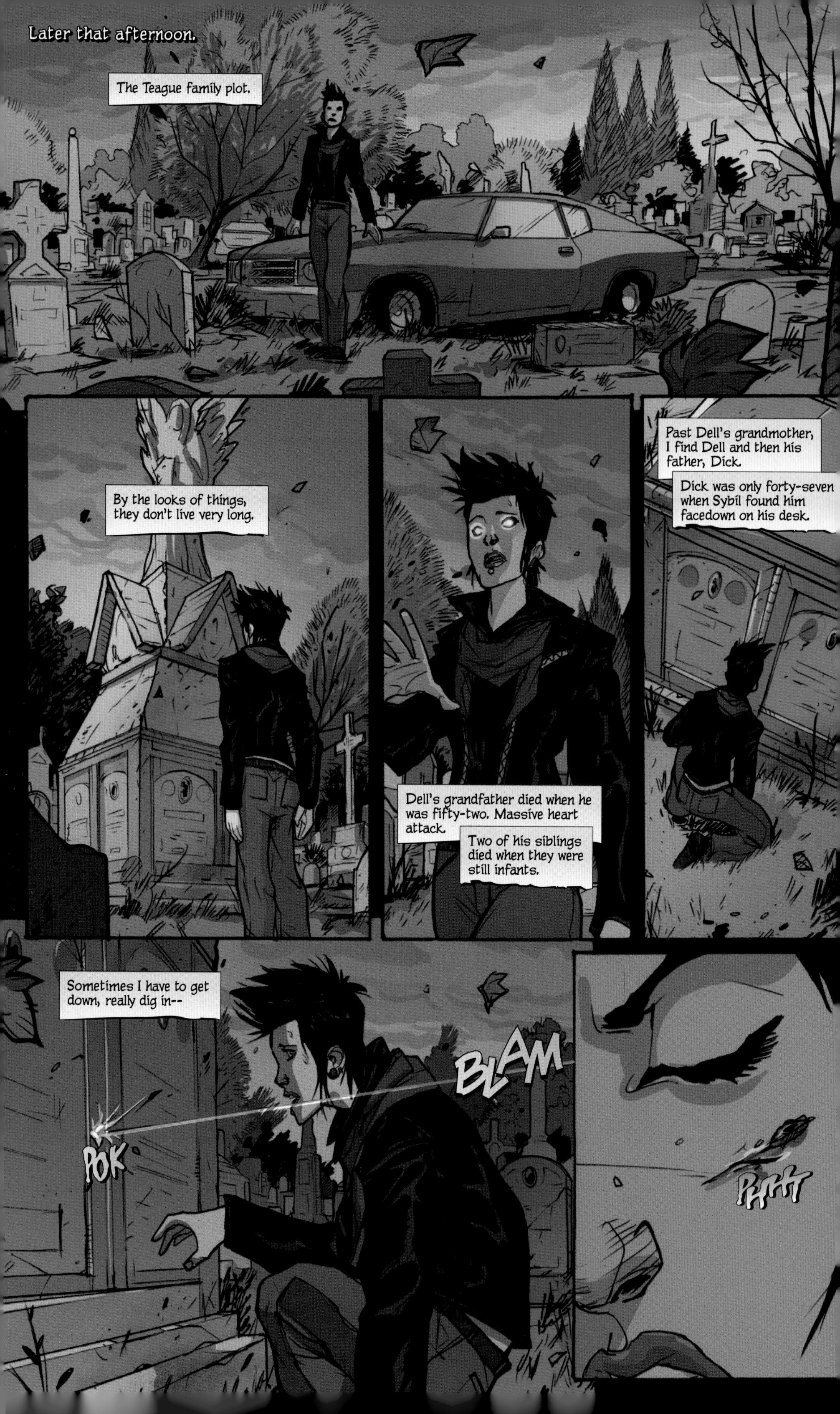
Later that afternoon.
The Teague family plot.
By the looks of things, they don't live very long.
Dell's grandfather died when he was fifty-two. Massive heart attack.
Two of his siblings died when they were still infants.
Past Dell's grandmother, I find Dell and then his father, Dick.
Dick was only forty-seven when Sybil found him facedown on his desk.
Sometimes I have to get down, really dig in--
BLAM
POK
PHHT

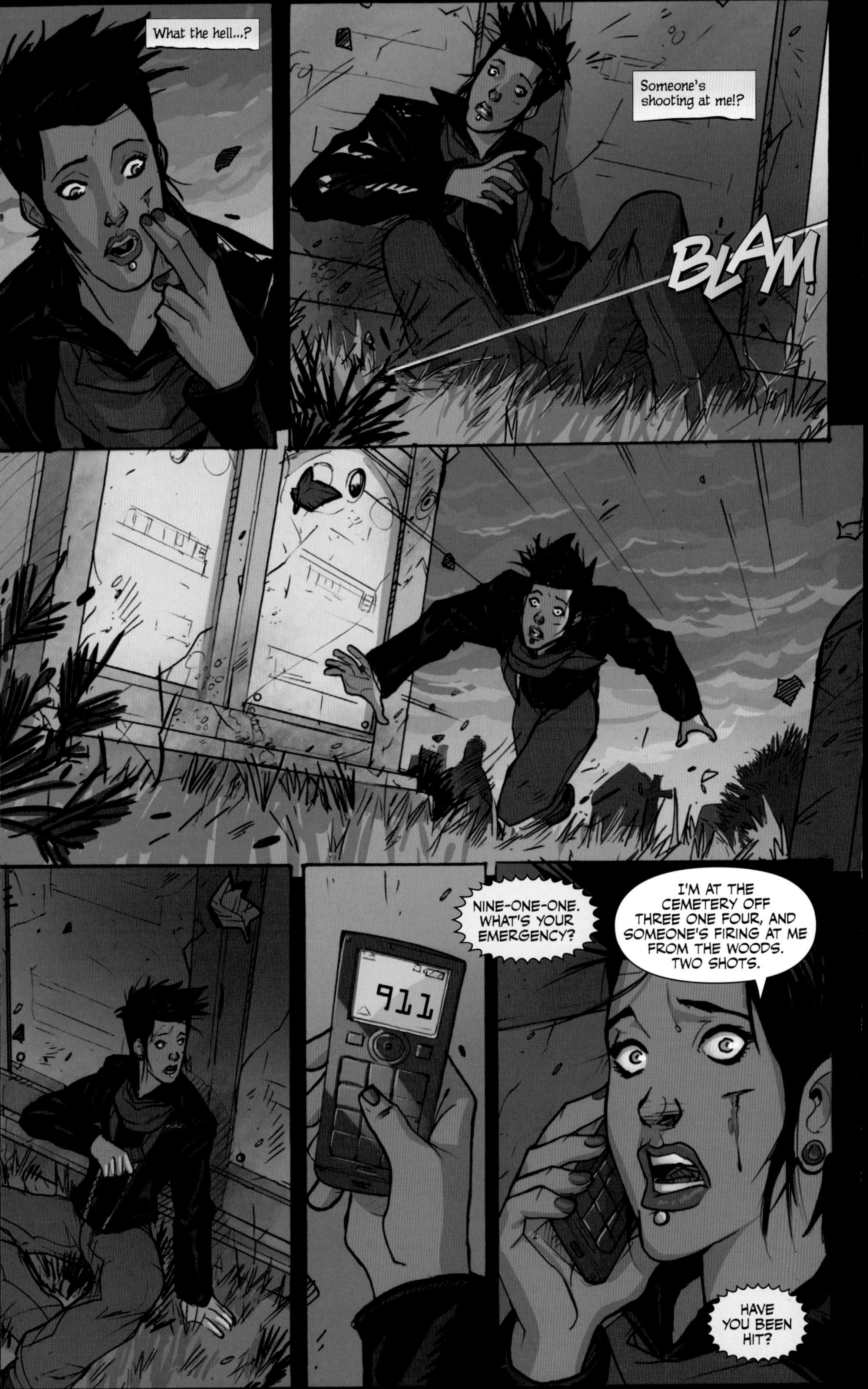
What the hell...?
Someone's shooting at me!?
BLAM
NINE-ONE-ONE. WHAT'S YOUR EMERGENCY?
911
I'M AT THE CEMETERY OFF THREE ONE FOUR, AND SOMEONE'S FIRING AT ME FROM THE WOODS. TWO SHOTS.
HAVE YOU BEEN HIT?

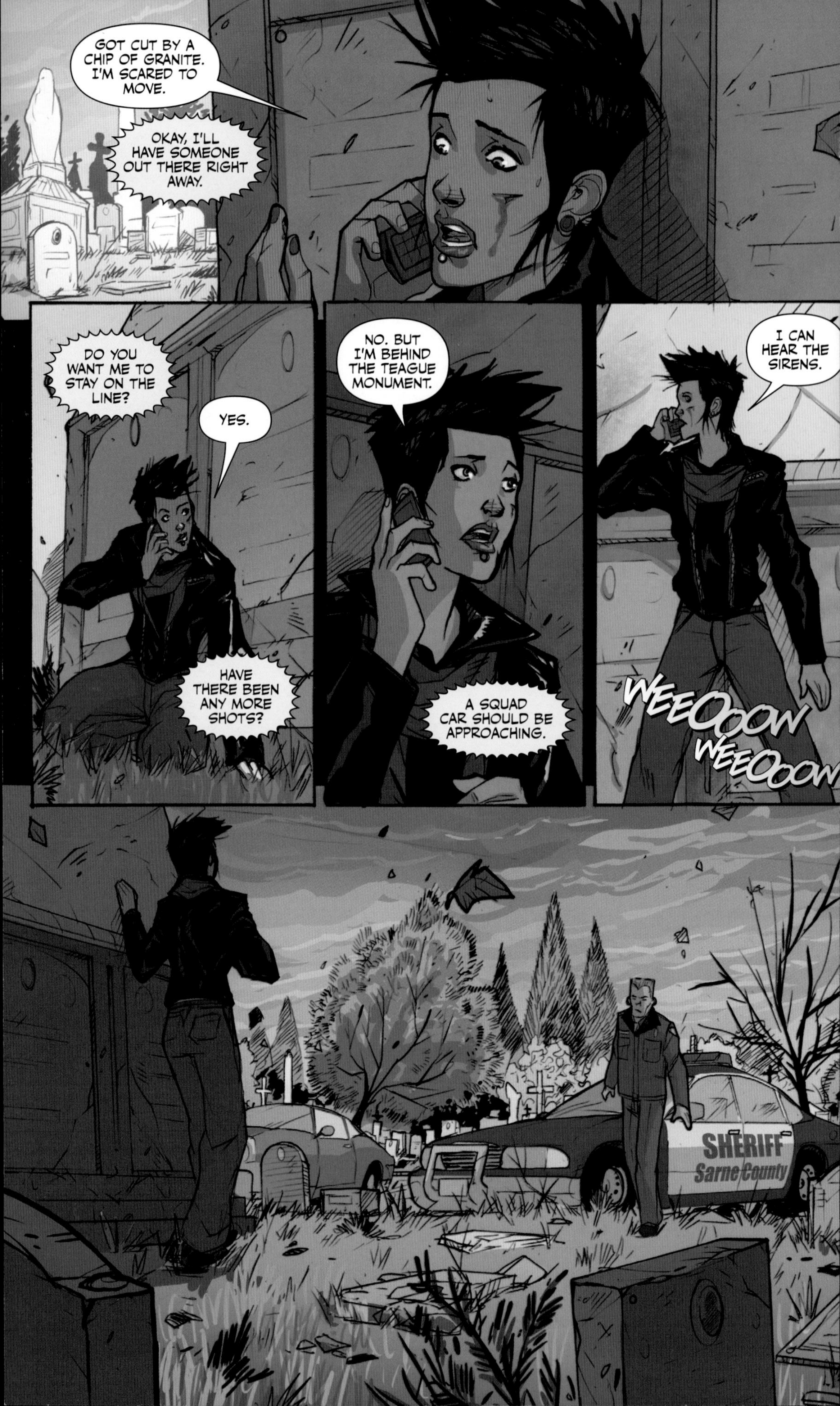
GOT CUT BY A CHIP OF GRANITE. I'M SCARED TO MOVE.
OKAY, I'LL HAVE SOMEONE OUT THERE RIGHT AWAY.
DO YOU WANT ME TO STAY ON THE LINE?
YES.
HAVE THERE BEEN ANY MORE SHOTS?
NO. BUT I'M BEHIND THE TEAGUE MONUMENT.
A SQUAD CAR SHOULD BE APPROACHING.
I CAN HEAR THE SIRENS.
WEEOOOON
WEEOOOON
SHERIFF
Sarne County

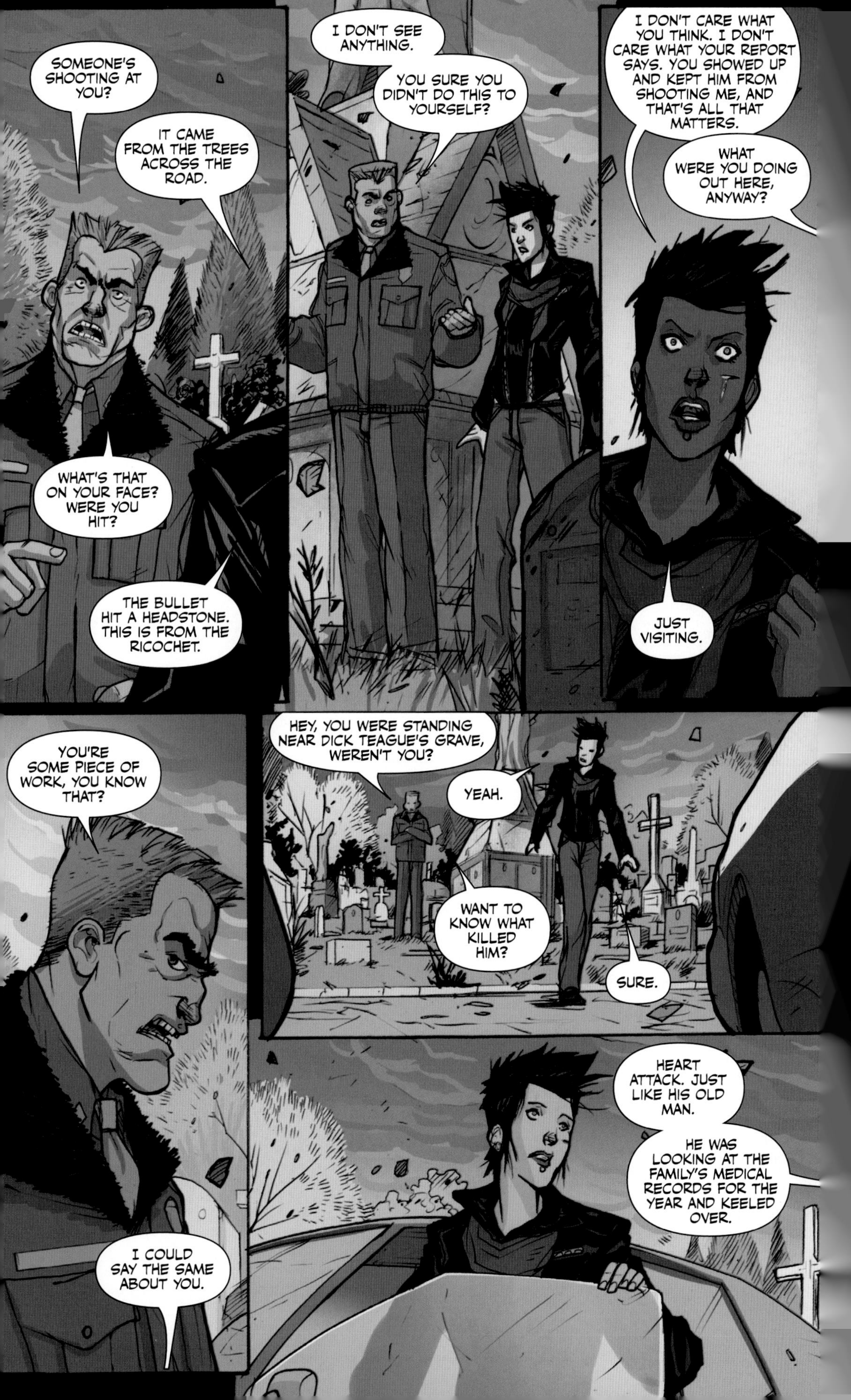
SOMEONE'S SHOOTING AT YOU?
IT CAME FROM THE TREES ACROSS THE ROAD.
WHAT'S THAT ON YOUR FACE? WERE YOU HIT?
THE BULLET HIT A HEADSTONE. THIS IS FROM THE RICOCHET.
I DON'T SEE ANYTHING.
YOU SURE YOU DIDN'T DO THIS TO YOURSELF?
I DON'T CARE WHAT YOU THINK. I DON'T CARE WHAT YOUR REPORT SAYS. YOU SHOWED UP AND KEPT HIM FROM SHOOTING ME, AND THAT'S ALL THAT MATTERS.
WHAT WERE YOU DOING OUT HERE, ANYWAY?
JUST VISITING.
YOU'RE SOME PIECE OF WORK, YOU KNOW THAT?
I COULD SAY THE SAME ABOUT YOU.
HEY, YOU WERE STANDING NEAR DICK TEAGUE'S GRAVE, WEREN'T YOU?
YEAH.
WANT TO KNOW WHAT KILLED HIM?
SURE.
HEART ATTACK. JUST LIKE HIS OLD MAN.
HE WAS LOOKING AT THE FAMILY'S MEDICAL RECORDS FOR THE YEAR AND KEELED OVER.

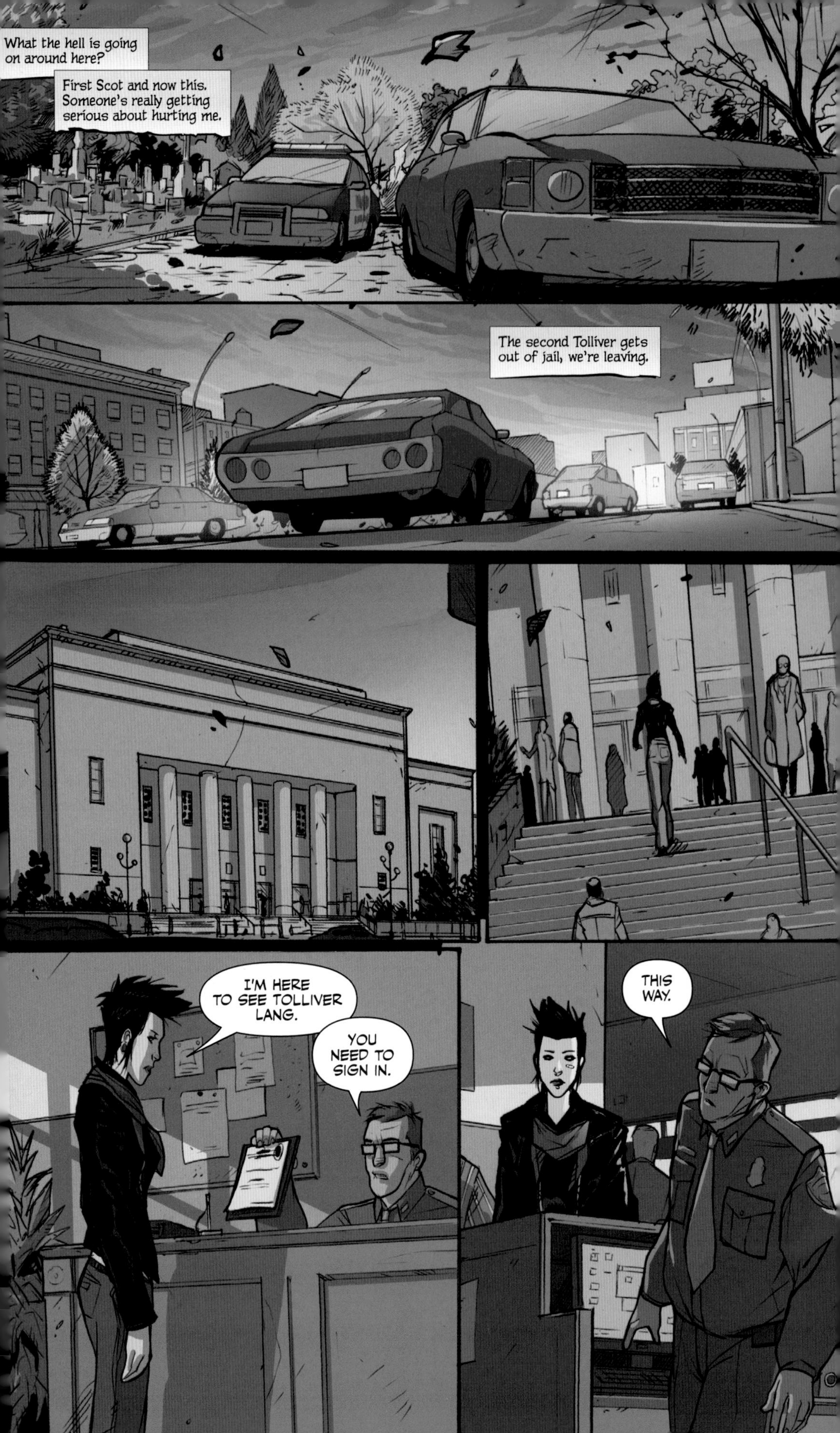

What the hell is going on around here?
First Scot and now this. Someone's really getting serious about hurting me.
The second Tolliver gets out of jail, we're leaving.
I'M HERE TO SEE TOLLIVER LANG.
YOU NEED TO SIGN IN.
THIS WAY.

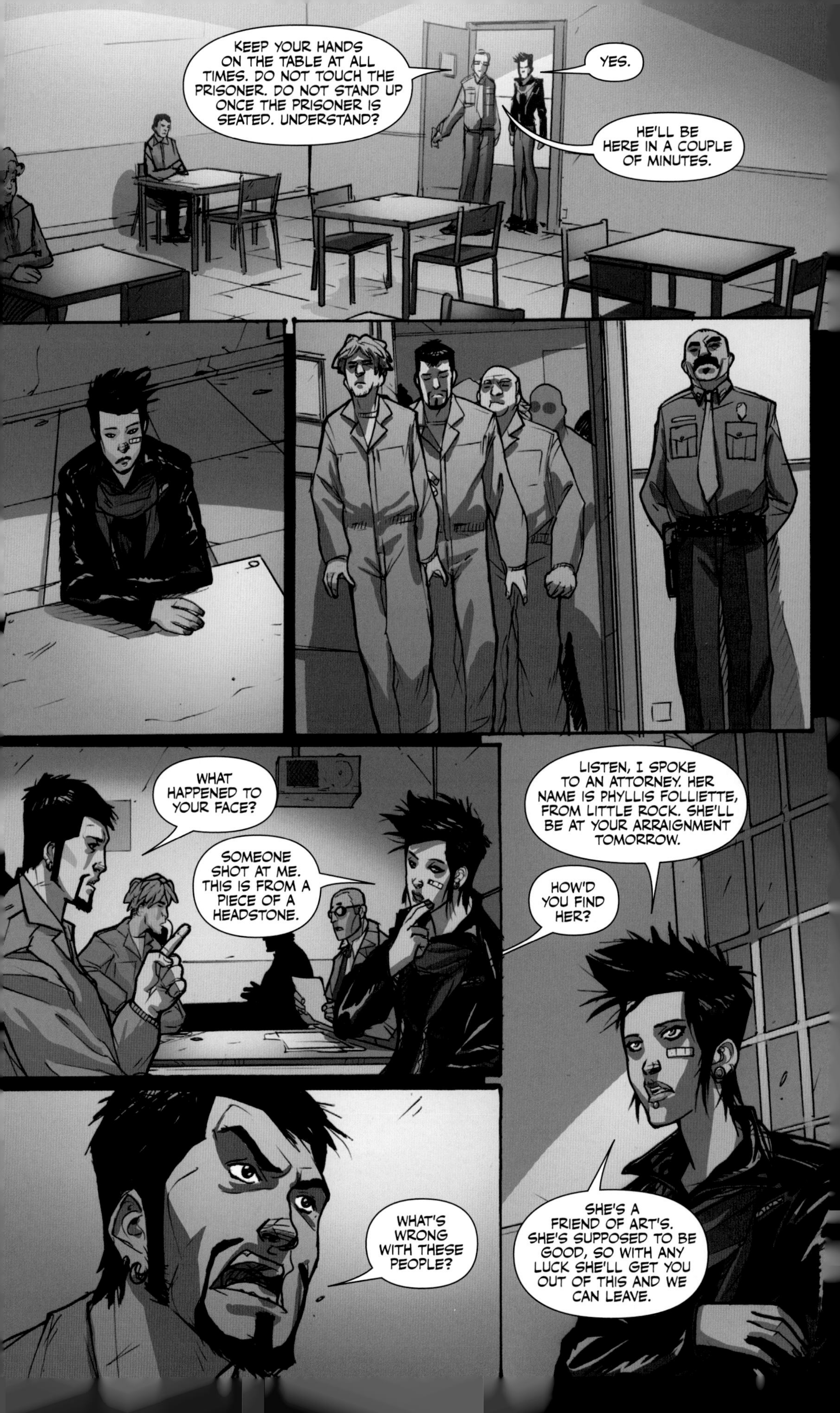
KEEP YOUR HANDS ON THE TABLE AT ALL TIMES. DO NOT TOUCH THE PRISONER. DO NOT STAND UP ONCE THE PRISONER IS SEATED. UNDERSTAND?
YES.
HE'LL BE HERE IN A COUPLE OF MINUTES.
WHAT HAPPENED TO YOUR FACE?
SOMEONE SHOT AT ME. THIS IS FROM A PIECE OF A HEADSTONE.
LISTEN, I SPOKE TO AN ATTORNEY. HER NAME IS PHYLLIS FOLLIETTE, FROM LITTLE ROCK. SHE'LL BE AT YOUR ARRAIGNMENT TOMORROW.
HOW'D YOU FIND HER?
WHAT'S WRONG WITH THESE PEOPLE?
SHE'S A FRIEND OF ART'S. SHE'S SUPPOSED TO BE GOOD, SO WITH ANY LUCK SHE'LL GET YOU OUT OF THIS AND WE CAN LEAVE.

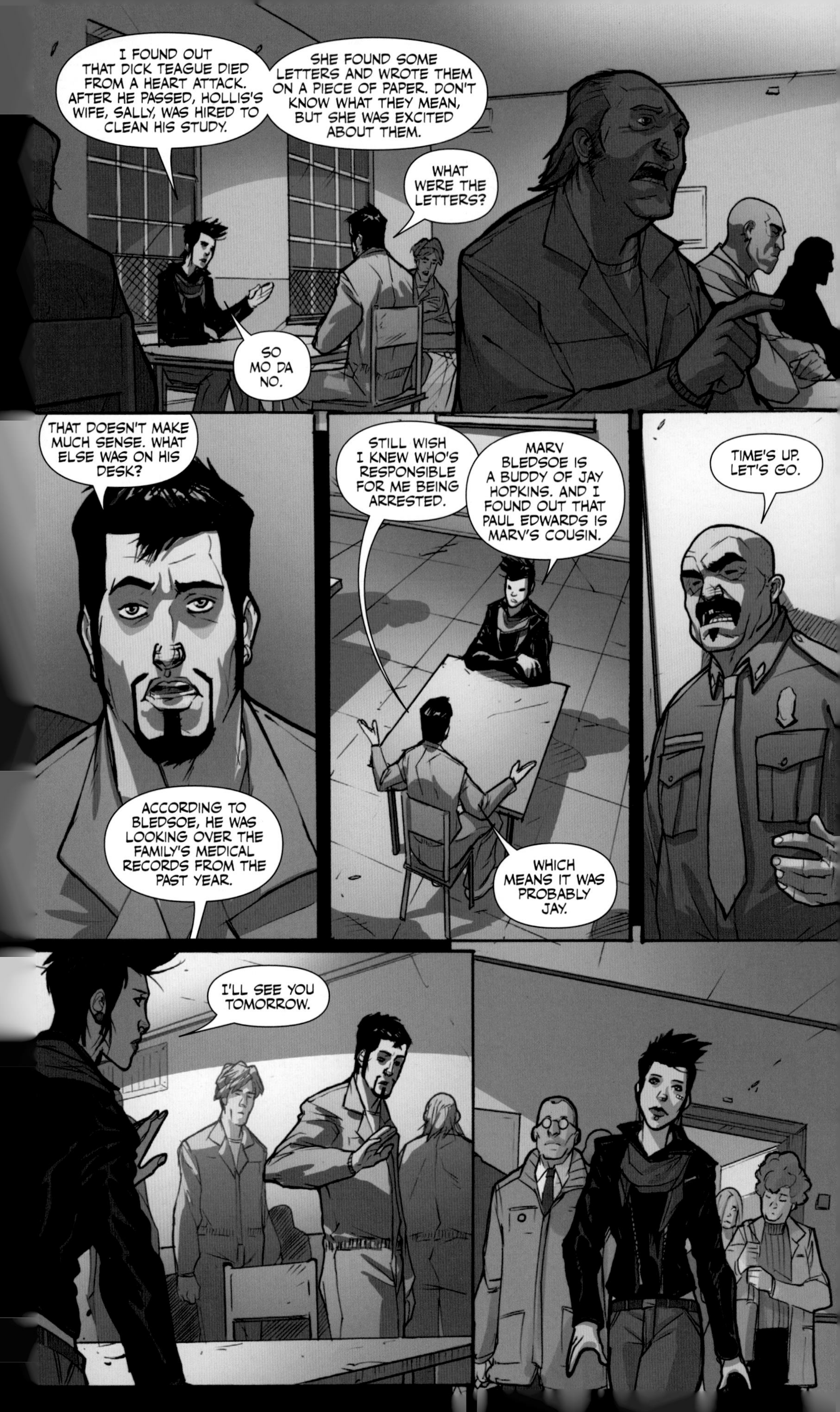
I FOUND OUT THAT DICK TEAGUE DIED FROM A HEART ATTACK. AFTER HE PASSED, HOLLIS'S WIFE, SALLY, WAS HIRED TO CLEAN HIS STUDY.
SHE FOUND SOME LETTERS AND WROTE THEM ON A PIECE OF PAPER. DON'T KNOW WHAT THEY MEAN, BUT SHE WAS EXCITED ABOUT THEM.
WHAT WERE THE LETTERS?
SO MO DA NO.
THAT DOESN'T MAKE MUCH SENSE. WHAT ELSE WAS ON HIS DESK?
ACCORDING TO BLEDSOE, HE WAS LOOKING OVER THE FAMILY'S MEDICAL RECORDS FROM THE PAST YEAR.
STILL WISH I KNEW WHO'S RESPONSIBLE FOR ME BEING ARRESTED.
MARV BLEDSOE IS A BUDDY OF JAY HOPKINS. AND I FOUND OUT THAT PAUL EDWARDS IS MARV'S COUSIN.
WHICH MEANS IT WAS PROBABLY JAY.
TIME'S UP. LET'S GO.
I'LL SEE YOU TOMORROW.

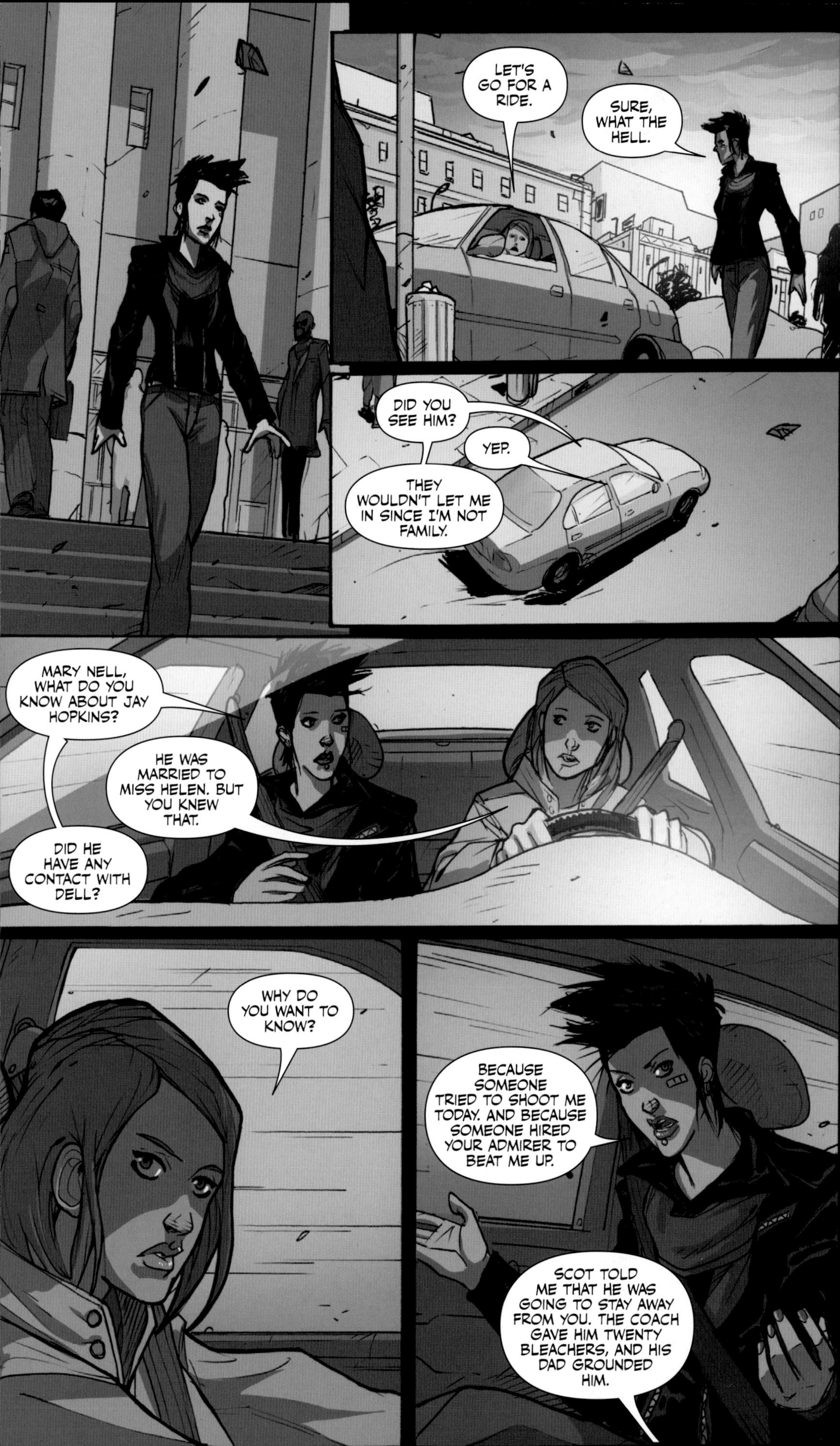
LET'S GO FOR A RIDE.
SURE, WHAT THE HELL.
DID YOU SEE HIM?
YEP.
THEY WOULDN'T LET ME IN SINCE I'M NOT FAMILY.
MARY NELL, WHAT DO YOU KNOW ABOUT JAY HOPKINS?
HE WAS MARRIED TO MISS HELEN. BUT YOU KNEW THAT.
DID HE HAVE ANY CONTACT WITH DELL?
WHY DO YOU WANT TO KNOW?
BECAUSE SOMEONE TRIED TO SHOOT ME TODAY. AND BECAUSE SOMEONE HIRED YOUR ADMIRER TO BEAT ME UP.
SCOT TOLD ME THAT HE WAS GOING TO STAY AWAY FROM YOU. THE COACH GAVE HIM TWENTY BLEACHERS, AND HIS DAD GROUNDED HIM.

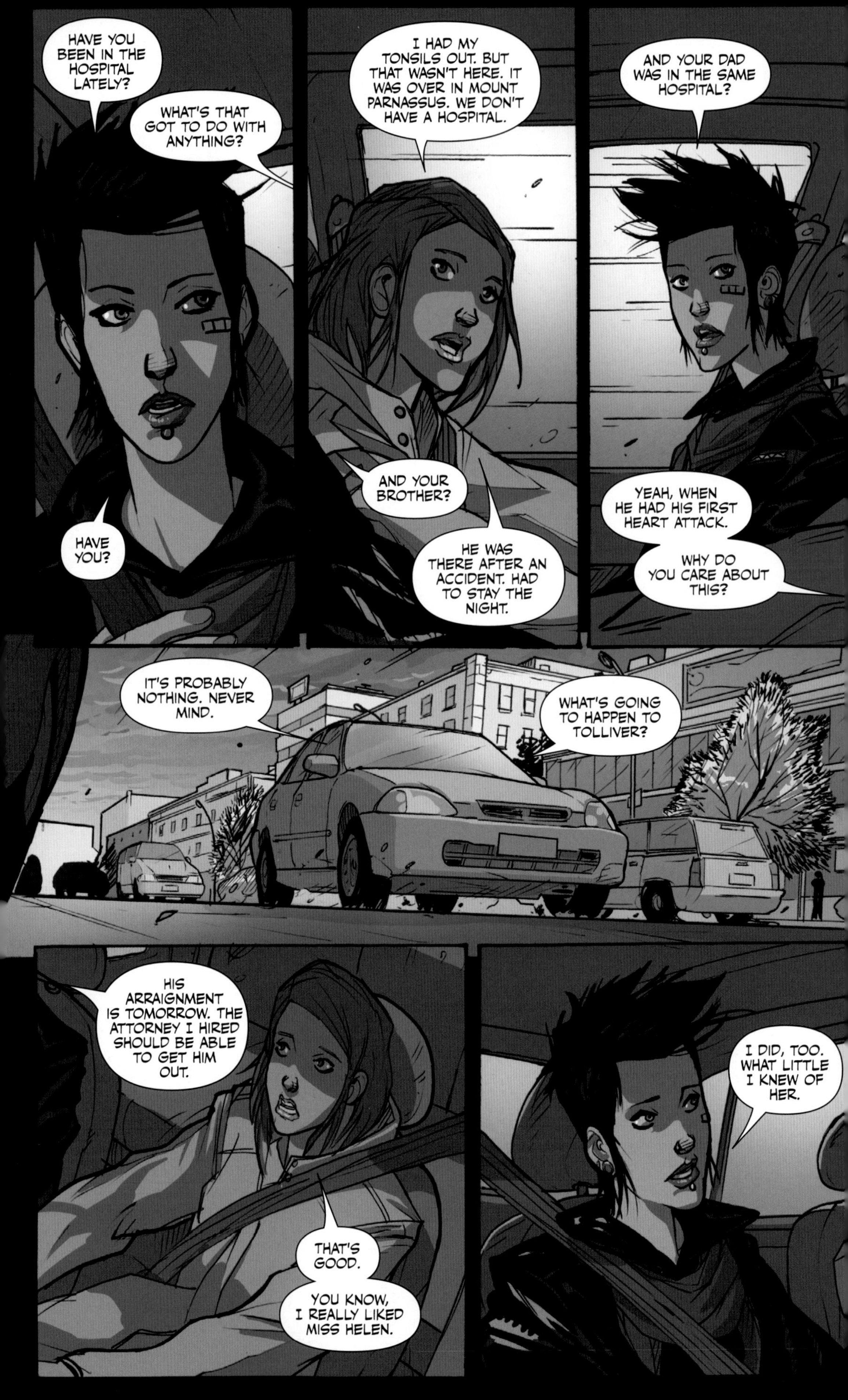
HAVE YOU BEEN IN THE HOSPITAL LATELY?
WHAT'S THAT GOT TO DO WITH ANYTHING?
HAVE YOU?
I HAD MY TONSILS OUT. BUT THAT WASN'T HERE. IT WAS OVER IN MOUNT PARNASSUS. WE DON'T HAVE A HOSPITAL.
AND YOUR BROTHER?
HE WAS THERE AFTER AN ACCIDENT. HAD TO STAY THE NIGHT.
AND YOUR DAD WAS IN THE SAME HOSPITAL?
YEAH, WHEN HE HAD HIS FIRST HEART ATTACK.
WHY DO YOU CARE ABOUT THIS?
IT'S PROBABLY NOTHING. NEVER MIND.
WHAT'S GOING TO HAPPEN TO TOLLIVER?
HIS ARRAIGNMENT IS TOMORROW. THE ATTORNEY I HIRED SHOULD BE ABLE TO GET HIM OUT.
THAT'S GOOD.
YOU KNOW, I REALLY LIKED MISS HELEN.
I DID, TOO. WHAT LITTLE I KNEW OF HER.

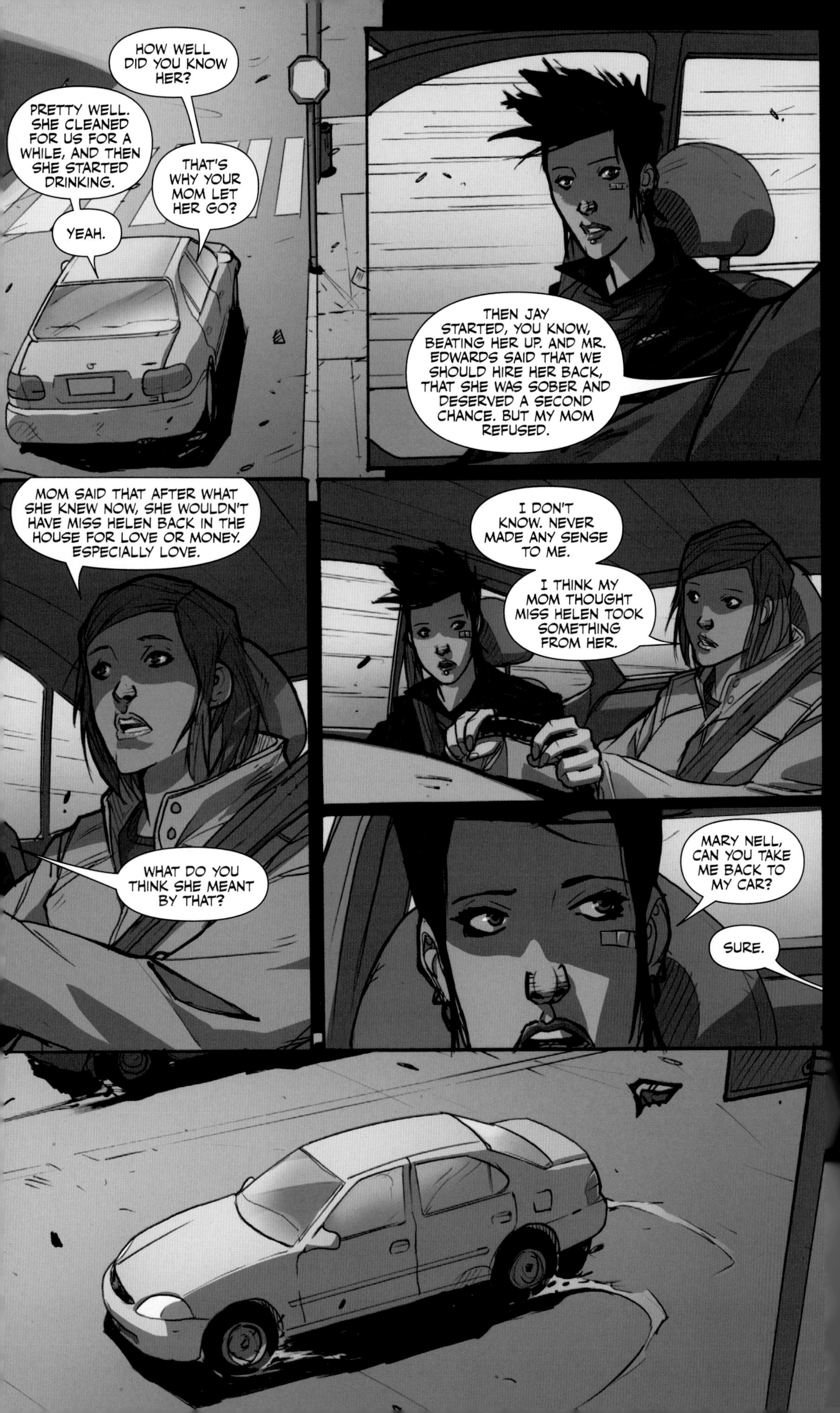
HOW WELL DID YOU KNOW HER?
PRETTY WELL. SHE CLEANED FOR US FOR A WHILE, AND THEN SHE STARTED DRINKING.
THAT'S WHY YOUR MOM LET HER GO?
YEAH.
THEN JAY STARTED, YOU KNOW, BEATING HER UP. AND MR. EDWARDS SAID THAT WE SHOULD HIRE HER BACK, THAT SHE WAS SOBER AND DESERVED A SECOND CHANCE. BUT MY MOM REFUSED.
MOM SAID THAT AFTER WHAT SHE KNEW NOW, SHE WOULDN'T HAVE MISS HELEN BACK IN THE HOUSE FOR LOVE OR MONEY. ESPECIALLY LOVE.
WHAT DO YOU THINK SHE MEANT BY THAT?
I DON'T KNOW. NEVER MADE ANY SENSE TO ME.
I THINK MY MOM THOUGHT MISS HELEN TOOK SOMETHING FROM HER.
MARY NELL, CAN YOU TAKE ME BACK TO MY CAR?
SURE.

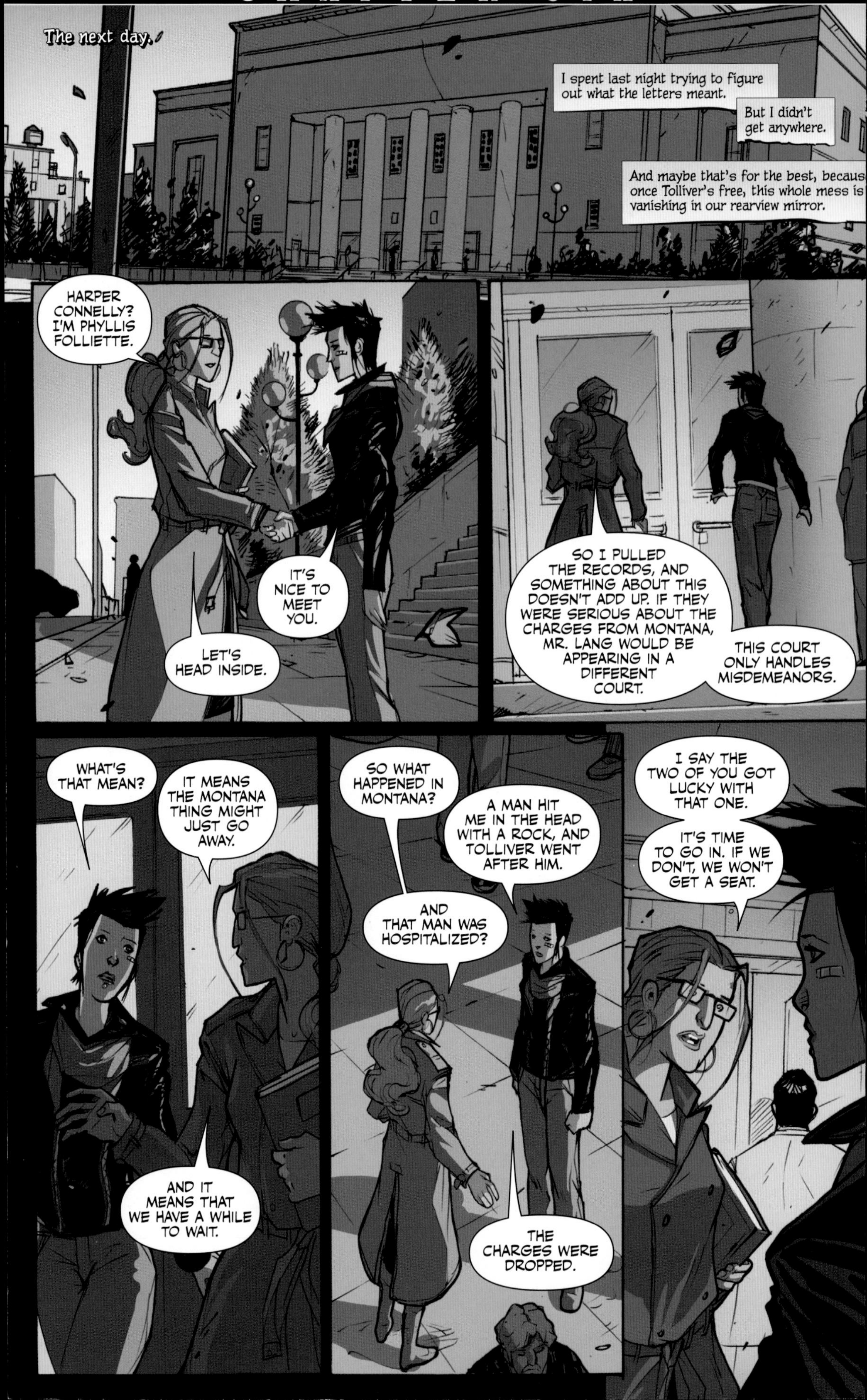
The next day.
I spent last night trying to figure out what the letters meant.
But I didn't get anywhere.
And maybe that's for the best, because once Tolliver's free, this whole mess is vanishing in our rearview mirror.
HARPER CONNELLY? I'M PHYLLIS FOLLIETTE.
IT'S NICE TO MEET YOU.
LET'S HEAD INSIDE.
SO I PULLED THE RECORDS, AND SOMETHING ABOUT THIS DOESN'T ADD UP. IF THEY WERE SERIOUS ABOUT THE CHARGES FROM MONTANA, MR. LANG WOULD BE APPEARING IN A DIFFERENT COURT.
THIS COURT ONLY HANDLES MISDEMEANORS.
WHAT'S THAT MEAN?
IT MEANS THE MONTANA THING MIGHT JUST GO AWAY.
AND IT MEANS THAT WE HAVE A WHILE TO WAIT.
SO WHAT HAPPENED IN MONTANA?
A MAN HIT ME IN THE HEAD WITH A ROCK, AND TOLLIVER WENT AFTER HIM.
AND THAT MAN WAS HOSPITALIZED?
THE CHARGES WERE DROPPED.
I SAY THE TWO OF YOU GOT LUCKY WITH THAT ONE.
IT'S TIME TO GO IN. IF WE DON'T, WE WON'T GET A SEAT.

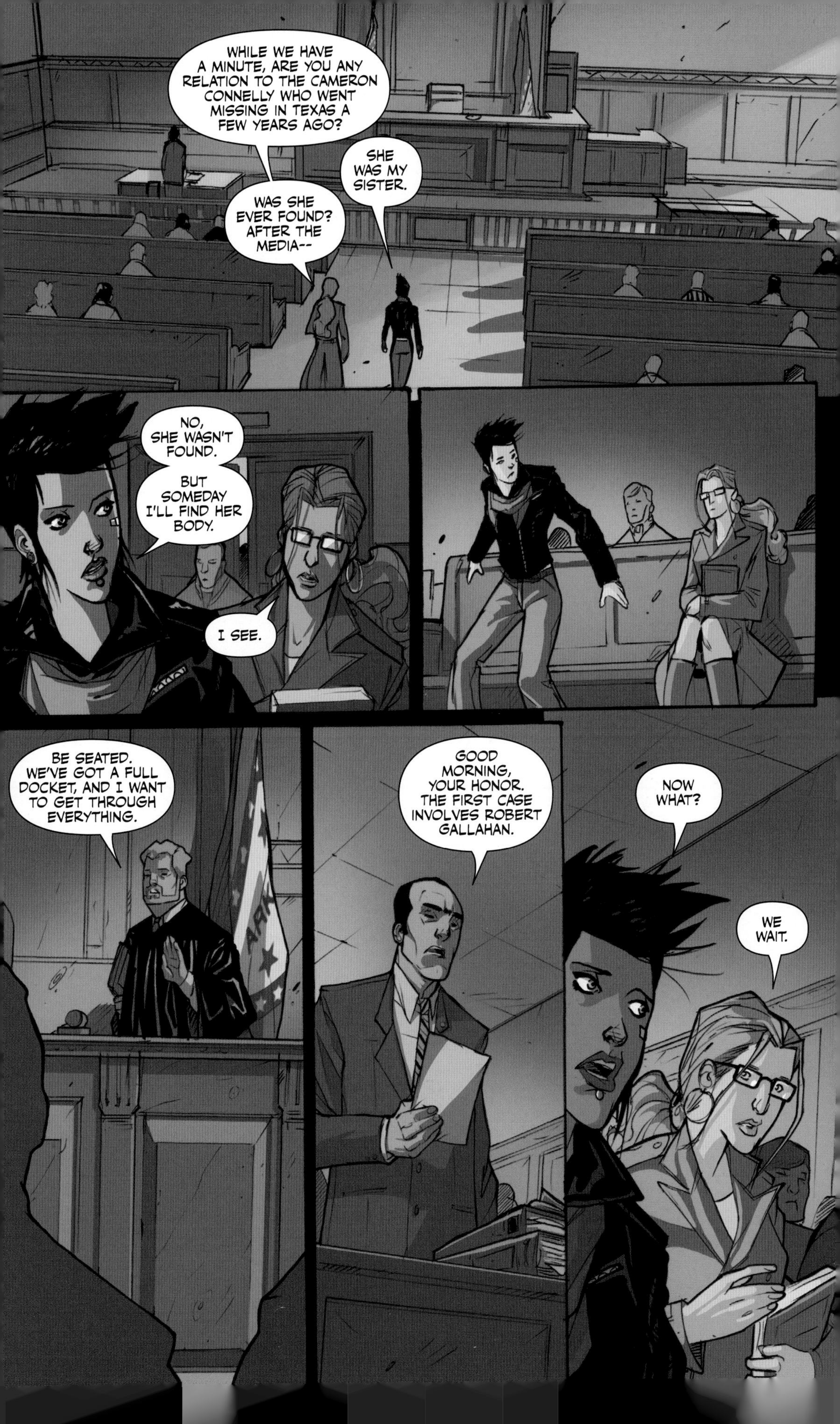
WHILE WE HAVE A MINUTE, ARE YOU ANY RELATION TO THE CAMERON CONNELLY WHO WENT MISSING IN TEXAS A FEW YEARS AGO?
SHE WAS MY SISTER.
WAS SHE EVER FOUND? AFTER THE MEDIA--
NO, SHE WASN'T FOUND.
BUT SOMEDAY I'LL FIND HER BODY.
I SEE.
BE SEATED. WE'VE GOT A FULL DOCKET, AND I WANT TO GET THROUGH EVERYTHING.
GOOD MORNING, YOUR HONOR. THE FIRST CASE INVOLVES ROBERT GALLAHAN.
NOW WHAT?
WE WAIT.

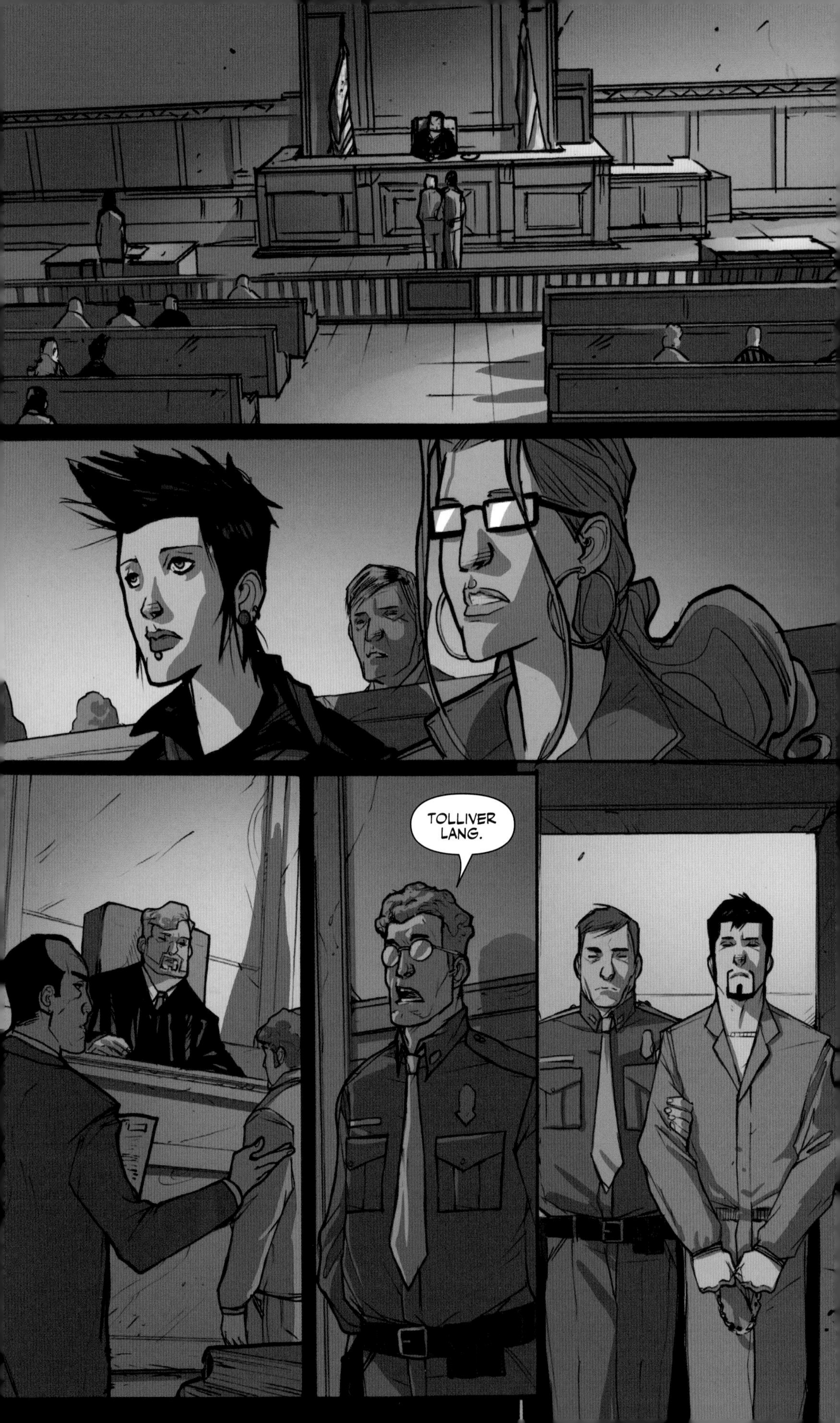
TOLLIVER LANG.

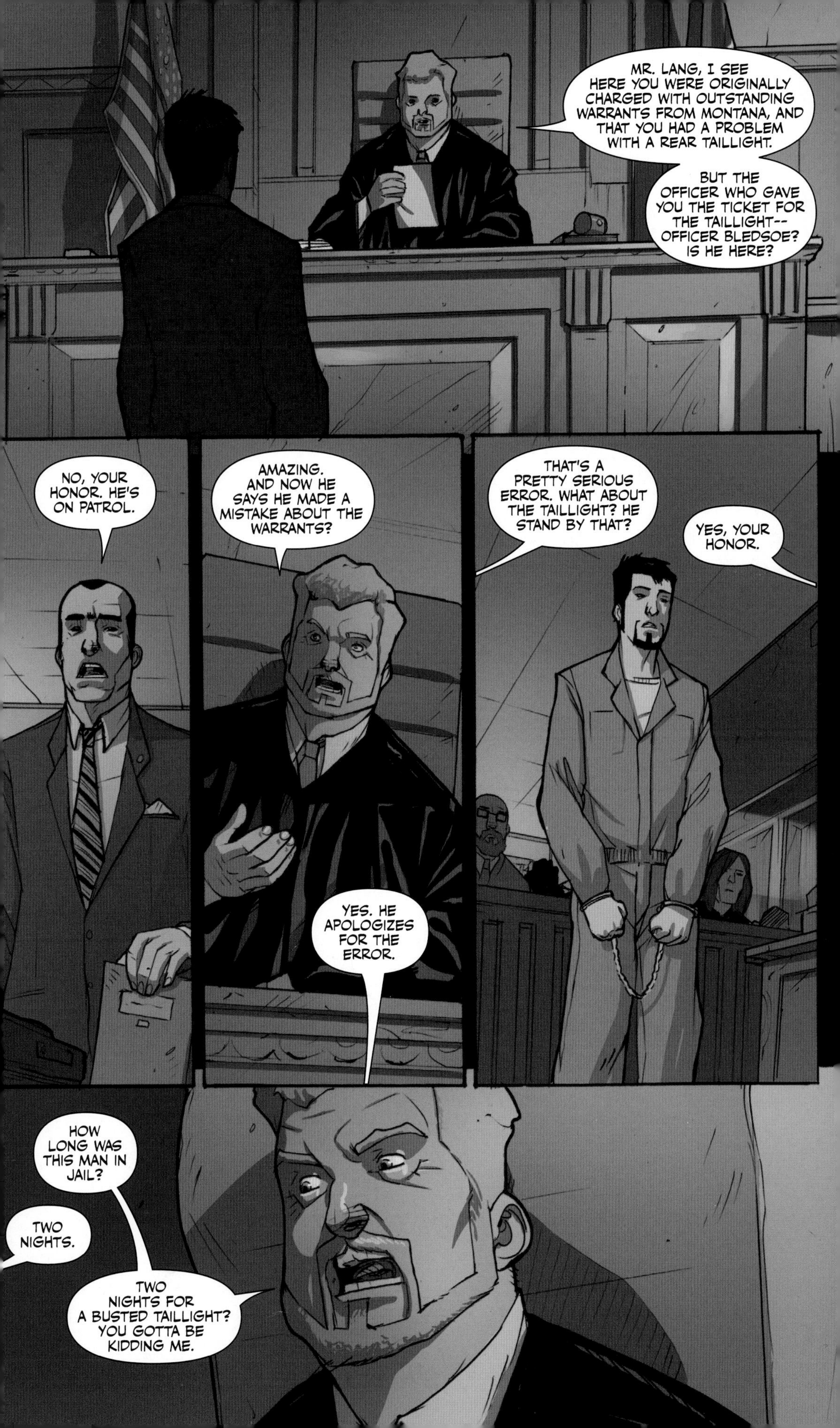
MR. LANG, I SEE HERE YOU WERE ORIGINALLY CHARGED WITH OUTSTANDING WARRANTS FROM MONTANA, AND THAT YOU HAD A PROBLEM WITH A REAR TAILLIGHT.
BUT THE OFFICER WHO GAVE YOU THE TICKET FOR THE TAILLIGHT-- OFFICER BLEDSOE? IS HE HERE?
NO, YOUR HONOR. HE'S ON PATROL.
AMAZING. AND NOW HE SAYS HE MADE A MISTAKE ABOUT THE WARRANTS?
YES. HE APOLOGIZES FOR THE ERROR.
THAT'S A PRETTY SERIOUS ERROR. WHAT ABOUT THE TAILLIGHT? HE STAND BY THAT?
YES, YOUR HONOR.
HOW LONG WAS THIS MAN IN JAIL?
TWO NIGHTS.
TWO NIGHTS FOR A BUSTED TAILLIGHT? YOU GOTTA BE KIDDING ME.

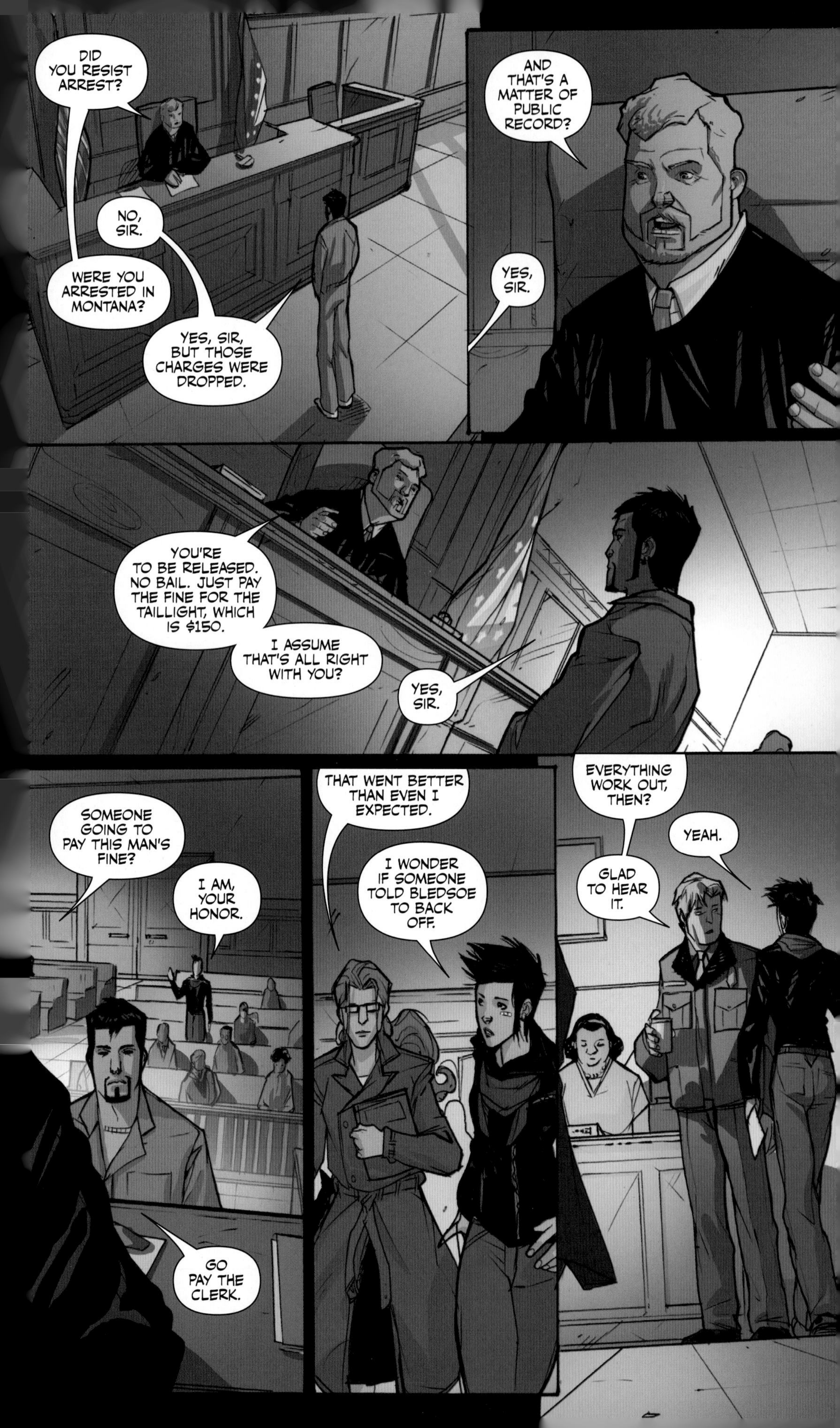
DID YOU RESIST ARREST?
NO, SIR.
WERE YOU ARRESTED IN MONTANA?
YES, SIR, BUT THOSE CHARGES WERE DROPPED.
AND THAT'S A MATTER OF PUBLIC RECORD?
YES, SIR.
YOU'RE TO BE RELEASED. NO BAIL. JUST PAY THE FINE FOR THE TAILLIGHT, WHICH IS $150.
I ASSUME THAT'S ALL RIGHT WITH YOU?
YES, SIR.
SOMEONE GOING TO PAY THIS MAN'S FINE?
I AM, YOUR HONOR.
GO PAY THE CLERK.
THAT WENT BETTER THAN EVEN I EXPECTED.
I WONDER IF SOMEONE TOLD BLEDSOE TO BACK OFF.
EVERYTHING WORK OUT, THEN?
YEAH.
GLAD TO HEAR IT.

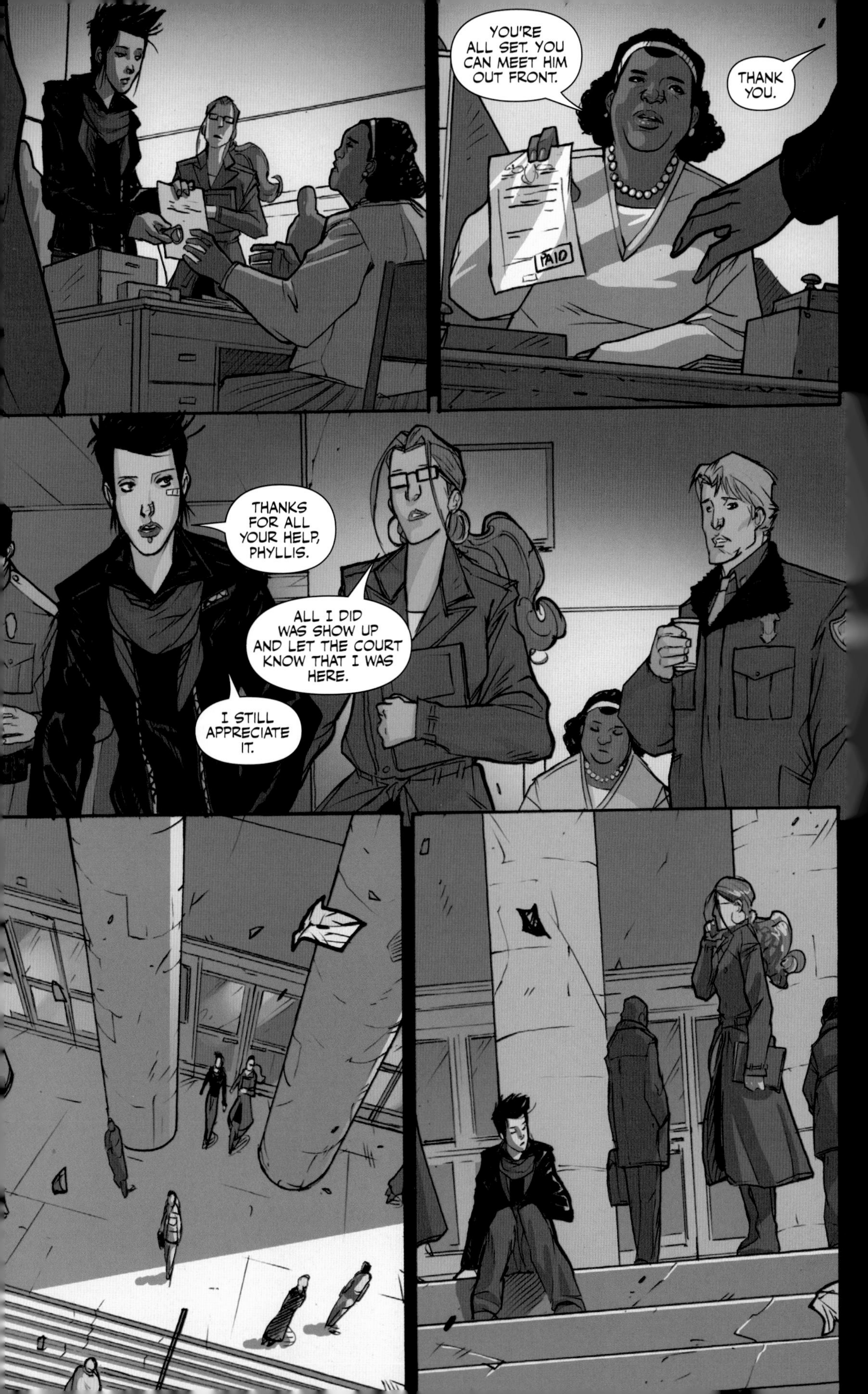
YOU'RE ALL SET. YOU CAN MEET HIM OUT FRONT.
PAID
THANK YOU.
THANKS FOR ALL YOUR HELP, PHYLLIS.
ALL I DID WAS SHOW UP AND LET THE COURT KNOW THAT I WAS HERE.
I STILL APPRECIATE IT.

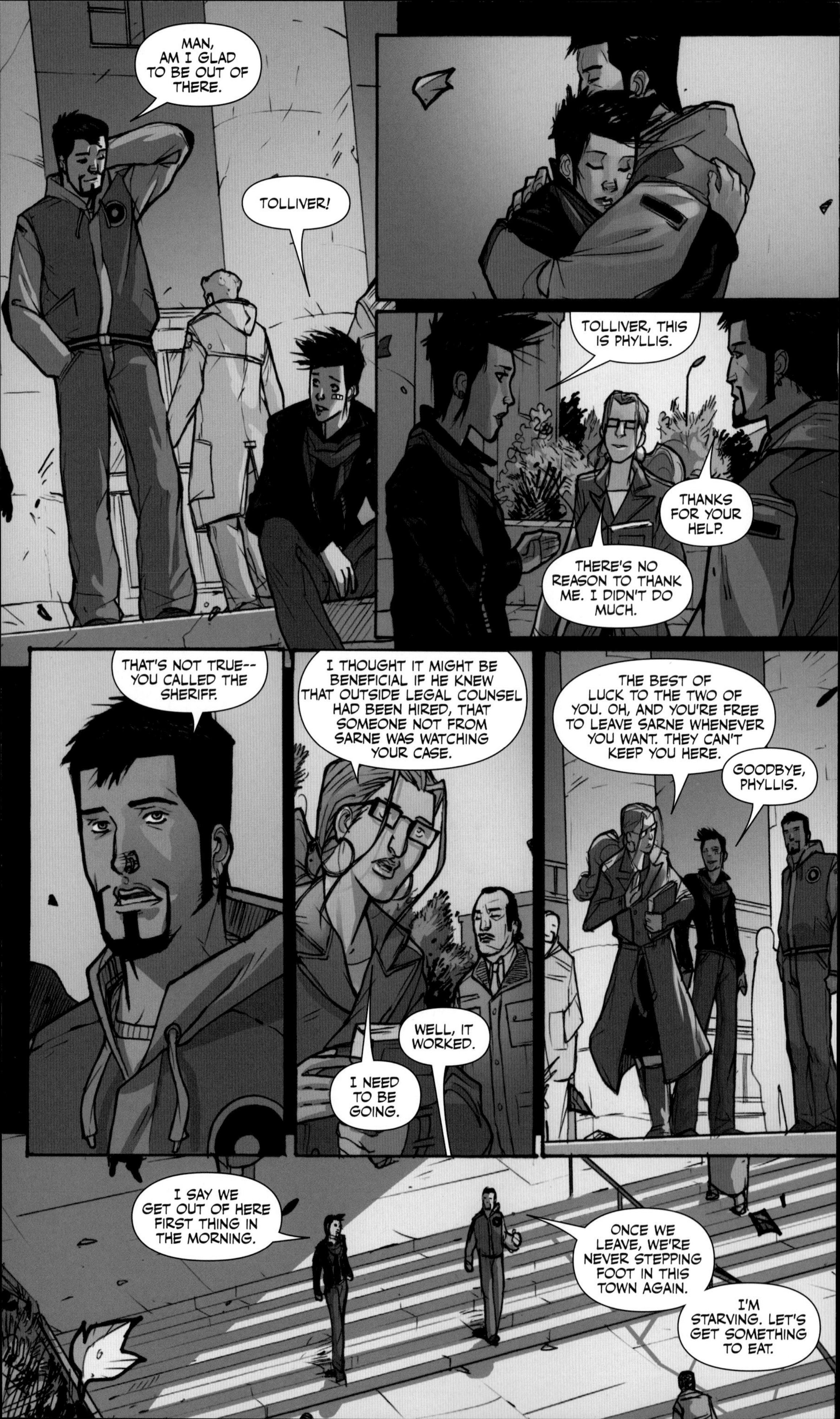
MAN, AM I GLAD TO BE OUT OF THERE.
TOLLIVER!
TOLLIVER, THIS IS PHYLLIS.
THANKS FOR YOUR HELP.
THERE'S NO REASON TO THANK ME. I DIDN'T DO MUCH.
THAT'S NOT TRUE-- YOU CALLED THE SHERIFF.
I THOUGHT IT MIGHT BE BENEFICIAL IF HE KNEW THAT OUTSIDE LEGAL COUNSEL HAD BEEN HIRED, THAT SOMEONE NOT FROM SARNE WAS WATCHING YOUR CASE.
WELL, IT WORKED.
I NEED TO BE GOING.
THE BEST OF LUCK TO THE TWO OF YOU. OH, AND YOU'RE FREE TO LEAVE SARNE WHENEVER YOU WANT. THEY CAN'T KEEP YOU HERE.
GOODBYE, PHYLLIS.
I SAY WE GET OUT OF HERE FIRST THING IN THE MORNING.
ONCE WE LEAVE, WE'RE NEVER STEPPING FOOT IN THIS TOWN AGAIN.
I'M STARVING. LET'S GET SOMETHING TO EAT.

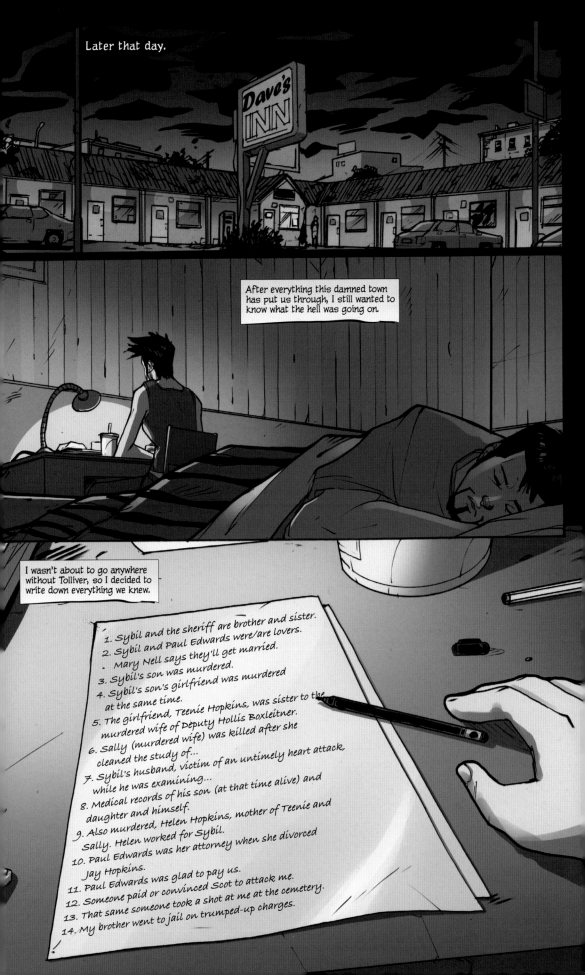

Later that day.

After everything this damned town has put us through, I still wanted to know what the hell was going on.

I wasn't about to go anywhere without Tolliver, so I decided to write down everything we knew.

1. Sybil and the sheriff are brother and sister.
2. Sybil and Paul Edwards were/are lovers. Mary Nell says they'll get married.
3. Sybil's son was murdered.
4. Sybil's son's girlfriend was murdered at the same time.
5. The girlfriend, Teenie Hopkins, was sister to the murdered wife of Deputy Hollis Boxleitner.
6. Sally (murdered wife) was killed after she cleaned the study of...
7. Sybil's husband, victim of an untimely heart attack, while he was examining...
8. Medical records of his son (at that time alive) and daughter and himself.
9. Also murdered, Helen Hopkins, mother of Teenie and Sally. Helen worked for Sybil.
10. Paul Edwards was her attorney when she divorced Jay Hopkins.
11. Paul Edwards was glad to pay us.
12. Someone paid or convinced Scot to attack me.
13. That same someone took a shot at me at the cemetery.
14. My brother went to jail on trumped-up charges.

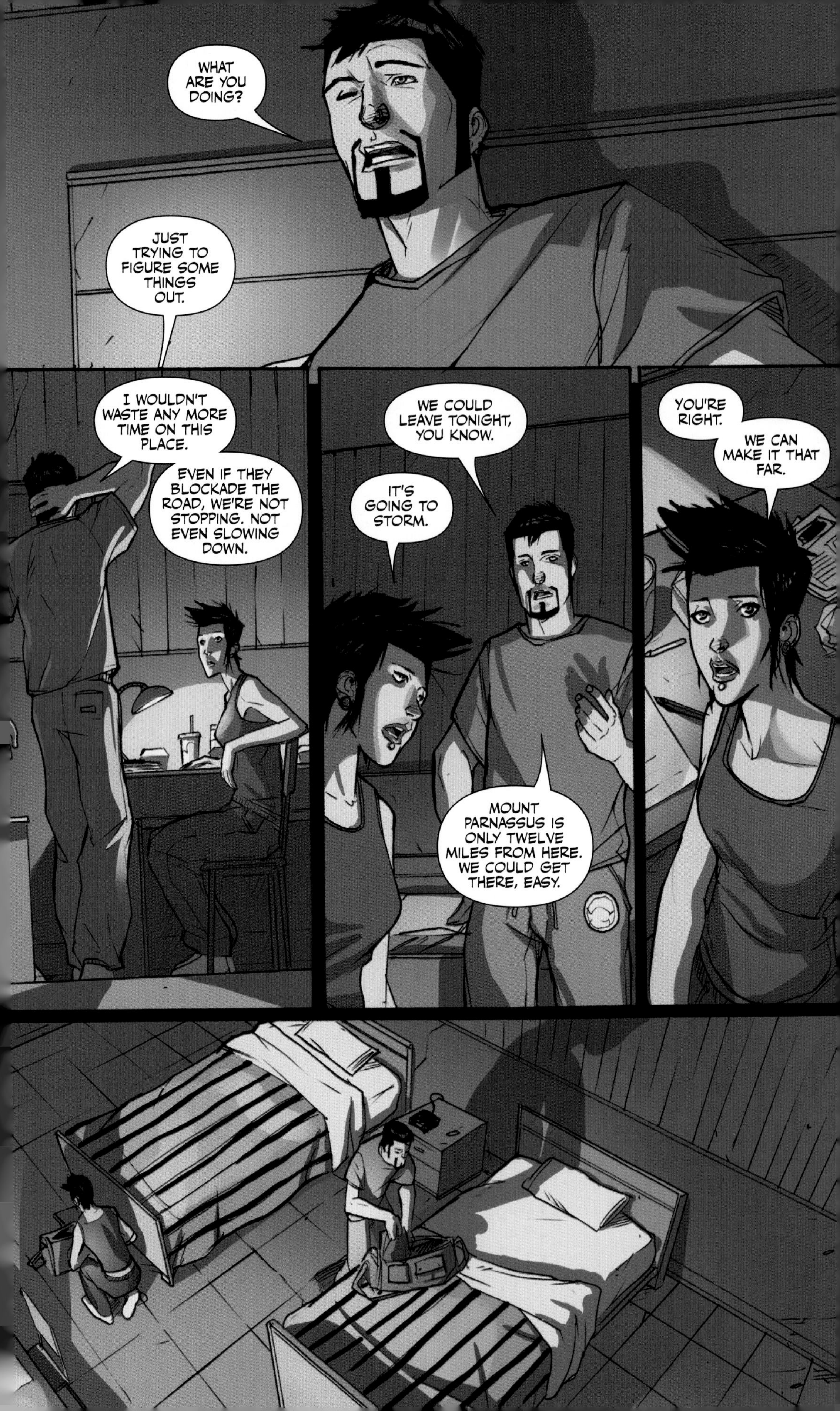
WHAT ARE YOU DOING?
JUST TRYING TO FIGURE SOME THINGS OUT.
I WOULDN'T WASTE ANY MORE TIME ON THIS PLACE.
EVEN IF THEY BLOCKADE THE ROAD, WE'RE NOT STOPPING. NOT EVEN SLOWING DOWN.
WE COULD LEAVE TONIGHT, YOU KNOW.
IT'S GOING TO STORM.
MOUNT PARNASSUS IS ONLY TWELVE MILES FROM HERE. WE COULD GET THERE, EASY.
YOU'RE RIGHT.
WE CAN MAKE IT THAT FAR.

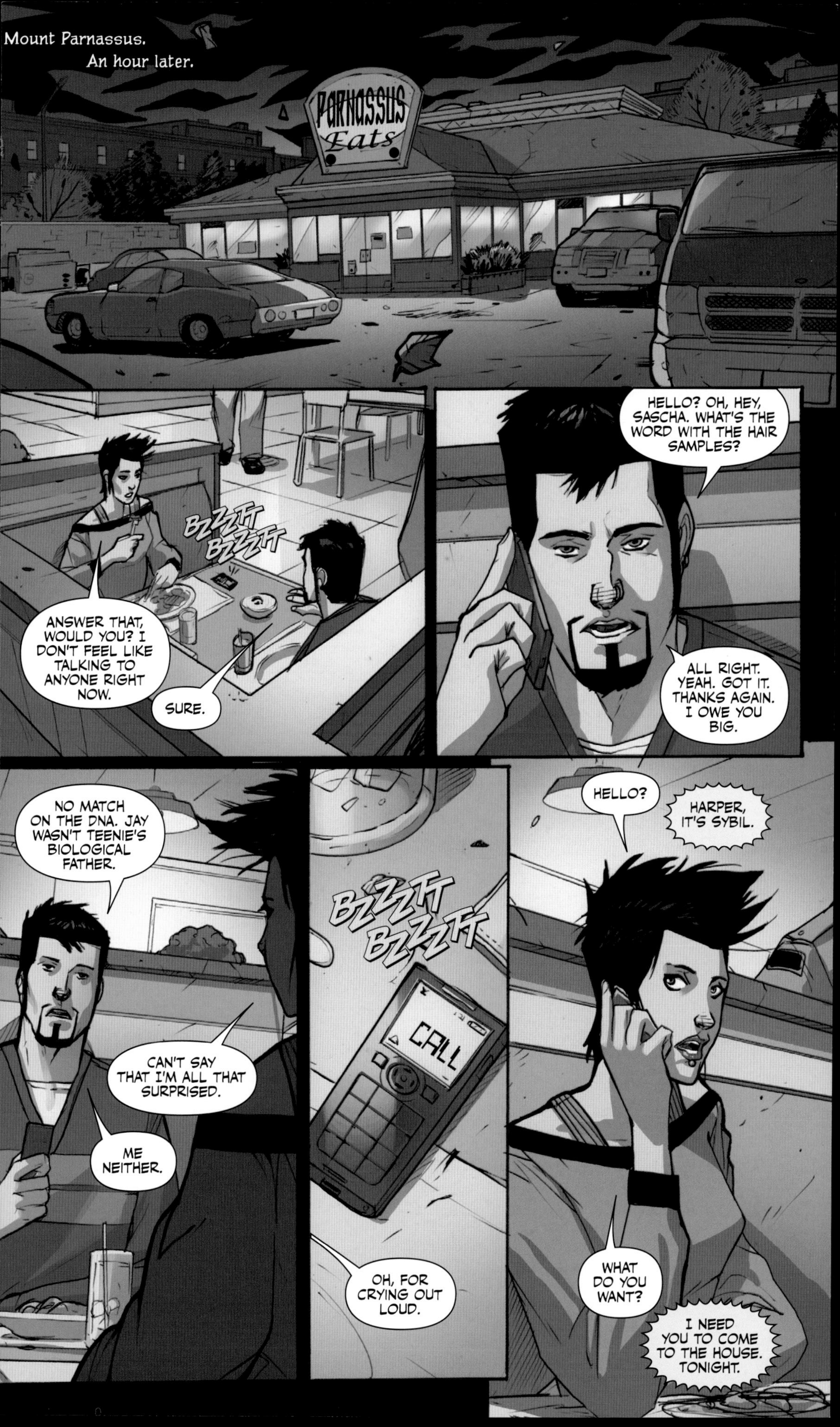
Mount Parnassus.
An hour later.
Parnassus Eats
BZZZFT BZZZFT
ANSWER THAT, WOULD YOU? I DON'T FEEL LIKE TALKING TO ANYONE RIGHT NOW.
SURE.
HELLO? OH, HEY, SASCHA. WHAT'S THE WORD WITH THE HAIR SAMPLES?
ALL RIGHT. YEAH. GOT IT. THANKS AGAIN. I OWE YOU BIG.
NO MATCH ON THE DNA. JAY WASN'T TEENIE'S BIOLOGICAL FATHER.
CAN'T SAY THAT I'M ALL THAT SURPRISED.
ME NEITHER.
BZZZFT BZZZFT
CALL
OH, FOR CRYING OUT LOUD.
HELLO?
HARPER, IT'S SYBIL.
WHAT DO YOU WANT?
I NEED YOU TO COME TO THE HOUSE. TONIGHT.

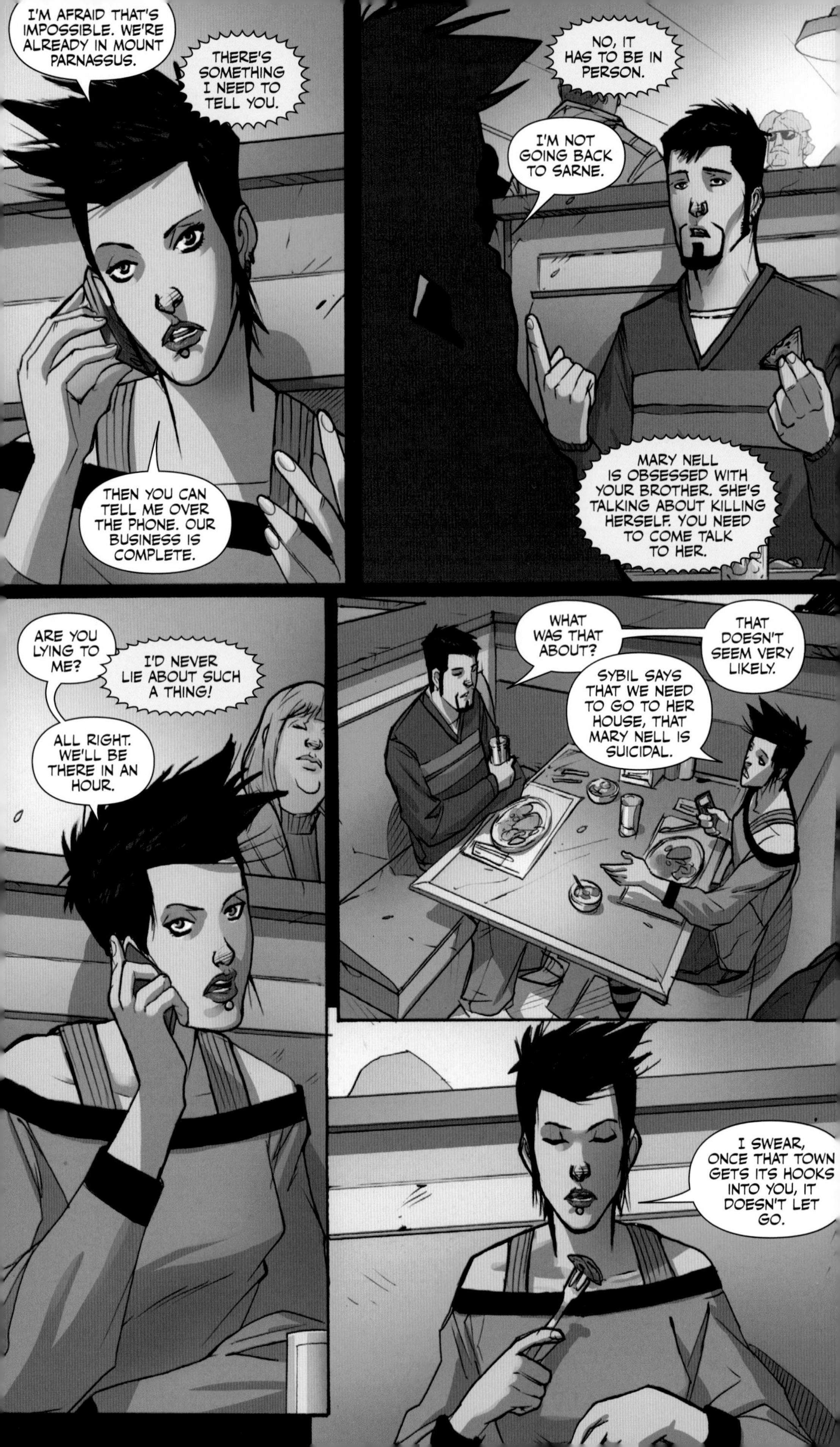
I'M AFRAID THAT'S IMPOSSIBLE. WE'RE ALREADY IN MOUNT PARNASSUS.
THERE'S SOMETHING I NEED TO TELL YOU.
THEN YOU CAN TELL ME OVER THE PHONE. OUR BUSINESS IS COMPLETE.
NO, IT HAS TO BE IN PERSON.
I'M NOT GOING BACK TO SARNE.
MARY NELL IS OBSESSED WITH YOUR BROTHER. SHE'S TALKING ABOUT KILLING HERSELF. YOU NEED TO COME TALK TO HER.
ARE YOU LYING TO ME?
I'D NEVER LIE ABOUT SUCH A THING!
ALL RIGHT. WE'LL BE THERE IN AN HOUR.
WHAT WAS THAT ABOUT?
SYBIL SAYS THAT WE NEED TO GO TO HER HOUSE, THAT MARY NELL IS SUICIDAL.
THAT DOESN'T SEEM VERY LIKELY.
I SWEAR, ONCE THAT TOWN GETS ITS HOOKS INTO YOU, IT DOESN'T LET GO.

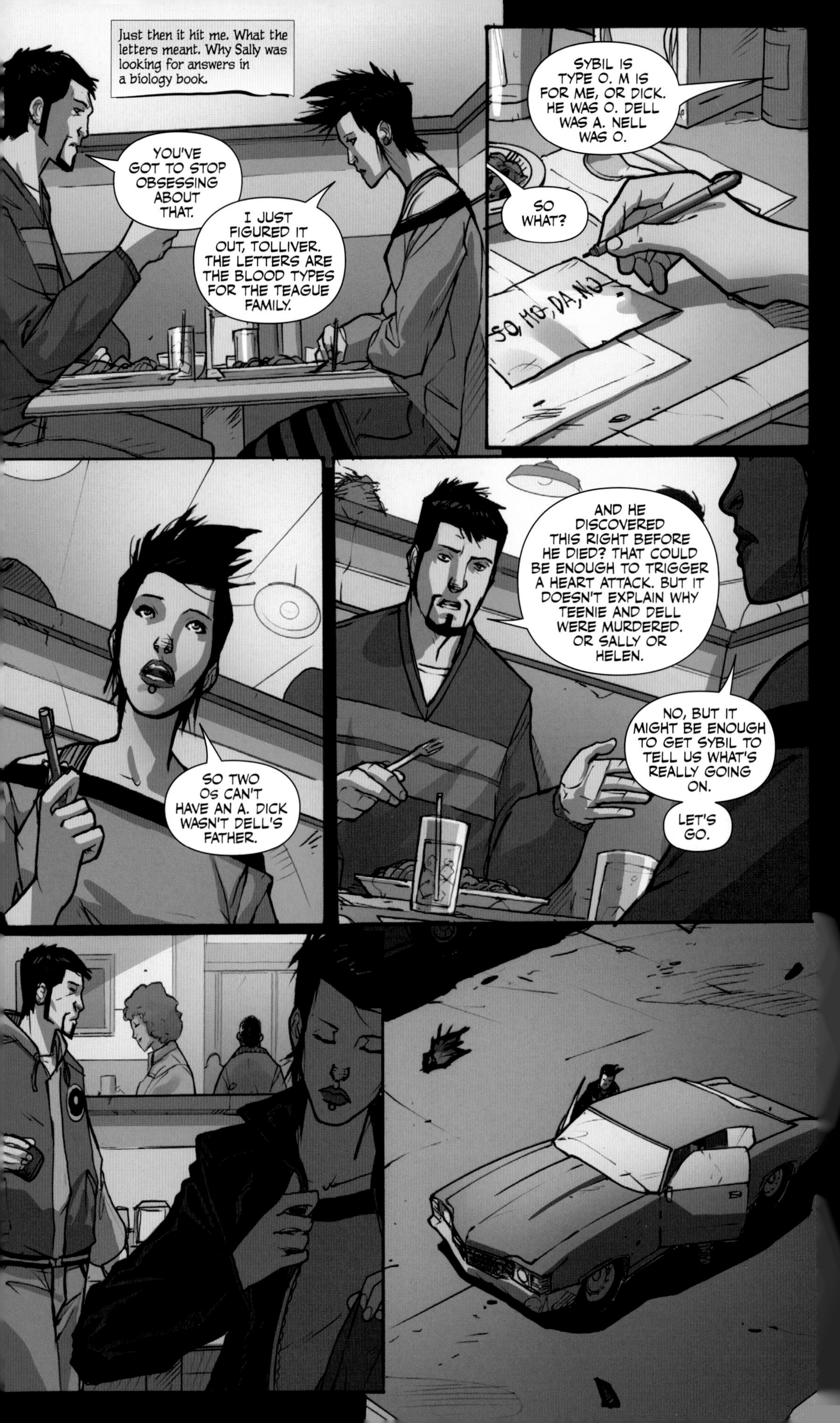
Just then it hit me. What the letters meant. Why Sally was looking for answers in a biology book.
YOU'VE GOT TO STOP OBSESSING ABOUT THAT.
I JUST FIGURED IT OUT, TOLLIVER. THE LETTERS ARE THE BLOOD TYPES FOR THE TEAGUE FAMILY.
SYBIL IS TYPE O. M IS FOR ME, OR DICK. HE WAS O. DELL WAS A. NELL WAS O.
SO WHAT?
SO, MO, DA, NO
SO TWO Os CAN'T HAVE AN A. DICK WASN'T DELL'S FATHER.
AND HE DISCOVERED THIS RIGHT BEFORE HE DIED? THAT COULD BE ENOUGH TO TRIGGER A HEART ATTACK. BUT IT DOESN'T EXPLAIN WHY TEENIE AND DELL WERE MURDERED. OR SALLY OR HELEN.
NO, BUT IT MIGHT BE ENOUGH TO GET SYBIL TO TELL US WHAT'S REALLY GOING ON.
LET'S GO.

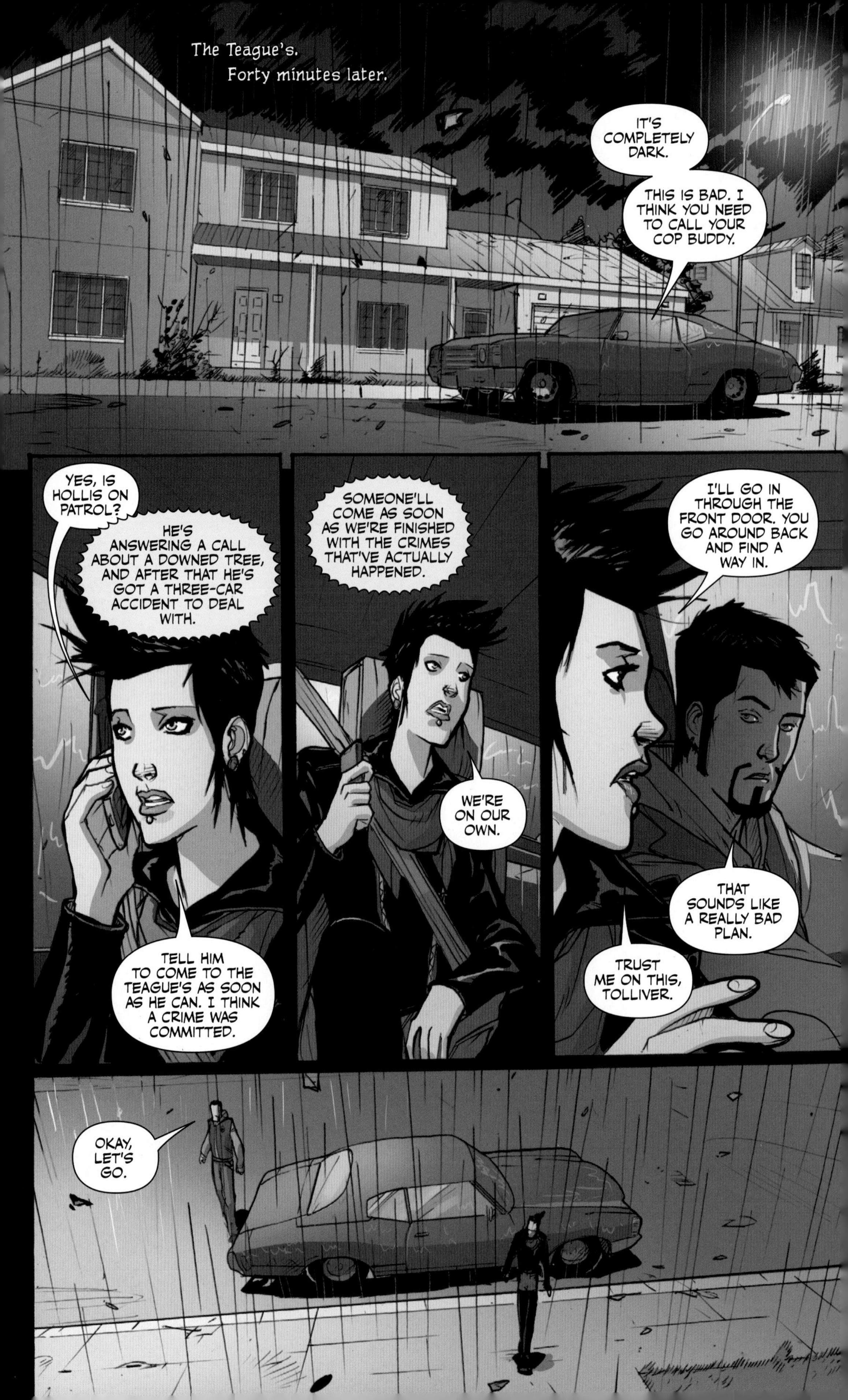
The Teague's.
Forty minutes later.
IT'S COMPLETELY DARK.
THIS IS BAD. I THINK YOU NEED TO CALL YOUR COP BUDDY.
YES, IS HOLLIS ON PATROL?
HE'S ANSWERING A CALL ABOUT A DOWNED TREE, AND AFTER THAT HE'S GOT A THREE-CAR ACCIDENT TO DEAL WITH.
TELL HIM TO COME TO THE TEAGUE'S AS SOON AS HE CAN. I THINK A CRIME WAS COMMITTED.
SOMEONE'LL COME AS SOON AS WE'RE FINISHED WITH THE CRIMES THAT'VE ACTUALLY HAPPENED.
WE'RE ON OUR OWN.
I'LL GO IN THROUGH THE FRONT DOOR. YOU GO AROUND BACK AND FIND A WAY IN.
THAT SOUNDS LIKE A REALLY BAD PLAN.
TRUST ME ON THIS, TOLLIVER.
OKAY, LET'S GO.

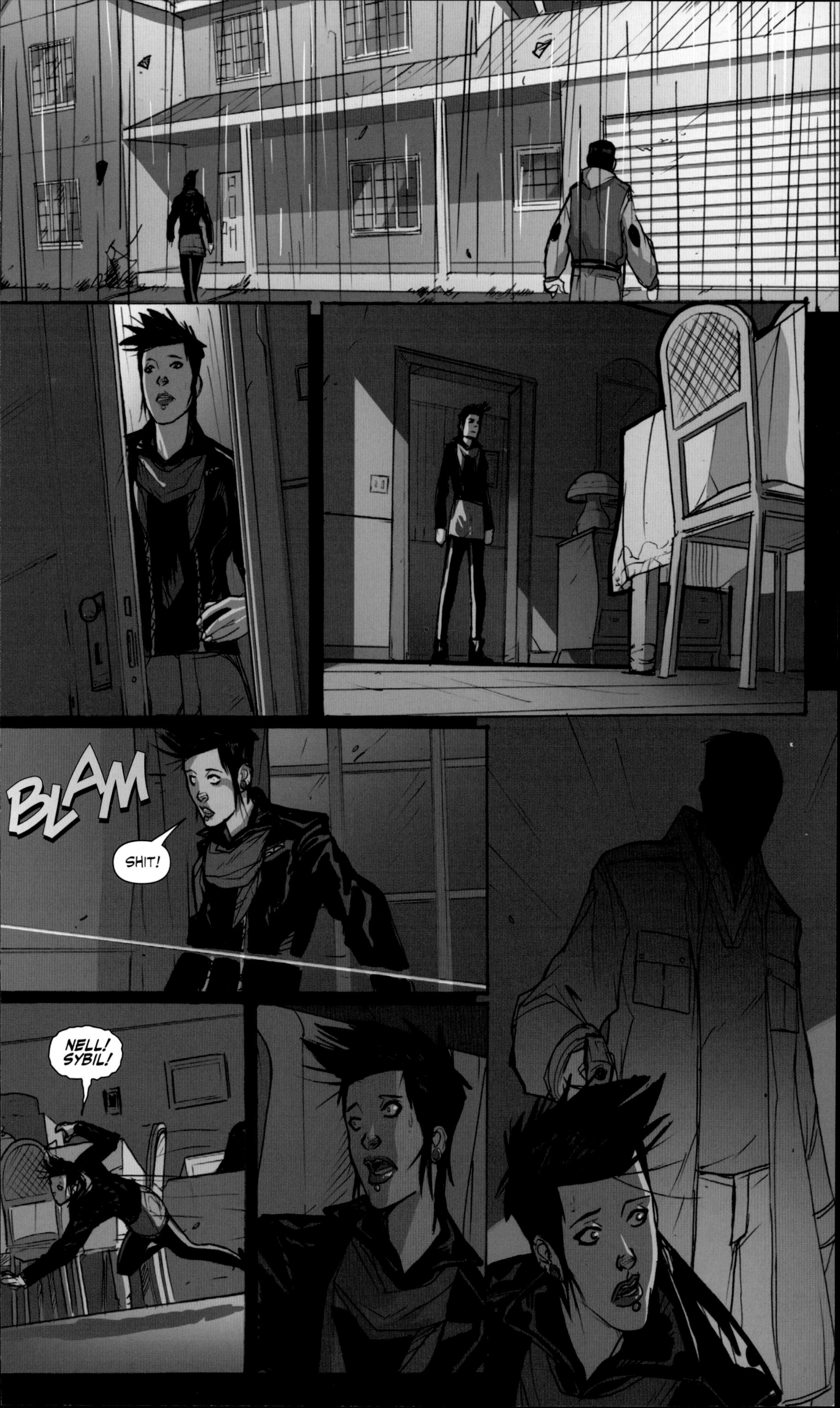
BLAM
SHIT!
NELL! SYBIL!

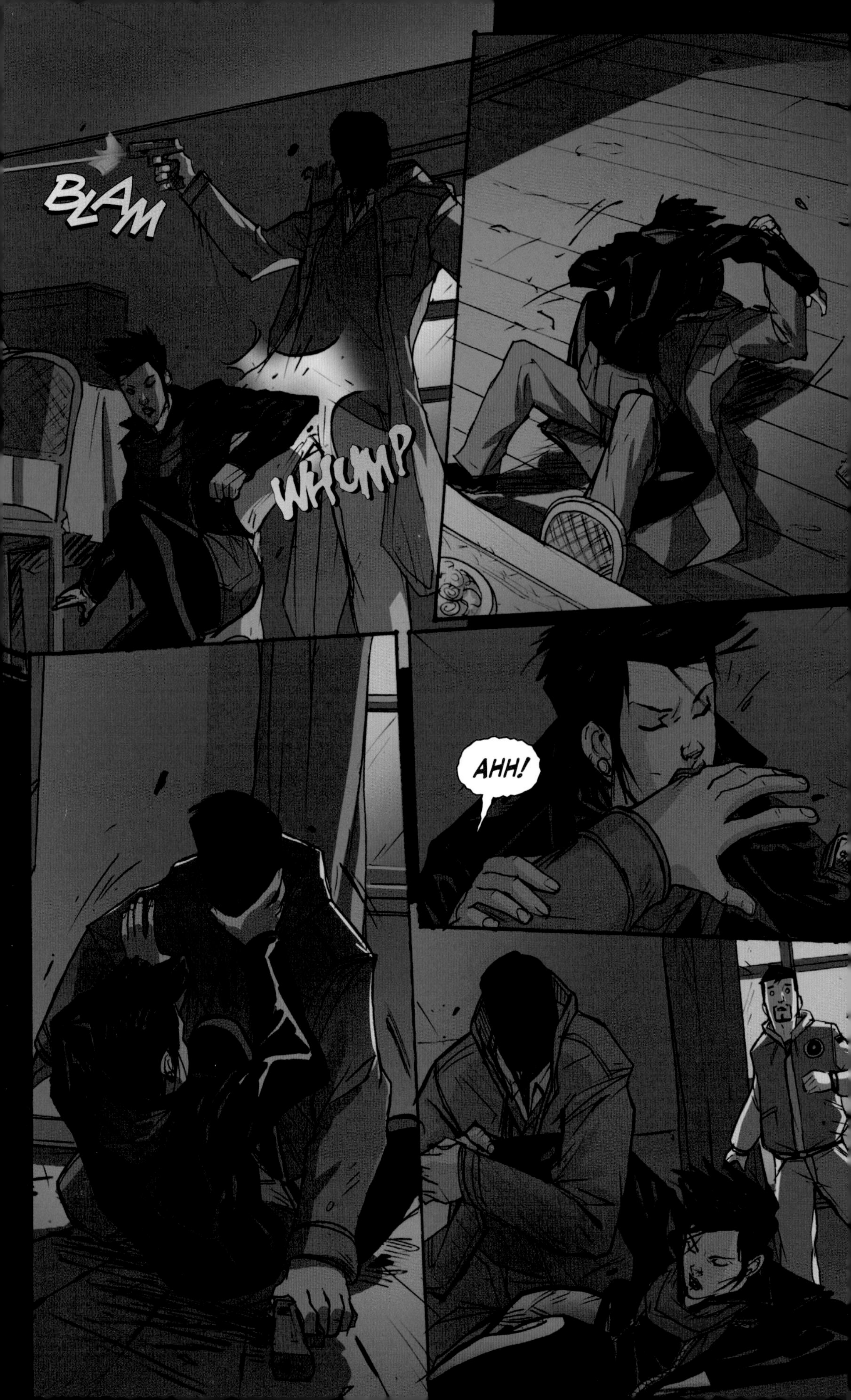
BLAM
WHUMP
AHH!

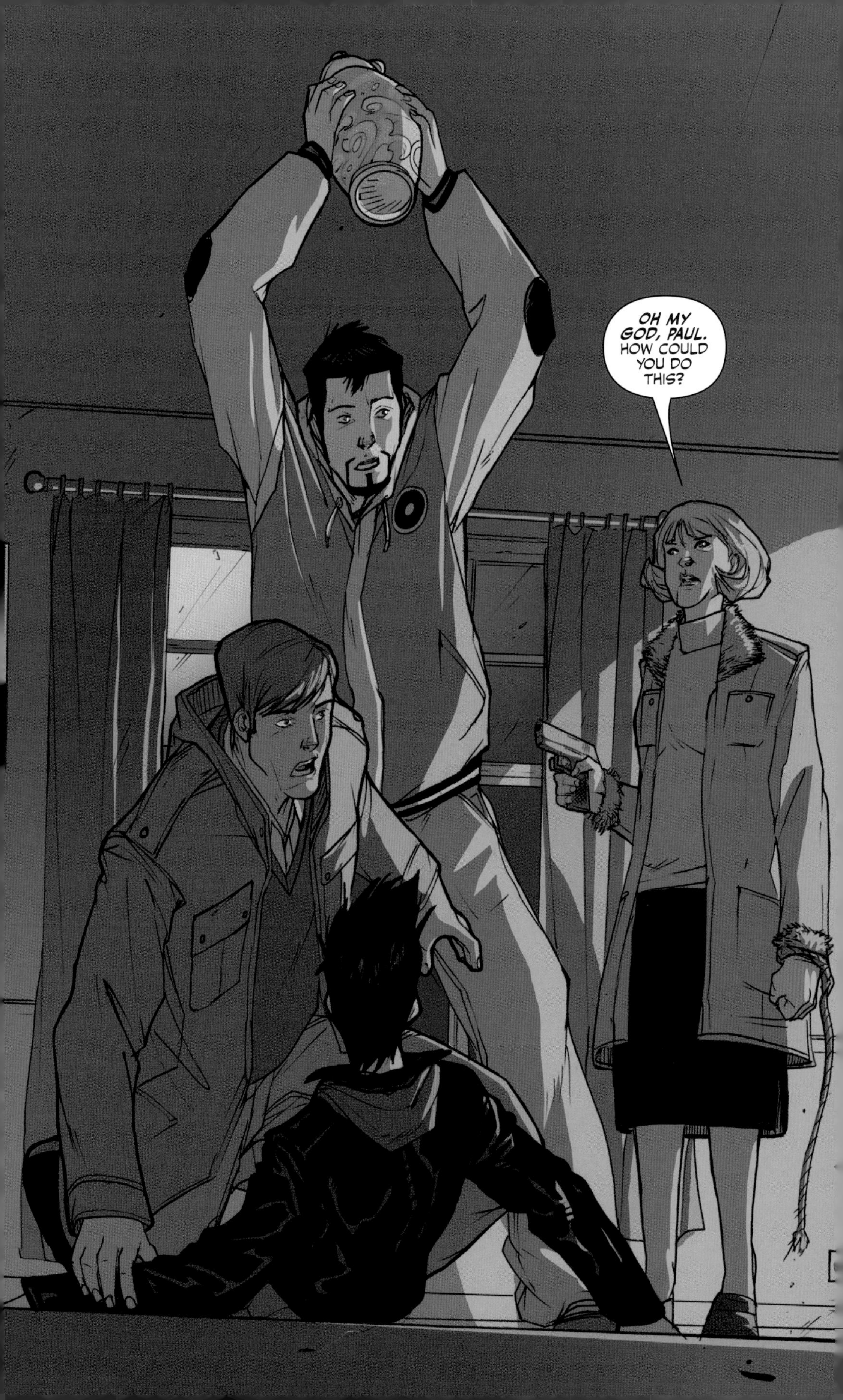
OH MY GOD, PAUL. HOW COULD YOU DO THIS?

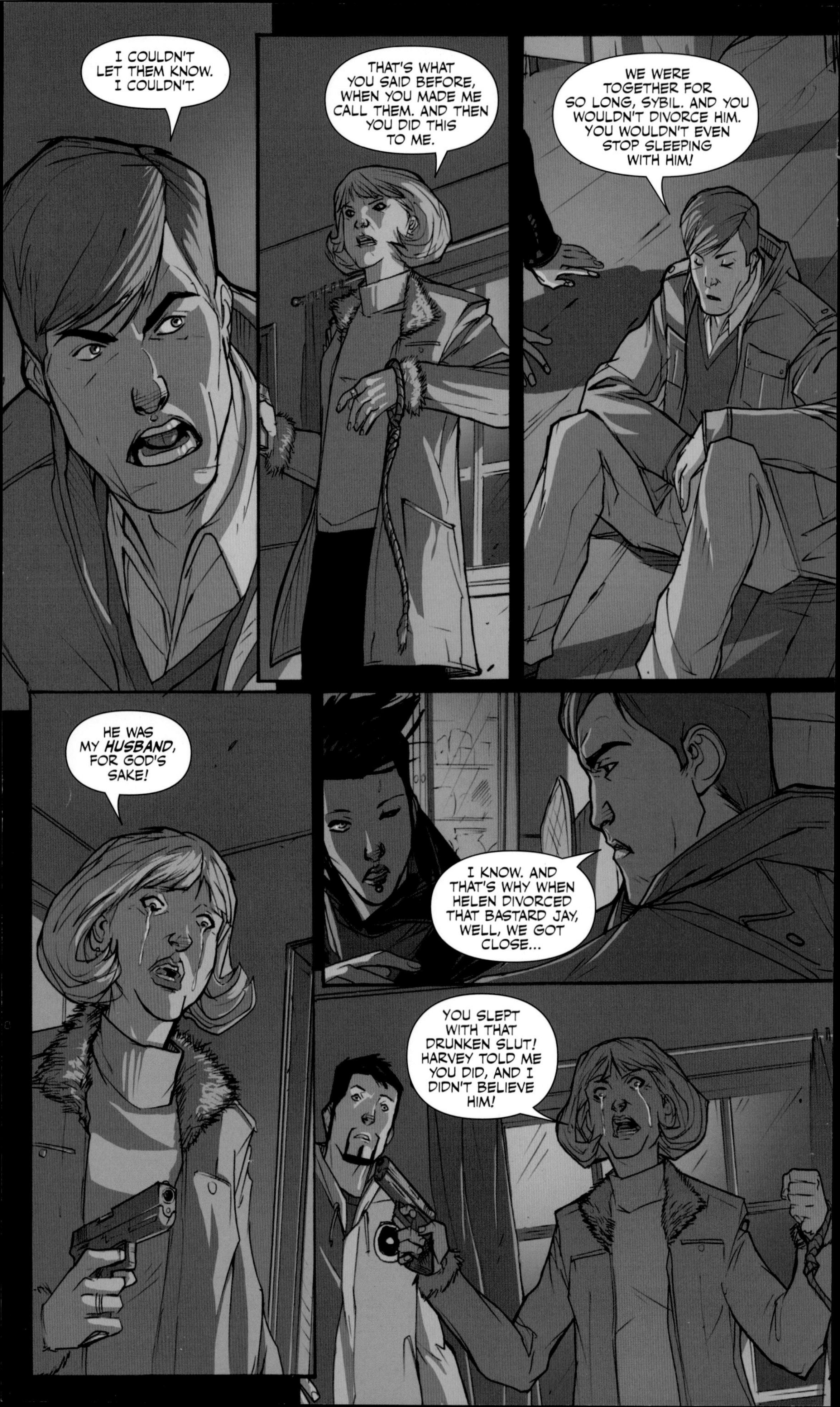
I COULDN'T LET THEM KNOW. I COULDN'T.
THAT'S WHAT YOU SAID BEFORE, WHEN YOU MADE ME CALL THEM. AND THEN YOU DID THIS TO ME.
WE WERE TOGETHER FOR SO LONG, SYBIL. AND YOU WOULDN'T DIVORCE HIM. YOU WOULDN'T EVEN STOP SLEEPING WITH HIM!
HE WAS MY *HUSBAND*, FOR GOD'S SAKE!
I KNOW. AND THAT'S WHY WHEN HELEN DIVORCED THAT BASTARD JAY, WELL, WE GOT CLOSE...
YOU SLEPT WITH THAT DRUNKEN SLUT! HARVEY TOLD ME YOU DID, AND I DIDN'T BELIEVE HIM!

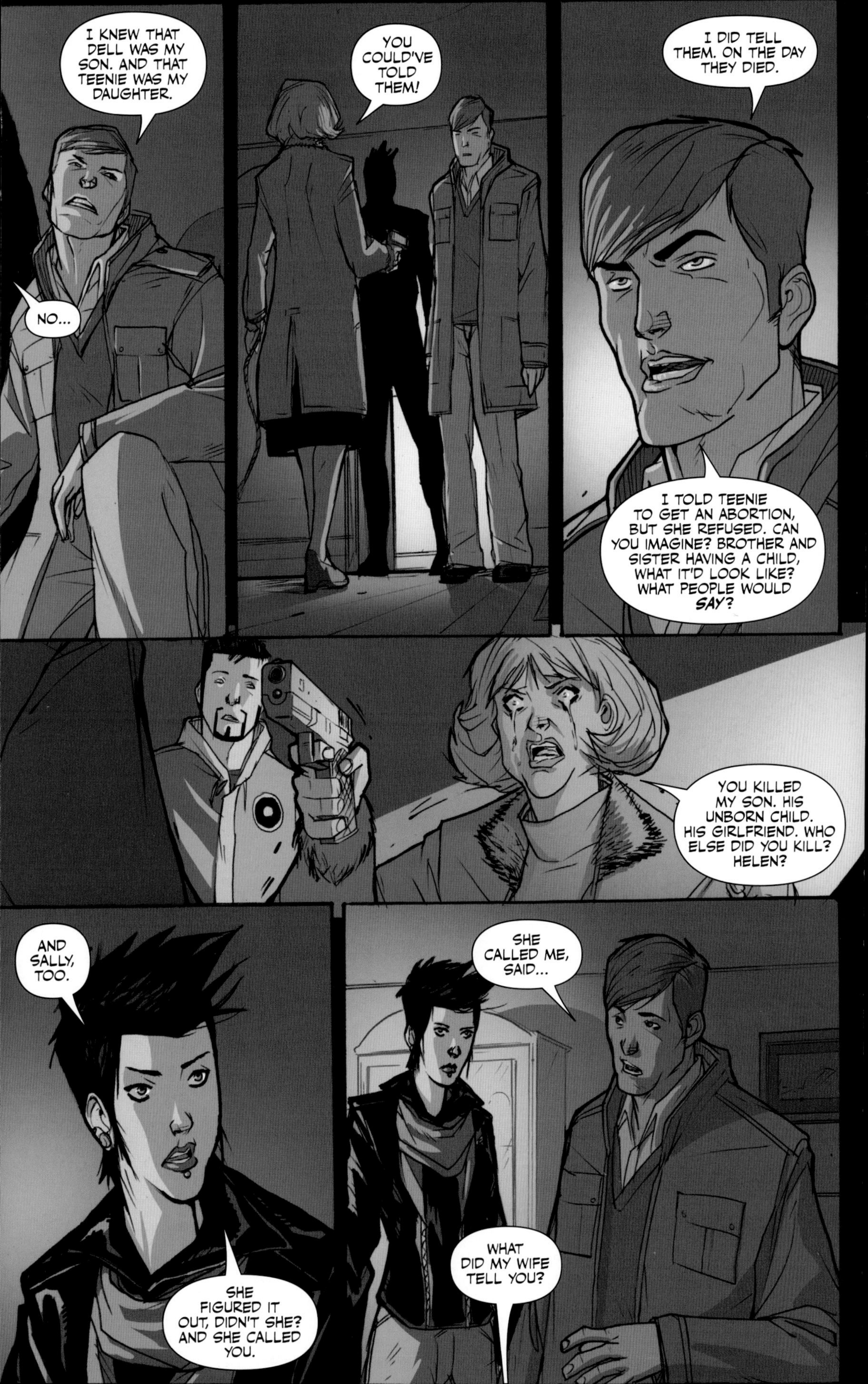
I KNEW THAT DELL WAS MY SON. AND THAT TEENIE WAS MY DAUGHTER.
NO...
YOU COULD'VE TOLD THEM!
I DID TELL THEM. ON THE DAY THEY DIED.
I TOLD TEENIE TO GET AN ABORTION, BUT SHE REFUSED. CAN YOU IMAGINE? BROTHER AND SISTER HAVING A CHILD, WHAT IT'D LOOK LIKE? WHAT PEOPLE WOULD *SAY*?
YOU KILLED MY SON. HIS UNBORN CHILD. HIS GIRLFRIEND. WHO ELSE DID YOU KILL? HELEN?
AND SALLY, TOO.
SHE FIGURED IT OUT, DIDN'T SHE? AND SHE CALLED YOU.
SHE CALLED ME, SAID...
WHAT DID MY WIFE TELL YOU?

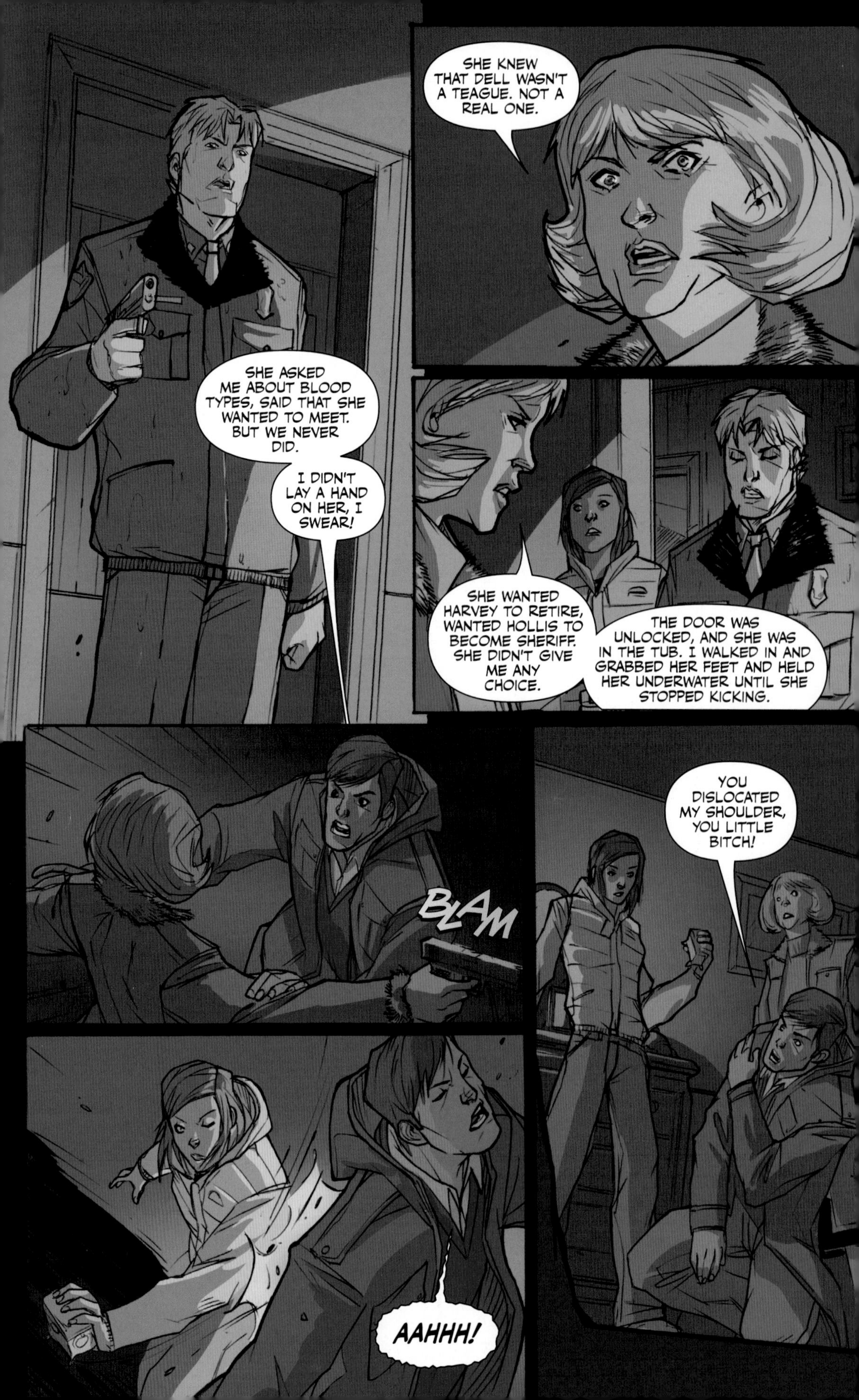
SHE ASKED ME ABOUT BLOOD TYPES, SAID THAT SHE WANTED TO MEET. BUT WE NEVER DID.
I DIDN'T LAY A HAND ON HER, I SWEAR!
SHE KNEW THAT DELL WASN'T A TEAGUE. NOT A REAL ONE.
SHE WANTED HARVEY TO RETIRE, WANTED HOLLIS TO BECOME SHERIFF. SHE DIDN'T GIVE ME ANY CHOICE.
THE DOOR WAS UNLOCKED, AND SHE WAS IN THE TUB. I WALKED IN AND GRABBED HER FEET AND HELD HER UNDERWATER UNTIL SHE STOPPED KICKING.
BLAM
AAHHH!
YOU DISLOCATED MY SHOULDER, YOU LITTLE BITCH!

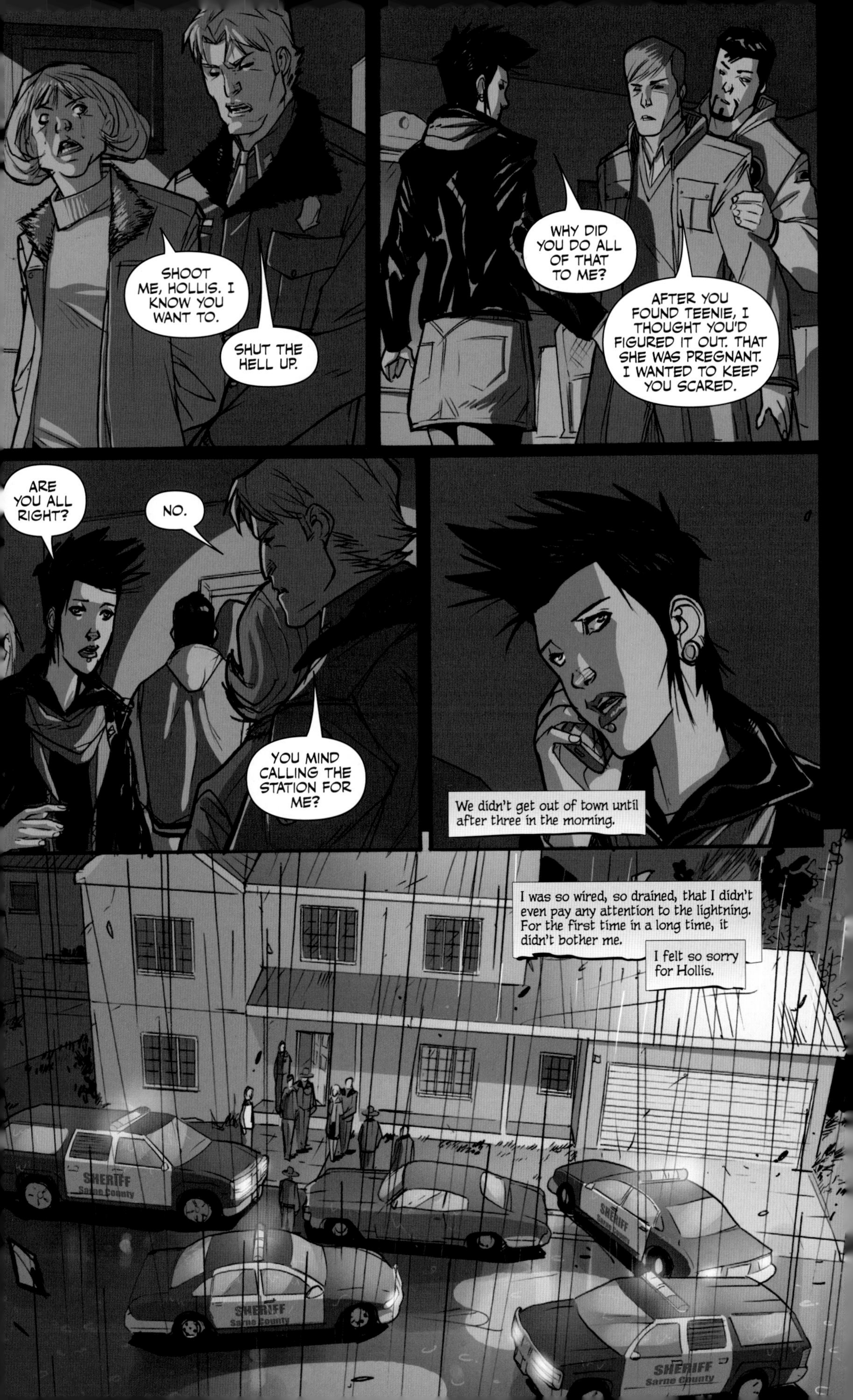
SHOOT ME, HOLLIS. I KNOW YOU WANT TO.
SHUT THE HELL UP.
WHY DID YOU DO ALL OF THAT TO ME?
AFTER YOU FOUND TEENIE, I THOUGHT YOU'D FIGURED IT OUT. THAT SHE WAS PREGNANT. I WANTED TO KEEP YOU SCARED.
ARE YOU ALL RIGHT?
NO.
YOU MIND CALLING THE STATION FOR ME?
We didn't get out of town until after three in the morning.
I was so wired, so drained, that I didn't even pay any attention to the lightning. For the first time in a long time, it didn't bother me.
I felt so sorry for Hollis.
SHERIFF
Sarne County
SHERIFF
Sarne County
SHERIFF
Sarne County

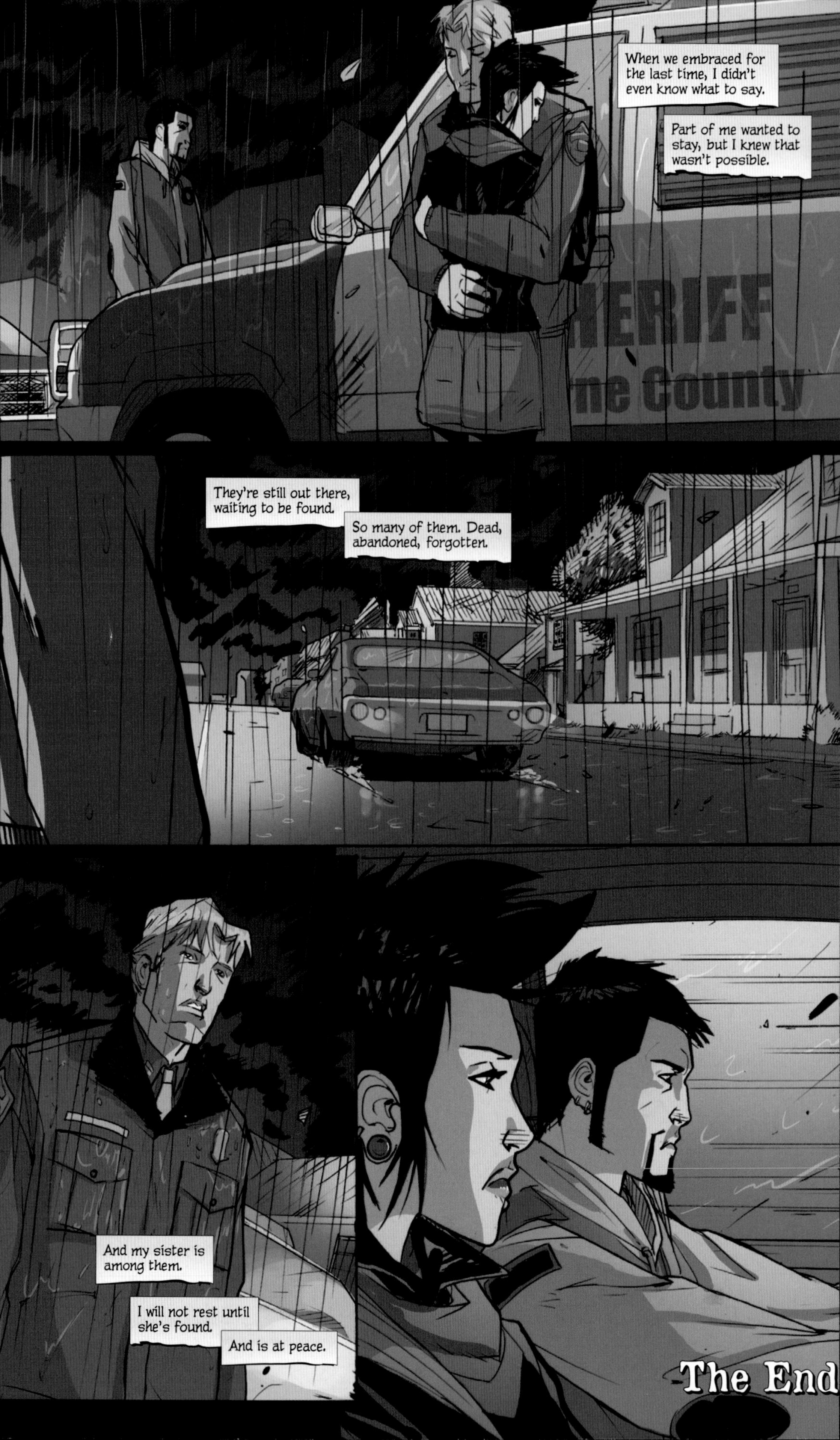

When we embraced for the last time, I didn't even know what to say.
Part of me wanted to stay, but I knew that wasn't possible.
HERIFF
ne County
They're still out there, waiting to be found.
So many of them. Dead, abandoned, forgotten.
And my sister is among them.
I will not rest until she's found.
And is at peace.
The End

Grave Sight

BONUS MATERIAL

COVERING *Grave Sight*

A LOOK AT THE COVERS FOR *GRAVE SIGHT*

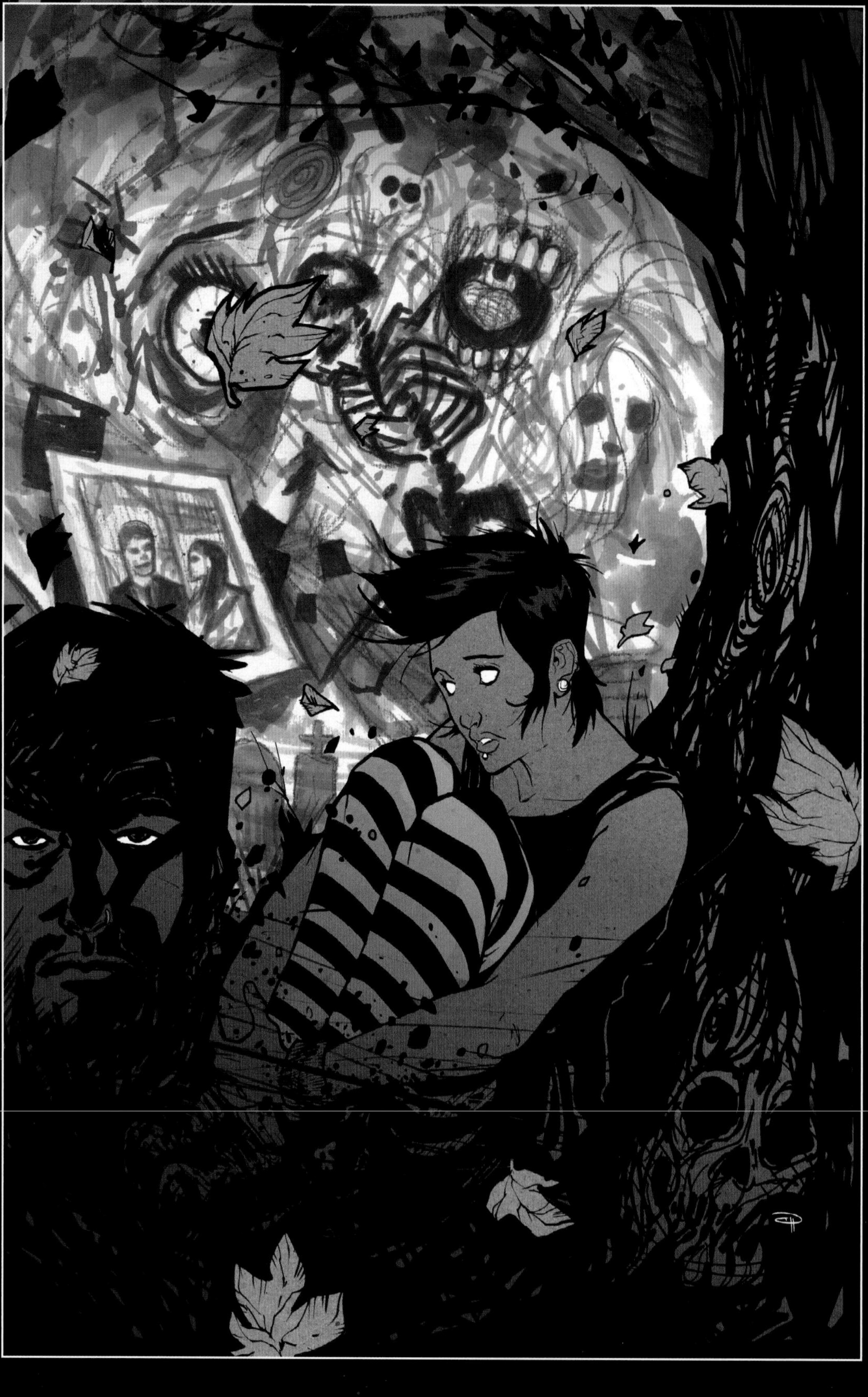

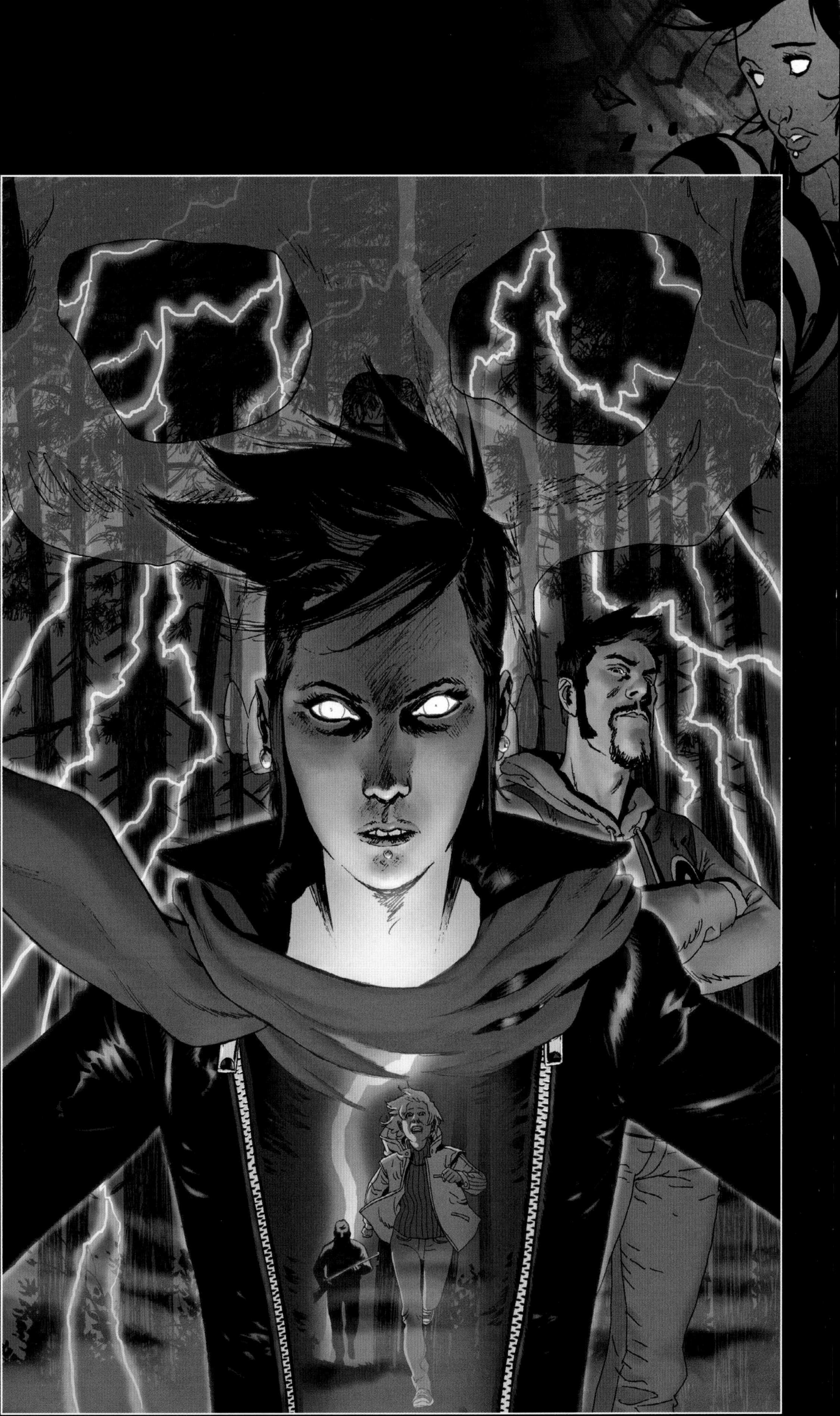

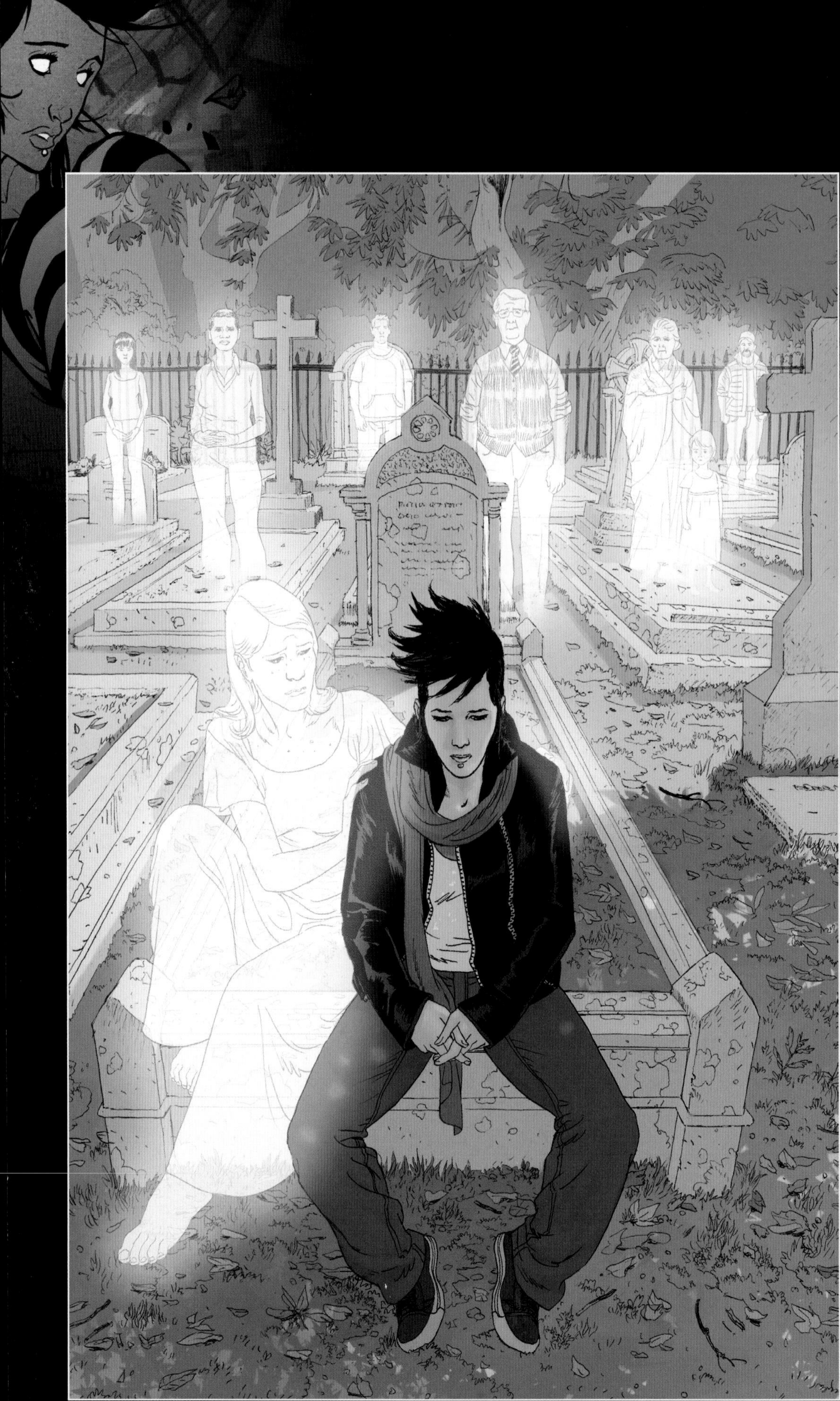

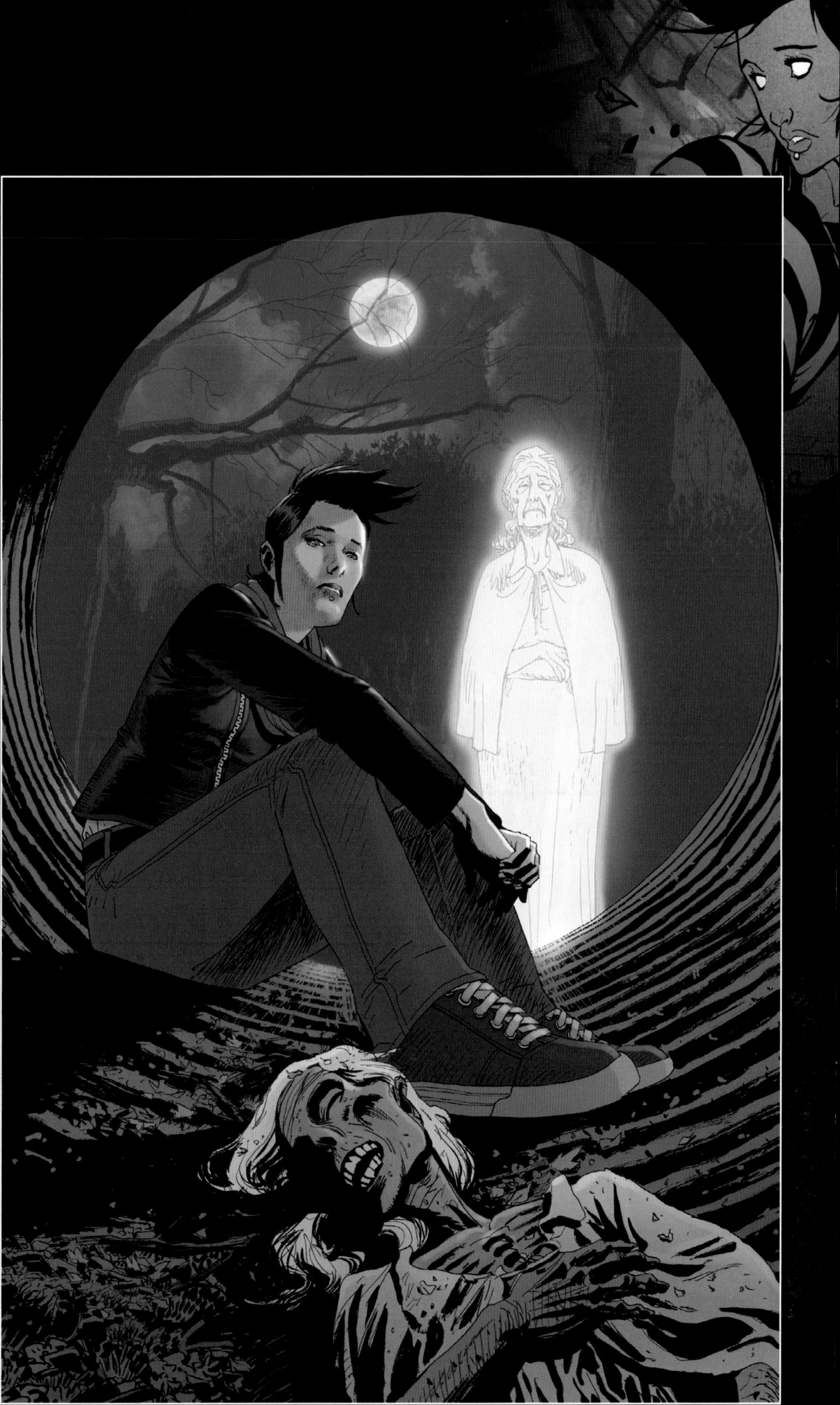

CREATING *Grave Sight*

A LOOK AT *GRAVE SIGHT*'S ART FROM PENCIL TO COLOR

Left: final pencils and inks by DENIS MEDRI
Right top: rough layout by DENIS MEDRI
Right bottom: final colors by PAOLO FRANCESCUTTO and final letters by BILL TORTOLINI

Left: final pencils and inks by **DENIS MEDRI**
Right top: rough layout by **DENIS MEDRI**
Right bottom: final colors by **PAOLO FRANCESCUTTO** and final letters by **BILL TORTOLINI**

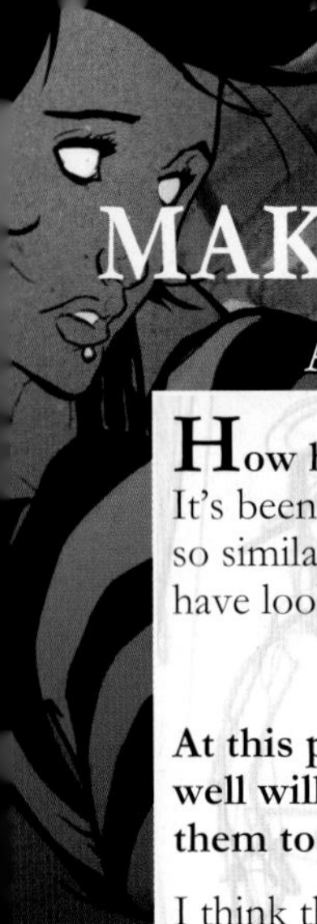

THE MAKING OF Grave Sight

AN INTERVIEW WITH NOVELIST CHARLAINE HARRIS

How have you enjoyed seeing Harper Connelly converted to the comics format?
It's been interesting. Sometimes I get pretty excited by what I see in the artwork, because it looks so similar to the pictures in my head. Sometimes I think, "Oh, gosh, I never thought it might have looked that way!" And that, too, is a pretty interesting perspective.

At this point in the Harper Connelly series, which is now the end of the first novel, how well will readers know Harper? And what should they know about what's coming up for them to discover?

I think that Harper is on her way to becoming a person who doesn't keep herself closed in, a person who connects more with the human race around her, and a person who is willing to admit the most emotional thing in her life. And I think that she also becomes a little more realistic in a lot of ways. I mean, in the books anyway, she comes to realize she can't maintain her two little half-sisters with any consistency. She comes to understand that they're well-off where they are. She comes to understand that a lot of the things she's been dreaming about are going to remain dreams but that she and Tolliver can have a life together. And I think she comes to be a little more at peace with herself.

Harper has the ability to see how and why people died...but not who killed them if they were murdered. How did you develop the parameters of her powers?

Well, it wouldn't be a very long book if she just said, "Oh, yeah, it was him!" [Laughs.] It had to be something that would work in a mystery setting. And, obviously, if you can see the identity of the murderer, that makes for a very short, boring book. So I had to put a limit to it. And her connection is with the bones of the victims, so I don't think that that's a totally unreasonable limitation to put on it.

Where did the inspiration for *Grave Sight* come from?

I was wanting to write something different from the Sookie Stackhouse novels, and I wanted to write something maybe a little darker—in my view anyway. I know that some people think the Sookie ones are quite dark, but they're not, in my view. And I've always been pretty interested in lightning. No matter how often I read an explanation of why lightning happens, it still seems like magic to me. I've always been interested in stories of people who have been struck by lightning and lived to talk about it. So I joined a LISTSERV for people who've been lightning-struck, and they were kind enough to let me lurk there for a while. I just found it really fascinating what a grab bag of consequences they suffered as a result of being struck by lightning. So my imagination began to take off from that.

Was Harper based on any real-life person you observed in that group?

No, she wasn't.

How would you compare Harper Connelly to Sookie Stackhouse?

Well, certainly Harper is a more grim personality who grew up without the love and caring that Sookie had when she grew up. Sookie grew up with a strong sense of community, and Harper didn't. Harper only had her siblings to help her, and they weren't really her siblings. Though Sookie had a very rough upbringing because of her telepathy, Harper was betrayed by everybody around her. Her parents, who should have taken the best care of her, were the ones who let her down the most.

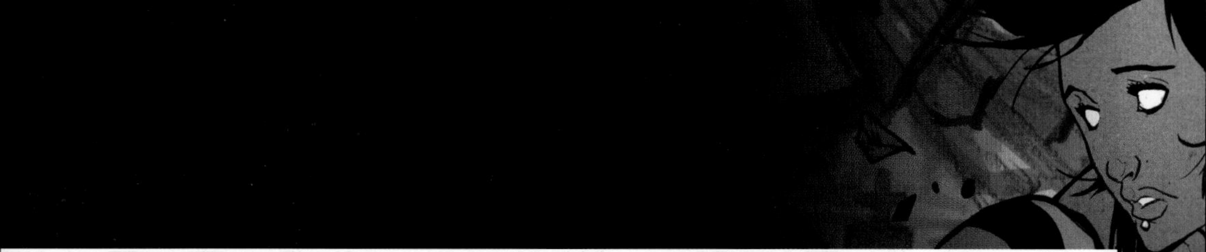

She's somewhat jaded, but she's not exactly alienated from the world—at least not on her end. Other people try to alienate her more than she tries to actively isolate herself.

I would agree. I think that she's made a very successful adaptation, considering her circumstances.

Both Harper and Sookie are similar in that they have this singular ability that really sets them apart. Is there something about crafting a heroine such as that, one who has a gift that seems enviable at first, that makes you identify with them as a writer?

Maybe that's a result of growing up as a writer in a society that didn't really believe I could do any such thing. [Laughs.]

But you proved them wrong.

Yeah, I did, but sometimes that's kind of a hollow victory, when you had a pretty intense teenagerdom to live through first. [Laughs.]

Are some of your life experiences mirrored in those of your characters?

Not literally, but maybe figuratively, yes. Maybe in essence the feelings are the same, but the circumstances are different.

Did you have any influence over the art for the book and how artist Denis Medri depicted any scenes?

I get all the artwork first when it's been "roughed in" and then when it's been colored and lettered. Seeing something in the various stages of development is really interesting for me. I feel like I'm learning a little bit about the business.

Have any scenes from the comic book really struck you as interesting, especially when compared to how you wrote them in the prose books?

Well, I think the scene where Harper and Tolliver are talking to one of Teenie's possible fathers, and he's sitting on the front porch of his wife's house after she's been murdered—there's something about that that really struck me. He looks so shifty. You can tell he's done something wrong. I just thought that was a very striking scene.

You wrote four Harper Connelly novels. Do you have any plans to go back to the series at this point?

I don't believe I will, because I'm usually pretty set on walking away when I feel like I've said everything about a character I have to say. And I'm pretty sure I've said everything about Harper that I have to say. Though something else might occur to me.

Did you enjoy developing her character and writing about her?

Absolutely. She's a very interesting person and quite a bit different from anybody I've ever written before. So it was kind of a challenge to represent her fully.

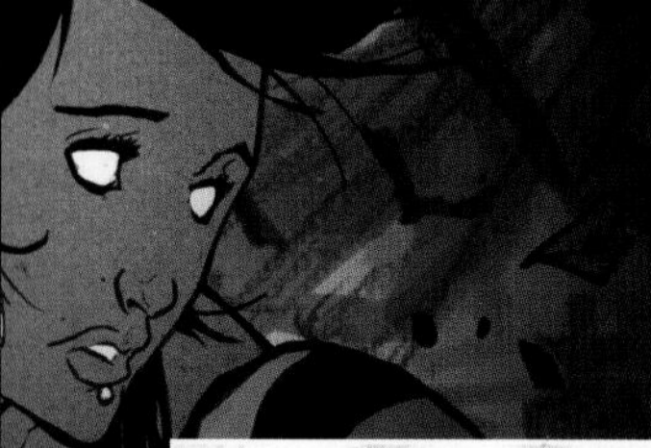

How so?

Well, certainly she had had a super-difficult upbringing—I think more so than any of my other characters—and she is not afraid to admit that she needs other people, which is not the norm for my heroines, who are pretty independent or at least never think too much about the people they do need. But she really needs Tolliver, and she's not afraid to admit it. At the same time, she is professionally stronger than any of my other protagonists. She says, you know, "I do my job and I do it perfectly." She's not afraid of death or afraid of her expertise, her own strong points. I like that about her a lot.

Her confidence in her work is kind of in stark contrast to how other people view her job. Even the people who hire her are often angry at her for it, and the fact that she charges money to tell people how their loved ones died. Is what she's doing a positive thing, in your mind, or is it controversial?

I don't know if I consider it controversial or not. I consider her a true survivor who's making her living in the only way she can think of to do so. She's essentially turning a disability into an asset by earning her living, and Tolliver's, by exploiting the consequences of the terrible thing that happened to her. It's really a case of making lemonade from lemons, I think. And I thought that was kind of admirable myself.

Speaking of Tolliver, her stepbrother, one of the interesting facets about the books is her relationship with him, which grows over the books. What do you think of how the comic portrays their relationship at this point?

I think it's absolutely like it was in the books. I'm really delighted to see that they're adhering to the story line in the books so closely and picking up all the essential markers that are leading to their eventual rapprochement.

Was Tolliver a character you enjoyed developing and writing?

Yes. He's not as clear to me as Harper is, but I think he finds happiness, too. He finds out more about his family, and he comes to understand that they've been living a lie in a lot of ways, which is sad, but it's better to know than to not know.

The *Grave Sight* comics are structured and paced a little differently than the prose books. How did you feel about the different setup of the comic?

Well, certainly after all my experiences, I know that different mediums require different structures. I've certainly seen that in the *True Blood* television series, and it doesn't surprise me at all that the comic-book series would need to be told in a different way.

Were there any scenes from the prose book that you were disappointed weren't able to make it into the comic adaptation?

I try not to second-guess the artist, the same way I've made my peace with the television show. Not everything from the books could be adapted—not every point I loved or felt was especially well done could be brought into the pared-down medium of the comic book. And the same thing with the TV show, which, of course, is very different from the original work. I guess I've really adjusted to the fact that if you translate my work into something different, there are going to be additions and subtractions.

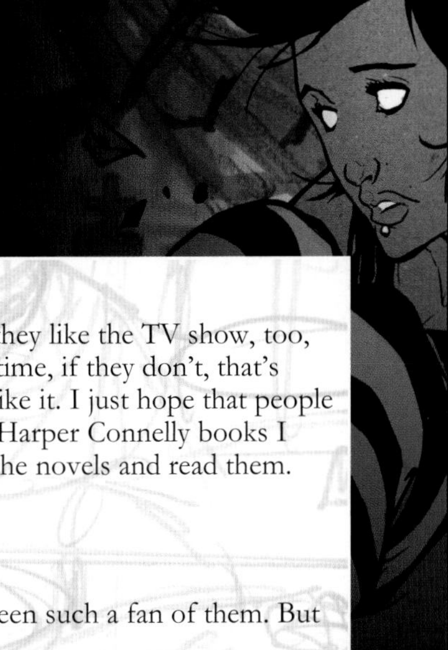

A lot of your fans aren't always so calm about those changes.

Oh, yeah! Oh, yeah. I hear about it a lot. And honestly, I hope that they like the TV show, too, because I think it's a fun show. I enjoy watching it. But at the same time, if they don't, that's okay, too. It's not the books. I don't take it personally if they don't like it. I just hope that people will always enjoy the books as well as the TV show, just as with the Harper Connelly books I hope that people will enjoy the comic books and again will pick up the novels and read them.

Were you a fan of comics before doing this?

I did read them as a child. I loved Archie! In latter years, I haven't been such a fan of them. But I'm seeing that the art is really extraordinary now.

In addition to working on this, you're doing another graphic novel, called *Cemetery Girl*, with writer Christopher Golden. What can you reveal about that?

It'll be released this year. It's about a young woman who gets dumped in a cemetery. She's completely lost her memory, and she doesn't know why she's there or where she came from. She doesn't know her name. But she does know, of course, that someone is trying to kill her. In fact, she actually dies for a minute and comes back. She's quite young, in her teens, and she starts living in the cemetery. She finds a crypt and lines it with the fake grass they cover the mounds with. She starts developing her whole life in this cemetery because she's afraid to come out into the open since she doesn't know who's trying to kill her.

Has working on *Cemetery Girl* affected how you look at the comic-book adaptations of your work?

Well, of course I'm looking at the comic books in a much smarter way now that I'm learning how they're being put together, and I'm chiding myself for my ignorance. When they send me the rough sketches, I had been looking at them going, "I can't really make sense out of these. I don't know why they show them to me!" But now I'm getting it a lot more, and I'm studying the way the panels are put together, and the lettering. And how they pick the right words for the characters to say. And I'm trying to learn from looking at the process of producing the Harper comic books with a view to making *Cemetery Girl* better.

There has been talk that the Harper Connelly books would be turned into a television series. Has that moved forward?

CBS and then Syfy had it in development. Both passed.

Would you like to see it adapted to TV?

Yes, I would, but I feel like I've had the Cadillac of TV experiences, so it would be really hard to match that again.

Do you interact much with Alan Ball about what happens on *True Blood*? Does he run things by you?

It's pretty much separate. If I hadn't trusted Alan, I wouldn't have signed the books over to him, because I had other offers I passed up. So Alan is doing his own thing, and I respect that. I admire his talent.

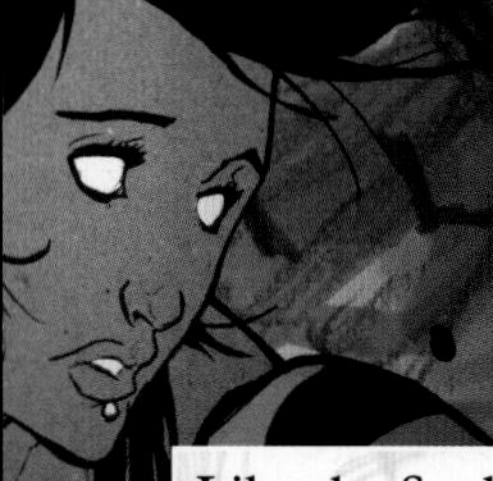

Like the Sookie Stackhouse books, *Grave Sight* is set in the South. Do you think the supernatural stories you write are better suited to the South?

Well, I have a couple of thoughts about that. Of course, I am southern and I write with a southern accent. But I think the supernatural is universal. I've read ghost stories set in Maine that were just as good as ghost stories set in New Orleans. Or California, for that matter. I think the supernatural is with us in every part of the United States. It's just a little prettier when it's got Spanish moss on it.

What first drove your interest in the supernatural?

Isn't everybody interested in the supernatural? Most people want to believe that there is something beyond what we can see and hear and smell. They want to believe there's more.

I would imagine that writing about these types of things allows you to hear some interesting supernatural stories from your readers.

You would think, wouldn't you? But I haven't heard anything that extraordinary. I am *ready* to hear! Bring it on!

Charlaine Harris is a #1 *New York Times* bestselling author who has been writing for thirty years. She was born and raised in the Mississippi River delta area. She is also the author of the successful Sookie Stackhouse fantasy/mystery series about a telepathic waitress named Sookie Stackhouse who works in a bar in the fictional northern Louisiana town of Bon Temps. The Sookie Stackhouse series has proven to be so popular that it has been adapted into *True Blood* for HBO. It was an instant success and is now filming its sixth season. Harris is married and the mother of three, and has lived in the South her entire life.

MEET

CEMETERY GIRL

An original graphic novel by
Charlaine Harris and Christopher Golden

Coming fall 2013 from InkLit

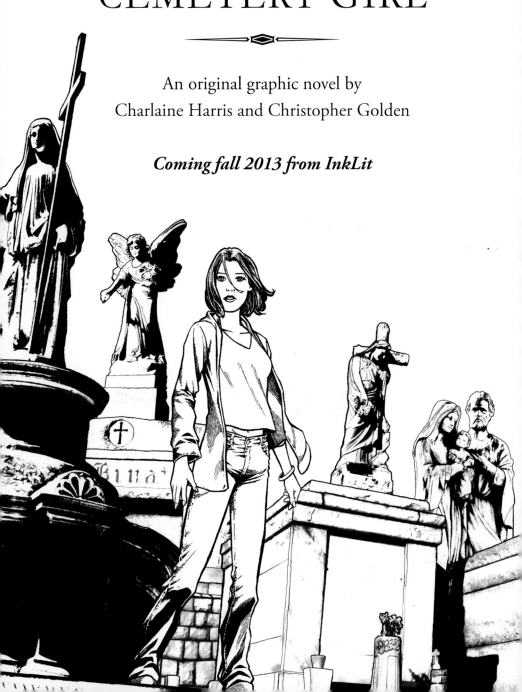

Zoom in on a tiny cocktail table in a hotel bar in Atlanta, Georgia. Two people sit on tall stools amidst throngs in wild, colorful costumes, an island amidst the madness of the annual revelry that is Dragon*Con. Charlaine Harris shares with Christopher Golden the idea she's had for a new novel called *Cemetery Girl*, along with her regret that she can't see a way to fit it into her schedule. Chris suggests that she consider developing the story for graphic novels instead. Charlaine has always wanted to try her hand at writing comics.

Months later, Chris's phone rings. *Cemetery Girl* has been haunting Charlaine. The more she thinks about it, the more the graphic novel idea intrigues her. Is Chris interested in collaborating with her to bring it to fruition? You bet he is.

And that's how it started, folks.

Together, we began to build the world around Calexa Rose Dunhill, to explore ideas about identity at the same time we were plotting our trilogy of murder mysteries. Each of the three *Cemetery Girl* graphic novels has its own insidious plot, but at the center of our story is the fourth and most important mystery—Calexa's. As the trilogy begins, she herself has been murdered. Fortunately, it doesn't take, but with her murderer still out there—and with no memory of her life before she was left for dead in Dunhill Cemetery—she struggles to find the courage to seek the truth. She feels safe hiding amongst the dead . . . until death itself shatters the sanctuary she's built.

The biggest challenge in turning *Cemetery Girl* into this trilogy of graphic novels was in finding the perfect artist for the project. We needed an illustrator who could put the reader right into the cemetery with Calexa, who could create the atmosphere with both detail and style, who could make us feel what Calexa feels, show us her horror and loss and loneliness and yet allow us to share more wistful, lighthearted moments. We needed an artist who could bring you, dear reader, into Calexa's story on a personal, intimate level, and from the very first day that he accepted the job, we have felt fortunate to have Don Kramer on board, bringing Calexa to life in Book One of *Cemetery Girl: The Pretenders*.

Now come along. Have a look at what's in store . . .

Charlaine Harris
Christopher Golden

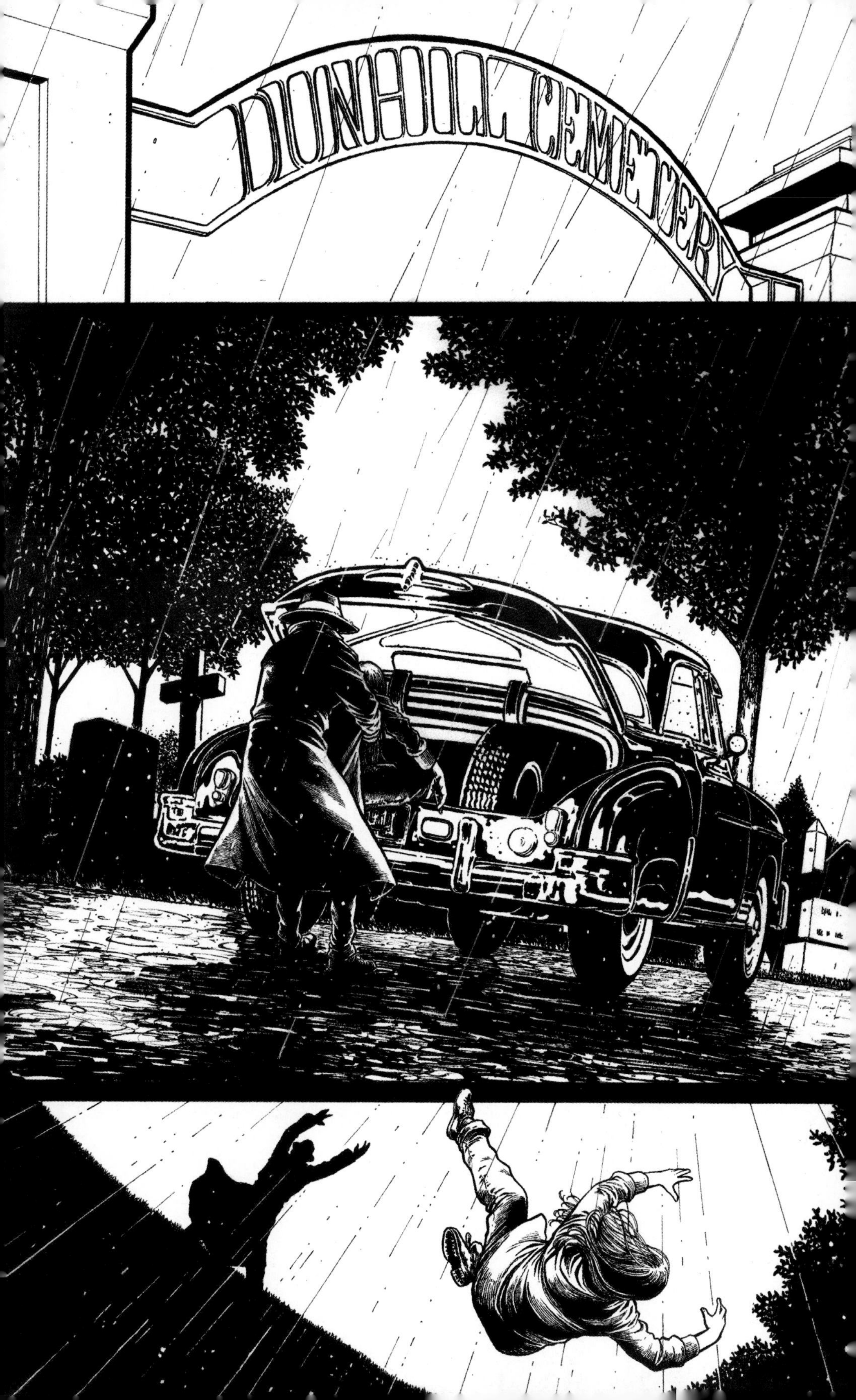
DUNHILL CEMETER

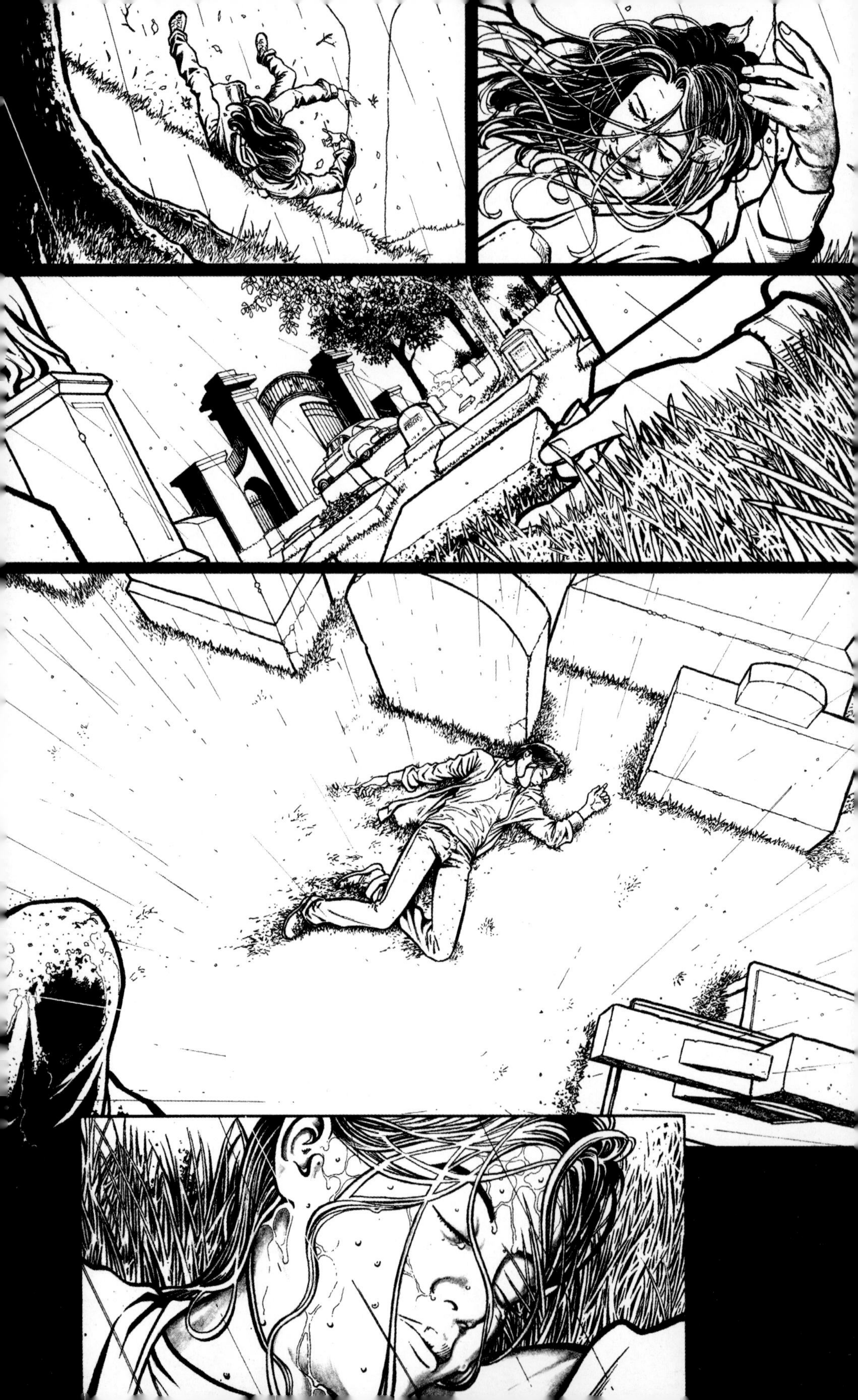

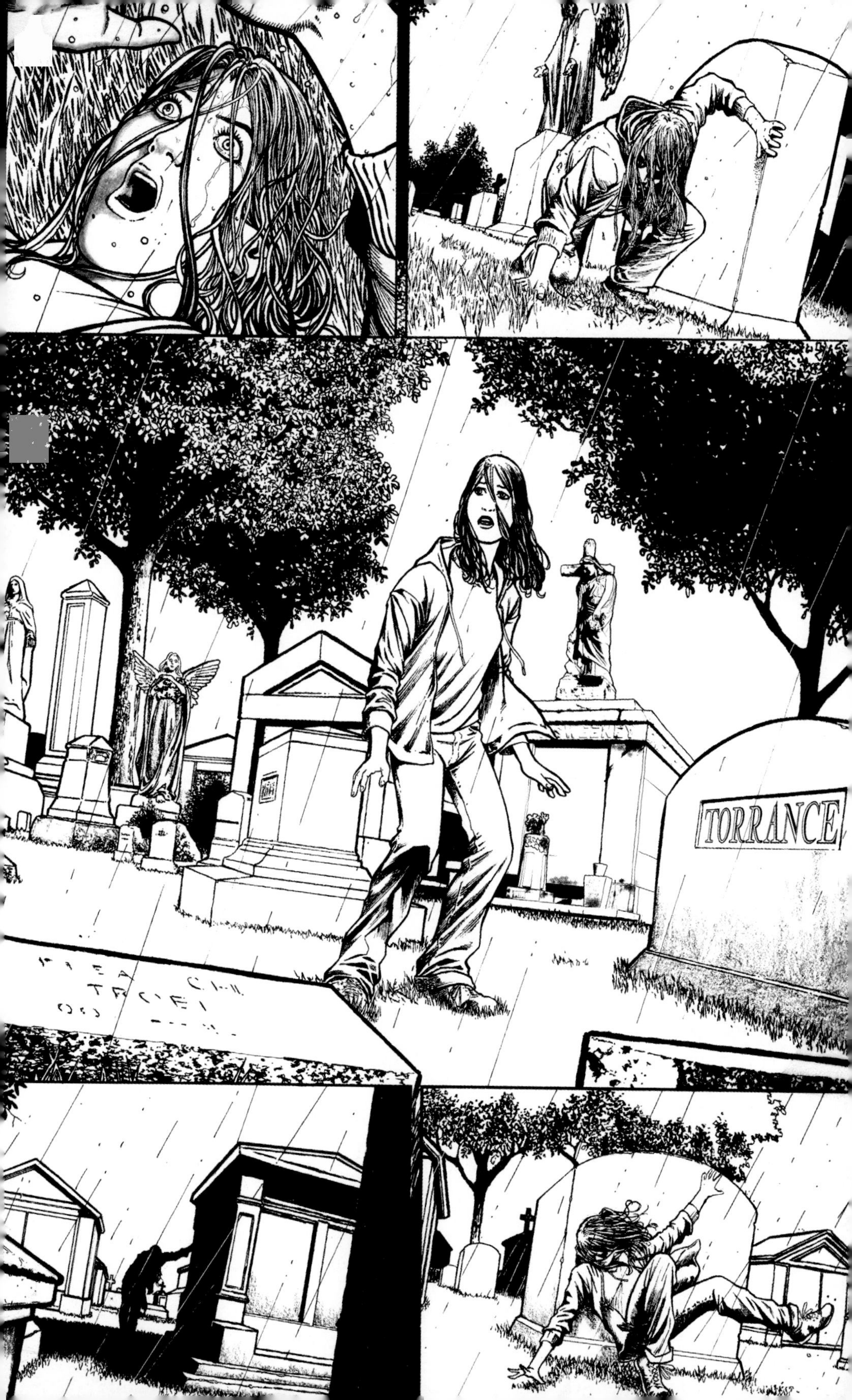
TORRANCE

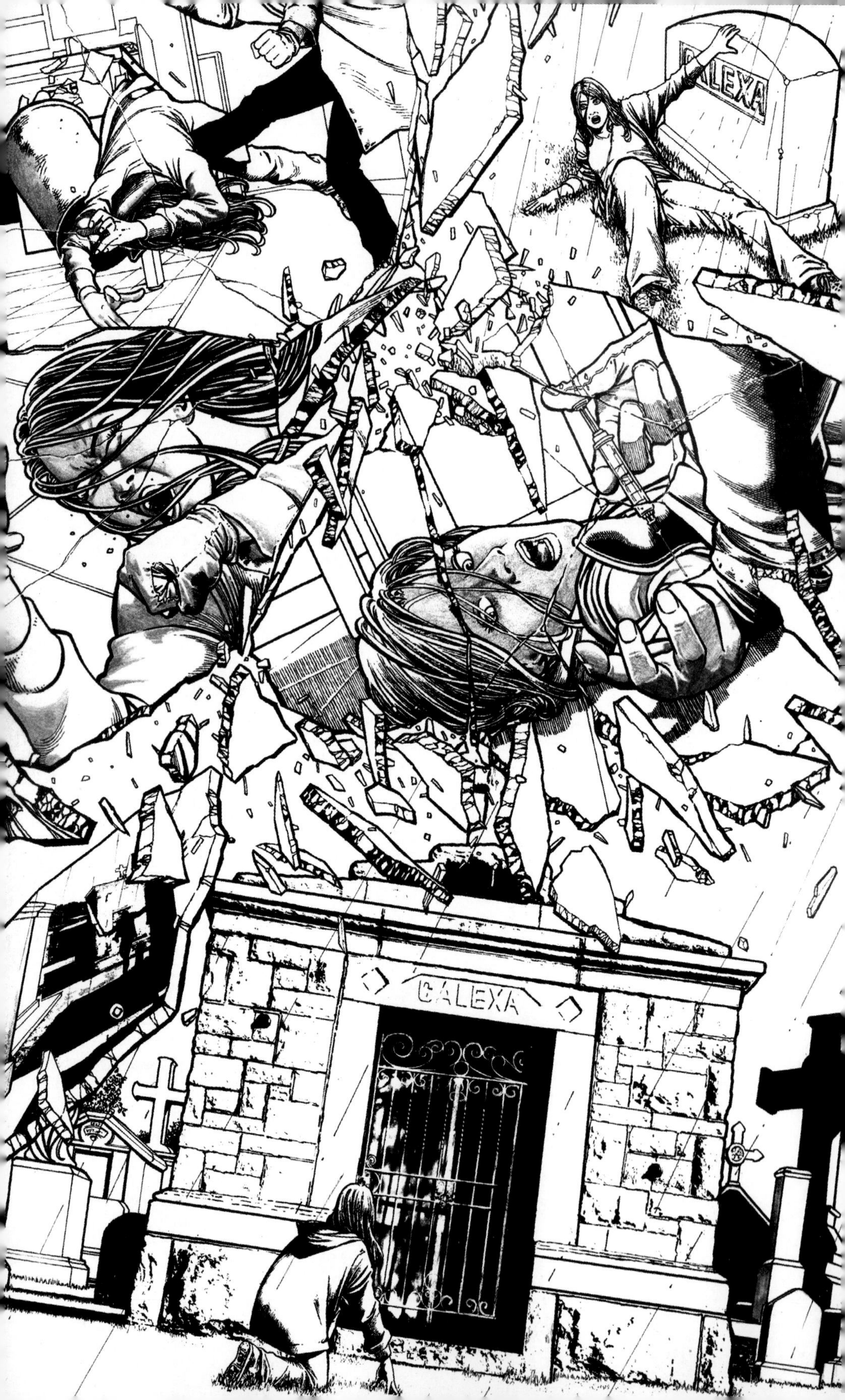
CALEXA

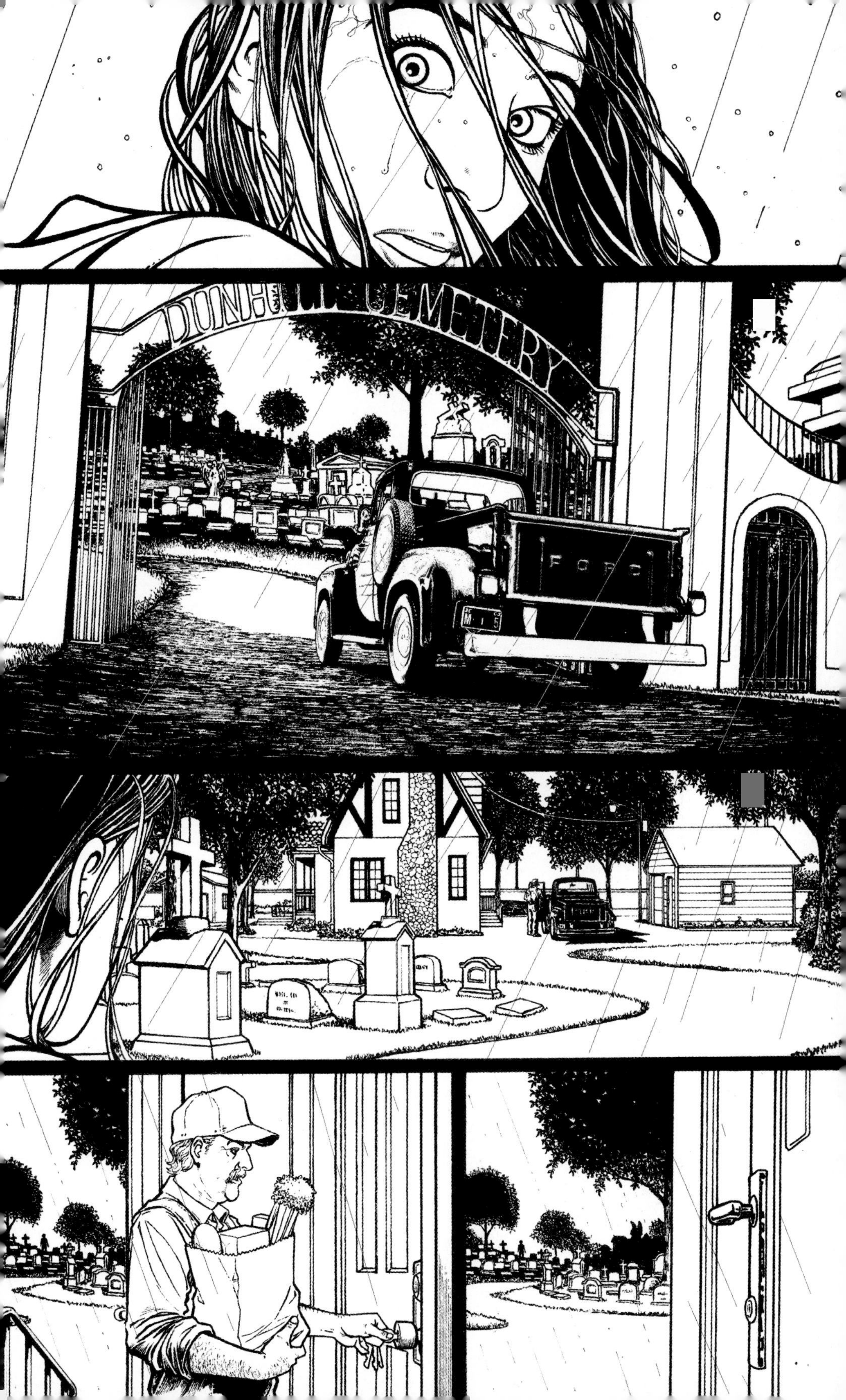
FORD

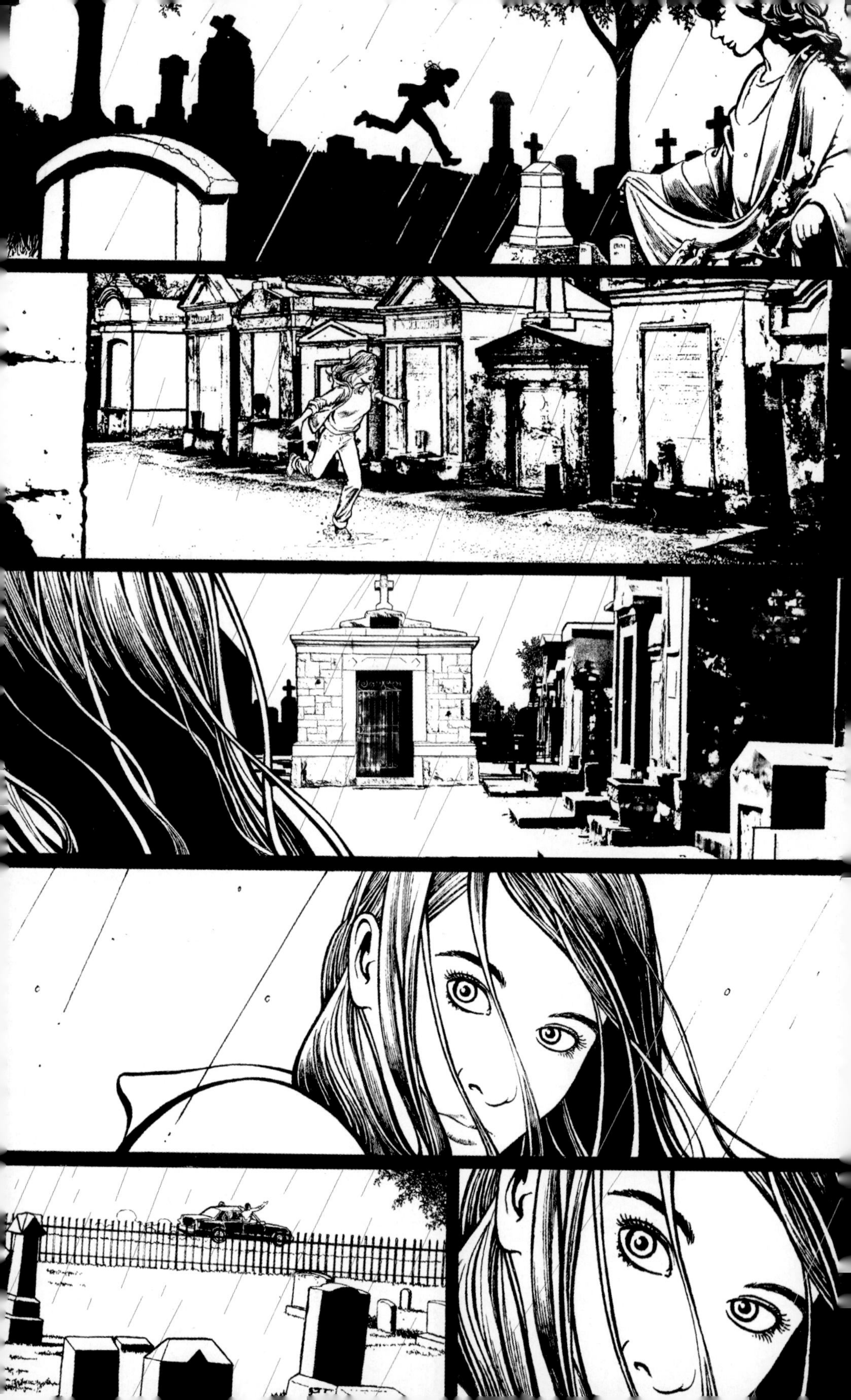

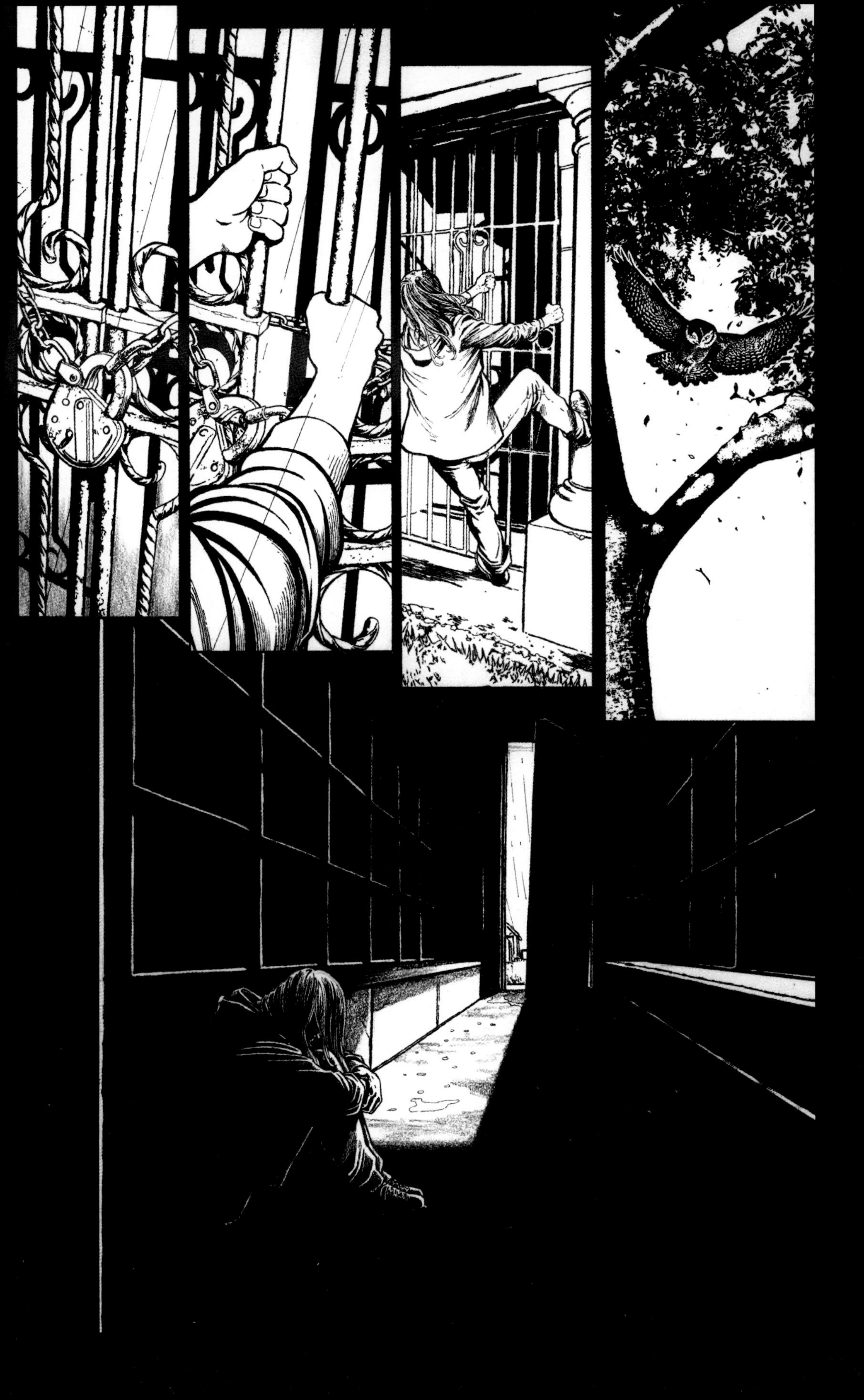

See where Harper Connelly began her adventures!

Read the books by #1 *New York Times* bestselling author

CHARLAINE HARRIS

New York Times Bestselling
Author of *Grave Surprise*
CHARLAINE HARRIS
grave sight
"Too much fun."
—*Wilmington (NC) Star-News*

Meet Harper Connelly:

When I was fifteen, I was struck by a bolt of lightning through an open window of the trailer where we lived... I recovered, mostly. Sometimes my right hand shakes. I have headaches. I have many fears. And I can find dead people.

"A winning supernatural caper...Should make Harper as popular as Sookie Stackhouse."

—*PUBLISHERS WEEKLY*

Find Charlaine online at
charlaineharris.com
and look for her on Facebook

Don't miss the rest of the series!

CHARLAINE HARRIS
grave surprise

CHARLAINE HARRIS
an ice cold grave

CHARLAINE HARRIS
A Harper Connelly Mystery
grave secret

"Too much fun."

—*WILMINGTON (NC) STAR-NEWS*

Available wherever books are sold

BERKLEY PRIME CRIME

A Member of Penguin Group (USA)

penguin.com/charlaineharris

T243-1012

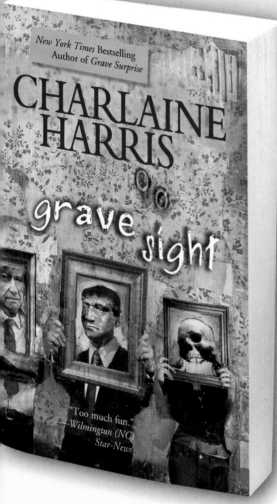